The
Keeper of Secrets

The
Keeper of Secrets

Julie Thomas

wm

WILLIAM MORROW
An Imprint of HarperCollinsPublishers

P.S.™ is a trademark of HarperCollins Publishers.

HarperCollins books may be purchased for educational, business, or sales promotional use. For information please write: Special Markets Department, HarperCollins Publishers, 10 East 53rd Street, New York, NY 10022.

FIRST EDITION

Designed by Diahann Sturge

Library of Congress Cataloging-in-Publication Data has been applied for.

ISBN 978-0-06-224030-9

13 14 15 16 17 OV/RRD 10 9 8 7 6 5 4 3 2 1

To Vicky—for inspiring me
with her passion for classical music;
to my mum—for providing me unconditional support;
and to my musical friends and family—for showing me
that anything's possible if you work hard enough
and want it badly enough.

Music is the language of the spirit. It opens the secret of life bringing peace, abolishing strife.

—KAHLIL GIBRAN

Acknowledgments

The roots of *The Keeper of Secrets* run back to my childhood and I have so many to thank. My best friend at school was Ruth Burns and her parents, Joe and the late Carmel, welcomed me with open arms into their Jewish home and shared their faith with their daughter's Gentile friend. Ruth, after forty years we're as close as ever and you're a true supporter and an honest critic.

This novel would not have happened at all without my late sister-in-law, Vicky Thomas, who was a music teacher with a deep and abiding love of classical music. Vicky's son, my nephew Paul, played the violin and she encouraged me to keep researching and writing when I felt overwhelmed and underqualified.

The incomparable Sir Michael Hill's International Violin Competition is held in New Zealand every year and was the basis for the competition chapters. Hill does so much to foster the love of the violin and happily shares his knowledge.

Many thanks to those who read versions along the way and

added their opinions and enthusiasm to the project, especially Reuben Aitchison, who is the best beta reader any author ever had.

Heartfelt thanks to my extraordinary mum, Thelma Thomas, who has always believed in my writing and been there through good and bad.

To my delightful editor, Carolyn Marino, and associate editor Amanda Bergeron, your patience and expert help and guidance and your passion for my story are appreciated more than words can express.

The
Keeper of Secrets

Prologue

Berlin
February 1935

"What does it mean when someone calls you swine?" Simon Horowitz asked suddenly, as his father's black Mercedes-Benz rolled to a stop at the top of a blind alley off the Friedrichstraße.

"Who called you that?" Simon could tell by the tone of his voice that his father was concerned.

"Not me. Joshua told us a story in school. A Nazi official passed his father in the street and said 'swine' and Joshua's father tipped his hat and said, 'Goldstein, pleased to meet you.'"

Benjamin Horowitz roared with laughter as Simon scrambled out of the huge car to join him.

"A very appropriate response. You tell Joshua I think his father is a genius."

This was a violin excursion. Sometimes his older brother, Levi, came with them but today he'd gone ice-skating with the girl who lived next door. Why would you choose ice-skating with a girl when you could come on a violin excursion? The twins, David and Rachel, were only nine, and they got bored when Papa played the violin. Mama said they were too young to appreciate the family treasures.

"Now come on, or we'll be late," his father said as he walked briskly down the alley, the violin case swinging from his hand. At nearly fourteen Simon was years older than the twins, and he was satisfied that these violin excursions made that difference clear. He slowed and let his father go on ahead.

It was midwinter and the shop displays were bursting with colorful and tempting fare. He moved from window to window: books, magazines, and crayons were displayed in one; glistening gold and diamond jewelry in another; and delicious cakes and pastries on round wooden stands in the third.

"Do you remember standing with your nose pressed to the glass watching the gingerbread house being built?" His father's question surprised him, and he looked up at the man's round, smiling face. It was Simon's experience that important men didn't have time for children and his father's patience and kindness were unusual. Still, if he had pressed his nose to a shopwindow, it must have been centuries ago.

"I remember the twins wanting to go inside. I've always preferred next door."

Next door was Amos Wiggenstein's Music Shoppe. Together they moved the few steps to the window. It was full of violins and violas, nestled on bright green satin, with sheet music spread artfully between them.

"Come in when you're ready," his father said gently and opened the door, setting off the chimes. They made a tinkling, silvery sound, like cascading water. Simon loved that sound; it meant the entrance to Aladdin's cave, and he felt the familiar excitement start to bubble.

A stocky boy in a dark blue wool coat that was just too small for him, Simon had black curls cut short and a plump face ending in a deeply cleft chin; his watchful, liquid brown eyes stared back at him from the glass. Finally he tugged the heavy door open and slipped inside.

Violins and violas of all sizes hung from metal hooks in the ceiling and were inserted into slats on the wall-mounted shelving that lined the long, narrow shop. The smells rose in clouds to meet his twitching nostrils—spruce, varnish, maple, beeswax, and dust. Rosin hung thick in the air, and the filtered sunlight formed golden shafts that bounced off the bodies of the instruments.

Simon turned his attention to the nearest violin; it was a rich orange-brown with lighter-colored purfling around the edges. He ran his finger over the body. The wood felt cool and smooth to the touch, yet welcoming and eager to share the music. A stab of intense longing to just pick it up and play almost took his breath away. Beside the violin hung a half size completely covered in gold paint, and farther along the row he could see a viola that was almost black.

When he was younger, he used to pretend he'd come here to choose his own violin, but now he understood that nothing on these shelves could compare with what he saw beneath the glass in the music room at home. The 1742 Guarneri del Gesú violin was one of the most glorious stringed instruments ever made, and the Horowitz family had owned it for one hundred and fifty years. Simon knew his career path, and every visit to this shop cemented it and made the vision clearer; he would play the Guarneri with the Berlin Philharmonic in recital.

Slowly he was drawn down the cluttered aisle. The wood shavings on the floor crunched beneath his feet, and he had to avoid empty violin cases and music stands. Passing the huge pigeonholed shelving, with its cleaners, strings, polishes, and chin rests stuffed into every available crevice, he hesitated in the doorway to the back room.

Amos's gangly teenaged assistant, Jacob, was bending over the silver saucepan of hide glue on the stove, stirring it gently and observing the two men cautiously. Amos and his father stood at the workbench surrounded by the tools of the luthier's trade: chisels, jack planes, scrapers, files, and gouges. Amos held the violin up to the light.

"As magnificent as ever. A true masterpiece," he whispered, seemingly oblivious to everyone else. His old fingers were gentle with the instrument, loving, reverential. Simon was used to this; he'd seen many adults hold the Guarneri that way. The intense oil varnish seemed to sparkle like new in the soft artificial light as Amos turned it over and over.

"I know that, Amos. But can you do it? Is it possible?" Simon could hear unfamiliar notes in his father's voice, impatience, uncertainty.

"Possible? Yes, certainly. Advisable, I'm not so sure," the old man said slowly.

Suddenly there was tension, and Simon could sense his father's indignation. No one questioned him about the instruments.

"When I want advice, I'll ask for advice. If you can do it, then do it."

"But you are changing important history, my friend."

Benjamin Horowitz stiffened. Simon knew that response well; his father was slow to anger, but his precious violin was always able to rouse him.

"It's my responsibility to keep it safe. The world is changing and we may have to make many pacts with the devil. This lowers the value and, maybe, I can give up other treasures and keep this one."

A question was forming in Simon's mind, a dark feeling of foreboding. It frightened him, and before it reached his lips, he turned back to the shop. Sometimes it was better to remember your place. He looked over his shoulder at the two men, oblivious to the world, bent over the violin that now lay on the green covering of the workbench.

Jacob followed him, took a violin down from its hook, picked up a bow, and handed them to Simon. He played a few notes and adjusted a couple of the pegs. Then he played a snatch of music. Jacob watched, delight on his face. Simon fiddled with the pegs again, then played some more, feeling suddenly exhilarated as the clear, sweet sound of Bach cut through the rosin-filled air. Amos and Benjamin emerged from the back room.

"He's a talented boy, this son of yours," Amos murmured. Benjamin smiled fondly at Simon.

"He's a good boy, he practices hard."

"Maybe so, but he has soft hands and a natural sense of rhythm and that's half the battle won already."

Simon stopped playing and handed the violin and bow back to Jacob. He could feel the blush rising in his cheeks.

"Thank you, sir," he said quietly.

"That's a French violin, made in 1810. Not as wonderful as your papa's Guarneri but still a precious thing."

Amos took down a box from the rack behind him and held it out to the boy.

"Here, son, have some rosin. Don't stop practicing, and one day you may be very good indeed. Then we hear you play your papa's Guarneri. Did you know the master himself described her sound as like the tears of an angel?"

"No, sir!" Simon couldn't keep the wonder from his voice. The master, Guarneri del Gesú, had described the sound of their violin? He exchanged a smile with his obviously delighted father.

They made their good-byes, leaving the violin in Amos's care. Halfway up the alley Simon touched his father's arm anxiously.

"What's he doing to it, Papa?"

Benjamin laid his hand on the boy's shoulder as they walked up the sidewalk toward the waiting car.

"Just a minor alteration, a necessary . . . improvement. You'll see for yourself when I collect it next week."

Talent

Part One: Daniel Horowitz

2008

Chapter 1

New Zealand
February 2008

The auditorium was in total darkness. You could've heard a pin bounce on the wooden floor; the air was alive with anticipation and the collective holding of five thousand breaths. Suddenly a large circle of light fell onto the front center of the stage, and Daniel Horowitz, fourteen years old, stepped out of the darkness into the middle of the white light. He wore a well-cut black suit and white shirt, complete with small black bow tie. In his left hand he held a full-sized violin and in his right, a bow. For a long second he blinked vigorously to adjust his eyes and steady his nerves. All he could see were rows of mysterious shapes in the darkness, but somewhere out there his father sat, his heart beating as fast as Daniel's. A bead of sweat ran down his face, and he brushed it away with the cuff of his shirt as he took a few deep breaths to control the butterflies in the pit of his stomach.

The stage lights came up to reveal a full orchestra seated

behind him, the tall, imposing figure of the conductor on the podium, his baton raised. The atmosphere in the hall was charged as every ear strained for the sound. With one dramatic sweep of the baton, the orchestra burst into the first note of Paganini's Allegro maestoso, the first movement of Violin Concerto no. 1 in D Major.

For over a minute the boy waited; then he gave the screw at the end of the bow one last twist, put the violin to his left shoulder, and raised the bow above the strings. The bow swept down and a strong, confident note rang out. His eyes closed and his body relaxed as the nerves vanished. His long fingers flew over the ebony fingerboard, and the smooth arc of the bow was mesmerizing to the entranced audience.

He was oblivious to everything but the music; his slender frame swayed slightly, more dipping and rising than swaying, as the sound climbed and fell in cascading waves. The conductor was half turned toward him and watched him almost constantly. Toward the end, the orchestra was silent and Daniel played the intricate music, trill after complicated trill, as the emotional journey built toward its climax.

Then seventeen spellbinding minutes later it was over. The last note was a flourish; his head jerked back, he dropped his arms to his sides, and he bowed from the waist. For a second there was a stunned silence, and then the audience rose as one, breaking into loud applause and shouts of "Bravo!"

Daniel stood in the wings watching the orchestra accompanying a young woman on her violin. It was finals night at the Samuel J. Hillier Foundation International Competition, and Daniel was the youngest competitor by at least four years. He was from Newbrick, Illinois, one of three Americans who'd made it to the semifinals stage, but the only one to progress on to the final.

His fellow finalists were Russian, Korean, Chinese, Australian, and Canadian. The competition was more than seventy years old and held in a different country every year. It worked on an annual rotation around piano, violin, cello, and viola; this year was the turn of the violin. Steeped in tradition and prestige, as well as a very good first prize of $20,000, the top award usually went to an up-and-coming musician on the verge of solo stardom. The first prize was regarded as an important step toward international recognition, and Daniel knew he was far from being at that stage.

He was an only child, tall for his age, with long arms and legs and a mop of black curls that fell into his eyes when he needed a haircut. Women adored his dimpled chin, his large brown eyes and long black lashes. He sometimes wished he looked more rugged and wondered if a broken nose or a small scar would make him look older and meaner. In many respects he was just an ordinary kid, until you heard him play the violin. His father had first put a tiny violin into his hands when he was four, continuing a male family tradition that went back over a hundred and fifty years. His great-great-grandfather, his great-grandfather, his grandfather, and his father had all played the violin, starting in childhood. But none of them was ever as good as Daniel already was, or so his mother told him.

Twelve months earlier, his school music teacher, who'd also been his violin teacher, had told his parents that Daniel now played better than he did and he could teach the child no more. He suggested that they allow Daniel to audition for the Hamilton Bruce Institute of Music in Philadelphia. He was younger than the school usually considered, but his talent was so obvious they made an exception and welcomed him with open arms.

This meant a new life, living in a small apartment with his mother, away from his friends and his father, going to a private junior high school and the Hamilton Bruce Institute, both on a scholarship. There were daily violin and piano lessons, weekly recitals and musical studies, and after six months the faculty had allowed him to participate in chamber music and orchestral work, although he was the youngest in the groups by far. It was hard work, on top of all his other studies, and sometimes he got very tired and homesick, but he loved it and playing always seemed to reenergize him. Even the practice was fun, and being immersed in a musical world gave him the confidence to express his opinions and dreams out loud.

His violin teacher, the former Italian concert violinist Maestro Alberto Vincelli, had decided to enter him in the Samuel J. Hillier because if he made the last forty it would be great experience. The semifinals had seemed highly unlikely, let alone a finals place among the best young violinists in the world, but life can be highly unlikely sometimes.

Daniel couldn't see them but he knew the judges were out there, five of them, sitting in the middle of the front row, listening to every note and watching every movement. There was a tight knot of tension in his stomach, his mouth was dry, and he wanted to cough. He took a swig from his water bottle; although it wasn't cold anymore, it was wet.

"Hello, darlin'."

He turned at the sound of his mother's whisper. She was wearing her favorite dress, the "lucky" dress they called it, a strapless green silk evening gown, and she clasped his violin case with two arms across her body.

"She's very cold, don't you think, Amy Funston?" she asked.

"But she's so great technically, that's her strength. It's a really hard piece."

"Just Pomakov to go"—it was a statement, not a question. He turned and looked at her and she smiled encouragingly. It occurred to him that she was very good at that balance, motivating and driving him and yet showing him she was proud. He'd love to win it for her, and the knowledge that he wouldn't made him feel guilty.

"He was awesome in the semis," he said softly.

"Not as awesome as my boy!"

He frowned. "Don't expect too much, Mom."

The girl finished with a long soft note and the audience responded with subdued applause. Cindy and Daniel moved out of the way quickly as a short, thickset Russian teenager scowled at them and strode toward the stage.

Chapter 2

Almost an hour later the six finalists were milling around backstage, moving to keep the tension at a level they could cope with. They spoke in hopeful whispers to their adult companions and avoided eye contact with one another.

Rafael Santamaria Gomez, the conductor and chairman of the judging panel, acknowledged each competitor as he walked past them toward the stage. He was tall, broad shouldered and barrel chested, clean-shaven, with smiling brown eyes, and his huge hand engulfed Daniel's. In that moment Daniel realized that this was the hand that held the baton and the thought thrilled him.

The prizes were donated by the estate of Samuel J. Hillier and presented by the old man's grandson, Grayson Hillier, who followed Gomez onto the stage. Daniel couldn't see them once they disappeared through the black curtains, but he could hear the conductor's deep Spanish accent.

"Ladies and gentlemen, it remains just for me to tell you the results. I know you are all waiting for them, thank you for being so patient! In third place, the very talented Canadian, Amy Funston." Applause broke out in the auditorium as the young woman squared her shoulders, kissed her teacher on each cheek, and walked out from the wings.

Curiosity overcame Daniel and he moved to where he could see what was happening on the stage. The conductor had his hand extended toward her and kissed her on each cheek.

"Well done; it was a beautifully played piece, technically brilliant."

Daniel couldn't hear her response, and he watched as the conductor guided her gently toward Hillier, who shook her hand stiffly and handed her the envelope without actually looking at her. She put her arm diagonally across her chest, with the slender hand at the base of her throat, and curtsied deeply to the audience, who clapped even harder.

"Wonderful! And now for the second position. It goes to a most impressive young man from Moscow. Ivan Pomakov!"

A ripple of surprise ran through the crowd; obviously they'd expected Pomakov to win. The Russian was standing quite close to Daniel and Cindy. For a moment the young man stood absolutely still; he looked stunned.

"Good Lord, not so awesome after all," Cindy whispered.

Daniel shot her a glance and her eyes were gleaming. He could feel the tension radiating from her body. The backstage staff pushed Pomakov toward the gap, and he stumbled before walking uncertainly into the light.

"Congratulations, young man. You played superbly."

The Russian leaned in toward the conductor's microphone.

"*Da* . . . ah, *khorosho* . . . *spasibo* . . . ah, thank you." He seemed to glide past and on to Hillier.

Daniel sucked in his bottom lip and stared unseeingly at
the cables snaking across the wooden floorboards. This wasn't
what they'd told him would happen, in the final four and the
hot favorite out of the running. Gomez's voice cut in over the
applause and the Russian stopped bowing to the crowd. Even
though Daniel could see the conductor from the side, he suddenly sounded a very long way off, and the boy strained to hear
what the man was saying.

". . . so exciting to be able to announce this winner. He is
the youngest winner we, this competition, has ever had, in
any category . . . one of, I believe, the youngest winners of
any of the major classical music competitions anywhere in
the world. From the United States of America, Master Daniel
Horowitz!"

Halfway through, his mother had cried out, "Oh my God!"
and started to hug him tightly. Her body was quivering and hot.
He felt suffocated. Suddenly hands pulled him away from her as
she was kissing his cheeks and he was spun around and pushed
toward the stage. His legs felt weak but he kept going, one step
after another.

"Go"—a female voice was loud in his ear—"to the stage,
now!" The lights seemed very bright, and the applause was
deafening. Once again his right hand was swallowed as the conductor's other hand came down gently onto his left shoulder.

"Well done, Daniel! *Muy bueno!* Such passion and maturity
in one so young!"

Everything he and his mother had rehearsed had gone out of
Daniel's head and he was reacting instinctively.

"Um . . . thank you, sir."

"This way, come, meet Mr. Hillier." The conductor stooped
to whisper in his ear.

"And don't forget, yes? To thank him for the money." Daniel shook Grayson Hillier's cold, limp hand and stared directly into the man's stomach as Hillier thrust a white envelope at him.

"Well done."

"Thank you very much, sir. For the money. It's a great competition, sir." He turned to the auditorium and bowed.

The house lights came up, and suddenly he could see that the crowd was on its feet, still clapping and cheering, and many were taking pictures of him. A rush of adrenaline surged through him and he smiled. Out of the corner of his eye he could see the Russian's pinched white face and blank eyes. He bowed again, more deeply. A young woman came from the wings with a huge bottle and a massive bouquet of flowers. She hesitated, then put them into his arms, and he could smell her perfume as she kissed him on each cheek. There were cellophane and roses and ribbons all around him and the bottle felt so heavy. The bottom of the bouquet reached past his knees and he struggled to see over the vast spread of flowers. A hand touched his arm, someone took the bottle and flowers from him, and he was free to bow again.

Still the applause continued. He glanced toward the side of the stage and could see his mother, clapping and smiling and crying, and he couldn't resist giving her a little wave. He looked up at the beaming face of Rafael Gomez and smiled back shyly. The conductor nodded briefly, and Daniel felt thrilled. Of all the strangers here, this was the man who mattered most to him. This was the man on the CD covers in his bedroom, the man posing with Joshua Bell on the poster pinned to his wall, the man whose autobiography he'd read countless times.

He could see the judges in the front row, the dark figure of Madam Francesca du Bouliver and beside her the silvered curly head of Itzhak Perlman in his chair; he didn't recognize the others. Wow, this was important and seriously cool! Wait till he could tell his fellow Cubs about this. As the thought exploded in his exhausted brain he knew his friends wouldn't understand, but tonight, he didn't care.

The postconcert gala was an outdoor affair. The hot summer air was very clear, and a million diamonds twinkled in the black velvet of the sky. Women in elegant gowns and men in tuxedos stood sipping Taittinger and gossiping. Every so often they broke from their conversation to take a new glass or an elegant canapé from the waiting staff. A string quartet played quietly in the background, competing with the lapping of the waves on the nearby lakefront. Huge snowcapped mountains glistened in the moonlight like brooding guardians.

Daniel sat at a round table by himself. He'd snuffed out the heavy gold candle and was tracing patterns of melted wax onto the stiff white cloth. The bouquet lay across the table, and closer to him stood the magnum of Taittinger Collection Brut, 1981. It was a black lacquered bottle covered with intertwined golden violins, a collector's bottle designed by the French painter and sculptor Arman.

His parents were standing a little way off, in conversation with a small, animated man who kept gesturing toward Daniel and was obviously trying to make a point to them. As usual his father was quiet and calm, but his mother, vocal and shrill, was still too excited. He sighed and took a gulp of Coke. Why wasn't anything cold in this country? Hadn't they heard of refrigeration? It was still hot. His jacket was on the chair beside him and, despite his mother's protestations, he'd untied the horrible bow tie and undone the top two buttons of the shirt. Now that the adrenaline had finally left his system, he was really hungry, tired, and bored and he wanted to go back to the hotel. All week he'd looked forward to the promised day out with his dad—tomorrow they'd go jet boating or ride a gondola and a downhill luge—so it was a surprise to discover that most of all he was ready to go home.

"Daniel?" He looked up as Rafael Gomez pulled back a chair. "May I join you?"

He sat up straight.

"Yes, please, sir."

"No more of the sir! How are you feeling now?"

"Fine. Thank you."

Rafael lowered himself onto the chair and put his champagne flute on the table.

"A little tired maybe?"

"Yes, a bit."

"So you should be; it's late, and you've worked very hard all week." There was a moment's silence. Rafael turned the bottle around and read the label.

"This is a nice touch."

Daniel shrugged.

"I'd rather have a case of Coke," he said without a hint of humor.

"I'm sure you can find someone who will swap it for several cases of Coke. I've just been rereading your notes. Do you like Maestro Vincelli?"

"He's a great teacher. That's what my mom says. We study a new composer every quarter and he loves Mozart."

"But what do *you* say about it? Do you like him?"

"Yeah, he can be fun, and he still plays really, *really* well."

"Oh, he certainly does. You know I conducted him once? Years ago and when he was a concert violinist and I was just a raw novice, not really knowing what it was that I was supposed to be doing. He won't remember."

"He told me. He said you were the best conductor he ever had. He knew you were destined to be great, he said that."

Rafael smiled softly. "I think he's employing—how do you say it?—selective memory. But I've been reading what he says about you. He thinks you're the most talented pupil he's ever had."

Daniel could feel the blush rising in his cheeks.

"Um, thanks," he said, taking another swig of Coke.

"No, don't thank me! I didn't say it, although I'm sure he is right. What's the best thing of all, do you think, about being a violinist?"

Daniel hesitated. The man didn't rephrase the question to make it easier; he just waited for Daniel to form his answer. Daniel really liked that the maestro knew he'd understood.

"I think . . . when they give you a new piece . . . and first you have to learn the melody and the timing . . ." Rafael nodded slowly and it was obvious to Daniel that he was concentrating all his attention on him. It was exhilarating and frightening at the same time.

"Then, when you get that, you explore the why, what it *means*. What the composer's saying and how to put the . . . feelings in. Suddenly the music kinda"—he broke off and looked up at Rafael, who still waited patiently—"I don't know if there's a technical term, sir . . . *sings* to you. Sort of makes perfect sense."

The big man beamed. "Absolutely right! And do you know why that is so, Daniel? Because it's in two languages, first the language of the brain, all the notes in the right order and the timing and the key and so on and so on. Then second, the language of the heart. This distinction, it is what separates all musicians. Some, like the young woman who came in third tonight, Miss Funston, speak the language of the brain perfectly, and so they sound, you know, technically correct, but the *heart*? It is a complete mystery to them. They don't understand the message, the *pasión*. When you do, it's a revelation. Every time you go back to a score you will find something new you didn't see before. I'm over fifty, ancient to you, I know, and I'm still a student!"

Daniel was entranced.

"So who's your favorite, sir? Composer?"

"All the time journalists ask me that question. I love very much Verdi and Puccini. What about you?"

"Vivaldi. Although I love Tchaikovsky and Paganini."

"What about Maestro Vincelli's little Wolfgang? And we mustn't forget Shostakovich and Brahms—"

"The Concerto in D Minor!" Daniel exclaimed.

Rafael laughed heartily. "See, you're a lot like me; you can never choose between your heroes! What about the future, Daniel? What do you want to do?"

"First violin in a world-famous orchestra and play baseball on the weekends."

"What? No solo career? You're not thinking about being a concert violinist?"

Daniel could hear the surprise in the maestro's voice and it made him feel guilty, as if he'd disappointed the great man.

"Sometimes. I . . . I don't know if I'm good enough to be a soloist."

"Do you know who that man is? The one who keeps badgering your poor parents?"

Daniel glanced at the man who was still talking. He had spiky, streaked hair and dark glasses sticking out of the pocket of his jacket instead of a handkerchief.

"No," he answered uncertainly.

"He's an agent. A powerful and thoroughly—you know—disagreeable little man. He is trying to persuade your parents that he wants to help them to guide your career and your life.

And he is just the first. They'll come flocking to you now, and they'll want to put you in front of an orchestra, onto the concert stage, and then maybe into the recording studio. And you know, you must always remember it is not you that they care so much about; it is themselves and the money you will make."

Suddenly Rafael thumped the table with his hand. Daniel gave a little start.

"In August I have a young artists' symposium at the Kennedy Center. Musicians from all over the world, singers, pianists, cellists, flautists, violinists, some trumpet and clarinet players, a candy store licorice mixture of beautiful music. I will talk to your parents and tell them to sign nothing and go with no one. All the best agents will hear you first. You must play, in the stringed instrument concert, okay?"

Daniel looked at his parents. His father had been watching and winked encouragingly at him. He wondered how Maestro Gomez would react if he asked how far the Baltimore Orioles' home ground was from the Kennedy Center.

"I'm sure they'll let me, if you ask them."

Rafael pulled himself to his feet.

"So, I bid you *buenas noches,* Daniel. Well done and we'll meet again soon."

"Good night, sir, and thank you." But the conductor was already halfway across the room.

Chapter 3

Illinois
July 2008

"Did you know there's a mathematical property named after Sosa, McGwire, and Maris?" asked Daniel as he rolled over onto his back and squinted at the cloudless blue sky. He and three other boys lay in the long grass beside a deep swimming hole. The relentless sun had dried the cooling water on their backs and now their skin felt prickly. A fly droned somewhere close by and the air was heavy with the rich smells of summer, sunbaked grass and tree-ripened fruit.

"A mathematical what?" Tony was obviously as bewildered as the other two.

"Just Dan being a nerd," said Billy as he, too, rolled over onto his back. "What do they teach you at that fancy school, anyway?"

Daniel flicked a piece of grass off his face and reached for the water bottle by his side. He was used to their gibes about his school; it was part of the ribbing you got when you did something different.

"A mathematical property—two numbers form the Maris-McGwire-Sosa pair if they are consecutive numbers such that when you add each number's digits to the digits of its prime factorization, they're equal! Sixty-one and sixty-two have it, and Sosa and McGwire both hit at least sixty-two home runs. And the record of Maris—"

Billy scrambled to his feet. "Who cares? Last one in carries the towels home." They all jumped up, followed him to the edge, and splashed into the water. Daniel was the last to surface. Tony and Billy were already wrestling, pushing each other under. Aaron was the closest to him.

"Who'd scored sixty-one," Daniel said. Aaron was treading water, his head bobbing up and down.

"What the hell you going on about now, math nerd?"

"Maris's record was sixty-one, and the other two scored sixty-two before hitting even more home runs in 1998."

Aaron launched himself at Daniel, spraying water in his face. Tony, Billy, and Aaron were Daniel's three best friends. They called themselves "the Cubs," as both official fans of the Chicago Cubs and also a group of kids bound by the fierce friendships of childhood, and this was their den. They spent long summer hours doing the things that really mattered: playing baseball, swimming, biking, fishing in the river that fed the swimming hole, playing computer games, strengthening the bonds after months apart.

During the holidays Daniel returned to his parents' home in Newbrick, Illinois, halfway between Peoria and Chicago. His father, David, owned a hardware store and they lived on a flat two-acre block on the outskirts of town. The house was cedar, the color of burnt umber, long and low-slung, with a porch and wide bay windows. The property backed onto a patch of thick forest that led to the river and swimming hole and was surrounded by other pieces of farmland that had been cut up into residential blocks.

The Horowitzes were part of a thriving Jewish community. They observed the basic food rules but didn't keep a strict kosher house, went to shul most Saturday mornings in the small local synagogue, and celebrated Shabbat, but not in the Orthodox style. As an only child himself, David understood how important it was for Daniel to have close friendships. David had grown up in New York and then Vermont, the son of a German Holocaust survivor and an American-born mother. His father had tried hard to become "American" and adopt the passions of his new homeland, but it always seemed to David as if he was trying to block something out, to replace horror with light. As a young boy he heard the nightmares and arguments through the thin walls of the apartment and grew to dread the times when his father became withdrawn and silent. Years of starvation during the war had left his father with digestive problems that led to frequent hospitalization.

David had come to understand that his mother's strong personality held the family together and that both his parents found comfort in the strict observance of their faith. His father was forever lecturing him on not taking things for granted and appreciating life's simple luxuries, like clean sheets and food on the table. No matter how full he was, he was never allowed to leave any part of a meal unfinished.

Music was their common bond. His father had put a small violin in his hands when he was very young and then told him solemnly that this same moment had happened to generations of his family before him. There were times when David caught a brief shadow of indescribable sadness on his deeply lined face as his father watched him practice. Something evil had extinguished the performance flame in the man, something dark that they didn't mention. Together they listened to LPs of famous violinists and talked about technique. When David reached high school, sports, girls, and good times became more important than the violin. His father cried, but said nothing, when he put the instrument away forever.

David had gone to work in a lumberyard and through hard work and luck he'd eventually gained the American dream: his own business, a beautiful wife, and a son. Although they'd tried for years, there were no more children. David, who looked more like his uncle Levi than his father, was tall and remarkably strong for his slender build, a good-looking man, with a quiet and thoughtful disposition. His son and his friends knew that he had a wicked sense of humor and wasn't above some gentle ribbing at his wife's expense.

Cindy, by contrast, was best described as vocal. She came from a large family and she knew that you needed to make yourself heard. Life taught her other lessons with surprising speed. She might have opinions and goals, but what people saw first was her physical appearance: thick, glossy blond hair, baby blue eyes that knew how to flash, and a body blessed with feminine curves. When she walked into a room, heads swiveled. Everything fell into place without her even trying. She was her parents' pet and, at school, a cheerleader and homecoming queen; she married her handsome childhood sweetheart, had a beautiful son—and then discovered the boy had a world-class talent. At last it was about something other than the way she looked, the way people expected her to act. At last she had an outlet for all those frustrated dreams of achievement.

Chapter 4

Mr. Dalley sat very straight in his chair playing his violin in time with Daniel. His room was plain, with just a piano, a stand for the music, a stereo player for recording his pupils' work, a small table with sheet music piled high, and the wheelchair. Apart from the wider-than-normal doorways, the lower light switches, and the ramp to the entrance of the house, it was a home just like Daniel's own. Daniel loved coming here, both for his lesson and Mrs. Dalley's homemade scones and lemonade. As an only child he was used to being adored and didn't really think about how much he meant to other people. He'd never asked why Mr. Dalley was in a wheelchair and, with the acceptance of youth, never bothered to pity him.

Daniel played an 1825 Jean-Baptiste Vuillaume French violin on loan from the Hamilton Bruce Institute. It had a beautiful, rich tone and he was particularly proud of the inlaid decorations on the back and ribs and the intricately carved scroll. The piece Daniel was playing was complicated, and he stopped twice, once as a reaction to pain in his finger. Finally he came to the end and lowered his instrument. Mr. Dalley lowered his and nodded.

"Much better. You still need to watch the timing of that last section. Mendelssohn intended you to feel the movement through the pace of the notes. Your fingering for the first part is almost perfect now, but don't forget that left thumb position; it can still be too high and that pulls your fingers down. Do you want to play the Bach again or something lighter to finish with? How's your finger feeling?"

Half an hour later there was a knock on the open front door.

"Hello? Just me," David called from the hall. Daniel and both Dalleys sat in the cool living room sharing their special postlesson treat: coffee, lemonade, and scones. David winked at Daniel as he sat down on the sofa.

"Hello, David, would you like a cup of coffee?"

"Am I going to turn down the best coffee in town, Mrs. D.? Everything okay today, Mr. D.?"

Mr. Dalley nodded. "Very good; Mendelssohn much improved and the Bach was excellent. We can put that one to rest for a while, I think, and move on to another. Daniel has chosen a rather lovely Corelli sonata, one of my personal favorites."

"How's Cindy?" asked Mrs. Dalley, her plump fingers fluttering around the coffeepot.

"Forever in the garden terrifying weeds; she really does enjoy being at home." David accepted the cup gratefully and said, "Thank you."

Mrs. Dalley turned to Daniel.

"Gary didn't collect the eggs at lunchtime. Remember how you used to love to do that? Would you be a dear and do it for me?"

Daniel sprang to his feet. "Is the bowl still in the second cupboard down?"

"No, it should be on the bench all ready for you. Rooster has been very noisy too, wakes the whole neighborhood, I shouldn't wonder, so you'll need to give him one of your good lectures. Let's go and see." Daniel grinned and followed her into the kitchen.

Thirty seconds later the men heard the door to the yard open and close.

"That should keep him quiet for a few moments. Hens have been particularly productive."

"Nice for him to do the things he remembers. So will he be ready for the symposium?"

"Oh, heavens yes. He could play tomorrow. He has several pieces at performance level now, but what I really wanted to talk to you about was his finger."

David looked up at him sharply. "What about it?"

"He has a nasty bruise on his left middle finger and although he tried to ignore it, I could see it was hurting."

"He's been out with the boys all summer—"

"Oh, I know. He told us all about the fish he and Aaron caught, but this came from baseball."

David gave him a sheepish grin. "More than likely."

"David, I know he's only fourteen and he likes his sports, but I think you should be seriously considering his future. Baseball could injure his fingers, *has* injured his fingers. If he broke one, it might set crookedly and that'd change his whole fingering pattern. It's my opinion that you should restrict him to watching. Do *they* know that he plays baseball in the summer? His teachers? If he had an agent, he'd tell you it must stop and Maestro Gomez would say the same. This symposium is a tremendous opportunity and his hands must be perfect."

David stirred the liquid in his cup and didn't answer immediately.

"I first took Dan to Wrigley Field when he was five, 'bout the same age I was when my dad took me to a ball game in New York. He wasn't American so he couldn't really *see* the whole baseball experience, but he took me, his American-born kid. I loved it passionately and so does Dan. The Cubs mean the—"

"And I'm not suggesting for a moment that he should stop going with you—"

"But playing is part of his commitment to the game. He acts out those games with his pals, just like I did. Part of coming home and being where he belongs is *playing* baseball." David looked across at the man to make sure he understood the point. The pale, narrow face was frowning, and the gray eyes looked tired and full of concern.

"How does Cindy feel about it?"

"She'd agree with you, one hundred and ten percent. She's the one who's battled with him when he didn't feel like practice, since he was four. I know she's told him to be careful of his fingers, but you can't approach a ball sport that way."

"Talk to him about it, please? He can still be a fan. All gifted people have to make sacrifices. They have to put their destiny first."

David shook his head. "Dan doesn't see himself as gifted and he wants to be like his friends—"

"He's not. He won the Hillier competition; his path in life is different. He'll see that if you explain it to him, I'm sure. You must help him to see it, otherwise you're failing him."

Two days later Cindy sat at their upright piano accompanying Daniel as he practiced. He'd done his usual selection of scales, major and minor, separate and slurred, melodic and harmonic; and now he was working his way through a lively Hungarian dance. He didn't need to look at her to know she was watching him closely.

"Good boy! . . . Watch that thumb . . . right through to the heel of the bow, give me a nice sustained sound . . . on the string, quite weighty, give it some strength . . . lovely! Nice flourish at the end."

It'd been their daily ritual for ten years, whether they were at home or in Philadelphia. She'd watched and listened to his teachers, read books, watched DVDs, and studied on the Internet; he respected her considerable knowledge. Pleasing her was as important to him as pleasing his teachers. He and his mother had such a well-refined shorthand that one look could convey whole conversations, and he knew what her likely reaction would be to almost everything.

As he was cleaning his violin she called him into the living room. It was a Sunday morning and he was surprised to see that his father hadn't yet left for the golf course. There seemed to be tension in the room and he paused in the doorway.

"What's up?" he asked, looking from one to the other. Cindy smiled at him and patted the sofa.

"We want to talk to you."

"Can't it wait till tonight, Mom? I'm meeting Aaron by the bridge."

"Going fishing?" his father asked.

"Playing ball. The guys from Stonyridge are biking over, then we'll go swimming with them. I'll be home for dinner. That's okay, isn't it, Mom?"

His parents glanced at each other, which meant they wanted to tell him something.

"Sit down, Dan," his father said, sounding suddenly serious. "That's what we want to talk to you about." Daniel felt a prickle of unease. He did as he was told, sitting down not beside his mother but in a chair opposite her. David cleared his throat loudly.

"When I picked you up Monday, I had a chat with Mr. D. while you collected all those eggs. He's very worried about the bruise on your finger. He thinks you should stop playing ball—"

"No!"

It was an instinctive reaction. He was driven to his feet by the force of the statement.

"Sit down, son. Nothing's decided, we're just talking. Mr. D. knows how good you are. He thinks you can go all the way to Carnegie Hall, be a concert violin—"

"But I don't *want* to be a concert violinist! And *he's* not my real teach—"

"Don't interrupt your father, Daniel. You can't know that yet. If you have the talent that everyone thinks you have, you must be what you must be." He could see his mother was losing patience and that meant an explosion was not far away. When she paused for breath, David abruptly took up the argument.

"Dan, you could break a finger. If it doesn't heal correctly, it'd change your whole fingering pattern. We've talked abou—"

"But I won't break a finger. No one I know has *ever* broken a finger playing baseball. I catch the ball with a glove."

He couldn't believe they could be so ignorant about something so important. His mother glared at him.

"Tony sprained his wrist last year and it took weeks to heal. And you know some of the boys have cuts and bruises."

"Oh, come on, Mom! They told me to be careful but what I did during the holidays was up to me. Maestro knows it'll never stop me playing the violin."

"But that's just the point, darling, it might. Forever. And we can't risk that; you're just too talented. We've put too much time and money into this. You won an international competition, for goodness' sake. What if something happened and you couldn't play at the symposium? How would that look to Maestro Gomez?"

His father came between them and stood over him. Through his anger Daniel registered that David was sweating slightly and the vein in his temple was throbbing, a sure sign he was agitated; his eyes were focused on a spot to the left of Daniel's face.

"So that's it, subject closed. But even though you won't play baseball anymore, we'll still go to the field and watch the Cubs, I promise you that."

Daniel slumped back and stared at them in horror. Anger and frustration and panic and loss swirled around inside his head. He could see his father was concerned, but there was something else in his eyes—guilt.

"Talk to me, Dan. Don't bottle this up. If you talk to me, you'll see I'm right—"

"So we're not actually *discussing* it at all, you're telling me what's been decided."

Cindy made her gesture of extreme exasperation. "It's for your own good, darling. When you can look at it coldly, you'll see that."

Daniel pulled himself to his feet.

"Where are you going?" she demanded.

"Out!" He spat the word back at her.

"Before you go I want your glove and your bat and your ball."

Daniel turned away and headed for the door.

"Daniel! Did you hear what I said?"

He spun around, his dark eyes blazing and his face flushed.

"I'm getting them, okay? You win, Mom, as always. They're no good to me anymore."

When he returned, the gear in his hands, he could hear the

raised voices still coming from the lounge. He paused at the door and listened.

"He'll cool down, David, and then he'll understand. He'll see we're right. He's a very bright boy and music is his life."

"Perhaps we're putting too much pressure on him. He's just fourteen, for God's sake."

"Precisely. He's fourteen and Sarah Chang was performing with major orchestras, in concerts broadcast worldwide, by the time she was eleven. He doesn't have time to waste on damn baseball."

Chapter 5

Daniel was so furious he could barely bike straight. He flew through the air and came down hard on the dirt bumps. The sudden thumps jarred his body and almost twisted the front wheel sideways. He liked the sensation, it suited his mood. They couldn't do that. They just *couldn't*. He'd known he'd have to choose someday but not yet; he was nowhere near ready to give a concert of his own. Besides, baseball was one of the few things left that made him feel normal, one of the gang. When he put on his glove, he wasn't some strange nerd who went to a special school; he was "Dan the Man," a baseball-playing Cub. He was good at third base; it was his special place on the diamond and he was a king there.

Perhaps he could appeal to Mr. D., make him understand, but he dismissed the idea in an instant; *he'd* never see how important baseball was. Nope, his father was the best hope. His father loved baseball too and he'd played the violin as a kid. But even Daniel knew his father didn't win the important battles in their house. He couldn't help feeling vaguely hurt and betrayed by his father's decision and what he saw as collusion with the enemy.

He burst out of the forest and onto the track to the road. Head down and legs pumping, he went as hard as he could, along the road and through the gates to the field. His teammates stood in a circle by the dugout. He threw down the bike and ran to join them.

"Nice of you to make it," Tony teased, and Daniel gave him a shove.

"Where's your stuff?" asked Aaron.

Daniel dug the toe of his Reebok into the dirt.

"Can't play."

"What! Why not?"

"You sick or something?"

All eyes were on him.

"Mr. D. told Dad it might hurt my fingers, so I've got to give it up—"

"No way!"

"But he's not even your real teacher anymore. Can he do that?"

"Man, that sucks!"

Among the general sounds of amazement, anger, and sympathy, one by one the boys drifted away to start the game. Soon only Aaron was left.

"Are you gonna do what they say?"

Daniel looked at him and he could see that Aaron understood.

"Guess so, you know what Mom's like."

"Well, we can still have catches and stuff, if you like."

Daniel shrugged. "Whatever."

"I . . . I better go. Come over later and I'll whip your ass at *Tomb Raider*. Okay?"

"Maybe."

Aaron hesitated. "Are you gonna watch us?"

Daniel turned away quickly. "Nope. See ya."

"Yeah."

He walked to his bike, picked it up, and rode away without a backward glance. He fought the tears for as long as he could—fourteen-year-olds didn't cry—but grief was a new emotion and he couldn't beat it. Eventually he didn't wipe the tears off his cheeks until he had to and only then because his eyes were so full he couldn't see where he was going.

The next morning Daniel had a rehearsal in the local hall for the youth orchestra's summer concert, an eclectic mixture of light classical, show tunes, and American favorites. The conductor, Mr. Simmonds the chemist, was as enthusiastic as he was amateur. But all the kids loved him because he imparted his passion for the music and explained the stories behind the pieces. The skill levels differed widely, so the odd extra note or early entrance was par for the course. No one really cared and they all ended up in the same place at roughly the same time. Daniel was the star attraction. His mother was concerned he might pick up bad habits from Mr. Simmonds and had taken some persuading to let him play this year. Normally Daniel enjoyed it, but today nothing could bring a smile to his face. His playing was mediocre and mechanical and he didn't stay for the postrehearsal Coke, cookies, and chat about the music.

His journey home took him along the main street, past his father's shop, past his old school, down the country road for a couple of miles, and then through the corner of the forest to the house. He had the violin case in a leather traveling bag on his back and his music in the saddlebag. As he reached the forest he heard the sound of voices. He stopped and listened; they were getting closer. He recognized the nasal twang of Richie, the leader of the Stonyridge gang. They were rivals of the Cubs and uneasy friends in the highly competitive world of fourteen-year-olds.

Suddenly a group of six teenagers broke through onto the path in front of him. Carlos and Richie, old baseball foes, were the only two he knew, but they were all older and stronger than him.

"Hey! Look at this." Richie walked over to him. The others followed and they formed a circle around the bike. Daniel felt a stab of impatience; he wanted to get home.

"Hi, Richie, guys."

"Daniel Horowitz. Thinks he's too good for Newbrick now. A big-shot violin player. I heard you don't play ball anymore."

The sneering note in Richie's voice made Daniel bristle.

"Who told you that?" he asked.

"Just heard it. Last night. Baseball too stupid for you now, with your fancy ways? You too busy playing crap music?"

Daniel was seriously outnumbered, and he didn't like the way this was going.

"Nah, I missed yesterday, 'at's all."

"Sure, whatever you say. You used to be quite normal, for a Cub. Now you're the weirdest one of the lot." The other boys laughed and one of them gave him a shove on the shoulder. Carlos reached for the bag on Daniel's back.

"Let's, like, have a look at this violin thingie, seeing as you're here, like."

Daniel pulled away. "Don't touch it! I'll . . . I'll show it to you." He slipped the bag off his shoulders and laid it across the handlebars of the bike. They watched as he unzipped it to reveal the black case.

"Looks old, kinda used," Richie said.

"Can't your parents, like, afford a new one?"

Daniel looked up at the boy, the contempt he felt showing on his face.

"No, you moron, the older the instrument, the better the sound."

"Don't call me a moron, you little prick! Let's, like, see this piece a junk." Carlos snatched at the open case and knocked it sideways off the bike. The violin case fell upside down on the earth. Before Daniel could get away from his bike to pick it up, the boys had it. They took the violin out and held it up. Carlos picked up the bow.

"Be careful!" Daniel demanded indignantly.

Richie laughed. "Ohhh, boys, we've upset him; maybe the nerd will cry. Doesn't look that flash to me."

"It's not. The flash one, the one that's worth *thousands* of dollars, is at home."

Daniel couldn't keep the smugness out of his voice.

Someone tweaked the strings repeatedly with his finger. "Can you play it like a guitar?"

Daniel tossed his bike aside and tried to retrieve his possessions. Carlos had the bow between his two hands. He held it away and snapped it in half. Daniel let out a howl of fury, but instinct told him that punching the boy would be a mistake.

"You jerk! That costs about three grand. Your parents'll have to pay for it." Carlos dropped the two bits, still joined by the horsehair, onto the ground.

"Did any of you, like, see me do it?" he asked the rest of group. They all shook their heads solemnly. Richie grabbed the violin off the boy who was plucking it, turned it over, and scratched a line down the middle of the back with his car key. Then he dropped it into the discarded case.

"Come on, let's split. Forget this stupid music crap, Horowitz; it's for chickens, girls, and fags. Go back to baseball."

They broke into peals of laughter as they ran into the cover of the trees and vanished. Daniel listened to the sound until it was gone. Then he picked up the two bits of bow and put them into the case. He turned the violin over and ran his finger along the surface scratch. It wasn't deep and could be easily mended but would mean a slightly altered sound. It was his second violin, but still . . . He closed the case, zipped it into the traveling bag, and slung it onto his back; then he retrieved his bike and continued on his way. For a while his mind was blank, numb with shock. Suddenly the rage and frustration at his situation bubbled up, and he let out a sustained scream of sheer resentment. The noise was lost in the wind rushing past his face, but the act of making it made him feel better.

Just before the gate to his house, he came to a screeching dead stop. An idea resounded through his agitated brain like a drum roll and he knew instantly that it was the right choice. It was so stunningly simple and logical. It'd solve everything. Why had it taken him so many hours to form a plan? All he had to do was find a way to tell his mother.

"I'm sorry but I can't believe you're persisting with this. It's just ridiculous!"

Daniel watched the three people sitting in a row in front of him. His parents were on the sofa and Mr. D. was in his wheelchair; they looked like a panel of judges. Daniel's French violin and bow sat on the coffee table between them. It was very hot and ominously still; there was an impressive thunderstorm brewing, both outside and in the living room.

"Why?" His mother's voice was full of the controlled exasperation he knew so well.

"I told you already, Mom, a hundred times. It's just not fun anymore; ball is fun. I want to play ball. I don't want to play the viol—"

"But you've always loved the violin."

"And don't you like the lessons?" Mr. D. smiled nervously at him, as if he was a disobedient toddler.

"Sure." He shrugged.

Cindy Horowitz rose and began to pace the room. Her long legs covered the area in a few strides, and her hands twisted around a handkerchief in a continual motion. He was reminded of something his father had said to him yesterday; his mother was not used to defiance.

"I've had enough of this stupidity, Daniel. Life is not all about fun. You're fourteen years old and you do *not* decide what you do. For ten years we've kept you focused on this instrument, no matter what. You *will* practice and have your lessons! You *will* play at the symposium and you *will* be returning to the institute." Her voice was crescendoing to something just under a shriek, and her blue eyes were full of rage, but he stood his ground. This was all she could do, yell at him.

"Or what? I don't want to, Mom, and you can't make me. I'll just refuse and you can't force me to hold it. I want to play ball and go to school here, like the other kids. I want to be normal."

"You're not just *normal*, Dan, you're extraordinary."

His father's voice was measured and calm, and Daniel knew it was meant as a compliment, but it grated on him.

"Only if I play the violin, Dad. If I don't play, I'm normal—"

"*Ordinary* is what you are if you don't play the violin." Cindy spat the comment at him.

"Okay, Mom, ordinary will do."

They stared at each other for a moment and then Cindy drew

a deep breath. "What if we ground you? No going outside this house, for anything, no friends, and no more ball games?"

Daniel shot a look of horror at his father, who held up his hand, palm facing her.

"No, I think that's a bit too drastic, honey. If we just give him time—"

"He's had two weeks and he still refuses to pick the damn thing up. We've been patient long enough. If you want to be stubborn, Daniel Horowitz, I'll show you stubborn. In ten days we leave for Washington, D.C. It's a *huge* honor, this symposium that Maestro Gomez has invited you to. You'll take your violin and you'll play. If anyone else asks you to play, you'll play. Do you understand me? If you refuse, we'll . . . we'll . . . we'll send you to a boarding school far away from your friends."

The threat sat between them for a full moment while mother and son continued to glare at each other. Daniel was pale but his expression hadn't changed. They'd had this argument, in some form, every day for two weeks.

"Boarding school exactly where, Mom? Philadelphia? Can I go to my room and read? I guess there's no point asking to go outside."

"Too damn right there's no point. Oh yes, I suppose you can go and read. How about finishing the book on Paganini?"

Chapter 6

Washington, D.C.
August 2008

"Here's to another successful symposium." Rafael Gomez looked up and smiled warmly at his wife. He sat at the grand piano playing one of his own jazz compositions. The rhythms echoed through the large apartment and bounced off the full-length windows, with their views across the Potomac to the sparkling lights of Washington, D.C. A very large black-and-white cat lay stretched across the top of the piano and blinked its amber eyes in conversation. His wife held a glass of Taylor's 1963 vintage port outstretched toward him and he took it from her.

"*Gracias*. If I keep out of the way, and everyone else just does their jobs, it will be another huge success, yes?" Their glasses clinked together in one clear note, like a bell chiming. He got up and followed her across the room. As he relaxed back into the comfortable chair and sipped the port, he studied her by the flickering light of a large candelabrum on the sideboard.

At thirty-two she was twenty years younger than him, lithe, long limbed, olive skinned, with thick dark hair, great bone structure, a wide mouth, and large soft brown eyes. She was a beauty, no doubt about it, a reflection of her varied gene pool— Hispanic, Caribbean, First Nation, and European. But he'd been surrounded by beautiful and sexy women all his adult life. What made Magdalena Montoya different was her soul. She was a gentle person with a calm, almost serene air about her, and she never spoke ill of anyone. A wise head on young shoulders, his sister had said.

He'd met her four years ago when her PR company had signed up as a sponsor of the Washington Opera and she'd come along to the opening night of an opera he was conducting. He'd been introduced to her at the postopera gala. When she finally accepted his dinner invitation, he'd discovered she had a passion for classical music and played the flute, but she wasn't a professional musician so had no interest in using him to further a career and he found this incredibly refreshing. Four months later he'd nervously proposed beside a huge decorated tree on Christmas Eve and she'd accepted. Everyone was amazed. It was her first marriage and his third.

"Dollar for your thoughts," she said softly.

"Oh, nothing very unusual, just thinking about what I am, such a lucky man. All this"—his arm swept the large open-plan room—"and you. I must have done something wonderful in a previous life to deserve it but I don't know what."

She walked across to the chair, her bare feet silent on the polished wooden floor, and pushed the coffee table away. Then she took the glass from his left hand and the Cuban cigar from his right and placed one on the coaster and the other in the ashtray and sat down astride his lap.

"Funnily enough, I was thinking the same. How much I love

you." She kissed him passionately, and his arms enfolded her as he returned her kisses. Then he stood up, lifting her into his arms at the same time.

"Time for bed," he said gently.

She put her arms around his neck and kissed him again.

"Cristina once told me that nothing distracts you from good port, a good cigar, or good music," she teased. "I nearly said, 'You want to bet?' But that's not the sort of thing a daughter should know about her father." Rafael laughed and carried her across the lounge into the bedroom.

It was the day before the symposium, a beautiful, sunny summer's day with a zephyr blowing in from the Potomac. Rafael walked quickly through the entrance to the Kennedy Center, acknowledging the smiles and nods from the people milling around. Occasionally he stopped to shake a hand, kiss a cheek, exchange a few words, or sign the odd autograph, but he was making his way purposefully to the office of Jeremy Browne, the artistic director of the Washington Opera.

Browne was a dapper Englishman, except for his wayward hair, which always looked as if he'd stuck his finger in a light socket and received a thousand volts to kick-start his day. He had a charming public persona, but those who worked with him knew him to be sophisticated, cunning, and highly efficient. Rafael considered Browne a fair, but demanding man. The Englishman had a strong vision for the company, and as long as you tried your hardest and demonstrated loyalty, he'd move heaven and earth to get you what you needed. Staging opera was an expensive operation, involving all aspects of the arts— singing, orchestration, acting, dance, and visual design—and Browne needed to walk a tightrope between artistic integrity and business acumen. He was on the phone and waved Rafael to a seat. When he made a gesture with his free hand as if raising a cup to his lips, the Spaniard shook his head to decline the offer.

"Have to go now, my darling girl, you'll never guess who's just walked in. Your favorite conductor . . . the very man . . . yes, yes, I will . . . and we look forward to seeing you in about ten days, we're all very excited. *Ciao, bambina.*" He hung up and extended his immaculately groomed hand across the desk.

"*Buenos días*, Rafael, sorry about that. Loredana sends you all her loving as usual."

Rafael smiled as he shook Browne's hand. "Wonderful, I certainly look forward to that. And how is her Violetta?"

"She says she's almost ready. Michael heard her and he said she's sounding sensational."

"*Muy bien.* I trust Michael's judgment. Let us hope that the audience, it is as discerning, or perhaps, as forgiving?"

Browne laughed and raised one bushy eyebrow. "Indeed. Are you ready for this media intrusion?"

Rafael nodded. "Of course, all for the good of the company."

"Working title is 'Making Classical Music Sexy.' No comment. I asked for the questions to be e-mailed; I'll run through them and you can practice your answers."

Rafael suppressed a smile. Browne micromanaged and he wouldn't let his star conductor give a lifestyle interview to a major newspaper without checking the responses first.

"Fire away."

"Where were you born and what was your childhood like?"

"In Spain. Madrid, which makes me a Madrileño, in 1956. My parents ran a restaurant, and my sister and I, we lived with them above it. I was a happy child. I loved football and bull-fighting. I used to go to sleep, you know, with the guitar music drifting up to my bedroom window."

"That'll lead on to if music was important from an early age."

Rafael smiled at a memory. "I have a nice story. My parents, they had a cabinet of records and before I was three years old I used to sit in front of the stereo player and conduct to the zarzuela with my grandmother's knitting needle."

"Brilliant! That's what they want."

"By the time I was ten, I was composing and conducting and singing in the church choir. Believe it or not, I had a pure boy soprano voice. I used to sing at local weddings and parties and make money."

"So why did you become a conductor?"

"I was at the Julliard and one day the conductor of the orchestra, he didn't arrive. He liked to drink, you know? So I had fifteen minutes' warning and I took his place."

Browne shook his head in wonder. "I've never heard that part of your story. Funny how fate takes a hand sometimes."

"Indeed. I was twenty-two when I made my professional debut, and so I have been conducting for thirty years now."

"And you still compose; I love that last CD of Hispanic songs."

Rafael beamed. "Thank you, Jeremy. I have four Latin and two classical Grammy Awards as a conductor or composer, but the one for my own work is the most precious."

Browne hesitated and Rafael waited patiently; he was well aware of where the conversation would go.

"What about the label 'charismatic classical-music sex symbol'?"

Rafael shrugged. "What about it? It's a fine line. I am a musician and that is how I wish to be seen. I want to present all the glorious composers of the past to the people. I understand the, you know, need for all the glitz and the hype, the marketing."

There was a long pause. Browne fiddled with his pen and didn't look up, so finally Rafael decided it was time to help him.

"How much of my private life should I share? I thought it would be okay to give them the—how do you say it?—bare bones."

Browne's expression was one of relief. "Which would be?"

"I was married to Lorenza and we had two beautiful children. Miguel, my son, was a brilliant pianist and he died of leukemia when he was fourteen. My wife was killed in a car crash two years later when I was away in Japan on a symphonic tour. For a long time I was very sad. I married again but it didn't work, and then I married again, to a perfect woman, and it did work. My daughter, Cristina, is an artist. I am now very happy, thank you and good-bye."

Chapter 7

The long Grand Foyer at the Kennedy Center was a mass of children, teenagers, and parents. Instrument cases of all shapes and sizes stood on the floor or leaned against the brass planters. The air was abuzz with chatter and laughter, both sharpened by anticipation. Daniel, determined not to show how fascinated he was, exchanged secret smiles with the kids carrying violin cases.

Rafael Gomez had established the annual Sergei Valentino Young Artists Gala Symposium three years earlier with the help of a Russian-born London resident, the billionaire philanthropist Sergei Valentino. It was by invitation only and was more of a celebration than a competition. Young classical artists came to Washington, D.C., for a week and played or sang. Cellists, flautists, violinists, singers, pianists, trumpet players, other assorted instrumentalists, and youth orchestras converged on both the Kennedy Center and the opera company's rehearsal facilities at Takoma Park to go to workshops and master classes and to perform auditions for invited agents, teachers, conductors, arts administrators, directors, and potential sponsors.

David led his wife and son over to the massive bronze bust of

JFK. Daniel stared up at the rough-textured metal face as Cindy scanned the crowd.

"He's very tall, so I'm sure we'll be able to pick him out," she said.

"He won't even remember me."

"Oh, don't be ridiculous! Of course he will. You only won the Samuel J. Hillier, remember?"

David was watching an attractive young brunette, carrying a violin case, who had a group of men clustered around her.

"Wonder who she is," he murmured.

"She looks important," Daniel said.

"Who?" Cindy's attention had returned to them.

"That girl over there; the people around her seem to know who she is."

"Humph," Cindy said. "I don't think she's a competition winner. Now, Daniel, isn't this exciting? Aren't you glad we came? You can't tell me it doesn't make you want to play!"

David bent down and put his mouth beside his son's ear as Cindy turned back to the crowd.

"If I were you," he whispered, "I would agree with her." Daniel didn't respond.

"Look! There he is." She pointed across the crowd to where Rafael had emerged from the Hall of States and was immediately surrounded by parents and children.

"God, doesn't he look . . . at home here," she finished quickly. They watched his slow progress across the foyer. About fifteen feet away Rafael appeared to scan the crowd, and when his gaze came to rest on Daniel, he smiled broadly and winked.

"He's seen us."

Daniel glanced at his mother; she sounded breathless. With an obvious effort Rafael excused himself and strode over to them.

"Daniel. Welcome to Washington." Daniel felt his hand engulfed, and he experienced the same thrill at the man's presence that he had felt at the Hillier competition.

"Mr. and Mrs. Horowitz, hello. Thank you so much for bringing him all this way." Rafael shook his father's hand and gave his mother a kiss on each cheek.

"Please, call us Cindy and David, and thank *you* so much for inviting us. Daniel's been really *so* excited about this."

The maestro's attention was focused on him, and that made Daniel blush. Rafael took the welcome pack from Cindy. "Very good. Have you got your program there? Your rehearsal schedule will be . . . yes, here it is, and, you know, I want to make sure I see a couple of your rehearsals. There is also one workshop that I wanted to recommend to you too. Ahh, here it is! Maria Wong. I'll ask her to pay special attention to you. Listen to her advice, Daniel; her fingering is legendary."

"Thank yo—" Cindy began.

Suddenly Daniel became aware of other people hovering and waiting for their turn. If he didn't stop his mother agreeing with everything, his future would be decided without him. This thought made his brain snap to attention, and the courage to speak rose from somewhere deep inside.

"Thank you for asking me, sir. It's a real honor. I know my parents thought that if they brought me here it'd make me change my mind, but it hasn't. I've decided not to play the violin anymore."

They seemed frozen, trapped inside a peculiar bubble of awkward silence. Daniel was staring calmly up into the maestro's startled face. It was Cindy who broke the spell, and her voice was heavy with anger.

"Don't be ridiculous, Daniel. You agreed to come and of course you're going to play. I'm so sorry, Maestro, he's just tired from the trip. . . . "

Rafael didn't answer her and just kept studying Daniel. It felt right to return his gaze unblinkingly and wait for a reaction.

"When was the last time that you played?" Rafael asked softly.

"About three weeks ago."

"What happened?"

Finally Daniel looked away, his jaw set defiantly, determined not to speak in front of his parents. Cindy opened her mouth, but Rafael laid his hand gently on her forearm.

"May I borrow him, just for a moment? I need to check the hall, if it is ready. We won't be away very long."

"Certainly, sir. I'm sure he'd like to talk to you alone." Daniel could hear the relief in his father's voice.

The Concert Hall is the largest of the four theaters in the Kennedy Center and its high-tech acoustic canopy guarantees incredible sound. Dramatic curves of blond wood sweep around the walls, triple-tiered crystal chandeliers hang from the roof, and at the back of the stage sit the massive pipes of the Aeolian-Skinner organ. Rafael paused to let Daniel take it all in and then walked with him down the aisle toward the stage. At the front row he gestured to a seat and sat beside Daniel.

"It thrills me, you know, every time I see this place, like it was the first time; and the Opera House—wait till you hear a voice in there."

A theater is a theater, Daniel thought.

"So why have you decided this?" Rafael waited for his answer, and Daniel turned his face away from the scrutiny.

"Just . . . not to. I don't want to play the violin and I don't want to go back to the institute. I don't have to, my friends don't."

"Your friends *can't*. There's a big difference, you know."

Daniel knew what he wanted to reply, "They don't want to, they don't envy me," but that might be rude, so he said nothing.

"Remember the last time we talked, Daniel? I asked you what was the best part of being a violinist? Then you told me that it was when you discovered what the composer had to say, and that was a very good answer, yes? Now I have another question for you—what is the worst part about being a violinist?"

Daniel sighed deeply but didn't respond.

"The practice? Or the lessons?"

"No. I like the lessons, I like learning. Practice can be a pain when you have to just stop everything, whatever you're doing, and do it. But once you start, it's okay, especially new pieces."

Rafael nodded. "So? What is the bit you really don't like?"

"They won't let me play baseball anymore," Daniel said softly, his gaze focused on the floor.

"Who won't?"

"Mr. D. told Mom and Dad that I might hurt my fingers, so I should just watch. And he's not even my real teacher."

The frustration flared up inside, and he could feel his face going red.

"And you love it? Playing ball?"

"More than anything. Dad and I have been going to Wrigley Field for years, and the Cubs are just awesome. I know people rag on them and call them the lovable losers 'cause they haven't won the World Series for years, but they have great stars. The atmosphere at the field is the best and my friends and I are all fans of the Cubs."

Rafael turned to face the stage. He stretched his long legs out, crossed them at the ankles, and locked his hands behind his head. Daniel glanced at him, wondering what he thought about this musical disloyalty, but the man's face was impassive. The silence sat between them and then finally the conductor sighed.

"You know, I grew up in a city mad about football—what you Americans call soccer. Everything was Real Madrid or Atlético Madrid. But Real, they were my heroes. I missed them so bad when we moved to New York. And then, you know, I found the Yankees and the Knicks, had to change my sport, but my heart, it is still with Real Madrid."

Daniel stared at him in amazement.

"So you do understand? They said you wouldn't."

"Sure I do. When did they decide this?"

"Um . . . three weeks ago."

"Make you angry?"

Daniel nodded.

"Then Richie and his gang jumped me in the forest on my way home from orchestra. They broke my bow and scratched my vio—"

"My God! No wonder you don't want to play anymore. Do your parents know about this?"

Daniel nodded again. "They were really pissed about the bow. Carlos denied it, but Mom threatened to have it tested for fingerprints and they paid up."

Rafael smiled. "Well done, Mom."

"The violin needs to be resurfaced, but it was my old one, not the Vuillaume from the institute. The guys called me names and stuff, said that I was weird, said only girls and fags played the violin. On the way home I decided to not play anymore. I thought it'd be a real simple solution, just stay home and play ball and be like the others. That's what I want, to just be normal. But ever since then I've been grounded and we argue all the time. I've never seen Mom so mad. And they *made* me come here."

Rafael was smiling at him.

"Well, I admire you, young man. I don't think I could have stuck to my guns for three weeks, if I was in your position."

Daniel grinned, and he felt the knot inside start to relax.

"Dad says I'm stubborn like her. I figure sometime soon she's gotta give up and let me play ball."

Rafael nodded. "If I ask you a question, will you give me an honest answer?"

Daniel shrugged. "Guess so."

"Forget the baseball for a moment; do you miss playing your violin?"

"Yep."

"Do you miss the music?"

"Yep."

"So, if they let you play ball, will you keep playing the violin too?"

"I guess, maybe, if I'm allowed to play real games, with the boys."

Rafael waited a moment before continuing and Daniel couldn't help wondering where this was going and if maybe he'd found his solution.

"When I was young, my *mamá* wanted me to practice piano and I wanted to shoot goals at the local football club, so sometimes we argued about it, *a lot*, we argued a lot. With lots of shouting! I had this mad idea, you know, that I could be a professional? But I'm not fast enough and my aim, it is lousy most of the time, but it was pretty important to me, this dream, very important. So my dad . . . he decided to . . . strike a deal. So many hours at the piano gave me so many hours with my friends. And I learned an important lesson, about compromise. Sometimes it works like this: in order to get what you want, you have to give in a little and do what you don't want to do. With me so far?" He turned his head and raised a quizzical eyebrow at Daniel, who nodded his understanding.

"So how about *we* strike a deal, young man?"

"Okay."

"If you come to the concert and the workshop and listen to what Maria tells you, but you don't have to play, no rehearsals, for the moment, okay? Then I promise that I'll talk to your mom and dad. I think I can persuade them. In my opinion the danger to your fingers, it is very small if you are careful. And if it means you agree to play, then it's a worthwhile risk. What do you say?"

Daniel took the outstretched hand and they shook.

"Deal!" Daniel said enthusiastically.

"Good." Rafael stood up. "Now, I have to say welcome to all these people out there, in this hall, so I guess we better let them in. When you come to the concert, make sure you listen hard to Tatiana. She'll play Paganini. She is Russian and she is still a raw talent, had very few lessons really. I want to hear most of all what you think of the violin she plays." Rafael guided him up the aisle with a hand on the small of Daniel's back.

"Why? What's so special about it?"

"It belongs to a dear friend of mine, Sergei Valentino, and it was made by Giuseppe Guarneri del Gesú over two hundred and fifty years ago."

Chapter 8

Two nights later the string concert started on time at seven thirty. Daniel and his parents were early so they could drink in the atmosphere of the Concert Hall. He'd told them about Tatiana and the violin she'd play. He was as excited about watching the maestro conduct as he was about the pieces on the program.

After a string quartet and a viola solo came Prokofiev's Sonata in C Major for two violins, played by sixteen-year-old identical twin sisters, born in China and raised in the United States. The performance was technically flawless and their synchronicity fascinated him. An obviously nervous male cellist played a stunning first movement from the Concerto no. 2 by Carl Davidov and drew a standing ovation from the capacity crowd; then the announcer's voice filled the hall again.

"Thank you so much, Mr. Psliwesky, surely another Yo-Yo Ma in the making. Next it's my very great pleasure to introduce to you a young Russian violinist with a huge future. She is known simply as Tatiana and she's nineteen. She plays for us the Allegro maestoso, the first movement from Paganini's Violin Concerto no. 1 in D Major."

The crowd applauded warmly as the tall, auburn-haired young woman stalked into the spotlight and gave a slight bow, her face almost a scowl. She wore a black velvet bustier and an emerald-green skirt. Daniel dug his father in the ribs.

"It's her," he whispered.

"Who?"

"The one we saw with the men; she's the one I'm supposed to listen to." David nodded his understanding.

Tatiana put the violin to her shoulder, tuned briefly, tightened the screw on her bow, and waited for her entrance to the piece. The sound that poured forth from the violin was extraordinary, very powerful and yet crisply and beautifully melodic, with a rich, mellow tone on the D and G strings.

Daniel felt the little hairs on the back of his neck stand on end. He closed his eyes, and the fingers of his left hand began to move. The music was flooding over his consciousness, and he felt awash in a sea of sound, tossed from wave to crescendoing wave, not aware of anything or anyone else. Then, after eighteen glorious minutes, it was over.

Abruptly he opened his eyes and stared at the stage. Tatiana was smiling shyly, with a look of relief on her face, holding the violin and bow in one hand. Everyone around him was standing and applauding enthusiastically, including his parents. Daniel rose to his feet and clapped as hard as he could. He felt a sensation he didn't really understand, like a sudden sense of panic; he had to tell Maestro Gomez how amazing that violin was, about the extraordinary sound, as if he was the only one who really knew.

Three acts later there was a twenty-minute intermission. His parents headed to the aisle and up toward the Grand Foyer. Daniel dawdled behind them. Instead of turning left, he turned right and wandered down toward the stage. He could see the maestro over in the far corner, talking to an African American woman who held a clipboard. She was nodding her understanding. He gave her a kiss on the cheek and she walked away.

Daniel stood by the aisle, waiting for his mentor to see him. But before he did a very tall, thin man rushed up to Rafael. He seemed agitated, or very angry, about something and began talking fast and gesturing with his hands, pointing to the stage, his movements jerky and dramatic. Daniel could see by the body language that Maestro Gomez was placating him, one hand on his arm, and speaking strong, convincing words, but the man would not be pacified. Everyone in the vicinity had moved away, unwilling to be drawn into the heated conversation.

Suddenly the bell chimed to indicate the imminent end of the break. Rafael abruptly excused himself and turned away toward the door. The man gazed angrily after him and walked to his seat. Daniel glanced over his shoulder and saw his mother standing by the entrance to their row, watching, fascinated.

Rafael was about to leave his dressing room for the night when Jeremy Browne knocked on the partially open door.

"Hello there, what a magnificent concert. May I steal a moment?"

Rafael managed a tired smile. "Of course, what is it, my friend?"

He gestured toward a chair and the Englishman sat down.

"I won't keep you long. There's a meeting scheduled Monday and I wanted to give you a heads-up. Give you time to think about it. What do you know about Egypt?"

"They have a lot of camels? And sand, I believe. I did see *The English Patient*."

Browne smiled. "About the Opera House in Cairo."

"Ah . . . I believe it is quite a modern building, very good acoustics, and a first-class orchestra. I've often thought it would be great fun to do *Aida* there. Why?"

Browne pulled a piece of paper from his pocket and dropped it on the coffee table between them.

"Because this is a very interesting letter, from their GM. In three years they hold a six-month global expo in Cairo, and all sorts of cultural and sporting activities are planned. There's to be a massive football tournament for one. And an opera extravaganza. For eight whole months. They're issuing invitations to several companies and we're one of them."

Rafael sat forward and focused his attention on the letter.

"And?" he asked softly.

"I've done some investigating and, although nothing's confirmed yet, I've managed to find out some of the intendeds. Teatro alla Scala will open the festival with *Aida*. The Met wants to do something relatively new and lavish, maybe even Tan Dun's *First Emperor*. Covent Garden has gone for popular and suggested *Bohème, Carmen,* or *Traviata,* and the Australian Opera is considering its options. I'm thinking it'll be something a bit more adventurous, maybe a Britten or a Donizetti. Vienna will go with their stunning *Otello*, Berlin, possibly that updated *Rigoletto*. And the *really* interesting one is the New Israeli Opera doing *Nabucco*."

Rafael didn't bother to hide his surprise.

"Oh my God, what a . . . brave call. Asking them at all, I mean. Where do you think they will put us?"

"Don't know, possibly between the New Israeli and Vienna. They'll want the big three spread out. Any immediate thoughts?"

"Well, one name springs to my mind straightaway, but it isn't a composer."

"It's going to take some careful juggling of singers, because some will be booked elsewhere already. Competition for top voices will be fierce, and they'll want a wide range, not the same few voices—"

"No, no, I was thinking of Sergei. You know, not so long ago he mentioned that he was looking for something new? A grand project, something to get him enthused again. He has a relatively short attention span. What if we offered a Russian opera? In his honor, of course; he so loves all that international recognition, and we could pull out a violin solo for the Guarneri."

Browne was suddenly animated. Rafael knew any mention of Sergei Valentino would have a positive effect on the conversation.

"Russian! Of course! *Eugene Onegin, Boris Godunov, Fedora*—"

"What about *Pique Dame*? It's dramatically different and Tchaikovsky, his darkness will appeal to the Egyptians. There's been something of a revival in recent years, you know, with Domingo, some fascinating productions still around. Do you want me to talk to Sergei?"

"No, I'll make the first move. Dinner and a chat. When I know he's keen, you can join the debate and help him to love our choice. You're so good at that."

Rafael nodded slowly.

"As you wish. Now, if there's nothing else, I must get some sleep. Tomorrow is another day of discovering the next generation of virtuoso." He smiled his innocent, beguiling smile at Browne, who clearly didn't know whether to laugh at the joke or respectfully agree with him.

"How much do you practice?"

Maria Wong sat on a high stool in the South Opera Lounge and faced the collection of young violinists sitting in a semicircle. She was Eurasian, dainty and fine boned, with lustrous black eyes and a genuine Strad in her hands. Daniel couldn't take his eyes off the faded violin and her very, very long fingers.

"Well, I think you could say I belong to the minimalist school of practice. I know some people insist on eight hours a day, but, you see, I regard practice as my best opportunity to identify problems in a piece and solve them. That can usually be done in two or three hours, and sometimes it's best done at the piano, without even playing your violin. Of course you need to build stamina, especially at the stage you're all at, so that's very important too. But you should be aiming at *quality* time, not *quantity* time, when you plan your schedule. Next?"

"Do you change style if it is new composer?" The accent was foreign, Russian. Daniel turned his head to look at the questioner. It was Tatiana. Maria smiled at her warmly.

"Interesting question. Let me demonstrate." She stood up.

"When you want to play something like a Debussy sonata, you play like this." She played a small piece of music.

"You can hear that I have a light bow, with minimal pressure on the strings and a vibrato that makes a rather spontaneous sound, but when I play something like Brahms, I want more depth, more sonority. So I play with a lot more hair flatter on the string, giving me more volume of sound, like this." She played another snatch of music.

"So to answer your question, yes, very much. Part of learning a piece is deciding what style you're going to use and also how you capture the sound the composer intended you to make."

Daniel kept sneaking glances at the battered violin case that sat at Tatiana's feet. What did it look like close up? How did it feel? How hard was it to play? These questions had been reverberating through his mind since the concert and he was dying to ask them.

Half an hour later he got his answers, or rather, didn't get them. Maria Wong asked Tatiana to play for her. Daniel watched closely as she opened the case and lifted out the violin, then he sagged back into his chair. This wasn't the concert violin; it was probably one she'd had for ages. The girl went through her routine quickly, rosin on the bow, wiping the strings, tuning at the piano with the accompanist, and tightening the screw on the frog, and then she began to play a piece of Mozart.

His attention wandered, and he began to look around the room. A crystal chandelier hung in the center and there were tapestries and paintings on the walls. The carpet was a pinky color, like salmon before his mom cooked it. Somewhere in the back of his mind he registered that the noise had stopped and she was putting the violin back in its case. He was too disappointed to look at her. Instead he wondered if every room in this place had a crystal chandelier and if the architects had argued over which chandelier to put in which room, and then his mind started to calculate how many crystals there might be in all the chandeliers in the whole building—

"I'm sorry, sir, but you can't go in there." The doors behind them burst open with a resounding crash, and a man strode in, followed by an agitated, large woman who was trying to stop him. Daniel recognized him instantly as the very tall man he'd seen talking to the maestro during the intermission the night before. He had a glossy black beard, curly black hair, and thick-rimmed glasses that sat halfway down a long nose. He stopped and his gaze swung around the occupants of the room.

"Sir! I must ask you again to leave. Now! There's a private master class going on in this room—"

Tatiana was hiding the violin case behind her back.

"There you are. I've been looking for you all over this building. Play it!" he demanded. His accent was English. She didn't move, and Daniel wondered why she didn't just tell him the violin wasn't the del Gesú.

"I said, play it!" he roared.

She hesitated a second longer, then with a sudden darting movement she leaped slightly sideways, ran around the semi-circle of chairs, across the room, and out the door.

"Come back!" It was an explosion of sheer frustration. He turned on his heel and was about to follow her when the woman blocked his path.

"I must protest most strongly, sir. You've upset one of our students, and I think you should leave the center now. I've called security."

"Didn't you hear it? It isn't the same violin," Daniel blurted out suddenly in a small but clear voice. The man spun around and looked straight at him. He was clearly angry, and Daniel could feel his own heart racing as the man towered over him.

"What did you say?" he asked sharply.

"I said, it's not the same violin. As the one she played last night."

"What do you know about her violins?"

"Nothing. I just know that the one she played today was ordinary."

"He's right." It was one of the other pupils, a girl sitting two seats away from Daniel. "It isn't the same violin. It sounds totally different."

The man turned to the woman who'd followed him in. "I'm sorry; please accept my apology for the interruption."

Chapter 9

Daniel wandered down the steps and into the Grand Foyer. He passed several groups of people, none of whom took any interest in him, so he sat down on the rim of one of the brass planters. It was nearly lunchtime and he wasn't sure where to go next. Two women walked into the foyer from the Hall of States. One of them was the African American woman he'd seen talking to the maestro during the intermission the night before—she worked here, she might know! The other woman was taller and had really long black hair.

"Excuse me."

They both turned toward him.

"Yes? Can I help?" asked the African American woman.

"I need to find Maestro Gomez. It's important."

"What's your name?" the other woman asked. Her voice was soft and her eyes were smiley, and he decided immediately that she might help him.

"Daniel Horowitz."

"Ah, Daniel Horowitz. You're the one who . . . the young violinist, the Hillier winner?" she asked, looking at him in a way he recognized. She'd heard about him and now she was putting a face to the name.

"Yes. I need to talk to him; it's very important. Do you know where he is?"

"As a matter of fact, I do." She extended her hand toward him. "I'm Magdalena Montoya; nice to meet you, Daniel Horowitz. I'm just about to hijack him. Why don't you come with me and we'll do it together."

He followed her into the Opera House. A young man was standing on the stage singing "Che gelida manina" from *La Bohème* to a loud piano accompaniment. He sounded very nervous and slightly flat. Several people sat down in the front, listening and scribbling in books. Magdalena stood just inside the door until the aria came to an end. Then she pointed to a figure over to the right in the back row. It was Maestro Gomez. He glanced over and gave her a little wave.

"Come on, this way," she said in a half whisper. They threaded their way through an empty row to the aisle and then up to where Rafael was stretched out.

"*¡Hola!*, gorgeous woman, fancy meeting you here." He extended his hand toward her.

"I came to make sure you have lunch and look who I found."

Daniel watched her take the hand in hers and bend to kiss the maestro on the mouth, before sitting down beside him. Rafael leaned forward and smiled at him.

"Hello, Daniel, and the lovely Miss Wong, how was she?"

"Very cool. She told me her brother was a semifinalist at the Hillier, on the piano."

"He was indeed. Matthew Wong—he's a very talented pianist."

Daniel wasn't sure what to do. He wanted to tell the maestro about the man who'd burst into the class but not in front of this woman.

"Do you know who this is, Dan?"

"No, sir."

"This is my very wonderful wife, Magdalena. Mags, meet Daniel Horowitz."

"Oh, we've met. I just didn't tell him that I have the dubious pleasure of being the *esposa*." There was laughter in her voice. Out of the corner of his eye, Daniel saw movement on the stage as a plump young woman walked out to the piano and gave the accompanist some music. Rafael watched her, glanced at a sheet of paper on the seat beside him, then seemed to make up his mind.

"We should leave these poor young things in peace." He pulled himself up and guided them out the door and back to the Grand Foyer.

"How about a plate of ice cream on the terrace?" Daniel nodded enthusiastically and Mags smiled playfully at her husband.

"Whatever you want to do, my love. You lead and we, your loyal subjects, shall follow."

Rafael laughed and took her hand.

"I make the mistake of telling a journalist that this woman makes me feel like a king, Dan, and she won't let me forget it."

They followed him upstairs to the KC Café, where Rafael ordered sandwiches for them and a vanilla and butterscotch sundae for Daniel, to be served on the Roof Terrace. While the staff set up the table Rafael showed Daniel the marble walls engraved with the words of President John Fitzgerald Kennedy and the amazing view down the Potomac River to the Jefferson Memorial. It was a cloudless day and the sky was a deep azure blue.

After they were seated and served, Rafael turned to Daniel. "So tell me, Dan, what did you think of Tatiana's violin last night?"

Daniel finished his mouthful.

"The absolute best thing ever. Better than any violin, even better than Maestro Vincelli's real Strad. It is the coolest violin in the whole world!" he said emphatically.

Rafael nodded his agreement. "She played the Pag rather wonderfully too, did you not think so? It rewards fury and fearlessness."

"It was my finals piece."

"I remember. I conducted you so I heard it right up close." They grinned at each other conspiratorially.

Talking to the maestro didn't feel like talking to an important adult; somehow it felt like he was just a friend who loved music, like he could say anything, Daniel thought. It was a satisfying thought.

"Who's the man you were talking to at the intermission?" Daniel asked suddenly. Rafael stopped eating.

"And why do you want to know that?"

"I saw him again, this morning. That's what I wanted to tell you. He interrupted Miss Wong's class." The sandwich dropped to the plate, and Daniel knew he had the maestro's complete attention.

"Tell me what exactly happened, son. Everything you can remember."

"Well, Maria asked Tatiana to play and she did—Mozart—but it wasn't the same violin. This one was ordinary."

"No, the Guarneri is back in the safe."

"He just came crashing in, with some woman telling him to leave. Tatiana had put her violin away but he told her to play, yelled at her. She looked really scared. Like she thought he was going to steal it. She ran out. But we told him that it wasn't the same violin."

"What did he do then?"

"Nothing, he just left. Who is he?"

"His name is Roberto di Longi and he's not a bad man, very intense, but not bad. He's a restorer and a dealer and he lives in London. He is a true expert. You know, I think he knows more about violins than anyone else I've ever met. Like any expert, he will tell you he can recognize any violin, only by its sound and the wood grain. But with Roberto I am more inclined to believe him, what he says, because he *really, truly* knows his violins."

"So why is he mad at Tatiana?"

"He's not mad at her; he is mad about the violin. It is a Guarneri del Gesú. We all know that much for sure. Sergei assures us the label says 1729, but Roberto, he is convinced it is actually a 1742, and every time he hears it, he tells me once again how convinced he is."

Daniel was eating slowly and watching him. Mags was sipping her coffee, also watching her husband with renewed interest.

"Do you think he could be right?" she asked.

"Don't know . . . maybe. If anyone can tell, he can."

"Does it matter?"

"If he's right, it matters very much. Seventeen forty-two is accepted as the best year; Guarneri del Gesú made his greatest ones ever then. He made only thirteen and they're all accounted for, except for the famous missing one. Destroyed in the war, they think, but no one knows for sure. When 1742s change hands, they sell for millions of dollars. Dan, have you read about Il Cannone?"

Daniel nodded, pleased he'd paid attention in the musical history classes.

"Paganini played it."

"He did indeed; it's a 1743, and the Lord Wilton, a 1742, and the sound, it is exquisite, sublime. You know, the Valentino family has owned this Guarneri for many years and Sergei assures me it is a 1729. A genuine Guarneri certainly, but one made in 1729. So one of them is wrong."

"How many Guarneri violins are there in the world, altogether?" Daniel asked.

"About two hundred and fifty by Giuseppe. There were several others in the family and they all made violins. But he was the master."

"Do they know where all of Giuseppe's violins are?"

"Pretty much all, I think. I am not an expert in this," Rafael admitted with a wry smile.

"But I could probably find out if I wanted, couldn't I? On the Internet."

"Sure, most of them. Some will be in private collections. Why this interest, Dan?"

Daniel was licking the last of the ice cream off his spoon.

"We had a Guarneri del Gesú once. But we lost it."

Rafael stirred his coffee slowly and didn't look up. Daniel wondered if the maestro thought that he couldn't see the interest the man was trying to hide. Adults could be very obvious when they were trying too hard to be subtle.

"We?" Rafael asked. Something in his tone of voice made Mags look at him sharply.

"My poppa. He grew up in Germany before the war, and his papa was a banker. His family had a music room with lots of beautiful old instruments, and two of them were violins. But the Nazis took everything away, the house and the bank, and he got sent to a camp."

"That's very sad. And one of these violins was a Guarneri?"

Daniel laid his spoon down on the saucer.

"Yep, a Guarneri del Gesú and an Amati. That's what Poppa told me. He was very proud of them. He used to play the Guarneri when he was my age."

"Do you know what year your Guarneri was?"

Daniel frowned; it was something he should remember. Whenever his poppa started to talk about it, his nana always found a reason to change the conversation.

"Seventeen twenty-something; I forget the exact year."

In one fluid movement Rafael sprang to his feet. He held his hand out to Daniel, and his excitement was obvious. "Come with me. I have something to show you!"

Daniel got up and hesitated, looking at Mags.

"Come on, hurry," Rafael ordered. They could hear the impatience in his voice. Mags gave a sigh.

"Okay, okay, we're coming. Better do as he says." She flashed a smile at Daniel.

Rafael walked them at a rapid pace to the lift and down to a dressing room. In one corner stood a large stereo system and a stack of CDs. He hunted through the pile, reading labels and tossing them aside.

"Raffy?" Mags stood with Daniel, watching. "What on earth are you doing?"

"Looking for . . . " His voice trailed off, then he found it and held it out toward them. "This. You *must* listen to this." He loaded the CD into the player and flicked through the tracks.

"Come here, Daniel. This is a 1742 Guarneri. This is Maestro Yehudi Menuhin playing the Lord Wilton."

The allegro from Bach's Concerto in E filled the room. Daniel felt the same sensation of wonder returning. It was a magical sound, urgent and sumptuous and yet wistful at the same time, and it completely engulfed him. Rafael instinctively began to conduct the orchestra, using smooth, broad movements to re-flect the undulating music. Daniel was as fascinated by the man's agile body, and his expressive hands responding to the melody, as he was by the sound. The allegro reached its con-clusion and Rafael sank to the ground, obviously spent by the emotion. When he looked up at Daniel, he was grinning with delight.

"That is your heritage, my boy. *That* is the sound you should be making, a genuine Guarneri. Then you would play and, oh my God, what a sound you would make! Everyone would stop to listen. You are a once-in-a-generation talent. *Don't you see?* It is the gift from your poppa. We must find that violin and we will find your heritage, Dan. *Then* you'll play for the whole world."

Chapter 10

Monte Carlo
September 2008

On the last day of the symposium Rafael had chosen and announced which of the astonishingly talented musicians would perform at Sergei Valentino's gala night, raising money for the Russian's favorite charities. Sergei rotated the venue around his homes and this year it was the turn of his hilltop villa in Monte Carlo.

Countess Ludevica de Savilla was a remarkably well-preserved eighty-year-old, with soft skin, delicious caramel-colored hair, and deep-set, cornflower-blue eyes. Not for the first time Rafael wondered if her carefully lacquered chignon would taste like the spun cotton candy he'd bought Cristina every year at the upstate county fair when she was a small girl. He pulled his mind back to what she was saying.

". . . so we thought this year we'd run a book on it. Would you care to have a guess, Maestro? Five hundred euros and you're in." Her voice was deep and throaty. He chuckled.

"Me? Now, what makes you think that I am a gambling man, Countess?"

"Oh, come now, dear boy. We're only a mile from the most gorgeous casino on earth. How many years have you been coming to darling Sergei's bashes, and you've never ventured inside the Monte Carlo Casino? And if he's going to tell anyone the subject of his ice sculpture, it would be you." He took a champagne flute from the gold tray on offer and smiled at the waitress.

"Thank you. I'll admit to a trip or two but only with Sergei, in a moment of . . . weakness. But I must protest, Countess, you know he hasn't told me anything about it. Not even a hint. He wasn't, to tell you the truth, overly impressed with Beethoven last year. The hair wasn't right; it looked more like Jeremy Browne. So I think it might be a more ancient theme."

"Older than the eighteenth century?"

"Much. My guess is . . . Bast." He sipped his champagne, his brown eyes twinkling at her. She blinked at him and he could see her surprise.

"What on earth did he write?"

"*She,* Countess. Bast was the Egyptian goddess of music. She's usually portrayed as a lion, or a beautiful girl with the head of a cat, I believe. She would look just magnificent in ice. And it is time we *had* a woman, no?"

She was about to comment when they were joined by Yuri Medvadev, a young artist who lived in New York and painted Mother Russia for a steady market of homesick compatriots. The countess turned to him.

"Tell me, have you heard of—what was it, Maestro?"

"Bast," Rafael said with a small knowing smile in the Russian's direction.

"An Egyptian goddess, a lion, or cat with a female head. I believe she was in charge of physical pleasure, er, sex and so on, so she was probably quite busy. But why do you ask, Countess?" Yuri sounded perplexed.

"Rafael! What have you been telling me?" The countess rounded on him in mock horror.

"I never said she was *just* the goddess of music. It is a very appropriate combination, music and sex, yes? Actually, I think it's more likely to be Chin-hua Niang-niang."

Out of the corner of his eye, he saw Valentino gesturing to him from over by the doors onto the terrace.

"But if you'll excuse me, I think I am being summoned," he added.

The countess laid her hand on his arm.

"You can't leave like that, my darling man. Who is this person? Another composer I've never heard of? I'm feeling positively ignorant tonight."

Rafael smiled a little guiltily.

"I could leave it for you to find out before next year's ball, but of course I wouldn't be so annoying. He's the Chinese god of the violin." With that he took his leave and walked across the room to the doors.

Valentino stood on the terrace, his enormous back to the room, gazing out at the sparkling city below them. As always, Rafael felt a fleeting sense of trepidation as he approached. Sergei Koylaovich Valentino was a vast man, six foot five and over four hundred pounds, his bulk hidden under impeccably cut Ralph Lauren shirts and Brioni suits. More impressively still, his attitudes matched his size. He lived life to the fullest and fulfilled his gargantuan appetites with boundless energy and enthusiasm.

Rafael had known him for eight years and during that time had watched him donate tens of millions of pounds, dollars, and euros to numerous artistic and educational causes. Of course, Valentino could afford to—the man was worth billions, courtesy of the mineral and gas reserves of his homeland—but his generosity tended toward the spectacular. Rafael had never managed to shake off his nagging uncertainty over Valentino's mental stability. On the surface the Russian was a charming, affable host with a huge laugh and Rafael knew many people considered him fortunate to be the confidant of such a remarkable man. Very few had seen the chilling, pale green eyes skewer an unfortunate employee with such swiftness it took Rafael's breath away, or heard the lashing from his tongue. Behind that charm lay a brilliant mind and a violent temper, someone who, Rafael suspected, would make a formidable enemy.

"I love this view. I never tire of it." The English was heavily accented and the bass voice deep and guttural.

"It is magnificent," Rafael said, drawing level with him.

"I sometimes wonder what my father would make of it. He was such faithful servant of the Party, and he lived such a gray life, an ordered life."

"But do you miss what you've never experienced? He was probably happy, yes?"

"I doubt that. He hated the rewards they gave my grandpapa for being a war hero; all he wanted was to serve the Motherland. Such limited dreams, no vision. For all we know, my friend, there may be gold in these hills. This house could be built on top of a billion-dollar fortune."

"Shall we bring shovels next time?"

Valentino turned to stare at him and then laughed, the cupid bow lips moist and red.

"Very good, Raffy. I get the license from the prince and you organize shovels for your orchestra."

Rafael laughed.

"Something tells me there's a joke here about the Anvil Chorus, I just can't quite find it. Have you added Tatiana to tonight's program?"

Valentino swung around to face back toward the room. His fleshy hand held a long glass of bloodred liquid. Rafael guessed it was Campari and soda.

"Do you want to hear her?"

"Of course."

"But you actually want to hear the Guarneri."

"That too."

"You are master diplomat. Yes, I had the violin sent over for her. She's doing very well, Maestro Montenagro says she has enormous talent. But she doesn't want to play the way he teach her; he's so structured, she plays by instinct. It's the gypsy in her."

"There must be room for all kinds of expression. I don't believe in limiting a young person's passion. If you restrict creativity too much, you know, shut it in a box when it's still developing, sometimes it dies."

Valentino glanced at him sharply. "She has said words like this to you?"

"No, no, nothing at all. I was actually thinking of someone else entirely. I will enjoy her sound, however she plays. She could play 'Three Blind Mice' on that instrument and it would sound heavenly, no? By the way, Sergei, have you had a call from Jeremy Browne?"

The Russian put his glass on the wall and lit a cigarette.

"About the *Traviata* gala? It is settled."

"He hasn't invited you to dinner then?"

"No, what does he want now? More money?"

"Quite probably." Rafael glanced at his watch. "I had better check on Mr. Psliwesky and make sure he can hold his cello. The preperformance nerves, they are going to play a big part in this young man's career."

"Give him vodka."

"He's Polish and he doesn't drink."

Valentino grunted.

"And he wants to be star? Tell Misha to start herding them into the music room."

Once again Tatiana followed Jan Psliwesky on his cello, and she waited impatiently for the enthusiastic applause to die down before she climbed the half-dozen stairs to the raised platform. There were around four hundred people standing in the vast room. The tapestries that lined the walls featured intricate designs of treble clefts in silver and gold thread, interspersed with famous musical figures playing their instruments. Heavy gold curtains hung at the huge windows, and the floor was dark polished wood. Above the audience the ceilings were covered in lavishly painted frescoes.

As well as the best emerging talent from the symposium, paintings by new artists adorned the public rooms of Valentino's huge house, and sculptures sat on pedestals where they could be admired. An invitation to participate guaranteed a flood of offers of work. At the end of the evening, he would announce some of his contributions for the next twelve months, sometimes without bothering to tell the recipients beforehand. He liked to surprise people and demonstrate the power that his money gave him.

Tatiana's sleeveless gown, in midnight-blue velvet with Swarovski crystals sparkling on the bodice, clung to the curves of her long body. Her thick chestnut-colored hair was held back in a large silver clip. There were murmurs of appreciation as she tuned with the pianist seated at the baby grand, then took up her stance, fiddled with the screw on the heel of the bow, and paused, bow above the strings.

Tchaikovsky's Mélodie demonstrated the spellbinding power of the Guarneri to perfection, as its complicated runs climbed to lingering top notes, then fell to an achingly sweet and soft finale. The woman's body moved gently with the melody and her face was a study of intense concentration. She played with admirable restraint and control.

Rafael Gomez, at the front of the crowd, was completely oblivious to the fact that people were probably watching for his reaction. The sound brought tears to his eyes. He was reminded for the millionth time why he'd chosen to make classical music his life—because it embodied all that was great and perfect and emotional. There were certain pieces of music that his son, Miguel, had played on the piano and his late wife had loved to hear; the light of pride had sparkled in her beautiful eyes—

Applause and shouts of "Brava" rang out all around him as Tatiana came to an end. Rafael coughed abruptly and shifted his stance, bringing the mask of impassivity down again. Suddenly he was aware of a movement in his peripheral vision, to his left. Tatiana had taken her deep curtsy and walked off the platform. At the base of the steps a tall figure stopped her and grabbed her wrist. It was Roberto di Longi.

"Let me look at the violin!" he commanded loudly.

Tatiana was surprisingly composed. The wrist he'd grabbed held the bow, and she put the violin behind her back. The people around them shrank away, and a hum rippled through the crowd. Rafael arrived at his side.

"Not here, Roberto," he said quietly. "She doesn't deserve to be frightened."

"I don't want to scare you," di Longi said impatiently to the girl. "Just let me have a look at this violin." In one movement he pushed her and she lost her balance. At the same time he reached around her, grabbed the instrument by its neck, and stepped away, the violin in both hands. He peered into the long, upright *f* holes and at the tool marks on the scroll, then ran his hand over the wood. The sparkling oil varnish made it look as if someone had dipped it in liquid toffee.

Rafael extended his hand and beckoned to di Longi to hand it over.

"Roberto, give it back to me. I'm sure we can—"

"No, no, Raffy, it is okay . . . let him look." The voice was unmistakable. Valentino stepped out of the crowd. He appeared very calm, but his eyes were icy cold. Tatiana ran to him and he enfolded her with one arm. Rafael thought she suddenly seemed very small clinging to his side.

"What are you looking for, my friend?"

"You know what I'm looking at." Di Longi's voice rasped with an edge of stress and something approaching desperation.

"And you won't find it. We've had this conversation before, Roberto. This is a genuine 1729 Guarneri. It is a magnificent instrument and I am proud to say it has been in my family for over fifty years."

But di Longi ignored him, turning the violin over and over in his hands, holding it up to the light and following the flame pattern in the grain with his forefinger. Finally he muttered, "I thought so." Then he walked over to the Russian and held out the violin. Valentino gave a dramatic bow and took it back in both hands.

"I'm sorry," di Longi addressed Tatiana. "I didn't mean to frighten you."

"She is easily frightened; she's Russian." There was a momentary pause as the two very tall men eyeballed each other, neither giving an inch.

"We both know what that instrument is, Sergei, and if you think I won't prove it, you're mistaken," he said. Then he walked the length of the room, making no eye contact on the way, and out the open doors. Before he reached the door, Valentino had thrown back his head and let out a huge roar of laughter.

"What fun, eh? I knew there was a reason why I invite him, such a pompous man. Play something for us, darling, play this mysterious fiddle!" He put the violin into Tatiana's reluctant hand. She hesitated but he gave her a gentle nudge toward the steps and slowly she climbed them again. A wave of noise swept around the room as people started to talk in hushed tones. She tuned the violin with the pianist and tightened the bow again. The lovely melody of Shostakovich's Romance from The Gadfly spilled out over the heads of the crowd.

Rafael was torn between the exquisite sound coming from the violin and watching Valentino moving from group to group, shaking hands and laughing, pointing at the stage and agreeing with the praise heaped on both his possessions. Suddenly it occurred to the maestro that di Longi might well be in a talkative mood, so he slipped to the edge of the room and walked briskly out the huge open doorway.

Chapter 11

Roberto di Longi was pacing back and forth across the gravel. The massive white stone mansion rose up behind him, lit by numerous burning pitch poles stuck into the lawn along a sweeping driveway. He was waiting for the valets to bring him his car and was obviously still extremely angry. Rafael stood in the shadows for a moment and watched him; if the Englishman was incensed enough he might answer questions without asking too many. As soon as di Longi saw Rafael walk down the wide steps he stopped dead.

"Arrogant, insufferable man! He's so infuriating," he exclaimed.

"We are in his house, so I guess he can be as infuriating as he likes. Are you going back to your hotel?"

"I want to get as far away from here as possible, why?" A sleek red BMW swung into the turning area.

"There's a café about ten minutes away, at the foot of the mountain road; let's have a drink. I want to ask you something," Rafael said as the driver opened the rear door.

"Fine. I have a question or two for you, come to think of it."

* * *

The café was almost deserted and they sat outside, savoring the cool breeze that rustled the trees, and drank Clés des Ducs V.S.O.P. Armagnac out of large glasses.

Di Longi had settled down a little and told Rafael all about his latest acquisition.

"Pietro Guarneri, 1735, Venice. Wonderful condition and the most beautiful honey varnish, superb color."

"How much?" Rafael asked casually.

"Too much, but I knew my buyer would be ecstatic. He missed out on a Bellosio only about a month ago. He loves those light honey-gold colors, and it has a magnificent sound."

He shifted in his seat, and Rafael could see he was weighing up his words.

"Just out of interest," he said, "what do you know about the girl, Rafael?"

"Tatiana? She's nineteen. She's very good, but impulsive, not technical at all. Sergei says it's the gypsy in her. I suspect that is Sergei being dramatic."

Di Longi raised his eyebrows and Rafael could tell that his comment didn't surprise the Englishman.

"How did he find her?

"He found her in a Moscow bar. He says she was playing, but it's a Russian mafia bar, you know? A dangerous lot, best avoided, and I think she was a regular . . . performer."

"Where did she learn to play, do you know?"

"She grew up in an orphanage in Archangel. I believe she ran away when she was thirteen so she did not have to, you know, go out onto the streets. But you have to think she hasn't had an easy life, yes?"

"How old is he?"

"Sixty-one."

"Are they lovers?"

"I've never asked but I'd be . . . surprised if he's promoting her solely because of her talent. Roberto, tell me again why you think this violin is not a 1729. You know what Sergei says."

The other man took a long swig of cognac and savored it before he answered.

"Several things. The grain of the maple, in the back, is wrong for 1729. And the varnish. It's an incredible color, quite a deep reddish tint on a yellow undercoat. The 1729s were quite a bit paler. And the texture is different too, softer. At his height Guarneri used thirty coats of varnish and sanded between each one, which built to an unbelievable depth of color. The *f* holes are long, obviously Guarneri, but clearly more refined than usual. The scroll is quite rugged and has his typical tool marks in the turns, clearly made *after* the death of his father, who had a major input into his scrolls, and he died in 1739 or '40. It's all simple deduction."

Rafael nodded thoughtfully.

"What about the sound?"

"More subjective. Has to be a comparison. I've heard several Guarneris live and some of them many times, including the Lord Wilton and even the ex-David, the one that Jascha Heifetz played. They all have the same kind of sound: dark, very robust, and with a beautifully resonant D and G. Once you hear it, you never forget it."

"Granted, but what about the label?"

"The Guarneris used a printed label, with the maker's details and the first two numerals, the century, which in their case was seventeen, block printed, and the last two numbers, the year, written in by hand. It's quite simple really; substitute a tiny piece of matched paper with alternative handwritten numbers and voilà! You've changed the date the violin was made. You couldn't tell, unless you tested the paper."

"And the del Gesú part, that is to do with the label, yes?"

"His name was Bartolomeo Giuseppe Antonio Guarneri and he added del Gesú himself. It's written IHS and is a reference to what they call the sacred name, literally an abbreviation of the letters that make up the words *Jesus Christ*. And he added the Roman Cross to the label."

Rafael was leaning forward, his attention absolutely focused on the information he was getting.

"So the label is distinctive and genuine, you think, just the date has been changed?"

The Englishman nodded emphatically. "Precisely."

"One thing I don't understand is why? What would be gained by changing the label?"

Di Longi seemed to have been expecting the question.

"To change the value, depending on when it was really made. It would make the violin more or less valuable and to hide its true identity. I'll tell you an interesting story, which not a lot of people know. The ex-Alard 1742, the one that's now in the Paris Conservatoire? Generally accepted around the world as a 1742 Guarneri. Did you know that the word *Cremone* on the label has a diphthong under the second 'e'? So what, you say? So *everything*. Del Gesú's father and grandfather used them, never Giuseppe, he used a cedilla. Yes, the label looks old and the characters of the printing are correct, but the fact remains that the Cremone is spelled differently, with an 'a' before the last 'e' and there is no other example, in all his work, of a label like that one. Plus the *f* holes are different from every other 1742. The closest match is a Vuillaume replica."

He sat back in triumph. Rafael was genuinely shocked.

"The Paris Conservatoire instrument is not a Guarneri at all? Is that what you're thinking?"

"I'm saying it may not be. There are serious doubts in the

minds of many experts. And if they were allowed to examine the Valentino instrument, I'm convinced they'd say it isn't a 1729."

"He'd never allow that."

Di Longi looked angry again. "I know, but he should. If enough people questioned it publicly, he might be forced to submit it for testing."

Rafael shook his head.

"If enough people question it publicly, he'll lock it away in a vault. Are there other del Gesús missing?"

"Oh God yes, from all the masters, and provenance is somewhere between bloody difficult and impossible. Many of them were looted during the war, first from their original owners and then from the Nazis as war spoils. They've been hidden, sold, maybe destroyed, possibly now owned by people who have no idea what they play. I read an article the other day about a woman in Iowa who found an old violin in her father's attic and gave it to her grandson to play when he started taking lessons. Didn't connect the fact that her father had served during the liberation of Germany with anything he might have hidden in his attic. The boy's father took it to a local antique store and a sharp-eyed dealer e-mailed pictures to Christie's in New York. What was it? A genuine Strad worth about two million quid. Proudly played by a six-year-old learning 'Twinkle, Twinkle.' "

Rafael nodded in amazement.

"Fascinating story. If you know a family who has lost a valuable violin—for instance, during the war—how would you go about finding it?"

Di Longi shook his head.

"You don't. You try something easier, like a manned expedition to Mars. Honestly, Rafael, I wish I could be more positive. So many instruments were taken, in all the occupied countries, and so few records survived the Allied bombing and the last-minute desperate destruction by the Nazis. They burned hundreds of thousands of records when they knew Berlin would fall. Then the Russians came in and the Yanks, and my lot too, come to that, and some of the stuff was just lying around, mostly in cellars, and they treated it as the spoils of war."

"So sad. The Internet would be the place to start, yes?"

"Absolutely, and some of the bigger museums have archives. Use your influence on the global network for private collections, all the people you know. Those kinds of avenues aren't open to ordinary people, but you might have some luck. Obviously, if someone owns it and knows what it is, the chances are they're not going to put their hand up and admit it; you'd have to catch them out."

He took a deep slug of brandy. Rafael stared into his glass. The man's comments spun around in his brain, and he couldn't escape the truth of the words.

"Any particular reason why you ask?" di Longi asked casually.

Rafael shifted suddenly.

"I'm not sure, maybe, maybe not. If it comes to anything, I'll let you know."

"If I can help, I'd be only too glad. I might narrow down the haystacks a little, but it's still a bloody small needle in a continent of hay, and while you're thinking about it, consider this. If Valentino's little masterpiece isn't a 1729, what is it? When *was* it made? Is it the priceless 1742?"

Chapter 12

Two hours later Rafael sat in front of his laptop in the lounge of his suite at the Hotel de Paris. He was surfing the Internet, reading articles about looted violins and the court cases raging around Europe and across the Atlantic over the provenance of recovered instruments. He'd found that one list of violins, identified as having been taken by the Nazis, was held at the Paris Conservatoire. But there was simply no one in any of the families left alive by 1945 to reclaim them. At first he didn't hear the soft knocking sound, but when it echoed a second time he looked up, frowned, then stood up and went to the door. He'd had a shower on his return from the evening's entertainment and was now wearing only a towel wrapped around his waist. Making sure the towel was tightly secured, he glanced through the peephole. A tall female in a black trench coat stood outside, her back to his door, but he knew who she was. "Tatiana! This is a surprise."

She turned around, and he could see uncertainty on her face. "Can I come in?" she asked in a small voice.

"Of course. Excuse me while I put a little more on. I wasn't expecting guests."

He stood aside and she walked into the lounge.

"I worried you be sleeping."

Her voice was heavily accented, and she pronounced the English slowly.

"My Russian's very rusty, but I'm happy to try to talk to you," he said cheerfully as he went into the bathroom and put on the large toweling robe hanging behind the door.

She smiled shyly at him when he reappeared. "I preferred it before," she said in Russian.

"A drink you like would?" he asked, his pronunciation better than his grammar.

She laughed, then swallowed it and looked guilty.

"No, thank you. I can do English better than you Russian. I shouldn't be here, so I just say what I say."

He gestured to a chair and sat down on a sofa.

"You don't have to be nervous, Tatiana. I'm just an old pussy-cat, yes? You played beautifully, you know. Did Sergei tell you that?"

"No. He was very angry, because that man look too close at violin."

She glanced back toward the door, and Rafael thought he saw real fear in her eyes.

"But he didn't take it out on you?"

"No. He always very kind to me. But he wouldn't want me here."

Still she wouldn't meet his gaze, and he wondered, not for the first time, what the huge Russian would be capable of if he felt his possessions were threatened.

"Maestro, I want to come to USA. I want to play in best orchestra. Maybe I'm good and play solo."

Rafael nodded his understanding. "Sergei has much influence, with many orchestras and conductors. No doubt he has plans to introdu—"

"No. He doesn't. He likes me play his violins for him, but not to have real career. He wants me to stay always with him."

Rafael nodded again.

"Ah, I see. Tell me, he will be wondering where you are, no? It's nearly . . . two A.M."

She was blushing. "No, he won't know what I do. We don't, I mean, I don't want to stay with him. I don't love him. I'm very grateful, but I want to live in USA."

"So what exactly do you think I can do? To help you?"

She didn't answer him immediately. Instead she got up and came to the sofa. Her hair was loose, and her large tawny eyes reminded him of his cat when Ludwig lay on the piano and blinked at him. She had a strong face, memorable rather than classically beautiful, with high, Slavic cheekbones, almond-shaped eyes, and a broad forehead. Her hand went out and caressed his arm through the robe.

"Such muscles." Her voice was husky. He could see where this was leading.

"It goes with the job, strong arms and strong wrists. Tatiana—"

"Find me job with orchestra and when I play, they will give me violin. I would be very grateful, Maestro. I show you."

Before he could answer, she opened the coat and revealed the complete nakedness of her exquisite body.

She glided forward and untied his robe as she pressed herself full length against him and slithered up to kiss him on the mouth. His arms came up around her instinctively and they kissed. She felt warm and soft, and her mouth was demanding. Her skill and experience was obvious. He put his hands on her shoulders and gently pushed her away from him. He stood and did up the robe, although he was acutely aware it wouldn't hide his erection. She looked up at him and he could see her confusion. He smiled at her as encouragingly as he could manage.

"Please understand, Tatiana, I am deeply flattered. You are, most definitely, such a very lovely young woman, but I love my wife very much—"

"So you won't help. You don't want to upset Sergei."

Her voice was monotone with no hint of a question. Upsetting Sergei was, indeed, an issue for him, but he believed passionately in personal freedom and Tatiana deserved to decide her own fate. Sergei knew he was a man of principle.

"No, no, I will see what I can do. Many of the orchestras in the United States, they have a high turnover and they are often looking for staff. I promise you, I won't forget that you want to come to America. I know what that feels like."

She stood up, belted the coat, and kissed him on the cheek.

"Thank you. You are very good man. Sergei say so."

"My pleasure." He knew the relief in his voice was obvious.

After she left, he poured himself two fingers of Jim Beam and went into the main bedroom. The call took a few seconds to go through and he smiled as he imagined the phone ringing through their apartment, then there was a familiar click.

"Thanks for calling. We're not home right now. Please leave a message with the time and date you called. Your call will be returned promptly."

Her voice was warm and softly melodic, and it made his heart rise. He waited for the long tone.

"¡Hola!, gorgeous. Just missing you, nothing new. The ball was fine. Sergei was . . . well, Sergei was Sergei, and everyone played well. Something a little interesting to tell you about the violin. How was work? My plane leaves first thing; shall we go to Oceanaire for dinner? Why don't you make a reservation for around nine? See you in a few hours, *te amo, adiós.*"

He hung up and stretched out on the bed, gazing at the ceiling. He'd never been a "player." If he were single, that would be a different story, but he was one of those men who always felt very "married." The temptations were obvious and if he was honest, flattering, but that wasn't how he wanted to be defined. At last the tabloid magazines had stopped asking those "wink-wink, nudge-nudge" questions about the gorgeous young musicians who threw themselves at the powerful and sexy conductor. He found the insinuation insulting and had to bite his tongue against sarcastic responses, which would've been interpreted as guilt.

This was the life of a professional musician: enjoying glorious surroundings in isolation, battling temptation, leaving messages on answering machines when your soul cries out to hear the voice of home, enduring constant plane trips and something that felt suspiciously like loneliness. To the outsider, his life looked luxurious and exciting, but the truth was that it was closer to hard work and discipline and more than a little sacrifice. Why did he do it? He knew the answer only too well, *for the applause.* But did he really want to persuade Daniel to live a life like this? Or any of them? How would they cope with the pressures and dangers of life in the public eye? Could they understand what life off the stage was really like, until they lived it? Perhaps it was better to let him play his baseball and go to school with his friends. And what about Tatiana? She was obviously sick of being a beautiful bird trapped in a cage, admittedly a gilded cage, but a cage nonetheless. Was she talented enough to make it without the patronage of Sergei? Secretly he doubted it. He saw hundreds of talented young musicians during the course of a year. What made Daniel Horowitz so special?

His mind went back to the conversation in the Concert Hall. The boy's body was stiff with resentment and fear, and when he spoke, his voice was tight. By the end of their chat there'd been a light of hope in the dark eyes that he hadn't needed to see to know was there. Daniel trusted him to make it better.

Then he'd discussed it with the parents. David had hardly said anything, but Rafael could see he felt guilty about the standoff. Cindy was polite but firm; the risks of ball sports genuinely concerned her. She wasn't just being a controlling parent; she truly believed she knew her son best and thought Daniel would give in and go back to the violin by the end of the holidays. Or was she just living vicariously through her child, watching him fulfill her dreams? Finally he'd persuaded her to consider a compromise, a grudging promise to think about allowing him to play ball when he came home next summer, if he went back to the institute now.

It didn't come close to the concession he'd promised Daniel, and the boy had been very quiet when they said good-bye. Somehow he felt as if he'd reneged on his part of the deal, as if there was so much more he could've done. Would it make a difference if he found the family violin? Was it even his place to encourage the child to continue along this difficult path? Didn't Daniel have a right to live his life his way and be whatever he wanted to be? Just as Tatiana did. Was exceptional talent enough of a reason to have your destiny decided for you by other people? Ultimately the power rested with the boy; no one could force him to pick up a violin. Why did he even care about the fate of this child?

Rafael took a sip of Jim Beam and let the mellow and smoky

liquor sit in his mouth before he swallowed it. At least he knew the answer to the last question. It was an echo that haunted him every day. A photo he carried in his wallet. Another child, also fourteen, just as talented, lost in the wonder of making music, at the piano for hours on end, a brilliant career stretching before him. Just as he'd started to question his destiny a deadly disease had snatched it all away and left a heartbroken father grieving forever. When we're chosen, do we really have any say in the matter?

Chapter 13

Illinois
September 2008

A slightly surreal early morning stillness settled over the whole town of Newbrick as Daniel rose and slipped away silently on a covert mission. It took him ten minutes of hard biking to get to the baseball grounds. He arrived at the same time as Tony and Aaron. Billy and the three newcomers were already there, wearing Cubs supporters' jackets to ward off the dawn coolness. Billy was holding his catcher's mask and mitt, and Aaron had two gloves and two bats. Tony organized them into a loose team arrangement, with Aaron on first, Chuck on second, and Daniel on third, Billy first catcher and Tony first pitcher. The other two were batting. No one won, but it was baseball, and the boys knew that was all that mattered to their friend.

For the next hour Daniel batted, pitched, fielded, and yelled his heart out. He hit a homer off Aaron and didn't even notice that Chuck hardly chased it; he was too busy sprinting around the bases. After sixty minutes of sheer bliss he said his good-byes, left his thanks unsaid but understood, in the way of teen-agers everywhere, and biked home. He was sitting on the swing seat reliving the homer, his bike lying on the grass, when his mother opened the front door.

"Been biking again?"

"Yep."

"Must make you hungry; want some waffles or eggs for breakfast?"

"Guess so."

She hesitated and seemed to want to say something else, but he looked away toward the forest and she closed the door. In a week he was due back in Philadelphia and she was supposed to go with him. They were still at a standoff. She refused to let him play baseball with his friends, although he did go swim-ming and fishing with them, and he refused to practice or play the violin. They'd both yelled and cried many times until finally David had decreed that the subject was closed for the moment and an uneasy truce settled over the house.

They'd go back to Philadelphia, and it was up to the teachers to persuade him to pick up the violin again.

Obviously, if his teachers couldn't, they would ask him to leave and he knew that would break his mother's heart. In the meantime, he was allowed to be with his friends, but not play baseball. Much of his day was spent at Aaron's house or by the swimming hole with his fellow Cubs. When Cindy tried to talk to him, he answered her in single words; and he spent as little time in her company as possible. It was a confusing mixture of anger and guilt and fear, which he just wished would go away.

Daniel kicked the floor of the porch with his toe. He could still feel the adrenaline rush of the baseball game, and it played across his face like a secret smile. He wondered yet again what

Maestro Gomez would say about his "civil disobedience." That's what Aaron called it, after some project he'd done in history last semester.

Daniel's mind often wandered back to D.C. and he could hear the man's voice, the accent, in his memory. He'd loved every moment spent in the conductor's company, and he missed the energy and the passion for music that surrounded the man, the way he seemed to understand everything. He knew that if he'd shared that with his mom, she'd say it was part of a bigger experience that he was missing, playing music, being a musician. Music defined him, it was the reason he was the way he was, serious, studious, a little old-fashioned and less worldly wise than his friends, more interested in the life of Paganini than the latest computer game.

Whenever he felt tempted to open the case and just clean his violin, just hold it, he remembered the prospect of a lifetime without the thrill of hitting a homer or taking a player out on third, and then he shut out that "missing" feeling before it really took hold. The only concession he made was time spent before he went to sleep, listening to Maestro Gomez's music on his iPod.

"Dan."

He looked up. His father was carrying golf clubs out to his car.

"Hi, Dad."

David put the clubs in the trunk and came and sat down on the porch.

"Been for a ride?"

"Yep."

"Everything okay?"

"Guess so."

Daniel stared out at the dusty road and wondered what was coming next. *Not another argument, please.*

"I thought I should come with you next week and be there for the discussions. Mom said she could handle it, but I feel it's best all around if I'm there too."

Daniel smiled at him. Maybe there were two people in his corner after all.

"I'd like you to come."

"I guessed you might. Don't worry, son, it'll get sorted. It won't go on—"

Cindy opened the front door.

"Breakfast's ready. Stack of waffles for whoever gets there first."

David stood up and extended his hand to Daniel.

"Just this once I'll give you a head start."

Daniel grinned. "Just this once. I'm starving."

Chapter 14

Washington, D.C.
September 2008

There's a great deal of rich, melodic music for the strings in the well-known and well-loved brindisi in Act One of Verdi's *La Traviata*. Rafael Gomez's left arm was working overtime encouraging the joyful emotion through, enticing the strings to put their heart and soul into it, while his right kept the fairly rapid beat. Glasses perched on the end of his nose and his shirt-sleeves rolled up, he stood at the podium guiding the orchestral rehearsal in the Opera House at the Kennedy Center. Once he added the singers and chorus to the mix, it would take all his concentration and energy to bring them in at the right moments, to keep them together and in time. The orchestra was superb, experienced and gifted musicians who knew this score as well as he did. They worked with him to the frenzied climax of the piece and finished in triumph.

"Bravo, everybody! Much better, cellos, I can't tell you the difference that makes. Watch about five bars from letter C, put more edge into it, rata ta ta ta ta! There is a brittle quality to her here, only she knows that she is sick, it needs to be frenzied. David, true pianissimo in that middle passage, please; you might drown Loredana completely if you're not careful. Now, let's do the Di Provenza once more please, from the top, and if you can all bear it, I will sing along."

Some in the orchestra chuckled; it was an old joke. His habit of singing along in opera rehearsals was legendary. He sang some and "lalalalaed" the rest, conducting at the same time. Halfway through he stopped and tapped the baton on the edge of the podium.

"Good, good, now don't get sloppy on me. I know it has been a long afternoon for everyone but you're a little late. And I'm getting lonely. From D please, and concentrate. Watch the rhythm, it needs to flow. This is the last piece."

After he'd given them a couple of extra details and then dismissed them with some words of encouragement, he noticed Jeremy Browne sitting in the auditorium, about halfway back. As soon as Jeremy saw the smile of recognition, he sprang to his feet and walked down to the edge of the pit.

"Lovely. Quite beautiful. And your singing's not so bad either."

Rafael laughed. "It's all smoke and mirrors. Plus the baritone midget I carry in my pocket, but he is our secret, yes? So what brings you down here?"

Jeremy watched him pack away the score.

"A brief chat, got a minute?"

"Of course, a coffee, maybe? I know I could do with one."

Ten minutes later they sat sipping espresso and looking out at the view of Washington. Browne lost no time coming to the point.

"I had dinner with Valentino, discussed the Egyptian opportunity."

"And what did he say?"

"He's very keen, took a minute to think it through, then he came up with a suggestion."

Rafael raised his eyebrows in surprise.

"Really?"

Browne nodded. "He seems to have shaken off the 'I don't want to influence repertoire' line of last season. I have to say I always thought those assurances were false modesty. Have you ever been inside the Egyptian National Cultural Center, Rafael?"

"Once, for a very fine *Le Cid,* Giovanni Donnatello's debut. I thought it was magnificent."

"And very . . . Islamic. Even the shape, a series of domed buildings. I don't know how much you know about Egypt. It's a deeply Islamic country. We follow the New Israeli Opera's *Nabucco* and that's a very, very brave step for the Egyptians. No matter how good the production is, there *will* be dissent. It's about exiling Jews, for goodness' sake! This whole exercise is supposed to promote the fragile peace in the region, to show outsiders that the Arab world is unified, and to make a stand against terrorism. Valentino assures me he understands all this, and he still wants us to do Wagner. One of the few truly anti-Semitic composers the West has produced. And not just any Wagner either. He wants the magnificent and very, very, very long hymn to Christianity—*Parsifal.*"

He'd gotten more and more dramatic as the speech had progressed and Rafael loved it. His look of utter fascination gave way to laughter.

"Perfect! Inflammatory, impossible, ridiculously expensive,

and completely crazy. And so very Sergei. Did you, you know, suggest something Russian at all?"

Browne nodded. "Oh yes, but he's not interested. Seen them all and they're dark and depressing. He suggests a brand-new production of *Parsifal*, the more controversial the better. That, and that alone, he is interested in funding."

"Can we do it without him?"

"Possibly, but it's a very hard ask. The board knows it'll cost a small fortune, whatever we do. It'll take funds earmarked for other things. Talk to him, will you, Rafael? He's your friend. Explain to him that it doesn't work that way, it can't."

Rafael stared sightlessly out the window as he tried to imagine what on earth he could say that would change Sergei's mind about anything.

"To be honest, Jeremy, I don't think he'll care. You know that line from *Gone with the Wind*? 'I don't give a damn'?"

Chapter Fifteen

Illinois
September 2008

"Daniel, it's for you. It's Maestro Gomez!"

Daniel sprang to his feet and sent books flying in all directions as he rushed past his mother toward the sitting room. The receiver lay on the table and he grabbed it.

"Hello, Maestro? It's Daniel."

"Daniel! How are you, son?"

His voice sounded tinny but still deep and with that slightly sleepy sound that Daniel knew so well.

"Okay. I'm going back to the institute tomorrow."

"Are you playing? Practicing?"

"No, sir. We're going to talk to them about it. Mom says they'll persuade me."

"Don't worry about that; you know they can't make you do anything you don't want to do, yes?"

"Yes, sir."

"Good. I've been thinking a lot about those violins, the lost ones of your poppa's you told me about."

Daniel was uncertain where this was heading. "Yes, sir."

"I wondered if you could do me a big favor. I want to talk to your poppa. Do you think he would see us? Would he maybe talk to us, just you and me, if we went to see him?"

Daniel looked at his watching parents and he knew there was a huge grin spreading across his face.

"Sure he would. He loves your music. So does my *feter* Levi, he's really my great-uncle, poppa's brother. They'd *love* to meet you."

"Good. Is your dad there?"

"Yep, he's right here."

"Okay, let me talk to him for a moment. The institute can wait. I'll see you soon."

Two days later a car pulled up outside a modest two-story home in Woodsville, a small town in rural Vermont. Daniel led the way up the concrete drive as the front door opened and three elderly people poured excitedly down the steps and onto the front lawn. The first was a small, wiry man, almost bald. He had fierce dark brows and sparkling eyes above a large nose, and his face was very lined. Following him was a petite, attractive woman with soft gray hair in a bun, steel-rimmed glasses, and pale blue eyes. She enveloped Daniel with a hug and kissed him hard on each cheek. He hugged them both with obvious affection. A little way behind stood another man, considerably taller and very straight; his wavy gray hair had a trace of faded auburn and his green eyes were still sharp and watchful.

"Maestro, this is my poppa, Simon," Daniel said proudly, indicating the small man. "And this is my nana, Ruth, and this is my *feter,* Uncle Levi. Everybody, this is my friend Maestro Gomez."

After a magnificent afternoon tea of *apfelstrudel,* macaroons, sweet blintzes, and chocolate baklava on the terrace, his nana took Daniel into the back garden to help her with the weeding. The conversation so far had revolved around composers, concerts, symphonies, sonatas, concertos, operas, and soloists; and Rafael had enjoyed regaling them with the stories they lapped up so enthusiastically. Both men were intensely musical and had earned his respect almost immediately with their knowledgeable questioning and opinions.

"Your delightful young grandson, he is a rare talent, sir, and a very bright boy. When was the last time you heard him play?"

"Last summer before he went to the institute, his parents brought him here for a holiday." The accent was unmistakably German, but the English was impeccable and the pronunciation clear and clipped.

"He can be a skilled orchestral player and, I believe, quite possibly, a virtuoso concert violinist. But right now, you know, he doesn't want to play."

"We heard. It's a hard life and he's still young, but he doesn't understand how lucky he is, to have the talent, the opportunity, how important it is to play. I have tried to tell him these truths, but he grows up with everything; he has no idea what it is to have nothing."

Rafael nodded thoughtfully. "I think I may be able to persuade him. But first, I wondered if you would be kind enough . . . for me . . . I would like to hear all you can remember about your violins, the Guarneri and the Amati? And how you lost them."

The two old men glanced at each other and Rafael could see the sad connection between them, shared sorrows that needed no words. What he was asking was difficult and painful, and they both had to agree. Finally Simon nodded. Rafael now watched as Simon took a battered old shoe box out of a hutch dresser and brought it to the dining table, where they were seated. He opened the shoe box and spread the contents on the table. There were sepia photos, folded pieces of paper, two miniature portraits in oval gold frames, a couple of lists handwritten in faded ink, two identity cards, a small black box, and a dog-eared child's drawing of a tall man seated at the piano. Simon picked up a photo of two smiling teenaged boys, each holding a violin, and held it out to Rafael.

"Certainly, Maestro."

Loss

Part Two: Simon Horowitz

1935

Chapter 16

Berlin
November 1935

"You're playing too slowly, again. *Look* at the tempo, Simon.
You should be able to play it the way it's written by now. I want it
fast with a nice strong, biting marcato articulation in your bow."

Simon stood in the middle of the room, his music on the
stand and the violin and bow in his hands. He stopped and
peered uncertainly at the sheet in front of him. A short distance
away his teacher, Herr Eisenhardt, was watching him. The man
tapped sharply with his highly polished boot.

"Now, concentrate, boy. From the beginning."

Simon took a deep breath and began to play again.

Three hours later he was much happier. His elder brother,
Levi, played the Steinway grand, and Simon and his papa played
their violins. It was a beautiful, melodic sound with the main
tune carried by the piano, while the violins rose and fell in harmony.

"All together, and finish."

Benjamin's bow made a theatrical flourish, which Simon almost succeeded in imitating, and they all finished together.

"Well done, both of you. Just a little more and we should be able to play it for family night. What would you like to finish with?"

He was a short, rotund man with a round face topped by bushy eyebrows and divided by a huge handlebar mustache. His deep smile lines and laughing brown eyes created the impression that he was always in a good mood.

"Play some Vivaldi, Papa." Simon wiped his violin and laid it in its case.

"Always Vivaldi. Very well."

Minutes passed and neither boy moved. They were both so engrossed in the haunting, sharp sound of the Concerto in B Minor pouring forth from the Guarneri they hardly noticed the wink Benjamin gave their mother as she paused at the open door.

The Horowitz family lived in the most beautiful house on a street full of beautiful houses. Just minutes from the Brandenburg Gate, it was an old seven-bedroom mansion set in a lovely, leafy garden. Benjamin Horowitz had bought the house on his first visit after the decision was made to move the family bank from Frankfurt to Berlin in 1925. He'd been promised important government and commercial accounts if they relocated, and it had proved a very wise move. In three years, the bank had nearly doubled in size and profit and moved to magnificent premises on the Pariser Platz. His brother Mordecai ran the public banking services, while Benjamin took care of the elite government and business accounts. Their elder brother, Avrum, had immigrated to the United States in 1930 and worked for a bank in New York. They heard from him infrequently, but he seemed happy and successful.

Then in 1933 the Nazis came to power, and slowly, but inevitably, the tide turned against Jewish businesses. At first Benjamin had thought they'd be immune, and it had taken a long time for the effects of the insidious policies to bite. But over the last twelve months the government had used the bank to force several important Jewish companies into bankruptcy. When Benjamin protested, he was told he'd be quiet if he knew what was good for him and he was advised to concentrate on strengthening his international client list. Then he was instructed to foreclose on a major department store owned by close Jewish friends, and when he refused, he'd been threatened with arrest until he complied. But he brought none of these concerns home with him at the end of the day.

The house was Elizabeth Horowitz's pride and joy. She'd completely redecorated it in creamy ivories, rich reds, and brilliant blues and restored much of its original grandeur. It was the perfect place to showcase their collective treasures, some of which had been in their families for over three hundred years. An Albrecht Dürer portrait of one of Elizabeth's ancestors, a Nuremberg nobleman, hung in the hall and a Sandro Botticelli woman, in a Christian pose, in the drawing room. There were huge silver tea services and ornate table centerpieces, fine china dinner services hand-painted with twenty-four-carat gold, Venetian glass, original Fabergé eggs, many porcelain figurines and delicately carved ivory ornaments, Persian carpets and silk rugs, and numerous artworks.

Simon's favorite room of all was the music room. The ceiling was a canvas for a magnificent homage to Apollo, playing a golden lyre and surrounded by cherubs blowing on trumpets. The

walls were covered with bloodred silk wallpaper decorated with
music notes in gold leaf; there were lots of floor-to-ceiling mirrors in gold frames, heavy red velvet curtains, and, in the center,
a magnificent Austrian crystal chandelier. A 1586 Flemish double
virginal, all intricately decorated panels and two keyboards,
stood in one corner of the large room. No one ever played it, but
it looked gorgeous when the setting sun struck the golden decora-
tion. The room was dominated by a huge Steinway grand piano,
and along the walls, several instruments sat on velvet in old glass
cases. They included a sixteenth-century tenor recorder, a 1788
wood-and-ivory serpent, a 1535 Italian lute from the famous Bologna school, and, in pride of place, two violins. The first was an
Amati and the second a Guarneri del Gesú.

At school the next day, Simon continued to think about his family's precious violins. Nicolo Amati was born in Cremona, Italy,
in 1596. He was the grandson of Andrea Amati, the founder of
the Cremonese school of luthiers, who made the first instrument
on the pattern of the classical violin. Nicolo's father, Hierony-
mus, and his uncle Antonio were also violin makers. When his
father died, Nicolo took over the workshop and improved the
model that had been adopted by the rest of the family. He used
a so-called big pattern, with higher ribs and flatter arching.
These changes resulted in a baroque sound that suited the compositions of the period perfectly. His violins had a beautiful,
sweet, penetrating tone, although they were not known for their
power. He also made violas, cellos, and three-string bass viols.
Benjamin Horowitz's Nicolo Amati was made in 1640 with a
sound as smooth as liquid honey, a light tone, and a lovely dark
varnish. Nicolo Amati's workshop was important because it
trained so many master craftsmen. His star pupils included Antonio Stradivari and Andrea Guarneri.

Like the Amatis, the Guarneris were a family firm. Andrea had sons, and they had sons, and they all made violins. The most famous of all was Giuseppe (or Joseph) Guarneri, Andrea's grandson. His violins were, possibly, the most glorious ever made. He was born in 1698 and lived only forty-six years. He produced around two hundred fifty violins, compared with Stradivari's more than six hundred. From the beginning, he had his own individual style and was often in a hurry, which meant that his workmanship was sometimes quite rough. His backs were maple and his tops spruce. He flattened the backs and elongated the *f* holes to make them more upright and longer, and he put more wood in the resonator, making the box and belly thicker. All this meant his instruments had tremendous personality and individual characteristics. The sound was deep, rich, and mellow, with enormous resonance and penetration, ideal for the concert violinist. They were not easy to play but they rewarded skill with a sound so amazing it took one's breath away.

The Horowitzes' Guarneri was a warm brown color, with just a hint of a reddish tint over a yellow ground, and had a marvelous bright luster to the oil varnish. Simon would sit and just gaze at it for as long as his mother would let him. When his father allowed him to hold it, he would marvel at the silky feel of the highly varnished wood and the sudden chill under his fingertips. The sound was haunting and melancholic, especially during the Russian pieces—

"Simon Horowitz! Pay attention!"

With a sudden shock, he pulled himself together and looked up into the furious face of his schoolteacher.

"You're daydreaming again."

"No, miss. I was listening."

"Liar. Little Jew boy liar. Do you know what we do with boys like you?"

He looked at her uncertainly. She'd never paid him this much attention before. Behind her glasses her blue eyes were bulging, and her face was turning a horrible puce color.

"Um, no, miss."

She reached out and grabbed his shirt collar.

"Come with me."

The force propelled him out of the seat and almost off his feet. She dragged him between the rows of boys to the front of the classroom. The collar dug into his throat as the rush of mortification burned his cheeks with a bright red flame. He could see the other faces laughing at him.

"Now, class, pay attention. This boy is a liar. *And* he is a Jew. How do I know this? Look at his nose; no Aryan has a nose that big. And his forehead is slanted backward. He has very brown eyes, almost black, and they are crafty, disobedient eyes."

As she pointed out each feature with her pudgy finger, she slapped the side of his head with the other hand and the impact knocked him slightly off his feet. He stared up at the venom on her face in astonishment. What on earth had he done to deserve this?

"If you read the new chart on the wall, it'll tell you how to identify a Jew, so you'll know to avoid con—"

With a sudden burst of strength, Simon pushed her away from him.

"Leave me alone, you fat old frau!" He ran out the door and down the corridor. Behind him he could hear her voice shouting and the class in an uproar. He ignored all the sounds and kept on running, the clatter of his footsteps echoing off the walls, down the main steps, and across the playground toward the iron gates. It was freezing cold and his lungs felt like bursting, and tears were smarting in his eyes. He rounded a corner and saw two teenaged boys sitting on a wooden bench at the tram stop across the road. He pulled up, hesitated, and then walked toward them, breathing deeply through his mouth. As he approached he could see they were eyeing him with interest, too late now.

"Why aren't you in school?"

Simon prayed silently that the tram would appear soon. It was too far to walk home, and his head was spinning from lack of oxygen.

"Didn't you hear me, boy?" the teenager repeated. A wiry boy with freckles and blond hair got up and walked around him.

"Are you a Jew?" he said, sneering. Fear spurted up again like bile, and Simon searched for an escape route. Levi's words came back to him, "Say nothing and don't look afraid."

"What's your name?"

In the distance he heard the clang of the tram.

"Is it Levi, or Saul, or Abraham maybe?"

The second one had joined his tormentor and just as the tram swung into view and glided toward them, Simon saw that the boy had a large clod of earth in his hand. Why did the tram take so long?

"Lost your voice? Dirty little Jew boy."

"Just you wait, pig, you'll get what's coming to you. My father says all Jews are filth, just vermin, to blame for everything, and we need to sweep them—"

The tram pulled to a stop and Simon jumped on board just as the earth hit him in the small of the back. The boys were laughing, but they didn't follow him. He found a seat and waited for his racing heart to slow down.

The house was silent and welcoming. He closed the front door behind him and went straight to the music room. The weak

November sunlight reflected off the virginal and made patterns on the walls, but today he didn't stop to look; instead he went straight to the glass case.

"Simon, darling! What's wrong?"

He looked up as his mother crossed the room. Her arms enfolded him in a hug, and he could smell her lilac scent.

"My violin"—his voice sounded small and forced in his throbbing ears, and his throat felt tight—"doesn't hate me. It doesn't call me a dirty Jew boy."

He felt his mother recoil beside him and heard the shock in her voice.

"A what?"

"That's what they said, and Mrs. Munz, she said I was a little Jew boy liar."

She stroked his hair off his forehead and looked down into his face.

"I think you had better tell me exactly what's happened."

Chapter 17

That night the Horowitzes held one of their special musical evenings. Berlin in the 1930s was full of artists, poets, singers, dancers, and musicians. Some had left for the States, but many felt themselves to be invulnerable, protected by their popularity despite the ever-growing Nazi oppression. The classical music "set" was no different. Benjamin and Elizabeth invited composers, conductors, instrumentalists, and singers to their home and held musical soirees for their friends. On this night they had Franz Reinhardt, an elderly German composer and gifted pianist who would play the Steinway, and Lillian Hauptman, an accomplished violinist who adored playing the Amati. A group of elegantly dressed men and women were chatting, sipping brandy, and taking their seats in the music room.

Simon sat over in one corner watching intently. He'd repeated his story twice, to his mother and then to his father. They'd promised him it would never happen again because they'd find him a new school and make sure he never had to ride the trams. Even more wonderfully, as a special treat, they'd allowed him to stay up and watch the performance. Now he was so excited his heart was racing and the palms of his hands were damp. His father stood by the piano and as he waited for the guests to settle, he winked at Simon, who grinned back. His papa was the center of his universe, and Simon knew how lucky he was to have a father as affectionate and involved with his children as Benjamin was; some of his friends hardly ever spoke to their fathers.

"Ladies and gentlemen, welcome to the musical part of the evening. I trust you've all dined well, now let us have a feast for the ears! And in Lillian's case, indeed, a feast for the eyes as well. However, before I ask Franz to perform his brand-new composition, I have a little surprise for you."

As he spoke he walked over to the nearest glass case and unlocked the lid with a key he kept on a chain attached to his pocket watch. Carefully he lifted out the Guarneri violin and its bow and shut the lid.

"This is my Guarneri, as most of you know. My son Simon is fourteen, and he is a wonderful little violinist. He practices very hard and he's going to have a special night tonight."

He went back to the piano and gestured to Simon.

"Come here, son." Simon walked slowly over to Benjamin and gazed from him to the crowd of smiling people and back again. He could see his father's dark eyes brimming with joy and something else, pride. His papa was proud of him! Then his father put the violin in his hand.

"The Guarneri can be very hard on a nervous player. This way he has no time to get nervous. Here, take the bow, son." He turned to the audience.

"You must understand that Simon has loved this violin all his life and he's held it very often. But he has never been allowed to play it, until now."

A sudden bolt of energy shot through Simon's body. Instinctively he stood up very straight and took the bow. Benjamin hit an A on the piano.

"Tune it with me."

He adjusted each peg until his father nodded and then moved on to the next string.

"What do you want to play?"

His mouth was dry and he licked his lips.

"Debussy."

"Don't think too hard, son, just do it. Don't worry about mistakes, just keep playing." Simon tightened the screw on the end of the bow. The swirl of confusion, shock, and delight dropped out of his mind as he put the violin to his chin. It felt cold, strange, and unforgiving. He closed his eyes and drew the bow across the string. The quiet, melancholic sounds of "The Girl with the Flaxen Hair" drifted out into the room.

Sometime later Elizabeth sat on the bed of her second son. He watched the moonlight dancing on her long string of pearls. It was a hairdresser day so her hair was swept up into a roll, and when she smiled at him, the dimples in her cheeks and chin were like exclamation marks. He liked the fact that he had a dimple in his chin too, but Levi didn't.

"Your papa wanted you to go to sleep with happy thoughts, not sad ones," she said.

"It was the best night ever. Papa said we can rehearse the Bach Concerto for Two Violins. He'll play his Amati and I'll play my Guarneri. Levi will be so jealous."

Her eyebrows shot up. "*Your* Guarneri?"

He grinned. "It'll always be mine. I'm going to spend my life playing it now, Mama."

She nodded gently. "I do believe you will, and you'll always remember tonight, for all the right reasons."

"I've just been going over every note in my head. After all these years, I played it! I knew exactly what it would feel like and it did."

She stroked his hair.

"I know you did, my clever young man, and you were wonderful. If you worry about Mrs. Munz or those awful boys, you just remember, none of them could play a violin at all, let alone a violin like . . . yours."

A slow smile spread across his face.

"I hadn't thought of that. They couldn't do it, but I can. And next time Papa and I will play together, for everyone."

Chapter 18

Berlin
November 1938

The doors to the synagogue opened, and people poured out into the weak late-autumn sunlight. Men, women, and children wore coats, jackets, and suits, with hats or yarmulkes on their heads and gloves on their hands. They were laughing and talking, walking in pairs, purposefully ignoring the small group that stood on the sidewalk at the bottom of the path. These people looked exactly the same, except there were no yarmulkes and no laughter.

"Jew!" one of them yelled as the people began to pass by.

Still the families ignored them.

"Dirty Jew! Get out, leave us all in peace!" As a woman passed close by him, one of the protesters spat at her face. She stopped, pulled a handkerchief from her pocket, wiped her face, and continued to walk, without looking in his direction.

"Jewish whore! Filthy bitch!" he shouted after her furiously.

The Horowitz family walked in three groups of two, Benjamin and Elizabeth arm in arm in front, the twins almost running, with Rachel's black plaits bobbing against her scarlet coat, and Levi and Simon together bringing up the rear. As he'd instructed them to do, Benjamin's children chatted to each other and ignored the abuse being screamed at them less than three feet away.

In four months, Simon Horowitz would turn eighteen. He lay on his bed listening to the sounds floating in on the night air, laughter and shouting and something that sounded like anger and then every so often the noise of a siren or a loud truck. It was early November and the city of Berlin was winding up into festive mode. His elder brother, Levi, was twenty-one and stayed out late almost every night. Simon, who took after his father, was not very tall but stocky and strong. Simon's face had lost the chubbiness of youth, and the flashing eyes and wild brows offset his hooked nose. He wasn't sure about the dimple in his chin; it was fine on his mother and as a child he'd been proud of it, but now he wondered if it made him look too young.

He switched on the light above his bed. His room was quite plain compared to the rest of the house, but he liked it that way. Two huge portraits dominated the pale walls. One was Paganini playing his 1742 Guarneri violin, Il Cannone, and the other was a late-eighteenth-century portrait of another of his heroes, Antonio Vivaldi. Simon's violin case lay beside the music stand and a box full of sheet music. The rest of the room was tidy; clothes were in the wardrobe, and the top of his nightstand neatly displayed his hairbrush and comb, a mirror, a china bowl and pitcher, and, in a wooden frame, a line drawing of himself playing the violin, by his younger sister, Rachel.

He picked up his book on composition and thumbed through

it. Officially, both he and Levi were waiting for things to improve before starting college; unofficially, they knew that in the current political climate, no college would take them. Levi was working as a clerk in his father's bank, and Simon was giving music lessons to the children of Jewish friends. It was hard to find Gentiles who would teach them; in fact, in some parts of town it was hard to find Gentiles who would serve them in shops. There were so many restrictions now—they weren't allowed to carry guns or own radios, and for several months they'd carried identity cards. It wasn't compulsory to do so, but that day wasn't far away.

Very few businesses were now openly owned by Jews, and most of those premises were being continuously covered in graffiti, as were many of their friends' homes. Simon was used to the Gentile reaction. If he was called names, spat at, or, worse, had things thrown at him, he just put his head down and hurried on. Things would get better; Papa was convinced of it. This Hitler was Austrian; he wasn't even German and the Germans would see through him and his sadistic thugs, vote them out in the next election, and everything would return to normal. Papa told them that it was just these extremists who made life difficult. Most people were as friendly as ever, and his customers had stayed loyal.

In fact, Simon suspected that his papa didn't really discuss the situation at the bank with anyone except Mordecai. Levi told him that accounts were being closed and funds withdrawn every day. People were very apologetic; it was nothing personal, but they'd been told it was unsafe to do business with a Jew. One woman even told him she hadn't known he was "dirty." Mama told them that when Uncle Avrum suggested they sell the bank and come to New York, their papa had been horrified by the idea. The current atmosphere might be very hard, but it was temporary and it would pass; it was no reason to leave their home and start again somewhere else.

At least they still had their musical evenings, although those attending were more likely to be just family now. Many of their friends were too frightened to go out at night in case they got assaulted by roving bands of Nazi youth. Simon and his papa played the violins, separately and together, and the old thrill was always there. His reverence for the Guarneri remained as strong as ever. Sometimes it sounded close to perfect, and at other times it made him look like a novice. His skill had been widely recognized, and he clung to his dream of studying music and playing in the Berlin Philharmonic when this madness came to an end.

"Good book?"

He looked up. Levi stood in the doorway.

"Not especially. Can you hear the noise out there? Sounds like another busy night for the police."

Levi sat down at Simon's desk and picked up a fountain pen. He resembled his mother, tall and willowy with long limbs and fingers. Her coloring, auburn hair, moss-green eyes, and golden skin dusted with freckles, made him different from the other children, who were like Benjamin, with his dark hair and almost black eyes. Levi would've made a beautiful female, as his mother was, and already seemed to posses her innate grace and elegance in his movements. Simon knew that many fathers would've struggled to understand Levi's passion for art, design, color, and fabric, all things exquisite and perfect, but Benjamin had a strong cultural flame in his own soul and he respected his eldest son's talent. His sons, in turn, respected him.

"Should be fun. Want to come?"

Simon hesitated. Levi was suggesting a covert operation, and he knew his parents would vent their disapproval in the morning.

"No thanks, too cold for me, and I want to practice the sonata again, for tomorrow night."

Levi shook his head with obvious amusement.

"You know what they say, Si, all work and no play. That bloody violin rules your life. If you change your mind, we'll be at Das Festmahl till midnight."

He pulled himself to his feet.

"Have fun and be careful," Simon said, returning to his book.

"Always."

An hour later, Simon stood in his room doing fingering exercises on his own Victorian violin. It was boring, repetitive, and time consuming but, according to Herr Eisenhardt, absolutely necessary if he was to achieve the dexterity he craved.

Suddenly the night was split by the sharp sound of glass breaking. Simon went to the window. A group of men were using a piece of wood to shatter all the windows of a Rolls-Royce parked up the street; the scene was almost as bright as day. Farther on he could see a big black police wagon with its rear doors open and men being manhandled into it. Downstairs he heard the telephone ring. He crossed the room and went out onto the landing. His father's conversation was brief, and then he heard his mother's voice. He moved farther down the stairs.

"He's out with friends," she said.

"Where?"

"I don't know, Potsdamer Platz or maybe the Friedrichstraße. Why?"

Simon could hear the panic in her voice.

"That was Franz. The bastards have launched a pogrom. He says we should get the children and come to his house. It's got a hidden cellar."

"Oh my God, Benjamin—"

"I'll take you and the children to Franz, and then I'll find Levi."

Simon ran back into his room. He grabbed his coat from the peg on the door and thrust his feet into his boots. He knew he had precious little time to get out of the house before his mother came. They'd never let him go alone, so he had to get out now and find Levi. He grabbed a piece of paper from his desk, dipped the fountain pen into a pot of ink, and scrawled a note.

"Mama, I know where Levi is. Get Papa to take you to Herr Reinhardt's. We'll meet you there soon. Don't worry, your loving son, Simon."

He could hear his mother going into David's room. He pulled the window up as far as the cord would allow, swung himself out onto the massive branch of the tree, and crawled along to where he could swing down onto another branch. In a few moments he was on the ground and moving toward the gate.

Chapter 19

The street was a seething mass of people. Simon stood on the sidewalk and watched the chaos with a mixture of horror and excitement. Groups of SS officers and storm troopers were running from window to window, smashing the glass with their truncheons or long sticks, and the sound was like a thousand bells all chiming at once. Men were carrying armfuls of furniture and books out of the shops to add to a growing pile heaped in the middle of the road. He could see two officers trying to set fire to one corner of the pile. Terrified people were running in every direction, yelling and screaming and trying to avoid the storm troopers' truncheons. A group of officers was clustered tightly around an Orthodox Jew, laughing and cutting his hair while he stood staring straight ahead, his hat in his hands, offering no resistance. A truck rumbled into the street and screeched to a halt. Uniformed policemen pulled up the back canopy. *Now we'll get some order,* Simon thought with relief. But, to his amazement, the SS officers and storm troopers started grabbing men as they ran past and pushing them toward the tailgate of the truck.

An icy dread trickled down his spine, and his legs felt suddenly weak. Without understanding how or why, he knew that this night was different from all the abuse they'd suffered before. This was on a new scale.

He began to run down the sidewalk, leaping instinctively over piles of glass that lay underfoot like snow. The cold wind was blowing it onto the folds in his clothes and up into his face and hair.

Suddenly a large man blocked his path. He'd run out from a shop doorway holding a piece of jagged glass in front of him like a weapon. Simon saw terror on the man's haggard face as the hand thrust the glass out and upward toward him, then a softening to some form of recognition and acknowledgment. The man was wearing a yarmulke.

"Run!"

It was a half-uttered cry, choked off in his throat, and he was gone. Simon forced himself to start running again. The truck passed very close by him, swerving to avoid pedestrians, and he could see the desperation in the eyes of the men sitting in the rear. As he passed the top of the blind alley, something in his peripheral vision caught his attention, a pile of familiar-shaped objects in the middle of the dimly lit street. It pulled him to a sudden stop and he turned back. Violins!

Curiosity overcame fear, and he ducked into the shadows on the far side of the alley. Carefully and quietly he made his way from doorway to doorway until he was opposite the building. Two storm troopers were carrying three or four instruments in each hand out of the shop and throwing them onto the pile. The wood splintered as it hit the cobblestones. Simon could see an officer beating a man with a truncheon and recognized the victim, Jacob, Amos's assistant. There was nothing he could do to save Jacob or the priceless violins from the fires of hatred, and his common sense told him that his intervention could prove fatal, but still the violence and desecration filled him with incandescent rage and a sense of complete helplessness. Breathing deeply against the desire to attack the thugs only feet away from him, he crept back to the main street and began to run.

"Simon!"

Ahead of him was a café with its tables and chairs strewn upside down on the sidewalk among the debris, bright tablecloths crumpled in the glass. Rolf, a friend of Levi's, was beckoning frantically to him from the open door. He sprinted inside. The lights were out, but the room was lit by the flashlights and streetlights outside. A group of young men and women were huddled in a corner, away from the gaping hole that had been the front window.

"Levi!"

The brothers embraced.

"What are you doing here?"

"Franz rang Papa and said the Nazis had launched a pogrom. They've taken the twins to Franz's, he has a cellar. I knew where you were. We have to get to the Reinhardts'."

Rolf grabbed Levi's sleeve. "You'll be arrested. If they find you on the streets, they'll take you. Stay with us, you're one of us."

"We can't stay here. It's not that far—"

"At least leave your cards behind and lie about your names."

Rolf was pleading with him. Levi pulled his identity card out of his jacket pocket and threw it across the room. Simon felt in his coat pockets.

"I don't have mine."

Levi and Rolf hugged each other, and Rolf put the palm of his hand against Levi's freezing cheek. "Try and stay safe," he said quietly.

Simon followed his brother out the door and into the mayhem.

They ducked around the corner and down an alley. About two feet to their right, a blond woman was flat against the brick wall and an SS officer, his trousers around his ankles, was raping her. When she saw them over his shoulder, she began to struggle again, twisting her head from side to side and beating her fists against his back, but his large body pinned her securely. Simon stood frozen to the spot until Levi pushed him roughly.

"Come on," he whispered, "we can't help her." Reluctantly Simon tore himself away and sprinted after Levi's departing shadow, through a stone arch and onto another main street. Billowing gray smoke was rolling toward them.

"It's coming from down there."

Levi pointed to the far end of the street.

"The synagogue."

"We can't go that way, they'll be watching it burn. Up here, we'll have to go in a circle."

Levi set off at a jog in the other direction. There was glass everywhere, crunching underfoot with every step. The freezing cold wind was blowing straight at them, but at least it was keeping the acrid smoke at bay. Just before the end of the street, they saw a large gathering of SS officers, mostly standing with their backs to them, smoking and laughing. Levi grabbed his arm and pulled him into a darkened doorway. Simon could feel his heart pounding against his ribs, and his breath was coming in short, ragged gasps. He pressed his back as flat as he could against the hard surface.

One house down, the door swung open and an elderly woman put her head and shoulders out, glancing up and down the street. She looked straight into the frightened faces of the two young men and smiled at them.

"You Jews?" she asked.

Levi hesitated and then nodded. The group of officers was

breaking up, and some were walking down the middle of the street, toward the clouds of smoke. She beckoned to them.

"Quickly, in here!"

She opened the door fully and they scrambled inside. It was a bare hallway with black and white tiles on the floor and a naked bulb hanging from the ceiling. Ahead of them was a steep staircase.

"Up there." She gestured toward the stairs. At the top she opened a door and waited for them to go past her into a cozy lounge. Two chairs and an overstuffed red sofa filled the room, and a large electric heater threw off a fierce heat. Floral curtains were drawn, and there was classical music coming from the radio on the table. It was Wagner.

"What are your names?" she asked gently.

Levi cleared his throat.

"I'm Levi Horowitz and this is my brother Simon."

"Well, hello, Levi and Simon. I'm Maria, Maria Weiss. Welcome to my humble home. Shall we have some coffee and chocolate cake while we wait for the morning?"

She was a plump woman, not as old as he'd first thought, with silver-streaked black hair pulled back in a bun, and she beamed at Simon as she picked up a large ginger cat from one of the chairs.

"Come on, Wolfgang, find yourself somewhere else to sleep. Take off your coats and have a seat; do make yourselves comfortable. I'll make some coffee and you can tell me all about yourselves. Since my Herman died I don't get many visitors, so it'll be lovely to chat with two young men."

"You're not Jewish, are you, Mrs. Weiss?"

"No dear, I'm not."

Levi looked at the door, and Simon could feel his uncertainty; who knew what it would mean for her if they were found here.

Some Gentiles lured Jews in and then betrayed their presence to earn a few extra marks.

"Are you sure about this? We don't want to get you into any trouble."

"Oh, fiddlesticks! No one worries about an old woman who lives up a flight of stairs. And I'll have any visitors I choose in my home. Now, how do you like your coffee?"

Chapter 20

Levi and Simon stayed all night with Maria Weiss. They discussed music, art, history, philosophy, and literature; drank real coffee; and devoured delicious chocolate cake and wonderful chicken sandwiches. She showed them Herman's collection of first edition books and played them his radiogram. They amazed her with their stories of prejudice encountered every day and had to explain that they weren't allowed to own a radio, although they would've dearly loved to have accepted her kind offer to take hers home.

Before she'd let them go, she made them have a wash and use Herman's old razor to have a shave. Then she calmly cooked eggs for breakfast. As they left she gave them each a kiss on the cheek and told them to come back if they, or their family, were ever in trouble and needed her help. They hugged her, thanked her profusely, and promised to invite her to see their instruments. Then they reentered the world of danger.

Outside it looked like another planet. Broken, gaping window frames, piles of charred furnishings and, everywhere, shattered glass. Half-burned books were blowing in the bitter wind along the deserted streets. At Simon's insistence they circled back to the alley and cautiously picked their way through the debris to the music shop. The front window was smashed, and a pile of charred wood sat in the middle of the alley. It was eerily silent. Simon knocked on the open door frame that hung half off its hinges.

"Hello?"

No response. The brothers glanced at each other and then stepped tentatively inside. The familiar, evocative odors were masked by the strong smell of burned wood. The hooks and the shelving were empty. In the middle of the room several sheets of music were soaking in a large pool of blood. Simon pointed to it.

"That's where he was beating Jacob."

For a moment they stood in silence, both wondering what had happened to the men they'd known since childhood. Then Levi walked through the deserted shop to the back room.

"Simon. Through here."

The area was empty and ransacked, but hidden amid the broken tools, spilled glue, and piles of wood were seven complete violins. Two were unvarnished, but the others had been, or were being, repaired. The boys retrieved them carefully and carried them into the front of the shop, where the daylight was better.

"We need to find something to carry them home in," Levi said, looking around.

"I think I know." Simon ducked back into the rear and came out carrying a wooden box. "Will this do?"

"Perfect. Is there any cloth or paper we can put between them?"

"Music?"

With their treasures packed away and taking turns to carry

the box, they started for home. There were no trams and be-cause they avoided the areas where trouble might still be smol-dering, it took them two hours. As soon as they shut the front door, Elizabeth flew at them and embraced them fiercely.

"Where have you been?"

Simon could hear the emotions in her voice, a mixture of fear, anger, and relief.

"We were taken in, by a woman on the Handerstrasse, and she looked after us. A Gentile. And see what we rescued."

Over coffee at the kitchen table the boys relayed their story and learned that their parents and the twins had set off for the Reinhardts' house but had been turned back by a fire truck chief who was still a client of the bank. He'd ordered them to go home, lock themselves in, and not answer the door to anyone. This morning they'd tried to ring Franz Reinhardt but there was no reply. Levi described the scenes in the central city and the men being carted away by the police. Benjamin demanded to know exactly where Maria Weiss lived and said he would send her a gift.

Then Simon told them about the destruction he'd seen at Amos's shop. Benjamin examined the violins and pronounced two of them to be excellent examples of Cremonese workman-ship from the early nineteenth century. Three more were French or English from the same period and less valuable, and the last two were brand-new.

"We'll keep them safe for Amos. I'm sure we have a couple of spare glass cases in the attic, and they'll be just fine all together. You did well to go back; that was brave, and I'm proud of you both."

Levi hesitated and then seemed to gain the confidence to speak.

"Papa, I was thinking. After everything that has happened,

should we not store some of our precious things? We could put them in the bank vault until—"

"No!"

It was Elizabeth who reacted, and they all turned to look at her.

"I will not give in to them. Our treasures belong with us."

Benjamin took her hand and squeezed it, then turned to his eldest son.

"Don't think I haven't considered it. Mordecai moved some of his art and instruments into the vault last month. We have many friends in the government and I've been assured that, provided we obey the rules, we will remain exempt. And now, *we* have some news. Some months ago we applied for an exit visa for you, Levi. In case things got worse, we wanted to give you the opportunity to choose whether you go or stay."

Levi was staring at his father, openmouthed, and Simon watched his mother blinking back tears. His father's words seemed distant as he tried to grasp the concept of his life, a difficult and dangerous life, without Levi.

"You're the only one old enough—allowed to go on your own, I mean—and it would take years for visas for the whole family to come through. We were told that you'd stand a very good chance of being granted a visa. And so it has proved."

"You mean—"

"I was advised two days ago that, if you wish to leave, there is a visa available for you now. From a good friend of mine in the government."

"And go where?"

"London. It's closer than New York, your English is good, and I have friends who will take care of you. When everything settles down, you can come back," his father said firmly.

Levi was digesting the news and shaking his head with obvious amazement. Simon looked into his father's face; his expression was very serious, with new lines of worry and stress and no laughter in the black eyes. So he didn't believe that everything would be fine anymore; in fact, he was so concerned he was prepared to place the life of his eldest son in the hands of a Gentile friend.

"I can't believe it, Papa! London! When do I go?"

"We were going to talk to you about it over the weekend, but after last night . . . " His mother's soft voice trailed off.

Benjamin covered her hand with his and addressed Levi, his voice calm and measured. "I've already been on the telephone this morning. You should go tonight. You're allowed one suitcase and a coat. I will help you pack. There are one or two things I will help you to hide. A letter of introduction to a good friend of mine and a little family treasure. To help you along your way."

Late that afternoon Simon watched as his father used an old cloth bandage to strap a packet to Levi's chest. It contained a letter to Mr. Peter Dickenson of London's Marylebone Bank, a complete list of all the family's possessions, and a letter to Avrum in New York. He also carried a small leather pouch that slid over his shoulder and hung in his armpit, taped against his side. It held several rings and brooches, two solid silver snuffboxes, two miniature portraits of Benjamin and Elizabeth, and a tiny black box with ten loose diamonds in it. Levi knew that he was to deposit them all in Mr. Dickenson's bank for safekeeping and bring them back with him, but if the worst happened, they would give him a good start in life. Simon helped Levi struggle into as many clothes as he could wear, and they packed the rest into a brown leather suitcase. Their conversation was stilted, neither of them knowing what to say and yet both wanting to say all the important things. Over the top of the pile of clothes Levi laid a photo of his family and one of him and Simon holding the two precious violins. Then, as he closed the lid, there was a light knock on the door.

"Levi?"

It was Rachel. The twins had turned thirteen a month before, and she was on the verge of puberty, small for her age, olive skinned and elfin, with glossy dark ringlets and huge, startled brown eyes.

"I wrote a poem about us. I want you to take it with you. I drew you a picture on the back."

She held it out to him, her face solemn. He opened his arms and she ran into them. Simon watched them and wondered how he would comfort her after Levi was gone.

"I don't want you to go; I'm scared," she whispered into his jersey. He stroked her hair.

"Shhh, don't worry, little bird, it won't be for long. I'm just going on a bit of an adventure and then I'll come back and we'll sing prayers again together, I promise. And Simon will take care of you while I'm not here. You must promise me that you'll take care of David."

She pulled back and held the piece of paper up to him. He opened it and read the poem, then turned it over and looked at the drawing of a tall man seated at the piano.

"Thank you, sweetheart, it's beautiful. I shall treasure it forever."

They ate beef and cabbage almost in silence. Elizabeth looked pale, and her eyes were red rimmed but she maintained her composure. David reacted to the tension by telling them a story about a cat his friend had rescued the night before and his parents said he could keep it, because having a pet was a very good thing for a child when everything was so uncertain. At six sharp there was a knock at the front door. Benjamin opened it to a close friend, a Gentile who worked in the government. He was nervous and glanced up and down the street repeatedly.

"Is he ready?"

"He is."

Levi struggled into Papa's best woolen coat and then they all hugged him hard. Elizabeth ran her hand down his clean-shaven cheek.

"God will take care of you, my precious firstborn boy," she said in a small voice.

"I'll be back for Pesach, Mama, Pesach 1939."

Simon stood on the front step and watched Levi climb into the back of the big black Mercedes. It was his papa's car. Suddenly he understood the price his father had paid to his Gentile friend to get Levi away to safety, and he felt the first real stab of fear about the future, a sense of vulnerability and danger.

Then, with a final confident wave, his brother was gone. But not forever, for somewhere deep inside he knew he'd see Levi again. Not a hunch, a deep, simple knowledge. He glanced at his mother, intending to share this happy thought, but Elizabeth was staring down the street at the disappearing car and her desolate expression told Simon that she believed she'd held her beloved eldest son for the last time.

Chapter 21

Berlin
November 1939

"Benjamin Horowitz?"

Benjamin looked up from his stack of papers and his smile died. A tall, gaunt SS captain stood in the doorway, carrying a black truncheon in one hand.

"Yes, I'm Benjamin Horowitz."

Something tightened in his stomach.

"You run this establishment?"

"I own it, yes."

"Stand up. You will address me as 'sir.'"

Slowly Benjamin rose to his feet.

"How can I help you, sir? Would you like to open—"

"Your bank is closed. My men have escorted all the customers out and locked the doors. You will now collect all your workers and bring them to the main area on the ground floor. Immediately."

"But wh—"

"Don't argue with me, Jew! Do it now!"

The order was barked at him and, as if to emphasize the point, the man tapped the end of the truncheon on his gloved palm. Benjamin moved quickly from behind the massive wooden desk and hurried into the teller area. The women looked frightened. Money was scattered on the desktops, and some had fallen to the floor. He smiled reassuringly and ushered them all around the barrier to the main customer area. Mordecai came through a side door from the stairwell, with terrified men and women trailing after him. In a few moments all the employees were huddled together. Armed soldiers watched them from positions around the walls. Benjamin approached the captain, and instinct told him to veil the anger he was feeling.

"They're all here now, sir."

"Good. Two of my men are checking the building; when they return, I will address your workers."

As he spoke two guards came through the back door, dragging a young man between them. Benjamin recognized him as Moses Guttmann, a clerk. One of the guards pushed him into the crowd, then turned and saluted his superior.

"All accounted for, Hauptsturmführer."

"Good." He returned the salute and then turned to the assembled.

"I want you to divide into two. All the Jews over here to the left and all the others to the right. Do it, now."

There was some confusion and chatter as they moved around the room until two distinct groups emerged. The captain watched them impatiently.

"Come on, come on, hurry up! This bank is the property of the Third Reich. It will be closed until we decide what to do with it. All of you on the right-hand side will go home now. You will not come back here again. Go, now!"

Two soldiers opened the front doors, and the people on the right began to reluctantly move toward them. Some were waiting for a sign from Benjamin or Mordecai, and they both gestured toward the doors, encouraging the Gentiles to leave.

"Good. There are two trucks outside on the street. You, Jews, will all file out and climb onto these trucks. Go, now!"

"Excuse me, but where are you taking us?" Mordecai asked.

"To be processed. Do as you're told and no harm will come to—"

"But this is our bank; we have a special exemption. You can't just come in here and take over. Tell him, Benjamin!"

The captain stepped very close to Mordecai and raised the truncheon.

"I can do whatever I like. This is not *your* bank. It is the property of the Third Reich. And you have no exemption from me. Now go outside and get into that truck, before I split your head open like a ripe melon, do you understand?"

Benjamin took his brother's arm. "Come, let's do what he says. When they've finished with us, we'll go down to city hall and see our friends. All this will be sorted out, you'll see. For now, we must set a good example, so people don't get hurt."

They walked out the door and into the freezing cold air. Two large army trucks were parked in the middle of the street and the men climbed onto the back, then turned to help their employees up. As the trucks rattled off over the cobbles, Benjamin blinked back tears and squeezed his brother's arm.

"Don't worry, we'll be back in business tomorrow. No one will take our bank away; it's just a mistake."

It was nearly sundown on a Friday afternoon and Benjamin still wasn't home. Elizabeth had everything ready for the Shabbat observation, and she and her children waited in the music room.

Simon played the piano and they all sang. He could see that her anxiety level was rising with every minute that ticked by, and he didn't know what to say to comfort her. She'd phoned the bank and got no answer; then when she'd rung her sister-in-law, Sarah, she'd learned that Mordecai wasn't home either. This was what they'd all dreaded for a year, ever since that terrible night when so many of their friends had been rounded up and arrested for no reason.

Suddenly the music was overridden by a loud banging on the front door. The twins instinctively went to their mother's side.

"Open up, Jews!"

It was muffled but quite easy to understand. Someone was standing on the doorstep, knocking and yelling insistently.

"Who on earth? Simon, be careful."

Simon had rushed out of the room toward the door.

"Open up, Jews! Open up, Jews!"

Elizabeth and the twins followed him into the entrance hall. The banging was constant; it sounded like a fist. Simon stood behind the door.

"Who are you? What do you want?" he called loudly.

"Open this door. By order of the Third Reich, open up now, Jew."

He looked back and could see his fear mirrored on their faces. "We must open the door to them. Be strong. Papa will be home soon."

Simon slipped the chain and started to open the door. Before he had it a quarter of the way ajar, it was pushed from the outside and a horde of uniformed men swarmed in. They fanned out into all the rooms. A large army officer, wearing the insignia of a major, thrust a piece of paper at Elizabeth.

"This residence has been commandeered," he shouted at her. "Jews will no longer live in such houses. You have fifteen min-

utes to pack one suitcase each, clothes and photographs only.
No valuables. Go!"

He screamed the last word in her face.

Simon ran into the hall in time to see a soldier lifting the
Dürer portrait off the wall. He hesitated for a second then kept
moving. In the drawing room, men were putting their possessions into boxes—candlesticks and vases, figurines and bowls.
Some were taking the paintings off the walls and carrying them
outside while others were lifting up chairs and tables. Understanding hit him with a blinding clarity, followed immediately
by fury. They were stripping his house. Looting it. Taking everything. Where was Papa? What was he supposed to do without Papa?

In the music room a slight man in a black leather coat was
leaning over the glass cases. He had close-cropped blond hair
and very fair skin. As Simon ran in, he straightened up.

"You, over here," he ordered.

Simon felt a rush of relief as he saw that the violins were
untouched.

"What are these? What year?"

"This . . . um, this is a 1545 tenor recorder. That's a 1788
wood-and-ivory serpent, very rare. And that's, um, that's a lute
from Bologna."

"What year?"

"1535."

The man held out his gloved hand.

"Keys," he ordered.

"I . . . I don't have them. My father has them and he's not
here."

"No matter."

He took out a small flashlight and carefully smashed the side
of the glass case containing the recorder. Gently he lifted it out

and turned it over in his gloved hands. Then he bent down and put it into a box at his feet.

"You can't just—"

"Shut up, boy! I can do what I like. You, out there!"

He called to two SS guards who had run past the door. They stopped, came in, clicked their heels together, and saluted him.

"Stabsmusikmeister," they answered in unison.

"Take that double virginal away."

They looked at him blankly, and he pointed at the virginal.

"There. And be very careful with it. It's Flemish, around 1580 . . . am I right?"

He turned to Simon, who nodded with a sinking heart. The man was a captain and a director of music. He watched as the man systematically broke the cases, lifted out the instruments, inspected them, and put them in his box. At one point the captain looked at him.

"Shouldn't you be upstairs packing some possessions?"

"These *are* my possessions."

"Not anymore," the captain muttered.

When he got to the Amati, he plucked the strings and looked at Simon questioningly.

"Nicolo Amati, 1640," he replied, his voice dull.

The man's bright blue eyes gleamed at him.

"Very good."

He laid it in the box and turned to the other case. Simon couldn't contain the cry of rage that rose in his throat.

"No!"

The man ignored him and carefully broke the glass. Simon was there before the captain's gloved hands could reach inside. The glass was jagged and sharp.

"Careful, boy. Don't be stupid, you'll cut your hands to ribbons. Let me do it."

Reluctantly Simon pulled back. He felt his heart would literally break in two as he watched the man. With infinite care the captain lifted it out and held it up to the last rays of weak autumn light.

"Oh my God, look at this," he whispered.

"It's a 1729 Guarneri del Gesú." The words burned in Simon's throat. "I want to tell you it's something else, but you wouldn't believe me."

"Quite right, I wouldn't. In every house like this, there's a priceless jewel. Do you play it?"

"Yes. It's very unforgiving. The master himself described the sound as the tears of an angel."

The captain picked up the bow and put the violin to his chin. He tightened the screw on the heel of the bow and played a long note. Simon's temper flared.

"My papa will kill you when he hears you've done that."

The man stopped and laughed. It was a cruel, humorless bark. Simon could feel a red mist descending over his brain.

"Your father is probably dead by now. Say good-bye to your violin; it's now *my* violin. You shouldn't own such a thing anyway."

He bent down and gently put the violin into the box, beside the Amati. Simon waited until he'd straightened up again and then he punched him in the face as hard as he could. The blow was completely unexpected and stunningly effective. The captain reeled backward into the wall and let out a ferocious roar. His hand came up to his nose as blood spurted out.

"You dirty Jew bastard! You'll pay for this, my God you will."

Two guards came running in.

"Take him! And take this box."

Two guards grabbed Simon by the arms and dragged him toward the hall. Other soldiers were pulling Elizabeth, David, and Rachel down the wide staircase. Rachael was sobbing, but David was struggling against his captors. The major was standing in front of the Botticelli portrait, held between two soldiers. He addressed Elizabeth directly.

"This is a religious subject. For Jews to own such a work is sacrilegious, a profanity before God. If the Reich had known you had it in your possession . . . were you not told to register all your important assets?"

She faced him defiantly.

"My husband is an important man; he owns the Bayer Bank on the Pariser Platz. We're exempt from registration."

"Not anymore. Your son has seriously assaulted one of my officers. Forget packing possessions." He turned to the soldiers. "Take the boys and turn the women out."

The men shoved Elizabeth and Rachel out the front door and threw them down the steps into the snow. David and Simon were marched toward the door, a guard on either side of them.

"Wait!"

The captain had a large white handkerchief pressed to his still bleeding face. The guards stopped in front of him. He took a truncheon from the holder on his belt.

"I wouldn't want you to forget me, you dirty Jew bastard," he hissed in Simon's face. "If you were in a camp or on the street, I'd put a bullet through your head, but I want you to think of me playing your precious violin."

He brought the truncheon down as hard as he could across the back of Simon's left hand. Excruciating pain sped up his arm like an electrical current. He swallowed the scream as the guards pushed him out the door and down the steps.

"Mama!"

David tried to break free, but the guards held him tightly. Rachel and Elizabeth huddled together, their faces white with terror. As the boys were pulled toward a waiting truck, Simon twisted his head and looked at them.

"Go to Maria Weiss, Mama. Remember, Rachel? She'll help—" He was cut off as hands grabbed him from inside the truck canopy and yanked him up.

"David! Simon!"

Her screams were the last thing he heard as he pitched forward into the blackness of the truck, fell on his broken hand, and passed out.

Chapter 22

Dachau
November 1939

The locomotive pulled into the platform, rolled to a stop, and let out a long sigh of steam and a piercing keen of whistle. Soldiers stepped up to the wooden boxcars, unhooked the metal bolts, and slid the sides open. Clusters of men of all ages stumbled out onto the frozen ground. They'd traveled south for days, squeezed so tightly together they couldn't turn around, and now their lack of balance was sending them reeling from side to side. Large dogs, held on chains, barked and lunged at them. Snow swirled in the cold wind, stinging exposed skin.

Simon, his hand bound in a bloodstained handkerchief, followed the man in front of him. David was at his heels. Both of them were drinking in deep gulps of the icy, but fresh, air. All around them men in greatcoats seemed to be yelling abuse and screaming instructions.

"Out! Out! Come on, move faster! Move, you dirty Jew."
Eventually they came to the end of a stationary line of men.

"Where are we, Simon?"

Simon turned back to his brother.

"I don't know."

A middle-aged man, standing in the line next to theirs,
scowled at them. "Dachau, someone said we're waiting to go
into Dachau."

"What's that?" David sounded confused.

"It's a work camp, a slave labor camp."

"Why did they take us away from Berlin?"

"Because we're Jewish, boy. When they ask you what you can
do, boy, tell them you're good at making things. That you like
building things."

He looked at Simon. "And you—tell them you're a cook or a
baker; they're always looking for cooks."

After waiting for three hours, the boys got to the head of their
line. An elderly man sat at a small wooden table, with a sheet
of paper and a pot of ink, a pen, and a blotter in front of him.

"Name?"

"Simon Horowitz, and this is my younger brother, David."
Their names were written down, and they were marched into
the camp through gates in the barbed-wire fence. The buildings
were wooden, rectangular, and low-slung. They were herded
across a large square of open ground and into a long room where
a man with foul breath cursed in their faces and told them to
strip naked. Then he gave each of them a set of striped fatigues,
with a red-and-yellow-colored Star of David on the jacket, and
no underwear.

In front of them more lines had formed, leading to a row of
chairs. The air was full of the metallic clicking of scissors. Simon

reached a chair and was pushed down onto it. First a man wielding scissors cut his hair, and then his head was shaved. It felt very strange; the man's hands were rough, and he pressed hard with a blunt razor. When it dug into Simon's scalp, it hurt, but the ache from his hand was so intense he hardly noticed. David's eyes were very round and full of unshed tears. Although Simon tried to send the boy a reassuring smile, he feared it looked more like a grimace.

As soon as the shaving was done they were sent in yet another direction and had to sit in front of a man at a table. This one looked weary and old and wore fatigues, with a Star of David on the jacket.

"What happened to your left hand?"

"It . . . I got hit. By a truncheon."

"Let me see."

He unwrapped the hand and tentatively held it out. The man lifted it into his hands, turned it over, and gently prodded the swelling. Pain shot up Simon's arm, and he yelped and pulled back.

"You're lucky. It's the metacarpals, the bones in the hand behind the knuckles. A clean break and not through all of them. It'll heal in a few weeks. Put some snow on it when you can to stop it swelling any more, and flex the hand to stop it getting stiff." He looked up at Simon, and his dull gray eyes were kind. "Try not to show the pain. If they ask you if you can work, say yes. If you're no use to them, they'll shoot you."

After that they were marched off to their barracks, bald, barefoot, freezing, and dressed in fatigues that looked like pajamas. The building was a single story with one entrance. Inside it was lined with long wooden bunks, four levels high and six feet wide, full of men, lying with their feet toward the wall and their heads pointing out to the center of the room. Each man had a horsehair blanket and a small metal bowl and lay on a thin sack. Simon stared openmouthed into the room. The guard gave them each a bowl, a blanket, and a sack and pushed them toward one of the bunks.

"In there."

They clambered up and lay down on their stomachs. Putting any pressure on his hand hurt, but he swallowed the pain and didn't flinch. He could feel David's small body shivering beside him, and he patted his arm.

"What must we look like, eh! Don't worry, we won't be here long, and what a story we'll have to tell. Papa will find us and sort it all out, you'll see."

David nodded vigorously.

"I know he will, and it's good to be lying down. I wonder where Mama and Rachel are. God, it's cold!"

Simon's overriding memory of his first night was the unrelenting noise. He wasn't yet in a position to realize that sleep deprivation was second only to starvation on the list of nightmares to come. All around him echoed a cacophony of coughs, groans, cries, farts, screams, and snores. After a while he created an orchestra in his head and allocated different instruments to the most defined sounds. He couldn't stop wondering what they'd do if he just got up, walked to the gate, and told them he'd had enough and wanted to go home now. He'd done nothing wrong; what gave them the right to hold him here? Or had he? It was easy to forget that surreal moment when he'd punched a captain in the army of the Third Reich. And who else was here? Franz Reinhardt, who'd simply disappeared during the Kristallnacht, was he here somewhere?

Just as Simon had finally fallen into a black oblivion, harsh voices were screaming at him and jerking him awake. It was still dark, but he could feel bodies moving around him.

"What is it?" he mumbled sleepily.

"Roll call. Three times a day, and for God's sake, don't be late."

The voice sounded frightened. He felt David moving next to him.

"Come on, Si. We'd better follow them."

The mass of men moved as quickly as it could, out the door and into the freezing night. Large spotlights lit the bare parade ground with a fierce white light. There were more men in great-coats and more large dogs on chains, snarling and barking. Simon and David stood in line toward the back of the ever-increasing square of men. Simon glanced around him—old men, young men, very thin men, very fat men, and all with shaven heads or a little regrowth, shapes disappearing into the dark-ness beyond the scope of the light.

After an hour, his legs started to ache but still they stood there, nothing to see but the back of the man in front of you. After two hours, he began to play violin pieces in his head, his fingers twitching as they hung by his sides. After three hours, dawn was breaking, and they were yelled at again until they all ran back to the barracks.

Over the coming days Simon and David learned the routines of the camp. There were endless hours wasted in roll calls and standing still in one place. The men had hats that they wore outside of the barracks, and when an officer addressed a man, he tore it off his head and stood with his arms by his sides and his eyes downcast. Prisoners were identified by num-bers and had to recite them from memory when addressed by anyone in uniform. They were fed once a day, stale bread and a thin, watery version of *kartoffelsuppe,* a soup with chunks of potato in it, sometimes a piece of sausage. After the first few hours, the hunger pangs abated into a dull gnawing sensation, an awareness that they were never full. Simon remembered his last meal at home with vivid clarity. For lunch that day he'd had a piece of *roggenbrot* bread, some cheese and spicy sausage, and a big portion of his favorite cabbage salad, with raisins, apple, and carrot and a lovely vinegar and sour cream dressing. In fact, he and David could recite all their favorite meals: sauerbraten, apple pancakes, baked veal cutlets, lebkuchen, and their mother's wonderful *neujahrspretzel* on New Year's Eve—anything, as long as it had no potato in it. All around him, Simon was conscious of men coping with the sudden withdrawal of substances they were used to ingesting frequently, smokers, heavy drinkers, those on medication, and those used to ample food. Some suffered in silence and some didn't. Fights over food were common.

He was astonished how quickly he and David seemed to adapt to their surroundings. They slept on the thin mattress, a sack full of wood wool, with a long-haired, scratchy blanket to keep out the biting cold, in close proximity to numerous other bodies. In fact, body heat was a godsend in the dead of night. The other prisoners taught them to hold their mattresses over a fire so the fleas, lice, and bedbugs would fall out into the flames. The latrines were trenches in the ground with a wooden plank laid over them. The planks had round holes cut in them, and a thin canvas sheet separated each hole. Showers and baths were distant memories, but they did "wash" themselves with snow when they got the chance. Their feet were always cold to the point of numbness and started to turn black after days of standing barefoot on frozen ground.

Fear was the most restricting aspect of their daily lives. The guards had complete control over every prisoner and made arbitrary decisions, seemingly on a sadistic whim. Simon saw men shot and hanged and beaten with truncheons every day. He worried about the effect this must be having on his thirteen-year-old brother and tried his best to convince David that their situation was only temporary and would be remedied as soon as their papa discovered where they were. Then, on their twentieth day, something happened that changed everything completely, forever.

"You and you and you and you, come, now. Come on, move!"

Simon was so used to the general din of shouting voices that it took him a moment to realize that the man was yelling at him. And at David. Almost subconsciously they followed the men in front of them, out the door, and across the open space. But this time there was no roll call and they kept on running, the dog at their heels. Eventually they came to another building. An officer with a clipboard stood outside watching them.

"Numbers!" he ordered.

They recited their numbers in turn and stood, eyes down, arms at their sides, caps in hand.

"You have been picked to do munitions work. In here, move!"

They found themselves inside a metal working room full of machines and tables manned by prisoners in fatigues. Simon was shown how to press metal shells, and David, with his smaller hands, was given the job of polishing them. The room was warm, and just the simple act of having something productive to do quickly lifted their spirits. His hand hurt at first, but he found a way to press down with his right and just adjust with his left. Sneaking sideways glances as he worked, Simon could see that the other men were equally absorbed in their activities and the guards seemed to leave them alone. After about five hours, a sharp, high-pitched whistle blew, and some of the men laid down their tools and stood beside their machines. The man with the clipboard reappeared and examined each man's work, then wrote something on his board. The men filed out the door, and another line came in. Simon returned to his machine, keen to get back to his work.

"David!"

Even before he looked up, he recognized the voice. His heart soared and then crashed, all in a split second.

"Papa!"

"Simon."

A terrible understanding crept through his numbed consciousness and seemed to freeze him to the spot. With a growing sense of finality he realized there would be no escape, no rescue from without.

Although Benjamin wore fatigues that barely covered his body, Simon could see that his father had already lost weight. His face was ashen, and his skin had a sheen of sweat. He was bald, and for the first time in his life Simon saw his father's face without the large mustache; his long upper lip looked naked. What was worse, he knew that his father's reaction to seeing his sons would be as mixed as theirs at seeing him. The joy of their reunion would be tinged with crushing despair at their plight and an overwhelming feeling of shame at his inability to protect his family. They were prevented from talking further until they were marched back to the barracks.

Without consulting the guard on duty, Benjamin collected his meager belongings and moved from his building to be with his sons. There were some initial complaints from the men next to them, but when the family relationship was explained, they welcomed the new arrival with enthusiasm. David took great comfort in his father's physical presence, and Simon couldn't help but feel the load of responsibility had lifted. Even if Papa wasn't going to charge into the camp and rescue them, they had a much better chance of surviving if they were psychologically stronger.

Benjamin explained that he and Mordecai had been driven straight to the railway station and processed, then put on board a train to Dachau with no opportunity to protest or communicate with their families. After comparing departure times, they decided that both men and boys were probably on the same train but in different boxcars, and the chaos at arrival, plus the sheer numbers in the camp, had prevented them meeting until now. Their initial experience was similar to the boys'. They'd stayed together for the first twenty-four hours until Mordecai suddenly developed a high temperature and started vomiting. The guards dragged him away and Benjamin hadn't seen him since. The other prisoners said he'd been taken to the hospital. No one ever came back from the hospital.

Simon told him about the house, the captain, and the looting. Benjamin was delighted by the punch in the nose, but his joy turned to despair on learning of the fate of Elizabeth and Rachel.

"They'll be all right, Papa. I told them to go to Maria Weiss. Rachel came with me when we took that first big box of supplies to her, and she's picked up books for me and had tea with Maria. Mama knows that Maria will help her."

Benjamin nodded slowly.

"Yes, of course she will. Dear Maria. And she'll find Sarah. Maybe the officers didn't go to Mordecai's house and Sarah will take them in?"

Simon knew it was important that his father believed this; optimism meant strength, and strength meant survival.

"You know, son, I just thought of something; you should be *glad* that the captain understood about our violins. He appreciates their importance; he'll take care of them and protect them from . . . hatred and ignorance."

Simon turned away and gazed unseeingly across at the men on the other side of the hut.

"I can close my eyes and hear it, as if it were right here. I can feel it in my hand. I pray every day that I never lose that."

His father touched him on the shoulder.

"And one day you will play it again; believe in that, son, because that's faith and it will keep you sane."

Chapter 23

Dachau
June 1941

Routine only becomes dull when it's safe; routine punctuated by terror remains as sharp as the first time you experience it. Over the next few months every day followed the same pattern: roll call, work, food, roll call, fitful sleep. Yet at any moment a wrong glance, a careless word, a misunderstood answer, a faulty machine that slowed a man's work rate or a sign of real illness and his life could end, suddenly and violently.

Simon's hand had healed almost completely. He couldn't stretch it out flat or turn his fingers back toward his arm as far, and he was in no doubt that he'd lost some agility on the violin fingerboard, but it didn't hurt anymore and could stand pressure.

His first thought on waking each day was the health and safety of his papa and his brother. Benjamin had lost 140 pounds in weight and was virtually unrecognizable. The fatigues that had been too small now hung on him like tents. It was the height of a sweltering summer, and many men had dispensed with their tops, using them as cloth belts to try and keep the trousers on their narrow waists and hips. At least the ground wasn't frozen and feet had a chance to heal and dry out. Simon couldn't remember the last time he'd felt pain in his feet, but they still carried him.

He'd become an expert on the illnesses and aliments of camp life and often reflected on how inconceivable some of his regular activities would have seemed twenty months ago. Now he regularly deloused his family, and they returned the favor, furtively crushing the lice between their fingers; and he had on occasion squeezed pus from boils and ulcers, especially David's, so the boy could sit and lie more comfortably. When he was given the job of feeding the dogs, he sometimes managed to distract the guard on duty at the kennels and then he could snatch a few dog biscuits; he'd discovered they had a nutty flavor. The camp became more crowded every week, and the conditions deteriorated accordingly, with food rationed still further and more bodies squeezed into the bunks.

To make room, the killing had taken on a more structured approach with mass executions carried out by firing squad; on some days six thousand Russian prisoners were killed. A year ago construction had been completed on a large brick building over in the northwest corner of the complex and the camp rumor mill was in overdrive as everyone had an opinion on what was going on over the bridge across the creek. No one who was sent there returned to talk about it, and obviously no one was going to venture where they shouldn't, so the true purpose was anyone's guess. The most feared place was still the hospital. Stories filtered back, via those on cooking and cleaning detail, of medical experiments that were always fatal. Certainly anyone who was sick enough to need hospitalization was either shot or disappeared without a trace.

Occasionally they met someone they'd known in their other life, their "free" life. The world where they'd taken the small luxuries of a civilized existence for granted and never given them a moment's thought, like being clean, sleeping in a bed between sheets, having a change of clothing, getting enough to eat and a change of diet, having some privacy for ablutions, and, most of all, not fearing that their next moment would be their last. Often these people were unrecognizable, invariably now skin and bone and with the slow, listless air so common among the desperate and those without hope.

One hot June day Benjamin's quiet, almost internal daily prayers were interrupted by Amos Wiggenstein. He was nearly bald and very wrinkled, but his back was ramrod straight and his cheeks still had color. The two men embraced warmly, and Amos stared at him.

"How long have you been here, Benjamin?"

"Nearly twenty months. I know, what a diet! I'll write a book one day. And you?"

"Only three. Hannah and I were hidden by my cousin's husband, a good man, a Gentile. But when my money ran out, we were betrayed by a Jew working for the Nazis, and then they put us on the trains. I don't know where they took her."

They exchanged family information, and Amos told him what he knew of the war. Sadly he knew nothing of Sarah, Elizabeth, or Rachel; and Benjamin took heed to make sure the brief flame of hope didn't show.

"They destroyed my shop, you know, in the pogrom, and I never had the chance to go back," Amos said, and Benjamin could hear the pain in his voice.

"I know, the boys were out that night, and they went by your shop in the morning. Simon and Levi, they rescued seven of your violins from the back room and took them home. We put them in our attic. One day you can use them to start your collection over. I'm sure the Nazis won't bother to look in our dusty old attic."

Amos was clearly delighted at the news and also to learn that Simon was reasonably well and coping.

"I am working for them, Benjamin, building things, working with wood. They can see that I am good at carving delicate things. Even with these old hands. And I have started my own project, hidden among the tools and the wood. I am making a violin."

"Oh, Amos!" Benjamin felt the tears pricking his eyes. "God bless you for being such a temple of the indomitable human spirit. Wait till I tell my Simon; he'll be so happy. Just the other day he reminded me what you said to him when he was just a boy: Guarneri himself said the violin sounded like the tears of an angel."

Amos frowned and seemed to be searching his memory.

"I don't . . . oh yes, I do. He remembers that? It was a piece of fancy, something I made up to excite a young boy's imagination, something that sounded Italian. You tell him to stretch his hands. When it's finished, I'll bring it to him. Then he can be in violin land, you know, where all is sweetness and delicacy and harmony?"

The old man's eyes twinkled with merriment, and Benjamin laughed out loud.

" 'The Red-Headed League,' Conan Doyle. I haven't thought about that story for years. Come and see me again, my old friend; you're so good for my soul."

Simon was thrilled by Amos's news and spent several nights dreaming he had a violin in his hands again. For many months he'd lulled himself to sleep with a sweet dream that saw him playing in public, guesting with the Berlin Philharmonic. Then, bit by bit, it'd slipped away, shattered by the daily horror around him. But after Amos's visit, the dream returned and with it the haunting, deep strains of his beloved Guarneri. Vivid dreams were his most treasured escape and he often saw himself, as a child, playing his violin; and then he'd see his mother and Levi applauding, as if through his own eyes. Every day he told himself that maybe today Amos would appear, but every day he was disappointed.

Meanwhile David was a growing concern. He was terribly weak, and at times Simon had to hold him up during roll call and answer for him. A painful cough racked his skeletal body, causing the other men to complain, and at night he sometimes burned with fever, then woke drenched in sweat. Simon gave him what food he could and still eat something himself, and if he feared that David's quota of polished shells would be down, he tried to do some himself when the guards were distracted. He knew that David missed his twin with a suffering beyond his comprehension. They'd always been two halves of a whole and even fought with a closeness that told others they could criticize each other but would defend their partnership to the death. In the end it hadn't been enough; he hadn't been able to keep her safe.

"Simon?"

He looked up. It was a man he didn't recognize, a very short man with a single colored triangle on his jacket, not a Star of David, and a cloth patch over one eye.

"Maybe," he answered cautiously.

"I'm looking for Simon Horowitz."

"Why?"

"I . . . I have something for him."

"You can give it to me. I'll see he gets it."

"No, I can't. My instructions were very specific; give it to Simon Horowitz and no one else."

Simon eyed him suspiciously.

"Instructions? Whose instructions?"

"From Amos."

Simon sprang to his feet. Although he wasn't tall and was now painfully thin, he towered over the small man.

"Where's Amos?"

"He's . . . he's dead. He got very sick, so he couldn't work anymore and they took him away. But just before, he gave me a package and told me to deliver it to Si—"

"I'm Simon. You can give it to me."

The man hesitated.

"But where is it?" Simon was puzzled. "How can it be so small?"

He watched as the man pulled a small cloth bundle from inside his jacket and thrust it into his waiting hands.

"If they catch me here, they might shoot me. He was good to me, and he took care of me. I wanted to do what he asked."

Simon looked at him closely and realized he was no older than David, but his visible eye was blank and his face filthy and lined. Simon spun around and lifted up his silver bowl. Underneath was a half slice of stale bread he'd been saving for his father, but this boy's need was greater. He cupped it in his hands and transferred it to the boy's grasp, keeping it covered.

"Here, eat it now or they'll take it off you."

The young boy's dark brown eye lit up, and he shoved it greedily into his mouth.

"Thank you," he muttered.

"No, thank *you*. Amos would be proud of you. How long have you been here?"

"A year and a little bit."

"Do you have any family?"

"No. All dead. Just me now."

"How old are you?"

"I'm fifteen, soon."

"What's your name?"

"Philippe."

"Where are you from?"

"All over, we're Gypsies."

There was pride in his voice, and he gazed defiantly at Simon, who smiled back.

"You have no more reason to be here than we have. I hope you're . . . come back and see me again."

The boy hesitated and then nodded.

"I'd like that. Thank you for the bread."

He moved like lightning; one moment he was there and the next, he was gone. Simon laid the parcel on his mattress and carefully unwrapped it. The violin was very small and very crude, a wooden body with a bridge, a neck, and tiny pegs in the scroll. The strings were stretched pieces of fuse wire. The bow was not very flexible, a piece of thin tapered wood with some string, which had been frayed like horsehair, stretched from tip to toe. He ran his fingers over the violin and tightened the tiny pegs, then plucked the strings. They made sharp, twanging noises. When he picked up the bow and ran it over the strings, they made a longer twanging noise. Then he wrapped the whole thing back into its cloth cover and hid it inside his shirt. The guards were used to him wandering around and hardly gave him a second glance as he made his way out behind the dog kennels to a patch of ground where he knew he'd be undisturbed. Where he could spend some time getting acquainted with his new possession and find a place to hide it.

Chapter 24

Dachau
September 1941

Several weeks later Simon stood at his machine, methodically and skillfully raising and lowering the levers. He was very concerned about David; the boy was withdrawn and vacant, not answering questions and hardly eating his food. It was more than the usual apathy, and Simon feared it was the beginning of a glazed semiconsciousness, a state he'd seen in others. In his head he practiced the piece he was trying to master on his secret violin. The wire was tough on his fingers, and the instrument was almost impossible to keep in tune, but he was pleased with the progress he'd made during snatched moments of practice.

Suddenly his reverie was broken by a loud thump. He looked up to see two guards converging on the table where David stood to polish the shells. Instinct told him to stay where he was as he fought a desperate longing to intervene. Both men were kneeling down; David must have fainted. Then the worst possible thing happened, the SS-*obertsturmführer* appeared and noticed the disturbance. He briefly inspected whatever it was they were kneeling beside and ordered it to be removed. Simon watched in mute horror as the two men picked up his brother and carried him out of the room. Perhaps once he was outside, where it was cooler, he might be all right. These men knew David well, they guarded him every day; surely they wouldn't shoot him simply because he fainted?

The rest of the shift crawled at a cruel pace while he forced his racing mind to focus on the job at hand. If he made mistakes, he'd be punished. Finally the whistle blew, the output was checked, and they were released. He sprinted back to the barracks. His father was sitting with a group of his friends, but David was nowhere in sight.

"Where's David?" Benjamin asked cautiously.

"I don't know! I thought he'd be back here. I think he fainted, and two guards carried him outside."

One of the other men looked up. "When was this?"

"About five hours ago."

"Then he's gone; they've taken him to the hospital," he said in a matter-of-fact tone.

The word drifted in the air for a moment, such an innocuous phrase in any other life. Simon could see his own agony reflected in his father's eyes. The thing he'd dreaded most, worked so hard to avoid, had happened, and the hurt was so intense he could scarcely breathe.

He turned and ran out of the barracks. He didn't stop until he came to his special place, behind the dog kennels. He often fed the dogs and they were used to his scent so they didn't bark when he passed by. He approached an old tree trunk, half decayed and hollow, the perfect hiding place. He'd buried the violin under a pile of sticks and moss. The cover was complete; no one passing would've seen anything out of place.

Bitter tears stung his eyes as he fiddled with the tiny pegs.

The four strings were always loose, and he fought a constant battle to keep it even faintly resembling an instrument in tune. He couldn't tighten the bow and some of the string had worn away, but with a little manipulation and some stolen tape on one end, it did the trick.

He glanced around one more time. Mozart was David's favorite and this hardly sounded like the sonata he'd loved the most, but it was enough. Ten bars in, he laid the violin in his lap and began to cry huge sobs that racked his thin body.

David Isaac Horowitz never returned, and the cause of his death remained a mystery. Simon knew that the guards on the factory floor had taken the boy somewhere. Every day they saw the mute pleading in his eyes, but he was too afraid to ask and they never said a word. Perhaps David was taken to the brick building over the creek and consumed in the dreadful pall of stinking smoke that issued forth from its chimneys. Or perhaps he was taken to the hospital and died in a medical experiment designed to help Luftwaffe pilots survive extremes of temperature. Or perhaps he was just taken somewhere and shot and thrown into a mass grave; there was always one in operation somewhere in the camp.

However he died, his brother would always remember David as a brave, clever, witty human being with a stubborn streak as wide as the Rhine, the courage to bear pain without complaint, and a fierce loyalty to his family, especially his sister. He also loved his city and his country. He was so proud when his father took him to the Berlin Olympics in August 1936, and it broke his heart that he wasn't allowed to join the Hitler Youth Movement because he was a Jew.

In the end, it was Simon's passion for music that betrayed him. Even this anemic version of the instrument he cherished had come to mean so much to him that he dropped his guard. He was completely absorbed in recalling a passage of Bach and trying to approximate its sound so that his grieving father would recognize it and he didn't see the faces hiding in the grass, listening. Food was a powerful motivating force, and fights regularly broke out over a scrap of sausage or a piece of potato skin, so it was no wonder that he was betrayed to a second lieutenant for a piece of buttered bread.

When he eventually stopped and listened to the distant noises of the camp, out of the corner of his eye he saw a figure moving. Before he could hide the violin, the guard had walked into his sight line. The man was tall and well built, with broad shoulders, narrow hips, and long legs. His blond hair was cut very short, and he had an angry red scar down one cheek. He wore the insignia of an SS-*untersturmführer,* a second lieutenant in the SS.

"Number!" he barked.

Simon scrambled to his feet, aware that his hat was on the ground beside him.

"8467291, sir," he recited quickly, his eyes averted.

"What is that?"

The man was almost beside him, holding out one large hand. Reluctantly Simon handed over the violin and bow. The guard examined it carefully.

"Where did you get it? You may speak."

"It was made . . . a worker in the camp, he was a violin maker, sir."

"Did you steal it?"

"No. He . . . made it for me, sir."

"You were a musician?"

"Yes, sir."

"Pick up your hat. This way, now!"

Simon grabbed his hat and ran in the direction the guard was pointing. Somewhere inside him iron fingers of terror had gripped him, but the thought roaring through his head was, *Who will look after Papa when I'm dead?* The guard marched him to a small square building next to the SS officers' quarters. He took a key from the pocket of his uniform and unlocked the heavy padlock on the latch.

"In here!"

Simon stepped uncertainly inside. It was one single room, lit by a central lightbulb. From floor to ceiling on all four sides were stacks of brown cardboard boxes. The guard shut the door behind them.

"Search through those boxes, start over there."

The guard began to look in the box nearest to him. Simon was frozen by the fear of the consequence of misunderstanding. He couldn't make himself move.

"Now, Jew! Are you deaf as well as stupid?" the guard roared.

"Search for what, sir?"

The man stopped and looked at him, his expression blank. In all the months he'd been there, Simon had never questioned an order and he knew other guards who would've whipped, beaten, or kicked him for such insubordination. In that moment their eyes locked, one pair icy blue and mocking, the other almost black and terrified. The guard wasn't much older than him, and yet he held Simon's life in his hand. Prisoners were summarily shot for questioning an order.

"That's a very good point. What's your name?"

It'd been so long since someone had asked, he'd forgotten what the question meant.

"8467291, sir."

Automatically he averted his eyes and held his hat in his hand.

"No, not your number, your *name.*"

"Simon . . . Simon Horowitz, sir."

"And you play the violin?"

"Yes, sir, and . . . and the piano, sir."

"What violin did you play?"

Simon hesitated; could he share his precious secret with such a man?

"A Guarneri del Gesú, sir."

The man whistled softly. Simon knew there was pride on his face, in spite of his situation, and that was dangerous. The guard closed the box and came closer to him.

"My God! What was it like?" he asked with genuine fascination.

"Very hard to play, sir." Simon's voice was steadier.

"I'll bet. Tell me, I think I read somewhere, about a wolf note?"

"Yes, sir, on the top C on the fourth string. The G was magnificent, sir."

The guard nodded.

"We're looking for a violin case. I know there are at least two in here; I just don't know where."

Simon acknowledged with a small nod of his head.

"So come on! Get on with it!"

Simon tried to focus his thoughts and breathe deeply through his mouth to slow his frenetic heart. What was this? What did it mean? Was he going to die? Was this man just playing with him? Frantically he dug into the nearest box and saw that it was full of spectacles, so he turned to a second and it was full of shoes. The third contained wristwatches and pocket watches. Suddenly there was a sharp cry from the other side of the room.

"Here!"

He spun around and saw the guard was holding a black violin case aloft. He watched as the man opened it and lifted out a full-sized violin. It had a very dark varnish and was covered in a maze of cracks.

"I'm afraid it's been left here in the cold and the heat and it may not be so great"—the guard was running his finger over the instrument—"but it will sound better than that piece of shit you were playing. Come, outside!"

He opened the door and Simon hurried out. He watched as the guard padlocked the door and glanced around.

"Follow me."

He did as he was ordered and didn't falter until they came to the entrance to the SS barracks. He'd never been close to this part of the camp before, and the smell of real food mixed with the sour stench of his own terror.

"Inside."

The guard shoved him in the ribs but with no real force and he stumbled inside. The room was empty. The guard put the case on a rough wooden table, opened it, and held the violin out toward him. Simon took it and turned it over. There were several deep cracks running vertically down the back and across the front. The strings were attached but completely slack. Everything else seemed to be intact. There were no cracks over the sound box, the bass bar was there, and the bridge seemed to be strong. He blew gently on the top and a cloud of dust rose through the sound holes. Then he turned his attention to the pegs and the peg holes. The pegs were very stiff, but little by little he tightened the strings until they sounded roughly in tune with each other. Without a tuning fork or a piano it was the best he could hope for. He held out his hand for the bow. The guard watched him intently, genuine respect and fascination on his young face.

"Will it play?" he asked enthusiastically.

"Yes, sir. It'll take a while to sound good, but it will play."

Simon examined the horsehair and found it was in remarkably good condition. The bow had been rehaired just before it was confiscated. He tightened the screw on the heel and looked up.

"The bow is good . . . I . . . I don't suppose there's any rosin, sir?"

"Um . . . just a moment . . . yes, look!" He held up a lump of golden rosin and beamed. "And a cloth to wipe the strings," he added.

"Thank you, sir."

Finally they were ready. Simon played a simple scale and adjusted the pegs. Then he played it again and nodded. It was as close as it was going to get. He hesitated and wondered what on earth should he play? What would this man want to hear?

"What are you waiting for?"

"I . . . I don't know what you want me to play, sir."

"Well, what can you play?"

"Vivaldi, Bach, Beethoven, Mendelssohn, Debussy, Brahms, Mozart . . ." His voice trailed off uncertainly.

"Do you know any Wagner? Perhaps the 'Bridal Chorus' from *Lohengrin*?"

Simon gazed back at him steadily, his face betraying none of the revulsion he felt.

"No, sir. I never learned any Wagner."

"A pity, but never mind. Some . . . Vivaldi perhaps? Quietly." Simon grinned.

"One of my favorites. Even if he is Italian, sir."

"Mine too. A little winter to make us feel cooler?"

So Simon began to play, shakily at first and then with more confidence. Soon the sound overtook him, his eyes closed, and he moved, rhythmically dipping and rising with the music. There were some wrong notes, fingering he'd forgotten, and bowing that was less than perfect, but it was unmistakably Vivaldi.

Something deeper, more elemental, seemed to course through his wasted body. A life force he'd all but forgotten that rose up and nourished him.

When he'd finished, he stood with the violin in one hand and the bow in the other, his eyes downcast, unsure of what to do next. The guard reached out for them.

"You'd better go."

The guard laid the violin and bow in the case and walked over to a bench on the side of the room. When he returned, he was carrying a large enamel cup that he held out to Simon.

"Here, drink this."

"Thank you, sir."

Simon took it and raised it to his lips. It was beer. The cold liquid, with its sharp distinctive flavor, filled his mouth and he gulped down the whole cup. It was the first taste of something real, something delicious, he'd had in nearly two years.

"Good?"

"Very, very good, sir, thank you."

"Go now"—he pointed toward the door—"and run back to your barracks. It'll be roll call soon. We will do this again."

"Thank you, sir."

Simon turned and went out the door, his heart still flying from the adrenaline rush of playing the violin. As he ran across the hard parade ground a laugh of pure astonishment and relief bubbled up and spilled out of him.

Back in the hut the young guard stood staring at the violin lying in its case. Then he picked it up and put it to his chin, took up the bow, and started to play a simple scale.

Chapter 25

It took Simon half an hour to recount his exploits to his father and their friends. They were far more excited about the beer than the violin. Heinz said he knew the guard with that scar, that he sometimes guarded the woodworking room and he was a quiet man, not as brutal as some.

Over and over again the Vivaldi cascaded through Simon's head, and his fingers twitched and stretched. Finally he fell into a disturbed sleep, peopled by tumbling musical notes and cracked violins being wrenched away by men with scars on their faces. The sound of the door and a beam of white light jolted him from the dream.

"Attention! Attention! Prisoner 8467291. We want 8467291."

He rolled over. His father hissed in his ear.

"That's you. That's your number."

Simon shrank back into the darkness beside the wall. A guard with a flashlight was shining light into the shelves.

"Attention! Come forward now or we will pull everyone onto the parade ground."

"It's me," he called out and started to climb down. The soldier's hand grabbed him and pulled him to the ground. He shone the light into his face, and Simon put his hand up to shield his eyes from the glare.

"Come. Now."

The guard pushed him hard in the direction of the door. Outside it was a beautifully cool, star-filled night with a gentle breeze blowing. He followed the man across the parade ground to the SS barracks. The room looked smaller now with about fifteen men sitting around, drinking and talking. The table was covered with plates and glasses, and the smell of food made his stomach contract with hunger.

"Hello again."

He raised his eyes a little and saw that the guard who'd found him earlier in the day was standing over by the bench. He was holding the violin and the bow. Did they want him to play? All the men were staring at him and the conversations had died. He lowered his gaze to the floor. His heart was pounding against his rib cage.

"8467291, sir," he said quietly.

"Yes, I remembered. Here, tune this."

The guard held the violin out to him. He took it and plucked the strings, not bad. He took the bow, tuned the violin as best he could, and then tightened the bow. The guard held out the rosin toward him.

"What can he play?" asked one of the other men.

"Plenty." The guard turned to Simon. "Play whatever comes into your head."

Simon looked at the impassive faces. He pretended he was in an eighteenth-century court and in front of him sat the all-powerful emperor and his courtiers. He was playing for his life; of that he was certain.

What should he choose to play on this cracked, barely in-tune, second-rate violin? He started with Massenet's "Médita-tion," then went on to some Vivaldi in "Spring," a little Bach, Beethoven, and Mozart, not whole pieces just passages that floated into his head from long practice sessions that seemed a lifetime ago.

During the entire thirty minutes that he played no one moved, and some seemed barely to be breathing. He was completely lost in the music, his eyes closed, his body moving gently, and when his mind told him he was back in the beautiful music room at home, a smile played on his lips. Finally he stopped and opened his eyes. Reality flooded back, and he lowered the instrument and his gaze. For another second there was silence, and then two guards started to applaud.

"Be quiet."

The order was barked by an older man who wore the insignia of a major and was sitting by the empty fireplace. The applause died instantly.

"Whatever he does, we never clap him. You were right, Kurt, he is a find. He'll do very nicely."

He got up and walked over to Simon. He had a cruel face, with a square jaw, thin lips, and a broken nose below sharp cheekbones and small eyes.

"How long have you been playing? You may speak."

"Since I was four, sixteen years, sir."

"And who was your teacher?"

"Herr Eisenhardt, in Berlin, sir."

"And Kurt tells me you had a Guarneri?"

"Yes, sir, a 1729 del Gesú."

Simon could see his boots as the major walked around him. Suddenly the man reached out and lifted up his left hand.

"What is that scar?"

"I . . . I was hit by a truncheon, sir. But it has healed now."

"Just as well."

He nodded to Kurt and returned to his seat. Kurt took the violin and bow from Simon and put them in the case, then he gestured to the door. Simon took one last look around the room and followed him. Once outside Kurt handed him a mug. It was beer again, and Simon gulped it down gratefully.

"Thank you, sir."

"We need to strengthen you up. Come."

Kurt led him back to the barracks. At the door he stopped, pulled a cloth-wrapped bundle out of his pocket, and thrust it into Simon's hand.

"Keep it hidden until you're lying down. You will play for us. Don't . . . be afraid."

Simon kept his bundle hidden all night by sleeping on top of it. The next day he met his father at his secret place, and together they shared squashed bread, sausage, and cheese. It was the most food either of them had had in one sitting since their incarceration, and for a few moments they feared they'd both be sick. The Simon of those early days in 1939 would've shared these riches with his fellow inmates, but imprisonment had taught him the cruel laws of self-preservation. The men he lived and worked beside would've fought him to the death for a share of such booty, and the Simon of 1941 understood that this golden windfall, this discovery of his talent, might yet be the thing that ensured his, and his father's, survival.

Chapter 26

Dachau
November 1943

The night had drawn in early. Snow fell from the black clouds overhead and swirled around the wooden buildings of the camp. Over the creek a steady stream of smoke billowed from the tall chimneys and floated off toward the town. Figures, bent over against the biting cold wind, scurried across the open ground, and in the distance dogs barked hungrily. Simon and Benjamin stood on the doorstep of the officers' mess waiting for the door to open. They were both painfully thin, but neither looked sick. Their skin color was good, they had no boils or open ulcers, and their feet were wrapped in strips of felt. The door opened, and yellow light flooded out onto the snow.

The room was deliciously warm, and a huge fire roared in the open fireplace. The officers were drinking and talking, sitting in small groups around the table and the fireplace. A large plate of food sat in the center of the table next to the two black violin cases. Kurt was standing with his back to the fire, and he strode over to the table when he saw them.

"I have some more sheet music. My brother sent it from Berlin; have a look."

He picked up a brown leather folder and gave it to Benjamin, then waited impatiently while the older man looked through it. Simon was preparing his violin and watching his father out of the corner of his eye.

"What is it, Papa?"

"Handel, the Violin Sonata in D. I know the larghetto; it is very beautiful, sir."

Kurt beamed.

"Excellent! You can practice it tomorrow. How's the Mozart?"

"Very good, sir. We're ready to play it."

They tuned their instruments with a tuning fork and prepared their bows. Simon still played the same instrument Kurt had found two years before, but Benjamin's was in better condition, a lovely Italian violin with a honey-gold varnish and a rich tone.

The officers turned their chairs around and faced the musicians. Kurt held the violins and gestured to Simon and Benjamin to warm their hands in front of the fire. This was one of the best moments for both of them; the chilling numbness of the day was replaced by golden warmth that flowed up their arms and into their frail bodies.

Carefully keeping their eyes averted from any of the officers' faces, they picked their way through the chairs and back to Kurt. It was the Allegro con spirito from Mozart's Concerto for Two Violins in C, KV190. Simon played the sweeping melody while Benjamin's violin danced around it in the cascading runs so typical of Mozart, until they combined for the beautiful climatic finish. Benjamin's violin sounded particularly magnifi-

cent; the music suited its sweet tone, and Simon could see the
rapt expression on Kurt's face.

Then they played the Bach Concerto for Two Violins in D
Minor, their best piece and one that was often ordered. Benjamin
finished with the Massenet "Méditation," the major's favorite.
As always there was a long silence and then an uncomfortable
shifting that took the place of applause. Kurt came back to them
as they wiped the violins and put them away. His blue eyes were
warm, and he nodded the appreciation he dared not speak.

"You may eat inside tonight; it's too cold outside."

Simon hesitated and shot him a worried glance. He knew
only too well how quickly the atmosphere could turn ugly.
When he was too weak to play for more than a few minutes
last winter, one particularly brutal guard had started to beat
him until Kurt had intervened. Eventually the major had agreed
that there was a danger Simon could lose the ability to play altogether. It hadn't stopped that guard from taking his revenge
two days later in another setting, and the cuts from that whip-
ping had taken weeks to fade. Kurt seemed to read his thoughts.

"It's okay. Come, sit down over here."

He'd moved two chairs into the far corner, away from the
soldiers, and he gave them a plate each and then stood between
them and the rest of the room, blocking the view. The plate held
a little cold meat stew, some potato, some bread and cheese.
They ate as quickly as they could, using their fingers. Then he
took the plates and gave them a mug of coffee each as he ushered them out the door. The cold hit all three men like an explosion of ice. Simon and Benjamin gulped the hot coffee down and
handed the mugs back.

"Thank you, sir," they said quietly in unison.

Kurt was looking at Benjamin.

"The Mozart was wonderful."

"It's a magnificent violin, sir. I'd love to know the history."

"So would I. But it isn't wonderful when I play it."

Benjamin smiled at him, and for a second they stared at each other, then Kurt looked away in embarrassment.

"You're not frightened of me anymore, are you?"

"No, sir. You're very good to us. No one eats as well as we do."

"I wanted you to know. Don't ever tell anyone I said this, it would get me court-martialed. But you're both so talented and when you get to know . . ." His voice trailed off and still he didn't make eye contact.

Benjamin touched Kurt's arm, and Simon marveled at his father's bravery.

"It's a simple truth. Prejudice is much harder to maintain when you break down the barrier of ignorance, my son. You see us now as individual people with talent, not subhuman vermin, and that makes it harder for you to hate us."

Kurt looked directly at him.

"I'm sorry for this. I'm sorry we did all this to you. I hope that when the war is over and Germany rules the world, I can persuade someone to make an exception for both of you and you'll be able to live and play in peace."

Simon was watching his father as Benjamin shook his head sadly.

"No, son, it'll never work like that. I don't want to be an exception. I am a Jew, I am proud to be a Jew. If I live as I used to and play my violins again, then all Jews must be allowed the same right. You like us because you respect us. What you *don't* know is that all Jews are like us. They are no more vermin than we are. That is the truth about prejudice."

Kurt turned away abruptly. "I must take you back. If you're

too late, the guards in your barracks will punish you. Come!"

His voice was harsh, and he drew his coat around his shoulders and followed them out into the snow-filled darkness.

Kurt walked a very dangerous line. He had to pretend to be brutal toward his friend when other guards were around. If just one senior officer suspected that he actually *liked* the young Jewish violinist, he'd be transferred to another camp or, worse, to the Russian front. He took Simon on a work detail to the farthest corner of the camp and they swapped stories of their childhoods and families. He was the son of a prominent doctor from Düsseldorf and had an older brother in the Luftwaffe Ministry in Berlin. They'd both played piano as children and Kurt had learned the cello, so they argued good-naturedly about which instrument was harder to learn. Kurt admitted that he missed his dog, an Alsatian called Meister, more than his family and talked of his passion for football, ice-skating, and fencing.

Simon told him about Levi, who'd set out so bravely for London but had never been in touch after that night in 1938. And about his mother and sister, left behind outside their house in Berlin in 1939, four years ago.

Despite their envied position as musicians to the officers, Simon and Benjamin still had to work in the armaments section. The extra food gave them strength, and the music gave them something to think about while they completed the repetitive tasks. Simon had considered suggesting that they find some more musicians among the prisoners, audition them, and request instruments for a special string quartet or even larger. Then he realized that the amount of food wouldn't multiply in proportion and they'd end up getting less to eat. And he doubted the officers would be prepared to go to all that trouble. The violin, and the reward and respect it helped them to gain, had become the whole point to their existence, and they weren't prepared to share.

One afternoon in December, Benjamin was carrying a box of antiaircraft shells from one side of the room to the other when an unidentified foot shot out between the machines and tripped him. He fell heavily, and the shells went rolling all over the floor. The guards pounced on him and dragged him to his knees. They yelled at him to pick them all up, but before he could finish the task the SS-*obertsturmführer* blew the whistle for a shift change.

By chance, Kurt was about thirty yards away, escorting a work party to the nearby building site and saw the *obertsturm-führer* and a guard dragging the struggling old man through the snow, followed some distance behind by a younger inmate whom he recognized instantly. He must have broken rank and followed them.

"Simon!" he murmured in horror. He sprinted across the open ground and reached Simon just before he caught up with the trio. "No!"

Simon was completely focused on getting to his father and hadn't heard or seen Kurt's approach. The tall man launched himself at Simon and pushed him into the side of the building, pinning him there with his body. The *obertsturmführer* threw Benjamin down into the snow. "Kneel, you filthy piece of scum," he yelled.

Kurt pushed Simon even harder into the wall.

"Don't move an inch, leave it to me," he whispered into Simon's ear. He pulled himself upright and walked over to the group.

"What is this?" he asked, as casually as he could.

The guard had pulled his revolver from its holster, cocked it, and had it pointed at Benjamin's lowered head.

"Stupid old fool, he ruined a whole box of shells."

"Before you do that, you should know that he's a master violinist, the major's favorite."

Kurt's voice was icy cold. The older man glanced at him.

"You mean those Jews who come and play in the mess? I never stay. I can't stand to breathe the air when they pollute it."

"Still, I wouldn't kill him before checking with the major. You wouldn't want him to be furious, and it's not like he can pluck another violinist out of the night."

The guard shrugged, started to turn away, thought better of it, and with one flowing movement turned back and fired a single shot at Benjamin. The old man pitched forward into the snow, a large red stain spreading from beneath his face.

"Too late."

Kurt met Simon's body hurtling forward toward the assassin. They collided and went flying into the snow. Kurt landed on top of him and stayed there.

"What are you doing?" The *obertsturmführer* sounded amused and surprised.

Kurt looked up. "Nothing, sir. Just disciplining a man who should be working faster and I fell over him. I'll deal with it."

He struggled up and pulled Simon to his feet.

"Don't say a word," Kurt snarled as he dragged Simon around the corner. Once out of sight of the guards, he let him go and the young man slumped to the ground.

"I'm sorry, Simon, I had to stop you. He would've shot you. What good would that have done your father? I'm going to take you back to the plant and tell them that I called you away but you're ready for your work detail now. They won't punish you. Do you understand me? You *must* work."

Kurt put his face very close to Simon's, and there was desperation in his expression.

"If you don't carry on, Simon, I can't help you."

"I was supposed to keep him safe," Simon mumbled.

"This wasn't your fault. He made a mistake and they punished him. You must believe in heaven; you must believe he won't suffer anymore?"

Simon didn't answer him.

"Come on." Kurt hauled him to his feet. "It's too cold out here, and you must go back to your shift. I'll take care of him, I promise."

Simon's world had come to an end. He seesawed between rage and numbness and accepted the condolences of his friends with a blank expression. That night he lay with his face buried in his filthy mattress and cried silent tears of pain and fury. He'd seen the terror in his father's body replaced by calmness as he'd accepted his fate and said his silent prayers. His papa was dead. After so much suffering and with a half life that was almost bearable, one mistake, one lapse in concentration, and he was gone. So was he the last one left? Or were Simon's mother and sister still out there, waiting for all this horror to end? Where was Levi? Where was God, for that matter?

It was five days before he was summoned to play in the mess again. There was only one case on the table, the violin his father had played. He gave them Mozart, Brahms, and a piece of Bach his father had loved, the allegro from the Concerto in E. He played as if by remote control and thought of nothing as the music poured out of him. Afterward the major came over to him and said it was unfortunate his father was no longer able to play. It was the closest an officer of the Third Reich was ever going to come to saying he was sorry the man had been killed. Simon knew the major could've been court-martialed for apologizing to a Jew so he accepted the statement with a nod and a "thank you, sir." Kurt escorted him back to his barracks in silence. At the door Simon turned to him.

"Can you tell me? Was the man who shot my father punished? Did it anger the major?"

"Very much. He would court-martial him if he could, but the army wouldn't allow it. But he gave him some private justice, I believe, and his justice is legendary. I think he would've preferred the court-martial."

Chapter 27

Dachau
April 29, 1945

Some photographs are deafening. Years later, the American first lieutenant would study the black-and-white photograph taken the day that he, and his fellow soldiers, liberated Dachau and relive the noise and the stench and the horror of it all and how it mingled with that peculiar sense of indescribable joy. He spoke German so he understood more of what had happened, and more quickly, than the others.

It had snowed the night before, and a dusting of white lay over everything, like fine confectioner's sugar. The sun shone brightly but it was cold, an early spring day, Sunday, April 29, 1945. He knew that, like all the men of the Forty-Fifth Infantry Division, he was battle hardened. He'd been in combat with a ruthless enemy for over two years, but nothing he'd so far endured or observed could've prepared him for the vision of hell that lay behind the electrified barbed-wire fence.

The first thing his division came across was a railway spur off the main line leading into the camp. There were over forty open boxcars sitting motionless, in complete silence, seemingly empty. It wasn't until they got up close that they saw them, over two thousand emaciated bodies, both men and women, who'd been shipped from camp to camp in the last days of the German stand, with no food or water. Some had been shot in the back of the head with pistols, but most had simply died of starvation, thirst, and cold. Now they lay, mute in their agony, covered by a smattering of pure white snow. Later the soldier described their arms as being broomsticks tipped with claws.

Then they moved on, past the imposing homes of the camp directors and through the large gates decorated with the German imperial eagle. The highest-ranking officers had fled, melted into the general public, but the lower ranks were still armed and in the watchtowers. The first lieutenant watched while a German guard, in full military regalia, a recent arrival from the war on the Russian front, saluted an American officer, barked out a "Heil Hitler," and handed over his pistol as a mark of surrender of the camp. The officer looked around him at the huge piles of bodies and spat in the German's face, calling him a "*schweinehund*." The German was taken away, and some time later the first lieutenant heard a pistol shot.

He remembered chaos more clearly than anything else, chaos and a dawning sense of horror. Slowly the living skeletons started to emerge from the long wooden buildings. Some were waving tattered Allied flags, symbols they'd pieced together from rags and patches of cloth. As word spread among the terrified populace that the Americans were there, the numbers grew quickly; eventually there'd be more than thirty thousand prisoners to account for. The walking dead became a milling, pressing crowd of cheering, groaning, shrieking humanity who were desperate to touch their liberators, climbing over one another to kiss arms and legs and touch the jeeps.

He found the approaches frightening at first, but then he realized that once they'd touched him, kissed him, shook his hand, they moved on to someone else. Those who weren't able to walk crawled toward the soldiers, and he picked some of them up and carried them to safety so they wouldn't get trampled on.

Reinforcements from the Forty-Second and Forty-Fifth Infantry Divisions began arriving. They, too, had encountered the boxcars in the railway spur first, and with a roar they ran into the camp on the double, their rage obliterating the usual concern for having adequate cover and concealment.

A full tour of the camp revealed all to the first lieutenant. A room no bigger than his mother's kitchen housed fifty men dying of typhoid who could do nothing more than smile at him. Kennels were filled with large German shepherds with their throats slashed and their heads crushed. And the dogs weren't the only ones to feel the vengeance of the imprisoned; guards had been stripped naked to prevent them melting away in civilian clothing. Some lay where they'd been drowned in the moat that ran through the camp; others were torn apart or shot while resisting arrest. Everywhere there were mounds of bodies, stacked up against buildings and spilling out of open doorways, and the stench of decaying flesh permeated his uniform through his skin to his very bones.

Next he came across the evidence he later feared would send him insane, in a brick building across a bridge, separate from the rest. First, he encountered a room full of clothing: shoes, pants, shirts, and coats. Then he came upon an area with tables covered in lines of soap and towels and an entryway into a shower room. And last he found the massive ovens, standing open, their contents spilling out onto the floor, mountains of ash, pieces of bone, bodies waiting to be fed into the yawning abyss.

He stumbled into the weak sunlight and gripped the wall while he emptied the contents of his stomach onto the ground. Everywhere around him his fellow soldiers were reacting the same way, and as they gasped for breath all they could almost taste was the sickly, sweet aroma of burned human beings. Blindly, with rage tearing at his heart, he made his way back to the open parade ground. Part of him wanted to just run and not stop until he was miles away; the rest of him knew he could never leave—it would haunt his dreams until he died.

Some measure of order was being imposed, and finally the message was getting through to the dazed prisoners. They'd have to stay here while they were processed and they couldn't eat anything until food could be found that they could digest safely: dried bread, crackers, and chocolate soup. Over to his right he saw a tableau of three people frozen in a motionless standoff and within a second had assessed the situation. A tall, well-built man stood holding a white flag. He wore only trousers but was unmistakably an SS officer. There were cuts on his face and arms, and blood ran down to the fingers clenched around the stained flag. Two feet away an American corporal pointed a pistol at the German's head, and the fury on his face was gut-wrenching. The young man had probably never felt this enraged in his life.

At his feet knelt a small, skeletally thin figure, covered in dirt and wearing rags that barely hid a fraction of his body. Beside him on the ground was an object so incongruous it seemed to shine like a lantern. It was a violin case. The first lieutenant strode toward the group.

"What's happening here, Corporal?"

All three men looked at him. There were tearstains on the American's square face.

"I can't let him live, sir. They're animals, all of them."

The small figure on the ground began to plead in German.

"No, please. No, please. Don't shoot him."

Gently the lieutenant knelt down beside him.

"What are you saying?" he asked in German. The old man's face lit up with recognition.

"Please stop him, sir. Don't let him shoot, please, sir."

"But it's over. You don't have to be frightened of him anymore; it's time for him to pay for all this."

"He's my friend. I'd be dead but for him. He isn't a bad man, he kept me alive. Please, sir, don't kill him."

There was a note of hysteria in his voice. The officer straightened up and stared into the German officer's face. His eyes were very blue, and he had a bright red scar down one cheek. He returned the gaze calmly; he clearly wasn't afraid to die.

"Name and rank."

"SS-Untersturmführer Kurt Walder."

"Is it true? Are you friends?" he asked skeptically.

"Yes, sir. This prisoner had special privileges, and he played the violin for us. I saw that no harm came to him. Gave him food."

"What's his name?"

"Simon Horowitz. He comes from Berlin."

He looked from the German to the pleading face below him. The eyes were very black in their sunken hollows but clear and bright, and the face was filthy, lined, exhausted, but the emotion was real.

"Very well. Take him away, Corporal."

The other man hesitated and then holstered his pistol.

"Yes, sir," he replied with obvious reluctance.

"He's your prisoner, Corporal. On my orders, see no harm comes to him."

"Yes, sir."

The corporal saluted, then stepped away. The SS officer bent down and helped the old man to his feet. They embraced, then the officer was pulled away and marched off across the square. The first lieutenant picked up the violin case and held it out to the old man, who was watching the figure disappear across the parade ground. When he turned back, there were tears in his eyes.

"Thank you, sir. I pray that he survives," he said softly.

"How long have you been here?"

"Since November 1939, sir. What is the date?"

"Good God! 1945. How did you survive this?"

"I don't know. I played my violin."

A sudden thought seemed to occur to him, and he smiled at the American.

"I survived! It's over and I'm still alive."

He looked stronger than many, still terribly thin and small but not diseased and with a straighter stance and more fire inside. The officer studied his face again and realized, with a sudden shock, that he wasn't elderly at all. He was an exhausted, lined, bald, filthy man of no more than twenty-five, clutching a violin case.

Chapter 28

Vermont
August 2008

They expected him to say something. The silence had gone on for some time and hung around the table like a curtain of uncertainty. Rafael gazed at the photo in his hand, the smiling, confident boys holding two large violins. When he looked up, the old men were waiting patiently, their faces impassive, understanding in their eyes.

"It's an amazing story. Thank you, thank you so very much for sharing it with me."

It seemed inadequate, but he suspected that anything would. He was looking at Simon, and the small man shrugged his shoulders.

"The most important thing to remember, Maestro, is that surviving the camp doesn't make you better than all those who died. It just means you were lucky and, perhaps, you had something more to live for. On one level it was about a strange kind of fate, an arbitrary and completely unpredictable sort of . . . karma."

Rafael nodded his understanding.

"I have some questions, and if I don't ask them, I will wonder forever. Do you mind?"

"Ask away. I'll answer them if I can."

"What happened to Kurt? Did he survive?"

Simon paused before he began his answer.

"I wrote to his father about ten years after the war and I asked him if he could give me Kurt's address. His father was a doctor in Düsseldorf. For a whole year, I hear nothing. Then one day I get a letter, from his brother, Carl. He said both his parents were dead, of guilt and shame, and that Kurt had not returned from the war. They'd been told he was killed at the very end of the war, perhaps even after the surrender. He was an SS officer, very unpopular job. So I wrote back to him and told him that I had been in Dachau and his brother was a very brave man, a good man, and that I owed him my life more than once. He should honor his brother's memory. He was very grateful for that and wished his parents had been able to read it. He didn't say as much, but I have always suspected that his father committed suicide. We keep in touch from time to time."

Again there was a silence. Rafael put down the photo and picked up the group one: a tall, beautiful woman, a shorter, round, laughing man, and four children, taken well before the dark clouds of war.

"And your mama and Rachel?"

"We know only sketchy details. After a short time in a displaced persons' camp, I was sent to London, to Levi. We waited a couple of years, and then we went to Berlin to find our old house. It had suffered some damage but was habitable and there was a family living there, a military man of some sort. We asked if we could have a look and they were very nice. They let us take the mezuzah and we have it now, on this house, and I said there might be a box in the attic, could I look for it? They agreed and there they were! Seven violins, the property of Amos Wiggenstein, still wrapped in the sheet music. You know, the ones we'd rescued the morning after the Kristallnacht?"

Rafael was fascinated.

"What did you do with them?" he asked eagerly.

"Brought them with us, to New York. We lived with our uncle Avrum for a while, and I went into banking, followed in my father's and my uncle's footsteps, I suppose."

Levi spoke for the first time.

"And I went into interior design and window dressing. Had my own company."

Simon took a deep breath.

"When we were in Berlin, we found Maria Weiss. Mama and Rachel had gone to her on that night. What we didn't know then was that she was a remarkable woman, on the fringes of the Berlin resistance, such as it was. They tried to get us out of Dachau, but the authorities wouldn't agree; it was too late. And she tried to find Sarah, our aunt, but her house was looted and she was gone. We learned later that Mordecai's whole family was hidden for ten months by the Grajerks, the Polish family of a teller in our bank, then betrayed and sent with them to Bergen-Belsen.

"But Maria knew people, and those people got false papers for Mama and Rachel. They lived quietly for a while as Catholic Germans, with friends of Maria's. But these people were also involved in dangerous endeavors, smuggling and hiding Jews and passing German secrets to the Americans and the Russians. Rachel lived with a glamorous young couple, Harro Schulze-Boysen, a lieutenant in the Luftwaffe Ministry, and his French wife, Libertas Schulze-Boysen. They were spies, part of the Red Orchestra network.

"In 1941, Mama tried to go to Switzerland and then on to Levi in London, but her group was stopped at the border and the Gestapo didn't believe their story, even though they had all the correct papers. Eventually one of them broke, and the Gestapo shipped the whole group off to Auschwitz. Rachel had decided to stay in Berlin. She was madly in love with a resistance fighter, a handsome young lawyer called Hans, according to Maria. When I last saw her, she was fourteen and the idea of my little sister being madly in love with anyone still astounds me. She did important document work for her friends—she was very good at drawing and copying—and I can imagine what sort of work she did.

"In late 1942, the spy ring was infiltrated and they were all arrested. Many of them were tried and executed in prison, guillotined, but when they discovered that Rachel was a Jewess they decided the blade was too good for her and sent her to Auschwitz. By that stage of the war they were killing twenty thousand a day and the average life expectancy of a Jew in Auschwitz was four hours—"

"Oh my God!"

Rafael's reaction to Simon's words was instinctual, almost visceral. The old man smiled sadly.

"I know, Maestro, that place was an efficient killing machine. People arrived and lived for as long as it took to process them."

Rafael shook his head. These men had seen human nature at its worst, such savagery and brutality, and yet they remained above it.

"I'm so sorry, Mr. Horowitz. I'd hoped very much for a happier conclusion."

"I survived, and Levi's is a happy story. That's more than many families can say."

Rafael turned to Levi. "I was going to ask, what happened to you?"

"I don't talk so much about it. I left home in November 1938 on what we thought was an official exit visa, but I'd been set up and was arrested at the border. You must understand that there was corruption everywhere in those days. One of the border guards tried to shoot me but the gun jammed, then I fought back and escaped. I fled on foot to Switzerland and, eventually, to London. I had the precious things my father had given me and that meant I could pay for my passage to freedom, so he did save me after all. I was in an internment camp for a while, and then I worked on the land, for a farming family in Somerset. They had sons in the air force and they were very good to me. They knew I hated Hitler more than they did.

"After the war, I went back to London and got a job in a soft furnishing store. I designed pieces of furniture and I learned upholstery. When the Red Cross told me Simon was alive, I applied for him to come to London."

He'd kept his head down and his gaze fixed on the table throughout his short speech, and something told Rafael that he felt uncomfortable talking about himself. Then he looked up.

"Compared to Simon I had a very easy war."

"He is the master of understatement when it comes to his war, my brother."

The men exchanged glances, and Rafael could tell it was a subject over which they had made peace long ago.

"So what happened to the violins you brought with you?" Rafael asked in a moving-along-now tone of voice.

"We sold them, all except one."

Simon got to his feet and went into the hall. He opened a large cupboard and lifted down two violin cases.

"This is the one we kept, a Cremonese violin from around 1810, and this one."

He opened the case and lifted out a full-sized violin with a lovely honey-gold glaze and one or two obvious tiny cracks. The strings were loose.

"This is the violin both my father and I played in Dachau. I don't play it, I just keep it. I haven't played a violin since the last time I played for the guards."

"May I?"

Rafael held out his hand toward the violin, and the old man handed it over.

"Certainly, sir."

It felt rough, and the cracks caught under the skin of his fingers. He turned it over and over and studied the beautifully tooled scroll and then handed it back.

"Thank you very much for showing it to me. I have one last question and before you answer, I want you to know that it is not at all my intention to stir up old hurts, not at all. I want to help your grandson to reach a place where he *needs* to play the violin again. It's now more obvious to me than ever that these violins are a vital part of his family history and Daniel inherits his extraordinary gift partly from you, yes? It would be a tragedy for him, and for us, his public, if he never plays again."

Both old men nodded their agreement.

"So is there anything more you can tell me about the Guarneri and the Amati violins? Anything at all that might help me to find them?"

"And you do this just for Daniel?" Levi asked.

"Absolutely. They are his legacy. It's an unbelievably hard thing to do, but if we don't try, we'll never succeed, yes? I believe that if we could find even one of them, he would want to play it more than anything else."

Simon nodded slowly.

"The Amati may be in France. There's a list of instruments we read about in an old French magazine, oh, it would be ten years ago now, and it mentioned a 1640 with a very light tone and a lovely dark varnish. That sounds like our instrument. It's in a private collection. I doubt we could get it, because we can't prove it's ours."

"And the Guarneri?"

He felt guilty about pushing them, but they were as open as he was ever going to find them, and sometimes elderly memories need a helping hand.

"It had the most amazing oil vanish; it shone. It was a red-tinted brown and there was a flame in the maple on the back and there was a wolf note—"

"That's not what he means!" Levi cut across his brother's description. "He means is there anything to identify it. The answer is no."

Simon turned him. "It's for Daniel," he said firmly.

"We don't know anything, Simon. That Nazi thug took it away, and we know nothing more."

"But if he doesn—"

"We promised Papa. We swore a solemn oath and I won't betray his memory. Besides, that was long before the war. It can't mean anything now."

Levi was suddenly agitated, and Rafael could hear the stubborn desperation in his voice. They were hiding something but he had no idea what.

"You can trust me, gentlemen. If something happened to the violin, you know I'll keep your confidence."

"We don't have anything more to tell you, Maestro. I'm sorry if your journey has been wasted," Levi said with finality. Again there was silence, but this one was more uncomfortable.

"Yes, we do."

Simon turned to Levi and touched his arm.

"He's my grandson, Levi, and I *want* him to play. He is the last Horowitz in the line, and there may be no more. His great-grandpapa would *want* him to play again. He would want us to find it, and if the maestro doesn't know, he'll never succeed."

He picked up the violin and gave it back to Rafael.

"Look inside this violin. There is a label; you can just glimpse it. That's how we would tell our Guarneri, by the date of manufacture."

Rafael looked into the *f* hole. There was something stuck to the inside back of the instrument, but he couldn't see what it was.

"I don't understand."

Simon gave a deep sigh.

"Years ago, before the war, Papa could see what was happening to us, to the Jews. He was concerned that the Nazis would make an excuse and try to take our possessions. He worried that we owned things the Nazis would say were too precious, too valuable to be owned by a Jew. He couldn't do anything about most of what he owned and he knew that if they took the house, they would also take the bank, so the vault was not the answer. So he took the Guarneri to Amos Wiggenstein and paid him to make it less valuable. That way the Nazis wouldn't care so much about it and they might, one day, give it back to him. And he would know it instantly when he found it again."

The two old men exchanged glances again. Levi was obviously angry but silent.

"So Amos changed the date on the label?" Rafael asked incredulously.

"Yes, sir. Amos was one of the best luthiers in Germany. My grandpapa had come from Frankfurt to bring him violins when he was young, long before we moved to Berlin, so he'd cared for them for many years. He was an old man, but he was very, very skilled."

"So although it is a 1729, it wouldn't read 1729, now?"

Simon hesitated, and Levi gave a deep sigh. "No, sir, it *would* read 1729, now."

"But it isn't?"

"No, sir."

Something was beginning to stir in Rafael's mind, a wondering, an excitement, a feeling of amazement, mixed with a strong sense of dread. His mouth felt suddenly dry.

"Do you know what it *should* read?" he asked, already knowing the answer.

"Oh, yes, of course. It *should* read 1742, and that's why the famous last one has never been found. It's out there somewhere, disguised as something else."

It was one of those you-could-have-heard-a-pin-drop moments, as Rafael reflected and turned the old violin over in his hands. Such a circle of coincidences, but then perhaps it wasn't coincidence at all; perhaps it was fate, or perhaps it was the strange karma that Simon had spoken of earlier. Roberto di Longi was right, and Rafael was in a bind deeper than he'd ever experienced before.

When he eventually looked up, he could see the relief of a long-held secret, finally shared, on both of the other men's faces. Rafael felt deeply sorry for them and yet humbled by their resilience and their courage. They'd told the story because he'd asked; they didn't expect, or want, his pity. How could he ever begin to imagine what they'd gone through? How could he

make any of it up to them? Could he restore something so precious, such a link to the past, to those loved ones viciously torn
away from them? And, at the same time, could he reestablish a
musical dynasty? His gut instinct told him that success in this
would be more important than any other part of his legacy.

"Gentlemen, if your Guarneri is, indeed, a 1742, then I know
where it is."

Possession

Part Three: Sergei Valentino

1945

Chapter 29

Berlin
Late April 1945

The bullet whistled past about three inches above his left ear. In a desperate reflex action, Willi Graf threw himself behind a pile of rubble and lay very still. He couldn't hear the blood thudding in his head because the sounds around him were too loud, but he was aware of his heart hammering in his chest. The artillery shells landing in the next street made the ground vibrate, and his nostrils were full of the stink of smoke from the fires raging in bombed-out buildings.

About three hundred meters earlier, he'd finally given up on the brown box, it was slowing him down, so now he held nothing but the violin case, clutched to his chest. It was covered in a fine powder of dust from the rubble, and almost instinctively he brushed it clean with the back of his hand. Very slowly he raised his head above the jagged chunks of brick and peered around. Large craters crisscrossed the street between the debris, and he could see several bodies lying where they'd fallen, some missing limbs. The sharp cracks of rifle fire, the deep boom of artillery, and the low rumble of tanks over cobblestone echoed through the city like a death rattle. Berlin was falling, and street by street, building by building, the great Red Army was getting closer to victory. There would be no rescue from German troops outside the city; all was lost and it was time to leave, to melt into the crowd. He knew he should feel something, anger at the incompetence of a high command that had allowed things to get to this, fear for his family or even for himself, shame or humiliation when he considered the past few years. But for the moment the only emotion coursing through him was a strong sense of self-preservation; he knew what he had to do to save his own skin and secure his future and that took all his mental capacity.

Up until a few weeks ago his war had gone very well. As a *stabsmusikmeister,* Willi Graf had enjoyed a position of rare privilege. He was part of the M-Aktion team and had spent the last seven years evaluating and cataloging precious musical treasures for the Sonderstab Musik, the führer's special task force for music. Their instructions were to prepare the collection for a music university to be opened in Linz, Austria, after the glorious victory. Graf had traveled all over occupied Europe and handled wonderful musical instruments and original manuscripts. In 1942, he'd been in Paris, helping compose a nine-page list, an inventory of the cream of the violins they'd found so far, including ten Stradivari, three Amati, and at least four gorgeous Guarneri.

But in January he'd been recalled to Berlin. The war was not going well, and his orders seemed less confident, more confused, every day. He knew there were lists of instruments in Berlin,

Leipzig, Amsterdam, and Brussels, but he also knew that they'd probably been destroyed when the enemy bombs hit the administration buildings. This meant there were now very few people who knew where the most valuable treasures were hidden—and he was one of them. The führer himself had commanded him to guard the knowledge with his life so that when the army came and the Reich was saved, the plans for a music university could continue.

This morning he'd decided it was time he made his escape, so he'd dressed in civilian clothing and donned his long, black leather coat to keep out the spring cold. Before packing the box, he'd caressed its contents one last time, lingering over the curves and marveling at the beauty of the varnish. Nothing in his life mattered as much as this, his constant companion.

His plan had been to make his way on foot to a garage on the southern outskirts of the city where he knew he'd find a car, fueled and ready for the journey to the Swiss border. Then, after a couple of quick stops to collect some possessions, which he'd carefully hidden away for just such a "rainy" day, he'd be on his way to freedom and a life of luxury.

Now he admitted that he'd severely underestimated the danger on the streets, and the journey to the car was far more complicated than it'd appeared from the relative safety of the führer's bunker, but Graf had survived so far on his nerves and his cunning, and he wasn't going to give in to some stupid Russkies.

Slowly he uncoiled from behind the mountain of broken bricks. Snipers were his immediate problem, German riflemen hidden from view picking off people not in uniform. Case clasped to his body and bent low, he sprinted across the street into the deep shadows created by the shells of the buildings.

Two streets from the garage, the gunfire sounded farther away, and he dropped his guard a fraction, rounded a corner, and walked straight into a raised Russian Tokarev semiautomatic rifle. The patrol was miles from where it should've been. In desperation, he surrendered and tried to explain that he was just a German civilian, but they hauled him away, still clinging to the violin case.

Chapter 30

General Vladimir Mikhailovich Valentino sat behind a temporary desk and studied a wall-mounted street map of Berlin as he stuffed tobacco into his pipe. He was a heavyset man, six foot four and over two hundred and eighty pounds, with thick glistening black hair slicked back from a high forehead, a large mouth under a hooked nose, and an impressive downward-drooping mustache. He sighed deeply and lit the bowl of the pipe. On the desk in front of him lay a report detailing a sector his division had "liberated" the day before: how many German soldiers killed in combat, how many taken prisoner, how many supplies confiscated, how many civilians shot, and so on.

One thing that surprised him was the number of civilian bodies his troops were finding, men and women hanged or shot by their own soldiers. They were a barbaric lot, these Germans. Many years of warfare had taught him that one important statistic was missing and would always be missing. It was one of the universal tenets of conflict, over two thousand years old, that the women of the conquered belong to the conquerors and he knew that German women were being raped all over the city every day. He accepted the fact but he disliked the secrecy.

"Where's that tank?" he muttered to no one in particular. "I should be out on the streets, in the battle. Not hiding down here in a bloody rat hole."

There was a sharp rap at the door, and the young captain at the other desk looked up.

"Here it is now, General. Enter."

The door swung open. It was a junior lieutenant. He looked both nervous and utterly exhausted.

"Excuse me, General. We have something I think you'll want to see."

Valentino's cold eyes narrowed in anger. "Is it a tank?"

"No, sir, it's not. But it is important."

The general slowly pulled himself to his feet.

"All right, Andrei. I'll come, but I warn you, it better be so bloody important you never forget it until your dying day."

Willi Graf glanced up and went very white. The man mountain in front of him wore the insignia of a three-star general in the Red Army and was looking at him with keen interest in his pale green eyes. Graf shrank back into the frame of the metal chair. He felt very exposed in the bare room with nothing between him and the Russian officer.

"What is your name?" the Russian asked in perfect German.

"Helmut Becker."

"Where are your papers?"

"I lost them." He raised a hand to the graze on his cheek. "Some men attacked me in the street yesterday and stole them."

"Where were you going?"

"Home. I live on the Weibberstrasse."

The only emotion on the large face came from the eyes that bore relentlessly into his skull.

"You're lying," the general said simply.

"I'm a teacher, not important—"

"What do you teach?"

Graf hesitated then decided to take a risk. "Music."

The officer smiled and nodded.

"Hence the violin."

Graf raised his hands in a gesture of supplication.

"Please, sir, can I have it back? I need to be on my way, and I've done nothing wrong. I didn't even like the Nazis. I'm a simple musician and my pupils call me the Violin Man."

The general walked to the door and clicked his fingers briskly. "Bring it," he ordered in Russian, and then he returned to the center of the room.

The junior lieutenant came in carrying a closed black violin case. He stood at attention. The general opened the case and turned the officer's body so the case was facing Graf.

"Your violin, Herr Becker."

Graf sprang from his seat, but before he reached the case, the general caught him in the chest with a massive hand and pushed him back onto the chair.

"Sit down!" he thundered.

Graf's fear was palpable. He glanced from the men to the violin. Then the general picked up the instrument and inspected it closely. Surely the man didn't know what it was; what were the chances of that? Graf's brain was doing rapid calculations as he watched for a sign of recognition. The varnish glowed in the pale light coming from the corridor, and he longed to snatch it back.

"How long have you had this?" the general asked abruptly.

"Years." Graf licked his dry lips repeatedly. "My parents . . . my . . . my father gave it to me for my birthday."

"Where was it made?"

The Russian was studying the back, running his finger over the vibrant flame pattern in the wood grain. Graf didn't answer immediately.

"It's . . . I think my teacher said it, it was Italian?"

Finally the man put the violin back into the case and turned to gaze at Graf impassively.

"You *think*? You're a music teacher, a violin teacher presumably, and you don't know the make of your own instrument?"

"I do. It's Italian, from Cremona."

"Play it for me," the general barked as he picked up the violin again and handed it and the bow to Graf. Graf stood up, tightened the screw on the heel of the bow, and played a couple of notes. His fingers slipped off the pegs as he fiddled with them. Then he put the violin to his chin and began to play some Brahms. He was a very average violinist, but the sound was luscious, dark, and melancholic. It filled the room and bounced off the walls. The Russian listened for a few moments, seemingly transfixed to the spot. Suddenly he held out his hands.

"Enough. Give it back."

Graf reluctantly handed the violin and bow to the general and watched as he laid them gently in the case. The reverence in his movements was ominous.

"I ask myself some questions, Herr Becker. Why would a music teacher venture out on a day like this when there is so much danger everywhere? And without your papers? And why would such an insignificant man have one of the great violins of the world in his possession?"

Graf's blue eyes opened wide in horror, and he ran a hand through his short blond hair. This was going very badly.

"It's nothing like—"

"You're lying to me again, Herr Becker."

As he spoke, the general walked over to stand in front of him, several inches taller and much broader, his presence intimidating.

"And that's very stupid. I will give you one final chance. My men arrest you on a Berlin street, in broad daylight, wearing a quality leather coat and carrying a genuine Guarneri del Gesú violin. Who are you and *where did you get it*?"

In a detached part of his brain, Graf recalled all the threatening conversations he'd held as he ripped possessions from their owners and he couldn't help analyzing the emotion.

"There's only one thing that will save you. If you know of other . . . items of interest, and can show us where they are, we will spare you. Otherwise you will be shot as a German spy."

By now the menace in the Russian's voice was plain, and the threat spurred Graf into life. He was no spy. He snapped his heels together and saluted.

"I am Stabsmusikmeister Willi Graf, of the army of the Third Reich."

The Russian smiled broadly.

"Better, much better. A music captain, well, well, that explains everything. And when and where did you acquire the del Gesú?"

Graf looked over at the case and licked his lips again. Perhaps if he shared some of his loot with this man, they could make a deal; he had quite a bit to trade.

"I've had it since 1939, General. It belonged to a Jewish family, a wealthy banker in Berlin. I was present when their house and possessions were reclaimed."

"And you stole it. As an insurance policy."

Despite his predicament, Graf felt his anger burn at the insinuation.

"I'd never sell it! It's the most magnificent instrument I've ever held, and believe me, over the last seven years I've handled some truly extraordinary examples. I was told that Guarneri himself said that the sound was like the tears of an angel. . . ."

The Russian was staring at him, and Graf's voice trailed off. What was the man thinking? Why was he so impossible to read?

"And what else have you kept?"

"One or two other things, some wonderful art, some silver and jewelry. I have it hidden but this I had with me—"

"While you desert your post and your country?"

Graf remained silent; he was admitting to nothing more than the obvious.

"In Russia you'd be shot for such insubordination. So where is the rest of your treasure housed?"

The Russian's voice was dripping with contempt, but Graf could hear his interest.

"Not far from here. I'll show you."

The general stepped back and surveyed him one last time, then he turned away. Over his shoulder he barked at Graf. "You will show my soldiers where this is, and then they will bring you back. When I'm convinced you've told the truth, we'll talk again. Bring the violin."

The officer picked up the violin case, followed him out, and banged the door behind them. Graf sank back onto the chair and rubbed his hands over his face.

The truck rumbled to a stop outside a row of deserted, bomb-damaged houses. Willi Graf and Junior Lieutenant Andrei Malenskvia climbed out of the back, and two Russian soldiers joined them from the front of the vehicle.

"Down there."

Graf indicated the ground floor of the second house. The

soldiers exchanged glances and raised their rifles to cover him. Malenskvia withdrew his pistol from its holster and waved it in the direction of the house.

Graf led them to a wooden door and down some stone steps into a dark, dry cellar. One of the soldiers lit his cigarette lighter, and a small flame of golden light split the darkness. Two squares wrapped in cloth and a long metal box leaned against the wall. Malenskvia pointed at the squares.

"What are those?"

"Paintings." Graf couldn't keep the hatred out of his voice.

"Give me that and take them up," ordered the officer, and the soldier handed him the lighter and picked up one of the squares. Somewhere in the distance a rat scuttled across the stone floor. There were a dozen wooden boxes stacked over by a far wall.

"Is that it?"

"Yes, that's all," Graf replied dully.

"What's in those boxes?"

"Wine, I believe, or scotch. I didn't put it there."

"Upstairs, and keep your hands where I can see them."

The men loaded both squares, the metal box, and the wine onto the back of the truck while Graf watched them, aware that Malenskvia's pistol remained trained on him. He wasn't exactly sure what he'd hidden where but, with the contents of their stop at another cellar, it should be enough to bargain with. He knew two paintings, silver, and jewelry from the house that his violin had come from—what he'd considered restitution for his broken nose—were probably in the truck by now; perhaps the Russian oaf had a mistress at home.

Finally Malenskvia waved his gun in the direction of the street. "Run," he ordered.

Graf was confused and didn't move.

"What? What do you mean?"

"Run! You have sixty seconds, starting now."

"But the general said—"

"Now you have fifty-eight seconds. Do you want to escape or not?"

Graf took a last look at the shapes in the back of the truck, then began to pick his way through the rubble as quickly as he could. Malenskvia raised his pistol and shot him once in the back. His body jerked and he slumped, face forward, into the mud.

"Too late, time's up." The Russian grinned at his fellow soldiers. "He really shouldn't have tried to escape. That wine'll be a nice surprise for the general."

Chapter 31

Sochi on the Black Sea, Russia
Summer 1947

The early morning sun sparkled off the waters of the Black Sea. Keen sailors were out already, making the most of the first breezes of the new day. The almost deserted beach was quiet and still, as the fine white sand awaited the next invasion of bodies and buckets and spades. Halfway along the beach a path disappeared into the lush vegetation and broke out again onto a lovely, manicured lawn. Perfect lavender hedges and colorful semitropical plants competed for space around its periphery as the grass swept up to a beautiful, two-story home. Large windows and French doors, surrounded by delicate wooden fretwork, opened out onto the gardens. A wide balcony enclosed the upper story of the house, and in one corner a young woman stood gazing out at the sea. She wore a cotton nightgown and wrap, her feet were bare, and her long chestnut hair was piled up on top of her head. She heard a door open and close on the level below her, and she watched as a large man, in a blue silk robe with a towel over his shoulder, strode across the damp grass.

"Morning, Papa," she called cheerfully.

He stopped and turned, searching the house until he saw her, then his face was split by a huge smile and he raised one hand.

"Morning, my precious! Sleep well?"

"Yes, thank you. The sea looks wonderful."

His voice boomed in the stillness. "I'll wait for you if you want to join me."

"You go on, I won't be more than a few moments."

He acknowledged with a wave of the hand and turned back to his journey. She smiled as she watched him disappear into the undergrowth, leaving two lines of large footprints on the dewy lawn. This was their time, a time to heal the wounds of the past few years and be a family again. A summer of golden days and laughter, of being grateful, and, as a family, they had a lot to be grateful for.

Ten minutes later Yulena Valentina stood on the beach, searching the water for her father. General Vladimir Valentino was a huge, powerful man, but in the sea he looked like a little black dot, bobbing in the silver-blue water. She slipped off her wrap and ran into the cool welcome of the waves.

As the day wore on, the temperature rose and the entire Valentino household took individual measures to combat the heat. Everyone was aware of how stifling it would be back in Moscow and how lucky they were to have this seaside dacha, bestowed on the general by a grateful Motherland after his faithful service to Marshal Zhukov during the Great Patriotic War, but it was still ridiculously hot.

The general himself took refuge in the summerhouse with his pipe and his papers and a tall glass of rye kvass, a nonalcoholic malt beverage that he found quenched his thirst admirably, and a plate of beef- and cheese-filled piroshki and fried *khvorost* cookies just to see him through until supper.

Born the same year as Zhukov, Vladimir came from humble beginnings; his father worked in a St. Petersburg printing shop, and his mother was a laundress. He fought in World War I in the Imperial Army and then joined the Workers' and Peasants' Red Army in 1918. His path to major was swift, and after the Manchurian campaign of 1939, he became a much-trusted Zhukov confidant and a two-star general. He was there during the defense of Leningrad in 1941 and Stalingrad in 1942/43, the Battle of the Kursk in 1943, and the sweep through the Ukraine and Belorussia and then into Berlin in April 1945.

When Georgy Konstantinovich Zhukov rode a white horse out of the Spassky Gate in the Kremlin for the Victory Parade on June 24, 1945, the now three-star general Vladimir Valentino was in his accustomed position, right behind him. Comrade Stalin seemed to like Valentino too, perhaps because of his lowly origins or more likely because of his earthy sense of humor, and he'd fit into the Red Army headquarters in Moscow quite easily. Now he had an unusually spacious apartment close to the diplomatic quarter, a car with driver, and the lovely dacha in Sochi, not far from Stalin's own holiday residence.

A few yards away, his wife of twenty-nine years, Nada, busied herself preparing for the evening celebrations. It wasn't official Party policy to employ servants, so she arranged for a couple of the local babushkas to come and help and gave them some food for their trouble.

Nada was Ukrainian, the daughter of two teachers from Kiev, and had gone to technical college herself. She was a quiet woman, educated and wise, and many in the Party agreed that General Valentino had been blessed in his choice of spouse. Occasionally she even wrote Party tracts, and they were generally well received.

When all was ready, she took her cross-stitch upstairs, for a rest and a nap. She was looking forward to tonight. Yulena would play for them, and they could have a good, old-fashioned sing-along. Music was Nada's greatest passion, and the talent of her daughter was the one thing of which she was enormously proud. Nothing would have tempted her to publicly admit to a belief in God, but she still thanked "something" every day for Yulena's safe return from her war adventure. And, of course, she was grateful that her husband and son had been spared as well. Many of her friends had lost some, if not all, of their families, and she'd come through unscathed.

She was a strong woman, mentally and physically, and she didn't tolerate weakness easily. Her brown hair was peppered with streaks of gray and there were lines around her hazel eyes, but her skin was still exquisitely soft and translucent. Her husband thought of her as Rubenesque and womanly. She reminded him of those magnificent paintings he wasn't supposed to look at, in the books he kept hidden in the summerhouse.

The birthday boy was their son, Koyla. He was twenty-four today, and this family gathering would celebrate, yet again, their completeness.

Koyla had finished his schooling before serving as an assistant to a *zampolit,* a political officer in the Red Army, responsible for the philosophical and political health of the soldiers as they defended the Motherland. This had brought him to the fringes, but not the heart, of combat; and his promotion to *zampolit* proper had coincided with the Great Victory. Since the war he'd worked in the Party's central office as an information officer. He was completely committed to the "cause" and chose to believe wholeheartedly in the utterances of Comrade Stalin. He was proud of his father's war record and enjoyed the way that people *he* was in awe of always took notice of him when they learned his father's identity. However, he'd watched the acquisitions of the past two years with growing concern and had even considered declining the invitation for a summer holiday. It was too easy to become "corrupted" by the rewards of the State and he didn't want to be labeled a hypocrite. But his mama had convinced him that they were still true believers.

He was tall, almost as tall as his father, but had not yet filled out. The combination of light green eyes behind glasses, pale skin, short black hair, and fine, aesthetic features made him look like an intellectual, a writer or a scientist. He saw himself as a simple workingman with a message for those comrades who doubted the direction of the Motherland.

Now Koyla went for a brisk walk along the beach until he found a shady spot to sit and read the Party documentation that had arrived by official courier just that morning. Back in the house his very pregnant wife, Ekaterina, had a long soak in a cool bath and then fell asleep on their bed, with pillows to support her ever-aching back. Koyla had spoken at a Party rally she'd attended on her second day in Moscow and she'd asked him for advice on literature. They'd married three months later and now she was on the verge of having their first child.

She seemed to be searching for something when they met, and Koyla sometimes wondered if she'd yet found it. She was an intelligent woman, fierce and outspoken, but she'd lost her entire family in the horrors of Stalingrad, and now all she appeared to want to do was forget it'd ever happened. If he saw flashes of anguish in her deep brown eyes and the occasional evidence of her hatred for anything German, he held his tongue.

With her sharp cheekbones, short black hair, and slightly almond-shaped eyes, she could look like a cold piece of sculpture; then, suddenly, she'd smile, and men of all ages became tongue-tied.

The last member of the household, Yulena, was helping her mother in the large kitchen. Then she spent the late afternoon practicing on her beloved 1729 Guarneri del Gesú violin. It was a present from her father after the Great Patriotic War ended, and she still couldn't quite believe it was hers.

Yulena had shown musical promise at a very early age on both the violin and the piano. On her tenth birthday, she'd started in the musically endowed children's class at the Moscow Conservatory and was playing her first violin solo, Brahms, at twelve. When she was eighteen, she'd headlined a concert in the Great Hall and her future seemed assured.

But one afternoon in early 1941, she heard a radio broadcast by Major Marina Raskova of the Soviet Air Force. Raskova had broken the international women's distance record in 1938 when she flew from Moscow to Komsomolsk-on-Amur, in the Russian Far East. This had made her a folk hero, so she was the obvious choice to front a recruiting drive for female pilots. Yulena was just twenty-one and she didn't hesitate for a second. Within hours she'd left the safe world of the conservatory behind and was on an air force base in the town of Engels on the Volga River.

A two-year course was packed into six months of intensive training. The women were issued men's uniforms that were far too big and had to stuff their boots with newspaper. Sometimes the instructors could be brutal, but Yulena felt truly alive for the first time in her short life.

When she graduated, she was sent to the 586th Fighter Regiment. These were extremely brave women. They flew without parachutes and agreed that, if they were captured, they'd shoot themselves rather than surrender. Their role was to engage the

Messerschmitt 109s escorting the bombers and then to drive the bombers away before the targets were reached.

Yulena had had five "victories" when she was suddenly transferred to the Seventy-Third Fighter Regiment, a squadron of men. At first the men refused to have a female pilot as a wingman, but when she proved her worth time and again in furious battles over the skies of Stalingrad, they had no choice but to accept her.

In July 1943, she transferred back to the 586th for the famous battle at Kursk. This proved to be the decisive point of the war. Between them, the two fronts had more than 1.3 million men in combat and over twenty thousand field guns. In the skies, four thousand aircraft operated in an area that measured only twelve miles by thirty miles, and at times Yulena was in the middle of three hundred planes. Below her, her father and Marshal Zhukov were winning the land battle. She survived, despite being shot down twice, and was awarded the Gold Star, Hero of the Soviet Union.

Almost as famous for her mane of deep chestnut-red hair and her long-limbed body as for her flying, she quickly became something of a legend. Through the intervention of Zhukov, she was recalled in 1944 and given a posting to her old camp in Engels, training both men and women. These months gave her time to reflect on her war experiences and come to terms with what she'd seen, so that the deepest emotion she endured was concern over the fate of the men and women she was training. It was a source of some pride that she never cried over the deaths of her fellow pilots.

When the Great Patriotic War ended, she returned to the Moscow Conservatory to resume her studies. After her first concert in four and a half years, her parents had treated her to dinner in a restaurant and then her papa had presented her with

a battered black violin case. There were one or two tiny cracks
in the body, nothing important, and she'd had them repaired.
The oil varnish was in amazing condition and the color was a
deep burnt sienna, with the merest hint of red. The sound had
reduced her to tears in seconds.

Two years later it was her pride and joy, her dearest friend,
and she bore the teasing of others with a good-natured smile;
no one understood what this "piece of wood" meant to her.
No one except her papa. He'd found it in a little violin shop,
miraculously saved from the bombing, and he'd bargained with
the owner to get it for a very good price. Yulena understood the
realities of war only too well and had decided almost immediately that she wouldn't question her papa too closely about just
how he'd persuaded the shopkeeper to part with such a treasure.
All that mattered was that he had; it was his gift to her, his way
of saying she had brought much pride to the name of Valentino
and he adored her for it.

It was still daylight when Nada finished laying out her son's
birthday feast. The long table was groaning with dishes of
Beluga caviar, chicken pudding, stuffed cabbage leaves, beef
stroganoff, fish rolls, stuffed carp, and bottles of fine Georgian
red wine. She knew that Koyla would comment on the amount
of food and the apparent extravagance but she didn't care;
Vladimir worked hard, and their ability to put good food on the
table was his reward.

"Good grief!"

She looked up to see Koyla standing in the doorway and
wiped her hands on her apron.

"It's your birthday, my boy. And it will be our one holiday
feast."

"It's wonderful, Mama. You must have cooked all day."

She smiled with relief and straightened a chair as he walked around the table to her side and kissed her warmly on the cheek.

"And all for me? Thank you, I'm very touched."

"It is my pleasure. How's your darling Kati?"

"Feeling better; she slept this afternoon. Her back hurts and the heat makes her ankles swell."

"Oh, I do remember that. It was so hot before you were born I thought the doctor would have to hose me down."

He laughed.

"She'll be glad when it's all over but she's very good, she doesn't complain. Shall I get the others? They're in the drawing room. Papa is telling us about Comrade Stalin's latest favorite artist; he sounds very good."

"Thank you, darling. Open the wine and then ask them to come."

Chapter 32

There were nine of them around the table, five family and four neighbors. They ate and laughed and talked and made toasts to General Secretary Comrade Stalin and to Marshal Zhukov. Yulena told them about her adored professor Dmitri Shostakovich, and the exciting plans for the conservatory's end-of-year concert. She saw Koyla's expression harden when she mentioned Shostakovich but ignored it. Mama had worked so hard and it was Koyla's birthday; the last thing they needed was an argument.

"Been fishing lately, Koyla?"

The question came from their neighbor Ivan Suvokinov.

"Not since the winter, Comrade; no time, and I didn't want to leave Kati once she came close to her date."

Fishing and the Party were the only passions her brother seemed to indulge in, and at times, Yulena was tempted to tease him about how the Great Father viewed his stories of the five-hundred-pound catfish on the river Don and huge salmon in Neva, but she knew that Comrade Stalin was not a subject for humor.

"My dream remains the Baltic sturgeon in the headwaters of the Elba," Koyla added.

"An admirable dream." Ivan was warming to the subject. "You know there are fish in the Elba with over eighty pounds of caviar inside them? I've seen them, with my own eyes."

"So tell me, Koyla, how is the farm policy seen by the Party in Moscow?" asked Pavel Volkov, another neighbor.

Yulena suppressed her amusement; the two neighbors were easily impressed by power: Ivan pandered to Koyla's interest in fishing, and Pavel knew he adored talking politics. Almost instantly her brother was on the edge of his seat and she could see his eyes bright with enthusiasm. *Here we go,* she thought.

"It's a brilliant concept, you know. Before the next decade, less than two percent of all our land will be in private production and with State-set targets and quotas, we will achieve higher levels of productivity than ever before! Vegetables, meat, milk, potatoes, grain, and eggs."

Yulena sipped her wine and smiled innocently across the table at him.

"So why are there so many shortages then? Why do we queue for hours for a loaf of bread?"

"We've been through a brutal war, Yulena. You can't expect an economy of this size, even one guided by the Great Father himself, to recover from years of war so quickly. Of course there are shortages. We need more people to work the land, especially men. Comrade Stalin says that far too many of the workers on the collectives are elderly, female, and illiterate. It's hard to teach them how to farm productively. But there are plans in place to encourage more men to move to the country and help produce food."

"Encourage?" she echoed. "How will he do that?"

The atmosphere was heavy with a sudden intruder who'd

slipped between the chairs, and his name was Fear. For all it took was one word, one question, one suggestion that you disagreed with any of the Great Father's policies. Nada moved a couple of spoons around in the now-empty serving dishes and looked sharply at her husband. Yulena saw him catch the glance and immediately raise his glass toward her.

"Enough of politics. We're on holiday and we should be celebrating. Yulena, my darling, will you play for us?"

She smiled at him affectionately. "Of course, Papa."

"Splendid! Let us all go through to the drawing room and take coffee in there. Thank you for a wonderful feast, my dear, it was spectacular."

Her mother accepted their congratulations and ushered them through to the large and comfortable drawing room. The doors were open onto the back courtyard and a welcome breeze floated in, heavy with the scent of flowers.

Yulena busied herself preparing the violin and tuning it at the upright piano in the corner. Out of the corner of her eye, she saw Ekaterina have a quiet word to her husband and her mother-in-law and slip away.

"Thank you for your patience. I'm ready now."

The audience took their seats.

"Tonight I will play two pieces. One very old and one quite new. The first is the canzonetta from the Violin Concerto in D by Pyotr llyich Tchaikovsky."

Her body moved constantly as she turned from her mother at the piano, to the audience, and then out toward the gardens. She played with power and passion, her technique confident if lacking in subtlety. The sound had an eerie quality, almost a gypsy refrain, and she put her heart and soul into it. When she finished, they all applauded loudly, especially her father.

"Thank you on behalf of my divine instrument. It is the interpreter of the composer's genius. I merely do its bidding. Now, for something a little more modern."

Without introducing it further, she launched into the refrain, melodic and light, yet with an undercurrent of something darker; a longing unfulfilled, passions unrequited. It echoed around the room and held everyone spellbound until the last hypnotic note. Vladimir let out his breath after what seemed like an age.

"My God! What was that?"

She lowered the violin and smiled.

"*That* was 'Liebesleid,' Papa."

Koyla's voice was tinged with suspicion, as she'd expected it to be.

"Who wrote it?"

"Fritz Kreisler."

He was on his feet before she'd finished the name.

"He's German. Yulena, how could you? I thought we agreed never to play anything Ger—"

"Actually, he's Austrian, born in Vienna; and he's now an American citizen. He hasn't lived in Europe for years, and he certainly had nothing to do with the Third Reich. This piece was written in 1938 and means 'Sorrow of Love.' It has a companion piece called 'Sorrow of Joy.' He's one of the most brilliant violinists of our age, Koyla, and he has a 1733 Guarneri del Gesú."

Her brother was glaring at her, his anger looking for an outlet.

"All the same, I've heard you playing Bach and Mozart—"

"Another Austrian. And a complete genius. For goodness' sake, Koyla, not even *you* can extend blame for the actions of Hitler onto the great composers of generations past. I flew against them, remember? They tried to *kill* me and I don't include people who lived two or three hundred years ago. It's plainly ridiculous."

"Are you saying the policy of Comrade Stalin is wrong?" Koyla asked. His voice was quiet and his tone measured, but she knew he wanted her to say yes. Maybe he wanted to report her? Again there was an icy-cold moment of silence broken by Nada as she rose from the piano.

"It's time for a sing-along, don't you think? I thought we'd start with Rachmaninoff. Yulena, play the 'Maiden Fair' and, Koyla, sing for us. Please, darlings!"

The two siblings had been eyeballing each other across the room, but now Yulena turned away and smiled at her mother.

"Certainly, Mama. I need an E if you would be so kind."

Koyla sang the words from the Pushkin poem "Oh, Cease Thy Singing, Maiden Fair" in his clear, rich tenor voice. He scowled at her as he watched for his cues, and Yulena wanted to burst out laughing at him. They were almost finished when the double doors to the hall swung open to reveal Ekaterina standing in the doorway, one hand gripping her lower stomach. Her face was very white, covered in a shimmer of sweat, and her eyes were full of pain.

"Forgive the intrusion"—her voice sounded rough, as if it was difficult for her to breathe—"but my baby has decided to . . . oh, God! Help me, Koyla!"

Fifteen hours later the local doctor and an ancient babushka delivered Ekaterina of a healthy baby boy. He was over nine pounds and the effort almost tore her tiny body in two, but she was conscious enough to hold him. Wrapped in swaddling and yawning with obvious exhaustion, he peered up at her through tiny slit eyes. Koyla strode over to the bed and kissed her forehead gently.

"What an effort, what a wonderful woman you are. Hello, my boy!"

He reached out and stroked the chubby face with one finger.

"What do you want to call him?" Ekaterina murmured. The pink-and-white bundle was beginning to swim before her eyes.

"He will be a great servant of the Party. I know this. He will achieve great things for the Motherland. I think we shall call him Sergei. It means 'servant.' Sergei Koylaovich Valentino."

She smiled happily, then her grip on the baby loosened as the room swirled into a dancing whirlpool of light and she felt a huge rush of warmth between her legs. Four hours later Ekaterina Valentina died from a massive postpartum hemorrhage, and the household was plunged from joy into profound grief.

Chapter 33

Moscow
February 1948

Yulena had truly believed that things would change after the Great Patriotic War. During the 1930s, as she grew from an uncertain young girl into a confident and articulate woman, she'd watched the purges of the intellectuals and the scientists and the military and always held her tongue. The horror grew throughout the decade, but then suddenly they were all united against a common enemy and the military restored her respect for men in power.

It was a freezing day in early February and, as she sat toward the back of the Great Hall at the Moscow Conservatory, her heart was breaking. This was the scene of some of her musical triumphs and she adored the place. With its intricate plaster decorations and portraits of famous composers in oval frames surrounded by laurel leaves, the high ceiling, and the lovely half-circle-shaped boxes, it seemed to enfold her in a sense of history and pride. What would the great musicians think of the debacle currently taking place on the stage? she wondered.

Through tear-filled eyes she gazed at her professor Dmitri Dmitriyevich Shostakovich, in his dark suit, striped shirt, and striped tie. He wore round black-rimmed glasses, his black hair cut short, and a serious expression on his long, thin face. One by one the others were taking turns to criticize him and his music. He was accused of being a "formalist," writing music that was too elitist and inaccessible to "the common people." Finally she could take it no more and she dragged herself to her feet and walked out.

When she got to the apartment, Mama was playing with Sergei in the lounge. As always the boy gurgled with delight at the sight of her and held up his chubby arms. He was eight months old and his father had seen him twice. Both Nada and Vladimir understood that Koyla was consumed with grief and didn't want to see the child. Fortunately for Koyla, his mama was delighted to take over the care of her grandson and told him she would continue for as long as was necessary. She believed that in time her handsome and talented son would find another wife and that he'd do his duty and choose someone prepared to raise a child that wasn't hers. Until that time Nada and Yulena made sure that Sergei didn't go short of attention and love, and Vladimir tolerated the noise and found him a captive audience for all his best stories of the Great Patriotic War.

Yulena swept Sergei up into her arms and hugged him.

"Hello, my little prince. When is Papa due home, Mama?"

"Soon. How did it go today?"

Yulena hesitated, but it was her mama and she understood musicians.

"Horrible. Secretary Andrei Zhdanov has issued a decree. Not just Dmitri; he also names Comrade Prokofiev and Comrade Khachaturian. You should have seen them, Mama, all standing on that stage and criticizing him. They have no talent. He has more talent in his littlest finger than they will ever have. His works are banned and his family will have their privileges withdrawn, and the concerto he's working on, Violin Concerto no. 1 in A Minor, no one will be able to play it. Honestly, I could—"

"Enough, sweetheart. I do understand your frustration and anger, but you must always remember your papa's position." Nada's face was sympathetic, but her eyes were grave, cautious. Yulena swallowed hard and rocked the baby in her arms.

"So what shall we talk about? How has Sergei been today?" she asked brightly.

"A little angel, as always. I took him to the Hermitage Gardens for a walk, but it was so cold we came home. But he does love the snow."

Yulena put him down on the carpet and gave him a well-chewed wooden rattle.

"I must practice. Can you tell Papa that I need to talk to him when he gets home?"

"Of course, my darling girl. Don't worry about the professor; they'll not stay mad with him. He'll repent and then everything will be forgiven, you'll see."

Yulena paused at the door, her violin case in her hand.

"I very much fear you're right, Mama."

An hour later Vladimir knocked on the door to his daughter's room. He'd stood outside for ten minutes and listened to the fascinating interaction between violin and human brain. For long passages it sounded close to perfect and then the flow was broken by a jarring note; she'd curse and start again. She played some Vivaldi and then some Brahms, and he couldn't help but wonder what his son would think of her choices. How could two children, from the same genes and with the same upbringing, be so unbelievably different?

"Come."

Her voice was clear and strong and confident. He opened the door and went in. She stood in the middle of the small room, barefoot, a music stand in front of her and sheet music lying on her single bed.

"Hello, precious. I do love to hear you play; it lifts my old heart!"

He kissed her on each cheek.

"How was your day, Papa?"

"Ahh, as always, full of paperwork. The people of the occupied zones have no idea how much paperwork they create. Give me an old-fashioned battle any day. And how was yours? Your mama tells me it was not a good day for the professor?"

He could see her choosing her words before she spoke, assessing how much and what to say. He knew she understood that he walked a fine line in an administration fueled by paranoia and secrecy. The people he worked for would expect him to betray his own daughter to them if she had unpatriotic opinions and not think twice about it, but it was an unspoken pact between them: he could never betray her and she would never really give him cause.

"They've denounced him for a second time and banned his works. When he finishes this amazing violin concerto, no one will be able to play it. But, as Mama said, he will repent and then all will be well again."

Her father shrugged heavily. "I know you don't agree with Comrade Secretary Zhdanov, but he has his reasons. What did you want to talk to me about?"

"Sit down, Papa."

She pushed the sheet music aside, and he lowered his massive frame onto the bed. She put the violin and bow away in the case and took her time; he watched her expectantly and patiently.

"I want to leave the conservatory. I know I've almost finished there, but I want to have private lessons instead. Mikhail knows everyone and he can find me a teacher who won't lecture me all the time about politics."

She was avoiding his gaze.

"Can he find you someone as good as the teachers you now have?" he asked thoughtfully.

She looked surprised; perhaps she'd expected anger?

"Oh yes. There are many wonderful teachers who have to work privately."

"You mean they're banned?"

"Some. Would that matter?"

At last her eyes met his. She was trying not to look too fierce, but he could see the hope and it hurt him. He sighed.

"Yulena, you know that the Great Father himself takes a special interest in me, and my family. He has guided Koyla's career and suggested him to Comrade Beria. Without the Great Father's interest, Koyla would still be writing Party tracts for farm workers; now he's doing important work. And he asks me often how you are and when you'll be ready to play for him. You simply can't leave the conservatory and learn from a teacher who's banned. They have subversive ideas—"

"How can you know that? You've never even met them."

"Neither have you. They're just recommendations from Mikhail, and he was a friend of Sasha's."

When he needed to make a strong point, one she could not refute, he brought up the name of Sasha. Her best friend for many years, Sasha had become increasingly strident in his criticism of the Party and Comrade Stalin. He'd started writing for an underground newspaper, and then one day he'd simply disappeared. His mother had had one letter, from a labor camp in Siberia.

"So am I," she said quietly.

He put his arm around her shoulder.

"Darling, I know that you're upset by what happened today, but it's a minor thing. It'll be over in months. Comrade Shostakovich knows what he must do to reinstate himself, and he will do it. Please, think no more about leaving the conservatory. It's your destiny." He pointed to the violin case. "*That* is your destiny, to play with the Moscow Philharmonic."

Chapter 34

Moscow
March 1953

Over the next few years, both Vladimir and Koyla traveled in the course of their duties to the Motherland. Vladimir was a military adviser and spread his considerable wisdom among the Communist bloc, East Germany, Poland, Romania, Bulgaria, Hungary, and Czechoslovakia. And then when Comrade Stalin agreed to help his ally Kim Il Sung in North Korea, he sent some of his most trusted military personnel, including Vladimir.

Koyla had traveled with the Great Father to China and was instrumental in generating the propaganda needed to explain the Party's help for North Korea. He grew more and more incensed by the West every day and took every opportunity to tell his friends and family about the corrupt capitalist foe that the Great Father fought so patriotically on behalf of the Motherland.

The trips and the importance of his work also gave Koyla a reason to keep his distance from his son. His mother was doing a wonderful job, and when he saw Sergei, the boy was respectful, quiet, and well cared for and listened to his father's opinions with solemn eyes. But those slightly slanted eyes reminded him of his beloved Kati, even if they were a light green like his and not deep brown like hers, and he couldn't spend long in the child's presence without feeling an emotion that he otherwise kept buried.

By early 1953, Koyla was deeply involved in some of the darker campaigns of the Party, things he wouldn't share even with his parents.

On a late winter day in early March, Yulena was playing the piano for a delighted audience of one five-and-a-half-year-old boy. He was large for his age and strong, his eyes were quick, and already his language skills were well developed and he adored music.

"What would you like next?" she asked.

"The lullaby," he cried happily, clutching his knees to his chest and rocking.

"Ah, my brave Cossack solider . . ."

She turned back to the piano and began to play the sweet, mournful tune. She didn't need to look at him to know that her voice and the music would hold him enthralled.

> *"Sleep, good boy, my beautiful,*
> *bayushki bayu,*
> *quietly the moon is looking*
> *into your cradle.*
> *I will tell you fairy tales*
> *and sing you little songs—"*

The door to the lounge flew open, and Koyla strode into the room. The delighted child launched himself upward and threw himself at the man's legs.

"Papa!"

"What are you singing?"

His face was white, his hair rumpled, and his clothes disheveled. He bent and scooped Sergei into his arms. She stood up, alarmed by his appearance.

"Nothing. Just a folk song. Koyla, what's wrong? What's happened?"

"Where's Papa?"

He handed Sergei to her without glancing at the boy. The child's little face crumpled with disappointment, and she felt a sharp stab of anger; why couldn't he even pretend to care?

"At the Kremlin, where would you expect him to be? Say hello to Sergei at least!"

Koyla ignored her request.

"He hasn't rung?"

"No. What's wrong? For goodness' sake, tell me what's happened. You're frightening him."

Koyla slumped onto the sofa and buried his face in his hands. Yulena stroked Sergei's hair. The child was on the point of bursting into tears.

"Shoosh, bubba, everything's all right," she said soothingly.

Koyla looked up. "He's had a stroke," he said in a dull monotone. "He's dying. They think he'll maybe last another day."

A strange mix of emotion began to stir in Yulena's stomach, but the strongest feeling was the beginning of joy.

"Who?"

His voice, when he answered, was raw with grief and disbelief and hardly sounded like Koyla at all.

"The Great Father. Comrade Stalin is dying. Yulena, he's going to leave us."

Two emotions hit Yulena at once. She knew she mustn't show her brother that this news was music to her ears, because he'd never forgive her. And secondary to that, she knew that Koyla was suffering the second great loss of his life and Stalin's death would leave him inconsolable. Instinctively, she sat down beside him, Sergei still in her arms.

"Tell me what you know, then we'll try and ring Papa."

He drew back from her, his body rigid.

"They found him last night, the guards. They hadn't seen him all day, but they didn't check on him until evening. He's unconscious . . ."

"Who do you think will succeed him?"

He looked at her sharply. "Why?"

"Well, Papa talks about them, Comrade Khrushchev and Comrade Beria—"

"What does he say about Comrade Beria?" he interrupted.

She shrugged. "Marshal of the Soviet Union and he has never held a military post."

Instead of contradicting her as she'd expected him to do, he seemed not to hear. Something was different about him and it was more than grief. . . .

"Koyla," she asked quietly, "what are you afraid of?"

He got to his feet and began to stride around the room.

"Yulena, I have to go away for a while and I need to know that you'll keep Sergei safe."

"Of course. Go away? Where? Safe from what?"

"Away from Moscow, just for a while."

"Why?" She knew the concern in her voice was growing. He hesitated and then turned to face her.

"This is between us. Whatever Mama and Papa ask you, you tell them nothing. Agreed?"

She nodded.

"I've been working on a very important campaign, something that the Great Father expressly authorized. Something that would benefit the Motherland and all true Russians. But now, with the Great Father about to leave us and someone else—well, there may not be such a level of understanding of what we've been doing."

Something akin to dread was replacing her secret joy. "What have you been doing, Koyla?"

"An anti-Semitic propaganda campaign."

She couldn't hide her shock. "But we have Jewish friends."

"I know, but this wasn't aimed at them. This was to condemn the Jewish doctors who've been trying to poison our great leaders. Thirty-seven Jews have been arrested."

"And you think Comrade Stalin's successor could disapprove?"

"If it's Beria, he will. I've heard murmurings that the Great Father had approved the plans of Comrade Ignatiev to deport all the Jews to the farthest camps, as far from Moscow as possible. But I have no proof. They might want me to incriminate . . . I don't know what methods they'll use. I just think it would be best if I went away for a while."

He bent down and kissed Sergei on the top of the head. She tried to grab his arm, but he pulled away and walked to the door.

"Make sure he doesn't forget me," he said simply and then he was gone. Yulena sat very still, her brain racing and tears starting to fill her eyes. She hugged Sergei to her and felt his little body shaking. They began to sob at the same time.

Chapter 35

Sochi, Russia
Summer 1962

Sergei sat on the warm sand and watched the water lapping at his feet. It was yet another scorching-hot day and he was counting to a thousand before he ran into the cooling water. He loved numbers and he loved setting himself tasks: how slowly could he eat his meal and not be scolded by his grandmama, how many times would his grandpapa walk around the lawn before he settled in the summerhouse, and how long could he hold his breath under the water, even how many days it would be before he got another of those stiff, formal letters from his father in Berlin.

He knew that his father was an important part of Walter Ulbricht's government and that they'd built a massive wall around the West German part of the city. When his grandmama had told him that his father was getting married to a German woman and asked if he'd like to live with them, his response had been instantaneous. He didn't know his papa at all, couldn't speak German, and couldn't imagine life without his grandparents. Although he hadn't been involved in the final discussions, he knew his opinion mattered to them, and they decided he was too old to adapt to his father's life. Nevertheless, his grandpapa told him he should be proud of his papa's work. He was a bright child, however, and he could tell that his beloved aunt Yulena wasn't so sure.

Aunt Yulena. How many hours would it be before she arrived? He tried not to be impatient and yet he wanted to see her so badly. She brought laughter and music into the house, and she took him on walks and talked to him as if he were already grown up. Damn! Now he'd lost count somewhere in the seven hundreds and he'd have to start all over again . . . or maybe not. He leaped to his feet and ran into the water, his tall body plowing through the delicious coldness.

"Where's Sergei?"

Vladimir laughed heartily. "Nice to see you too, precious. He's outside in the garden, with your mama. She had to do something to keep him distracted. He's been counting the seconds until your arrival."

She left her suitcases in the lounge and walked through the open French doors onto the lawn. Nada was showing Sergei something in the flower bed, their heads very close together. He was thickset and long limbed, with black hair and his father's high forehead. Her heart leaped at the sight of him.

"Hello there."

They both looked up at the sound of her voice. Sergei ran across the grass and threw his arms around her.

"Aunt Yulena!"

She kissed him on each cheek.

"Hello, handsome. How tall you are. I swear you've shot up in four months."

She could see by the blush that he liked the compliment.

"How was it? I want to know everything."

She laughed and broke away from him to kiss Nada. "Hello, Mama."

"Hello, my darling. Come into the house. I'll make some iced tea."

Sergei took her arm and walked with her. "Which city did you like the best?"

His voice was lower than she remembered, and there was a trace of dark down on his upper lip.

"Oh, Paris. It was amazing and they just loved us. We played an extra concert and they applauded for what seemed like hours—"

"How's the violin?" he asked suddenly.

Yulena smiled at him.

"She's just fine; she loved the trip, but she missed you. I will play for you later."

After dinner Yulena told them all about the tour of Russian and European cities that her quartet had undertaken. It wasn't easy to get permission to leave the country, although Comrade Khrushchev's policies were considerably more liberal than those of his predecessor. Vladimir had used his influence to secure the necessary visas, and she knew he took a measure of responsibility for the success of the venture. Yulena was a regular first violin with the Moscow Philharmonic, but she loved the quartet more than anything.

Sergei hung on her every word, his pale eyes shining and his expression one of rapt concentration. He bombarded her with questions about the sightseeing she'd done, the monuments she'd seen, and the food, the shops, and the hotels. At last Nada called a halt and reminded them all that it was late, Yulena was tired, and they could start again tomorrow. Reluctantly Sergei kissed her good night and went upstairs to bed.

"He's growing up, Papa," she said as she accepted the glass of brandy he gave her.

"Yes, he is. He's a good boy, bright and interested in his studies. He plans to go to the State University and study geology and material sciences."

"Still? I thought his passion for mathematics would've taken over . . . or music," she added with a wry smile.

"He has an eye for the future, and he knows that the Motherland has enormous natural resources. There'll always be work in extracting those treasures. He also knows that our comrade secretary has had meetings in the West and sees them as a rival, not as the evil we were led to believe they were. In time they'll need those resources and they'll pay. He knows that between us, Koyla and I, we can get him a good job in that line of work."

"And music will never give him the kind of life he could have working in an industrial company," she added as she watched the moonlight dancing on the water.

"It's given you a good life."

"True and I'm very grateful. And now I'm off to bed. We'll talk more tomorrow."

Sergei woke early in the morning and read for a while, did one of the math puzzles in the book his aunt had brought him all the way from England, and then got dressed and went down to the beach to watch the water. There was an onshore wind and the green water was whipped up to decent peaks with frothy whitecaps. He was fascinated by the patterns in the wave sizes and how what appeared to be random was actually very regular. Then he made some geometric shapes out of small rocks and tried to change them by moving as few parts as possible. Finally, hunger got the better of him and he wandered back to the house.

As he stepped onto the lawn he heard voices. He stopped and listened. It was his aunt and his grandpapa and they were talking in the summerhouse. Something in the tone of their voices told him it was not a normal conversation. Very quietly he followed the vegetation around to the back of the outbuilding, so he could listen and not be seen.

"You can't," Vladimir said with an unmistakable note of finality.

"Ever? Or not just yet? I told you, I wouldn't do anything until Sergei was an adult. He's fifteen, so that's another five years at least."

"Ever."

"But, Papa—"

"But Papa nothing!"

It was a roar of fury, and it made Sergei shrink back into his hiding place. He'd never heard his grandpapa so angry.

"All your life you've lived for yourself. If we hadn't stopped you, you would've expressed your views without thought to anyone else. God knows what that would have done to your brother's career and to mine. I know you disapprove, Yulena, but you can't leave, it is just . . . unthinkable."

"It's not because of my views, I've explained that. It's because of my career, my music. There are so many more opportunities in the West. Amazing orchestras and gifted conductors—"

"And Comrade Kondrashin is not gifted?"

"Of course he is. He's wonderful, but he's one conductor and one orchestra. In the West, I could play with many and maybe even make a recording. Other artists are doing it, Papa. They request to leave and the government lets them go."

There was a silence.

"And their families pay. I see what happens in the government. Yulena, I know how these men work. It's the disgrace, the shame. A child of mine not wanting to live in the Motherland. How could I explain that? When the country of your birth has given you so much, nurtured your talent and trained you—"

"And I *am* very grateful."

"Then show it. And what about us? We'd never see you again. Sergei would never see you again. How could you think about doing that to him? You're all he has. You've been like a mother to him."

Sergei couldn't hear what his grandpapa was saying; the voice had been replaced by a roaring noise in his head. It was too awful to think about, his beloved aunt Yulena, gone? He stood up and ran across the lawn toward the pathway to the beach, and something inside him just wanted to keep running forever.

When Sergei didn't come back to the house for breakfast, Yulena set out to find him. He was at the end of the beach, sitting on a rock watching the boats racing each other in the distance. His back was to her, and he didn't turn around as she approached.

"Sergei?"

"Why do you want to leave me?"

His voice sounded small and frightened. She sat down beside him.

"I don't," she said simply.

"You do. I heard you talking to Grandpapa. I know he won't let you, but why do you want to go anyway? Everyone leaves me."

"I want to be a better musician than I can be by living here. I want to play with the best orchestras and have instruction from the best conductors. It has nothing to do with wanting to leave here; it's more about wanting to be there. In an ideal world I'd be able to learn and have all those experiences and then come back. Bring my knowledge home and teach it to others. But the Party doesn't allow that, not for the likes of me. If I left, it would be forever. Go if you must but don't come back."

"That's unfair."

"Yes, it is. Life isn't fair, and sometimes I think it's less fair here than anywhere else in the world. Sergei, darling, look at me."

He turned to meet her gaze. He'd been crying.

"I'm going to make you a promise, and I swear to you I will never break it. Okay?"

He nodded. She picked up his hand and cradled it between her palms.

"I promise that I will never leave. I'll never do anything that means I can't see you anymore. Whatever happens, I will always be right here."

Slowly his face was split by a smile, and she could see relief in his eyes.

"That's very good," he said quietly.

"Nothing in the world means as much to me as you, not even my precious violin. Now, I bet you're hungry."

"Starving."

"Good, because there are sausages and *grenki* with your name on them!"

The music swirled around him as he closed his eyes and listened. The scherzo had sounded technically demanding and frenetic, as if the man were possessed. When the passacaglia started, Sergei stirred suddenly in his seat, because it was a motif he recognized. It was the Stalin theme from the Seventh Symphony and a little bit of—what was it? He knew it, almost there. It was Beethoven! It was the fate motif from the Fifth Symphony. Aunt Yulena would be so impressed that he recognized it. As the movement progressed, the violin seemed to cry above the deep resounding notes of the orchestra, as if its heart were breaking.

Sergei sat in the Great Hall with his grandparents, mesmerized, listening to David Oistrakh play Dmitri Shostakovich's Violin Concerto no. 1 in A Minor with the Moscow Philharmonic. Somewhere on that stage his aunt was playing her Guarneri violin; he couldn't see her but he was sure he could hear her. Oistrakh played the 1702 Conte di Fontana Stradivarius and Sergei definitely agreed with his aunt's opinion: her instrument was superior. But this piece of music was important and Sergei understood why.

Between 1948 and 1955 the piece was banned after Shostakovich's second denunciation, but now the world could hear it, in all its glory. Music was the rhythm of life, and no matter what the Party did or said, they could never suppress the soul and spirit of the people, expressed in music! His heart swelled with pride at the thought of all those people sitting behind them listening to this exquisite composition, and some of the most beautiful sound was coming from his aunt and her violin. One day she would be center stage and he'd be right there to cheer her on.

Chapter 36

Russian Embassy, London
Winter 1965

It was a freezing cold concrete room with just one small table and two chairs. Yulena shivered and drew her wrap tightly around her body. She wore a thin black evening dress, her performance dress. At her feet sat the violin case and she glanced at it regularly, as if to reassure herself that it was still there.

So they'd ordered her to return to Moscow. Why? And why had she been brought here instead of taken to the hotel to collect her things? The guard had said they'd take her to the airport. She hadn't argued, much.

Other guards were talking to the remaining three members of the quartet independently, and she assumed they'd meet up again at the airport. But this room truly frightened her; this room had a bad feel. It wasn't in the dungeon, it had no sense of the Lubyanka, and besides she was a war hero, with a Gold

Star, they wouldn't dare. The door swung open, and a man in a military uniform stepped into the room. His insignia told her he was a captain.

"Comrade Valentina." His voice was cold, his eyes blank, his face expressionless.

"Good evening, Captain."

He sat down.

"What do you know about ideological subversion?"

"What?"

Her astonishment was genuine. His expression, or lack of, didn't alter.

"How long have you been a practicing lesbian?"

There was a sudden stab of fear through Yulena's chest.

"I want to talk to my father on the phone," she said quietly, "Colonel General Vladimir Valentino."

The day that changed Sergei's life forever started like any other. He was in his first year of getting a *bakalavr*'s degree in geology at Moscow State University, and he loved the work. It was his aim to finish this degree inside the normal four years and then work for another two years to get a *magistr*'s degree, before taking a job in one of the huge State-owned mineral refining companies.

His grandparents supported his plans and were considering retiring to the dacha in Sochi, which would leave the large Moscow apartment his alone. His father had returned to Moscow to work for the new general secretary, Comrade Leonid Brezhnev, leaving his German wife behind. Koyla didn't want to live in such luxury and couldn't imagine living day to day with members of his own family, so he had been given a small apartment close to the Kremlin. Yulena was in Europe with the quartet, and Sergei knew his grandpapa kept in regular contact with her. Sergei loved to speak to her on the phone, and she told him all the new English words she'd learned, even if there was usually a terrible echo.

On this day he finished class and walked briskly across the frozen ground to catch the Metro home. He was already showing the build of his grandfather, but his body was heavily muscled from the ice-skating and football he loved. As he reached the apartment building he stopped. Something was different. There was a plain black car parked outside, innocent enough, but his lifetime of experience told him this was a Party car. He took the steps two at a time and paused again outside the main door; there was a muffled sound he couldn't identify coming from inside. Quickly he unlocked the door and opened it.

They were in the lounge. His grandpapa stood at the window, his back to the room, his broad shoulders slumped. His grandmama sat on the sofa, her face in her hands, sobs shaking her whole body. His father was beside her, his face pale, his hair streaked with gray, and his cheap, ill-fitting suit straining against the muscles in his arms. A man Sergei didn't know stood apart, in one corner, a hat in his hands, his eyes downcast. Sergei recognized instantly that it was a tableau of grief.

"What's happened?"

Everyone looked at him.

"Sergei."

His grandmama's voice almost caught in her throat, as if the thought of him had suddenly occurred to her. His grandpapa strode over to him and hugged him very tightly. Sergei could smell pipe tobacco and old sweat. What could've upset them all so much, something too awful to contemplate, too terrible to articulate into a question?

"Sit down, my boy."

He guided Sergei to the sofa, beside his grandmama, who reached out a hand and stroked his hair. His father spoke for the first time.

"We have something to tell you."

"Who's died?"

"What makes you ask that?" His father's voice was sharp.

"Whatever's happened, it's very bad and that usually means someone's died."

"Your aunt has had an accident in London. She was told to return to Moscow and two security guards were escorting her to the airport—"

"Is she dead?"

Sergei shouted at his father, rising to his feet at the same time. It was his grandpapa who intervened and turned the boy around to face him.

"Yes, she's dead. We don't know—"

Sergei wrestled away from him, ran straight to his room, and slammed the door, throwing himself on the bed and screaming into his pillow. An emotion he'd never felt before was forcing its way up his throat. He could taste the acid bile in his mouth. He felt sick, and he wished the ugly sound he could hear would stop. Someone was screaming. The door opened and his grandfather walked quickly to the bed. Sergei sat up and threw himself at the old man's chest. The large arms held him tight, and the screams turned to heartbreaking wrenching sobs from deep, deep within his soul.

They weren't told much more. She'd begun to party with the European jet set and had slipped away from her escort to meet regularly with a Soviet exile, Sasha Orlov, who was living in

London. When she was warned about her behavior, she ranted to her escort about lack of freedom and Party oppression. They feared she was going to defect so they ordered her back to Moscow, but on the way to the hotel to collect her belongings there was a car accident. They would send her body back for burial, and all her possessions would be returned to her family. Vladimir applied for permission to travel to London and bring her home himself, but that was declined. Comrade General Secretary Brezhnev himself told him to be patient and to wait for her to be returned to the Motherland, where she'd be buried with all the honor due a Soviet war hero.

Sergei was inconsolable. He refused to believe that his aunt had had any intention of defecting. She simply would not have left him, of that he was certain. He told everyone about the promise she'd made to him three years earlier at the dacha, and then he decided she'd been murdered by the KGB. Finally his grandpapa had to talk severely to him and tell him that such stupidity must stop. It was a tragic accident and that was that.

In the end, Vladimir declined a military funeral and they buried her in the Novodevichy Cemetery, within the leafy gardens of a tranquil convent situated inside a bend in the Moscow River. She was surrounded by some of Russia's most famous poets and writers, and Nada remembered that Yulena had once told her that her beloved professor Dmitri Shostakovich had expressed a desire to be buried there. Her headstone had a violin engraved on it and a quote from Beethoven, "To play without passion is inexcusable!"

Sergei visited her grave as often as he could and brought her flowers and poured out his heart to her. When her possessions were delivered to the apartment, he took the violin to her and plucked the strings, held it in his arms, and promised her he'd always keep it safe. Vladimir wanted to discuss what to do with the violin, but Nada persuaded him to leave it for now, to let the boy keep it as a comfort until his grief had abated.

There were a hundred things he wished he'd said to her and now it was too late for all but one. When no one was around to overhear, Sergei swore an oath to his aunt that he would discover the truth about her death, that one day someone would be held accountable.

Chapter 37

Moscow
Spring 1990

Something inside of him made him feel like running, or skipping, or cartwheeling, an unusual emotion for a large, forty-three-year-old man. He was wandering through the Hermitage Gardens, his favorite park. You could keep Gorky Park; this place had an air of culture and refinement about it. People sat and played chess in the early spring sunshine, stretched out on the banks of the pond and read books, or strolled arm in arm through the stunning gardens. It made Sergei feel alive just being here, being back in Moscow after so many years.

He'd graduated in 1971 with a *magistr*'s degree and joined the exodus to the Urals but more willingly than most. The Urengoy gas field was in need of prospecting, and instinct told Sergei it'd turn out to be worth the trouble. Discovered in 1966 just south of the Arctic Circle, it was to be the world's second-largest natural gas field with over ten trillion cubic meters in deposits.

After a short, successful career in natural gas, he'd moved on to something more glamorous, diamonds. It meant moving east, to Siberia, but the Mir diamond pipe was a strong pull. And so he found himself in the town of Mirny. Once again it was just below the Arctic Circle, where winter could last up to ten months of the year with the temperature -50°C or colder, and the brief summer would bring temperatures in excess of 40°C. Nowhere else on earth was the temperature range so extreme.

After the war, the Soviet Union had found itself totally dependent on the De Beers cartel for the supply of industrial diamonds; without diamond drilling stones you couldn't prospect for oil and gas, without diamond die stones you couldn't produce precision parts, and without diamond abrasives you couldn't grind machine parts or armaments. So prospecting had begun in earnest and eventually resulted in significant discoveries in one of harshest climates on the planet.

When Sergei first arrived, he was confronted with environmental problems that seemed insurmountable: steel tools frozen and brittle, oil frozen into solid blocks, and rubber tires that shattered when you tapped them. Then when summer came, the permafrost became a sea of mud. What began as a search for industrial diamonds had become a huge source of gem diamonds, two million carats a year, a production rate that rose dramatically over the years to come.

Sergei worked long, dirty hours in the mine and learned quickly what to look for; he rapidly progressed to identifying the stones and sorting them. Then he caught the eye of management and began to climb the ladder of promotion. Eventually he applied for a transfer to Moscow, and now he was working in the cutthroat business of polished diamond trading.

After a short walk through the gardens, it was time to return to his office on the Kalinin Prospekt. He had clients from Japan,

Belgium, and Italy to see and deals to do. As he sat down at his large desk the telephone rang.

"Hello?"

"Sergei? It's Papa."

Almost imperceptibly his heart sank. What could his father want at this time of day?

"Hello, Papa."

They never wasted time with small talk.

"I'm at Sochi, got here an hour ago. Your grandpapa's very ill; I think you should come."

"I'm on my way."

He flew into Adler-Sochi International Airport, his papa picked him up, and they drove to the dacha in silence. Vladimir was ninety-four and had been a widower for six years. He lived quietly at the dacha, and his son and grandson visited him when they could. His heart had grown progressively weaker during the last few months, and he'd suffered several little strokes over recent days. He could still speak but with difficulty, his breathing was labored, and the doctors had given him morphine. Sergei asked why he hadn't been transferred to a hospital but Koyla was adamant that he'd expressed a strong desire to stay at home.

"His time has come."

Sergei didn't argue with his father; he knew his grandpapa missed his beloved wife terribly and that life had become a burden. Nothing much had changed in the house in over forty years and Sergei loved returning to it. He'd been born here and his mother had died soon after. He'd spent many happy childhood days here with his grandparents and Aunt Yulena. Now he sat in the sparsely furnished lounge, drinking tea and waiting for his father to come down from his grandpapa's room and invite him to go up.

If he closed his eyes, he could trawl back through the clouds of memory and find the sound that he held dearer than anything in the world. The sound of a violin. He could see her standing beside the piano, her slender body swaying in time to the music, her hair cascading around her shoulders, her face a picture of concentration and joy. As always, the music was indescribably sad when he remembered her.

"You can go up. It won't be long."

His father's measured tone crashed through the reverie and shattered it. He opened his eyes.

"Thank you," he said stiffly.

Sunlight filtered in through the gap between the curtains and the room smelled of medicine and urine. His grandpapa was resting on large pillows, raised at an angle off the big bed. His face was drawn, and his eyes had sunk into the sockets. His hands, bony and covered with liver spots, lay limply on the covers. Sergei crossed the room and sat on the chair beside the bed.

"Grandpapa," he said softly.

The old man stirred and moved his head slightly toward the noise.

"Sergei?"

His voice was hoarse, and his lips were cracked and dry. Sergei dipped the cloth into the bowl on the bedside table and gently wiped his face. Then he took a teaspoon of water from the glass and dribbled it into his grandpapa's mouth.

"I'm here, Grandpapa."

"Thank you."

For a few moments neither man spoke, and then his grandfather stirred again.

"I'm . . . very proud . . . of you. Always be your own man."

"I will, Grandpapa."

"Not like . . . your papa; he belongs . . . to the Party."

This surprised Sergei and he smiled.

"No chance of me being a Party man, I'm afraid."

Suddenly the thin hand moved across the bed and grasped his with a rush of strength. At the same time he turned his head toward his grandson and his eyes opened; they were clear and bright.

"I have to . . . tell you something, son. About . . . the violin."

"I have it, Grandpapa, at home, in Moscow. It's locked in my safe—"

"There are things . . . things . . . you don't know."

The pressure on his hand was strong, pulling him closer. Sergei felt a wave of curiosity. He turned and glanced at the door. It was shut, and they were alone.

"I'm listening," he said quietly.

Vladimir was accorded a full military funeral. Sergei and Koyla stood side by side in their very different suits and masked their grief behind impassive expressions. They were complete opposites, with different loyalties and opinions.

Koyla was retired now and lived in his small apartment in Moscow. The reforms of Mikhail Gorbachev had devastated him, and he'd watched the last four years with growing horror. First the Chernobyl disaster occurred in 1986; then the next year a German, Mathias Rust, had flown a plane into Red Square and Gorbachev had used it as an excuse to revamp the military; then glasnost brought freedom of speech and the release of thousands of political prisoners; and finally laws were instituted that allowed limited private ownership of businesses in the services, foreign trade, and manufacturing sectors.

To Koyla it felt like everything he believed in, everything he'd worked for, everything he would gladly have died for was being undermined and unraveled. Sergei knew this, but his opinions were so far removed from his father's he avoided discussions on the subject. He believed in the new Soviet era and the vision that Comrade Gorbachev had. Despite the food shortages and the increased lawlessness and no matter what the future held, he believed that the dragon Gorbachev had awoken would not be held back and Sergei intended to ride it for all it was worth.

Had Sergei known what direction that dragon would take he would've been astonished. His ambitious goals had been to reach the top of the State-owned diamond trading company that employed him, to own a large house in one of the best Moscow suburbs, wear designer suits, drive an Italian sports car, and to one day travel to Europe, to complete unfinished business. Instead he witnessed the attempted coup to replace Gorbachev, the reunification of Germany, the sudden collapse of the Soviet Union, and the rise to power of Boris Nikolayevich Yeltsin.

Sergei summed up the new leader very quickly; Yeltsin was from the Urals and had a background in construction. Sergei knew these men and he knew how to manipulate them. He gained a position of influence with Yeltsin's inner circle and became a regular supplier of top-quality gems and a financier for the thriving black market in luxury goods. When the reform policies began to bite and skyrocketing prices were combined with heavy new taxes, Sergei started a sideline in the provision of credit and the manipulation of loans.

Then in 1995 Yeltsin passed a presidentail decree allowing businesses to be privatized by a series of auctions. Sergei's considerable wealth was kept very well hidden, but political influence and power helped him to buy a large multitiered State company in the mineral extraction industry. It took two years of secret bidding to acquire complete control, but when he got Yeltsin's final approval, he pounced. The company had noncore assets in the construction, agriculture, and medical fields, and he spun those off and sold them. He was left with oil exploration rights, a thriving natural gas pipeline and field, very productive diamond mines, and a laboratory that created synthetic industrial diamonds.

It was beyond his wildest dreams, and Koyla was incensed. After some furious rows, he cut off all communication with his son and died six months later, bitter and alone. When Sergei heard of his death, he paused for a moment and then kept reading the report in front of him.

But the master stroke was yet to come. He was supplying Gazprom, the largest Russian company of all and the biggest extractor of natural gas in the world. Gazprom supplied nineteen different countries with natural gas and ran the world's longest pipeline network, more than 150,000 kilometers of pipe. In one deal, Sergei sold his natural gas assets back to Gazprom and catapulted from being very rich into the rarefied air of a billionaire.

He lost no time in moving his base to London and buying a magnificent Mayfair property and a country estate in Sussex. Six months later, he added the Monte Carlo mansion and an apartment in New York. The world outside of Russia was a revelation to him; his opportunities had expanded at a terrifying rate, and he greedily embraced all the experiences on offer. Life became a heady round of gambling, champagne, fast cars, women, cocaine, and luxury adventures. But there was a reason why he'd chosen London as his base, and at last he was ready to fulfill a certain promise.

The first step was a visit to a small semidetached house deep in the East End of London. He dressed casually and took a taxi, unsure what he'd find after all these years.

Sasha Orlov was nearly eighty, but his blue eyes twinkled with fun and his handsome face had aged well. With his wife, Olga, he greeted Sergei warmly and invited him into the comfortable front room for coffee and a banquet of Russian food. Sergei sampled the honey cookies, blintzes, strudel, and *rogaliky* pastries filled with nuts and fruit and complimented Olga on her wonderful cooking.

It was the framed picture on the sideboard that afforded him the opportunity to raise the reason for the visit. His aunt, young and carefree, her hair blowing in the breeze and her strong face smiling happily at the photographer, drew him like a magnet. As he gazed at it he was aware of Sasha watching him.

"I remember the day that was taken as if it was yesterday," the old man said quietly.

Sergei replaced it carefully and returned to his chair. "What can you tell me about her last trip? Was she planning to defect?"

Sasha shook his head emphatically.

"Absolutely not. We talked about it, constantly. I admit I tried to persuade her, for lots of reasons. But she was adamant and she never wavered. She had to return to Russia."

Sergei felt a sense of relief and something else he couldn't quite identify, closure perhaps?

"She loved us too much, I believe."

"Especially you; she talked constantly about you. She adored you."

Sergei smiled at him. "Thank you, Sasha. I can't tell you what that means to me."

"Is that what you came to ask me, son? If I believed she was going to defect?"

Sergei hesitated, weighed up the old man's likely reaction, and then made up his mind.

"How did you hear about her death?"

"The exile community was very strong. We had contacts,

even then, people who knew people, within the embassy. I heard the truth, almost immediately."

"The truth?" Sergei asked sharply.

"About her death."

His heart was pounding and he tried to control the emotion roaring inside his head.

"How did she die?"

"She was murdered, Comrade, by her own people. By the KGB."

Chapter 38

Cornwall
Summer 2002

Yuri Slatkin was just finishing his lunch dishes when his doorbell rang. It was a glorious summer's day and he'd decided to go for a walk. His farm was about half an hour's walk from the village of Boscastle on the north Cornish coast. Perched up on the cliffs, with a stunning view out to sea, he farmed the land, owned by the National Trust, in much the same way that generations of Englishmen had for a thousand years. It was a good life, quiet and simple and hidden from view. If he chose, he could drop into the Cobweb Inn for a pint of ale and a cheese-and-onion pasty with chips; otherwise he was happy with his own company and the radio.

For ten years he'd made this little corner of England his home, ever since that day when he'd boarded an Aeroflot jet at Sheremetyevo International Airport bound for Heathrow, and never once had he regretted the decision. It wasn't his first trip to the United Kingdom; in fact he'd spent the whole of the 1960s in London attached to the Russian Embassy. He was a captain in the army and his responsibility had been security, but unofficially he'd aided the KGB officers when they had less-than-pleasant tasks to do and had gained a reputation as something of a "fix it" man. Consequently he didn't sleep as well as he might've wished. When the nightmares plagued him, he liked to sit up and watch the moonlight reflected on the Atlantic Ocean. After years of State-reinforced atheism, he'd decided to read the Bible and been so fascinated by the concepts inside, he'd availed himself of repentance and forgiveness, just to be on the safe side.

He opened the door to an average-looking man in a suit, slightly on the short side, not heavy but not thin, anywhere from thirty-five to fifty, wearing sunglasses and carrying a briefcase.

"Yuri Slatkin?" he asked in Russian.

Yuri paused.

"Captain Yuri Slatkin?" the man repeated.

"Yes. What do you want?" It felt strange to be speaking Russian after all these years.

"To talk to you. It won't take long."

"I'm on my way to the village. Could you come back later?"

"Five minutes and I'll be out of your way."

Reluctantly Yuri stood aside and let the man in.

"Thank you."

The man sat down at his kitchen table and glanced at the kettle.

"Would you like a cup of tea, sir?" Yuri was careful not to let the irritation show in his voice. He could be a Party man, wouldn't be a good idea to upset him.

"Thank you."

"Have you come from Russia?"

"I travel, wherever my services are required."

Something in his voice made Yuri look at him; the man was taking off his sunglasses and putting them in his jacket pocket. His movements were very precise, clinical, and they made Yuri nervous.

"What would you like to talk to me about?"

"I have some questions to ask you, for a book."

Yuri put the teacups on the table and sat down opposite him.

"A book? On what?"

"Thank you. The Russian Embassy."

Yuri relaxed and took a sip of tea.

"I worked there, you know, when it was the Soviet Embassy, keeping the staff safe."

The man put his briefcase on the table and opened it. The lid was toward Yuri so he couldn't see what the man was doing.

"Safe from what, Captain Slatkin?"

"I'm not a captain anymore, I'm a farmer now."

"My mistake. Safe from what? What were the threats to the Party in 1965?"

As he spoke the man rose to his feet and with lightning speed he moved around the table. Before Yuri knew what was happening, his arms were behind his back and he heard the loud click of handcuffs closing. Instinctively he tried to rise, but the man had already attached another pair around the wooden chair and locked them into the pair on his wrists, holding him in a sitting position. The metal bit into his flesh.

"What the he—" he cried out, but the man pushed him back on the chair.

"Sit still. I have some questions and I will get answers. I always do."

There was an expression in the cold eyes that Yuri recognized instantly. The man took a square of paper out of the briefcase.

"Do you know this woman?"

Yuri looked at the black-and-white picture. He said nothing but knew he was betrayed by his reaction. His mouth was dry.

"This is Yulena Valentina," the man said coldly as he laid the picture down on the table.

"In 1965 she died, in London, and you"—he swung the brief-case around so that Yuri could see the tools inside—"are going to tell me what happened to her."

If Yuri hadn't been seventy-seven years old and out of prac-tice with the techniques he'd learned in the army, he might have lasted longer. As it was he agreed to talk before the man got to his third fingernail. The man told him he was disappointed; he was hoping he'd pull at least one tooth. He watched as the man pulled a cell phone from a suit pocket and dialed a number.

"He'll talk now." The man put the phone on the table and hit the speaker button. There was no sound coming from it, but he could tell someone was listening, breathing heavily.

"The KGB brought her in. They said she was going to defect and they wanted to send her back to Moscow, but someone had other plans. I don't know who, I swear. One of the operatives said that she was a lesbian and they were going to jail her, or send her to a gulag. She was beautiful and he taunted her. She got angry and he slapped her. It got out of hand."

"What happened then?" The man in the room asked; the other stayed silent.

"She was raped."

"Did you?"

Yuri raised his head; this man was an idiot.

"Did I what?"

"Rape her."

His head sagged down again.

"We all did. It happened sometimes, not often, but sometimes; the men called it a perk of the job. When it was over, we killed her."

"How?"

"They had a dozen ways, untraceable poison, injecting an air bubble, pressure to the carotid artery, a nick to the jugular vein—"

"Who killed her?"

Yuri didn't answer. The man leaned forward and picked up the bloodied pliers with his free hand.

"You have two choices, Captain Slatkin. You can tell me or I will string you from that beam and pull your testicles out of your scrotum, cut off your dick, and leave you to bleed to death."

"Romans chapter twelve, verse nineteen," Yuri said softly. "Dearly beloved, avenge not yourselves, but rather give place unto wrath: for it is written, Vengeance is mine; I will repay, saith the Lord."

He looked up at the man and was met by a dry, humorless laugh.

"*You're* quoting scripture?" There was an obvious note of incredulity in the voice.

"You're going to kill me anyway, so I might as well tell you the truth. I did."

The man picked up the phone and held it to his ear.

"Yes, sir."

Yuri watched as he clicked the phone shut and put it in his pocket.

"And now it's time to pay for that, Captain."

Half an hour later the man stuffed Yuri's mutilated body into the trunk of the farm car, doused the vehicle with gasoline, and set it alight. It exploded and burned fiercely. He put his sunglasses back on, picked up his briefcase, and walked up the drive to his car.

Chapter 39

Moscow
Summer 2006

Sergei stood outside the bar and looked at the flashing neon sign. It wasn't one of his usual haunts, and his well-honed internal radar told him it was owned by the Russian mafia. He kept his distance from them, at least in public, but it was very late and he was thirsty and, besides, he felt like some company. He didn't come back to Moscow often, only when business compelled him, and with every trip he was amazed at the changes.

Oh well, a quick Campari and soda and then back to the apartment to catch the news on CNN, unless something else took his fancy.

Inside, the decor was surprisingly modern and luxurious, with thick carpet, comfortable leather booths around silver-colored metal tables, dominated by a massive granite bar top. Halfway through his second Campari and soda a familiar sound cut across the babble of voices and clinking of glasses. It came from the room next door and it was a violin. The music was Sibelius, the Violin Concerto in D Minor, and it was being played by someone who really knew how to play.

He got up and followed the sound, through a beaded curtain and across a room where four men sat playing poker at a table, to an open doorway, and into a lounge area. Three men sat on a banquette against the far wall, and an older man sat in a large leather chair. In the center of the room a young woman played a violin. Several things registered with Sergei simultaneously. She was tall and slender, with auburn-colored hair and golden eyes like a lion; she had some Slavic blood and she was absolutely stunning; she was playing a genuine antique violin; and she looked remarkably like Yulena would have looked at that age. He stood and stared while she finished the piece. The four men clapped, then the older man spoke.

"Very good, my sweet, go get a drink."

She put the violin and bow into a case and walked toward Sergei, then past him and out the door without looking at him. He could see bruises on her arms, and her eyes looked dead and lifeless.

"Can we help you?" one of the men asked.

"No, thank you. It was the music."

Sergei turned on his heel and followed her.

The first time he tried to talk to her she ignored him, and then she got angry and told him to leave her alone. He could see she was frightened, so he changed tack and approached the owner of the bar, offering a cash incentive to let her drink with him. To his surprise, she was intelligent and articulate and knowledgeable about music. It took three visits before she told him her name was Tatiana and she'd grown up in an orphanage in Archangel. When she was thirteen, she'd been thrown out to earn her living on the street so she'd boarded a train to Moscow. She was now seventeen, and Sergei could see she was far from a naive virgin. When he asked her where she'd learned to play like that, she went silent and the fear returned to her eyes so he changed the subject.

Within a week he'd persuaded her to come back to London with him. He promised her he'd replace the clothes she left behind and give her an even better violin to play and no one would ever hit her again. There were many things he didn't know about her, but the one thing that mattered was that when she played, she made his heart stop.

On their first day in London he took her shopping and bought her armloads of clothes, some fine pieces of jewelry, and many pairs of very high-heeled shoes.

Then he brought out the violin and showed it to her. She was quiet and somber and examined it thoroughly before she began to tune it at the piano. He watched her from across the room.

"No one has played this violin for forty-one years," he said suddenly. She stopped what she was doing and looked at him.

"Why not?"

"It belonged to my aunt and she . . . died. I've kept it ever since, and no one has been good enough."

She smiled at him shyly. "Thank you. What would you like me to play?"

"Can you play 'Liebesleid'?"

She nodded.

"That was my aunt's favorite piece."

"Then I would be honored to play it for you."

She tightened the screw on the bow and put the violin to her shoulder.

"How does it feel?"

There was a hint of anxiety in his voice he couldn't hide.

"Right."

He smiled at her and wondered if she had any idea of the mixture of emotions he was feeling.

"I know it sounds weak, but I love to hold it and feel the wood, so smooth and cool, so many secrets locked inside."

"It doesn't sound weak at all; you love fine instruments, and this is the most beautiful violin I've ever seen."

She started to play. She was assured and confident, the bow sweeping over the strings and her fingering precise and accurate. The music took hold of her lithe body, which was turning and dipping in time with the lilting melody. Sergei stood very still, his arms folded across his colossal chest, watching, his expression betraying nothing. He didn't move when she finished.

"I'll play a little Paganini and maybe some Mozart," she said and then began to play again. Her fingers flew through the Paganini Caprice no. 5 and then some of Mozart's Violin Concerto no. 5. Finally she lowered the violin and he stirred.

"Thank you."

"Did it please you?"

"Very much. Tatiana, would you like to have lessons? From a maestro?"

Her eyes widened. "On this violin?"

"I know she's difficult to master, but she rewards diligence. I would like to see you perform in public and there's someone I want you to meet; he's a friend of mine, Rafael Santamaria Gomez. He'll know the right career path for you."

In every house Sergei owned, the Guarneri had its own keypad-controlled glass case and beside it sat a framed photo of Yulena. He smiled at the photo as he put the violin back. Tatiana's resemblance tugged at his heart. Long ago he'd accepted that he didn't have the capacity for a monogamous intimate relationship and that wasn't what he had in mind—the thought of

Tatiana rejecting him was just too painful to contemplate. She would become his muse, his past, his present, his piece of perfection, if he could only keep her in a glass case with the violin.

"All good things come to those who wait," he murmured to Yulena.

By October 2008, Tatiana had fulfilled that initial promise and was performing at Sergei's private parties and concerts. He could deny her nothing, and she wore haute couture gowns and shopped at the most expensive stores in the world. He encouraged her to read about all the composers and discuss their work with him and with Maestro Carlo Montenagro, her teacher, and Natalia Petrova, a gifted Russian violinist who lived in London. Tatiana was a sponge, thirsty for knowledge, and she knew it delighted Sergei when she found joy in a new composer.

She was also aware that everyone else speculated on the nature of their relationship— she was nineteen and he was sixty-one—but she never commented on it to anyone. The truth was he hadn't laid a finger on her, and she knew now that he never would. He used women when he needed them, but she didn't see them and didn't ask about them. There were aspects of him that frightened her. Like Rafael, she'd seen his temper directed at others, and at times she felt like a possession, but she knew he'd never hurt her. She dreamed of living and working in the United States, playing with a major orchestra and being a soloist. But, no matter what, there was always the violin and that drew her toward him more magnetically than anything else. She didn't love him, but she was in awe of him, and when he was away, she missed him.

On a warm early fall evening, Tatiana stood in front of the full-length mirror in her suite at the Hay-Adams Hotel in Washington, D.C., and surveyed the results of an afternoon of pampering. Her gown was Gucci and her sandals Manolo Blahnik. Her hair was in a simple French roll, and her makeup was subtle. Sergei came into the room from the balcony.

"I've been watching the White House, across the road. He's doing what we're doing, getting ready for the opera."

She gave a small laugh.

"And he will go by limousine too?"

"With a few extra cars. You look wonderful, my dear."

"Thank you."

He picked up the diamond necklace and examined it.

"South African blue whites," he said as he put it around her neck and fastened the clasp. She was putting large diamond earrings into her ears.

"Very sparkly"—she smiled at him in the mirror—"no matter where they're from."

He held out his hand to her.

"Come, it's time to see what these artists do with my money."

Restoration

Part Four: The Violin

2008

Chapter 40

Washington, D.C.
October 2008

The sound began softly and almost eerily, with melancholy notes, hinting at the heartache to come, echoing around the packed auditorium and building to an aching intensity. Over two thousand people settled expectantly into the plush red seats and focused their attention on the spectacle that awaited them.

At the podium Rafael's body was in total harmony with the music, arms moving rhythmically to coax the very best out of the orchestra. Suddenly the bright swell of the strings took over and carried the preludio to its gentle conclusion. The curtain rose slowly on a party scene in nineteenth-century Paris, the women in exquisite evening gowns, the men in tails, all moving to the swaying music and toasting their frivolous lives. A large chandelier hung over the lush salon, candles glowed in the ornate candelabra, and the light sparkled off the heavy gilt mirrors and the raised glasses. Loredana di Carlo took center stage in a soft off-the-shoulder gown encrusted with crystals, her dark hair in ringlets and a champagne flute in her right hand. She looked stunningly fragile, but her powerful lyric voice soared out into the theater.

Aria by aria, duet by duet, act by act, the story of Violetta Valéry, a courtesan dying of consumption, and her ill-fated romance with a handsome young nobleman, Alfredo Germont, took the audience on an emotional journey.

Rafael was complete concentration; sweat poured off him, rolling down his face and into the collar of his evening shirt. This was what he lived for, the opportunity to take truly sublime music and bring it to life. His right hand held the baton and kept the beat while his left clenched and pointed and encouraged and indicated where he needed more power or a note of heart-wrenching softness. He knew the orchestra trusted him completely, and the music was as old a friend to them as it was to him. Onstage the world-class tenor, soprano, and baritone followed him, and he followed them in the perfect symmetry of well-rehearsed art.

Reunited again, the lovers played out the last moments of Violetta's tragic life in the bedroom of her Paris home, and after the dramatic music of her death, the opera came to an end with a rousing last few bars from the orchestra. Rafael's arms dropped to his sides and his head slumped forward onto his chest, eyes closed, passion spent. For a few brief seconds there was complete silence before thunderous applause broke out.

The opening night postopera gala was always a glamorous affair and an important one in the financial life of any opera company. Donors needed to be thanked and sponsors recognized. Tonight Rafael had another purpose in the back of his mind, and he moved from one group of well-wishers to the next more rapidly than usual, accepting congratulations and kisses and agreeing with the comments. He was almost halfway across the crowded room when the circle he'd just joined parted suddenly. A familiar booming voice cut through the excited noise around him.

"Raffy."

The Russian embraced him in a strong bear hug, and the arms felt like bands of iron as he was held against the massive chest.

"Sergei. I've been looking for you."

"It was magnificent, my friend. Stupendous. Wonderful cast."

"Thank you, it did go well. Have you seen Loredana?"

"Yes. You were right, as always; she was perfect for the role. I tell her this."

Rafael gave a chuckle and accepted a salmon canapé from the tray offered by a waiter.

"Thank you. And I'm sure she'd agreed with you. Sergei, come this way, come with me, I want to talk to you."

Rafael led him out onto the terrace. Slowed momentarily by people wanting to offer congratulations, they eventually found a corner away from the crowd. The night was still unseasonably warm with a slight breeze off the river gently moving the air. The lights of Georgetown glittered toward the north.

"What is on your mind, Raffy?" the Russian asked congenially.

"I want to tell you a story and then, maybe, ask you a favor. You know, some months ago I judged the Samuel J. Hillier—it was the turn of the violins this year."

"I've heard of this. The winner was very young, I seem to remember."

"He's extraordinary, Sergei. He's fourteen, Jewish, from Illinois; his name is Daniel, Daniel Horowitz. I invited him to the symposium last month. He has an excellent technique but more than that, expression you would expect from a twenty-year-old, yes? He *really* understands what he plays, and his interpretative skills, they are extremely advanced."

"Another Joshua Bell?"

"At least, with a much pushier mother. I do, you know, truly believe this boy is a once-in-a-generation talent."

Rafael could feel Sergei watching him intently and when he turned to face him, the Russian took a sip of champagne and then raised an eyebrow at him with a quizzical expression.

"For you, who hears so many, to say such a thing? I must hear him."

Sergei was sometimes hard to read, and Rafael had no idea how he'd react to the request.

"He has a problem. And that's where you come in, my friend."

"Really?"

"He's given up. Doesn't want to play anymore, and no one can get him to pick up his violin. He's at the Hamilton Bruce in Philly. I've spoken to his teachers, because you know this happens sometimes when children hit this age. A child, he has to . . . to make the decision to be dedicated and that means sacrificing things; in Daniel's case it's baseball. But he's also frightened by his own talent, by his potential future."

"It's a young age to have everyone make a fuss of you."

"And to have self-discipline. You know, I think he's learning he can say no, and there's nothing his parents can do about it. That gives him some power, a sense of control over his life."

"And you want to help him?"

"I do. He's a very good kid, and he reminds me of myself, you know? I too loved sports, football, I argued with my parents, the music won. But I didn't have a tenth of the talent he has in his little finger."

"So what can I do?"

Rafael paused, and then took a deep breath; it was too late to turn back.

"I know you love to foster young talent, and without you I couldn't stage the symposium. I want Daniel to feel the power of his gift. More than that, I want him to experience true genius, to . . . to hold it in his hands. If he plays a real masterpiece, once, just once, it might inspire him. You know, Sergei, I want to be able to say to him, 'work hard and one day you could own a violin like this.' It might make the difference, yes?"

Sergei was looking straight at him, and Rafael could see his pale eyes had begun to dance with excitement. He knew that look.

"You want him to play the Guarneri."

"Yes," the Spaniard answered simply.

Sergei was thinking, processing the options, weighing up what was in it for him. Rafael was very familiar with the process, and he knew the brilliant mind would miss nothing, including the possibility it was a setup. That was why he'd declared Daniel as Jewish at the very beginning, so Sergei couldn't accuse him of subterfuge. Finally the big man smiled.

"Perhaps Maestro Montenagro should give him a lesson or two? So he knows what to do with her? She is very hard to play. And then, if he's good enough, this little protégé of yours, he could give a concert, no? . . . In my music room, for invited audience, his family, Roberto, James Keller, that Swedish fellow who wants to buy my beauty so badly. I will draw up a list. It will be fun! But first, you understand, I must hear him play, Rafael. Can you bring him to me?"

Rafael nodded thoughtfully.

"I can do that, if you tell me where and when, yes?"

"After the next Sussex concert. He can hear Tatiana play her."

"Excellent. You won't be disappointed, I promise you. And there is one other matter. Egypt. Sergei, come on, *Parsifal*?"

The Russian threw back his large head and roared with laughter.

"Absolutely. Of all the opera companies invited and all the glorious productions from all round the world, who will they remember? The one who dared bring Wagner to the party."

"And we would offend the Muslims with a Christian theme, and the Jews, who hate Wagner, and maybe end up with pro-testers outside the house? An injunction against us? You know it's happened to companies before."

Sergei laid his hand on Rafael's arm. "Yes, but the *people* will flock to see, and the media will congratulate us on our cour-age," he insisted.

"Jeremy won't do it."

"So he takes my money, but not my advice? This is not your argument to have, my friend. Just put time aside to revise your *Parsifal* and leave bargaining to me."

Two hours later Rafael lay on his stomach, stretched out on the huge bed in his apartment as Magdalena massaged his back and shoulders. The adrenaline still coursed through him and the music whirled inside his brain, and every so often his fingertips tapped the covers.

"So what will you do once Daniel has played the violin?" she asked suddenly.

"Hhhhmm? I'm not absolutely sure, yet. I think I need to talk to his poppa again and maybe Roberto."

"Who'll want to rip it away from Sergei immediately and restore it to its rightful owners, then convince them to sell it to *him*."

"They won't sell, ever, I could see that in their eyes."

"Do they have any idea what it's worth? Do you?"

"If it's the lost 1742, my research says anywhere from four to eight million dollars, probably closer to eight, you know it's in fantastic condition. Many collectors would be desperate to own it."

She stopped massaging.

"Good God, Raffy! And you expect him to just hand it over?"

"No, I don't, not at all. You know, I think it could get very ugly. Their word against his word."

"And what about Jeremy? The opera company?" she asked as her fingers and thumbs resumed their regular pressure on his rhomboids. "What'll happen when *he* finds out what you're up to? The company needs Sergei, you need him."

He sighed.

"I know. I have been thinking about that side of it too. To be fair to Jeremy I need to tell him what is happening, don't you think?"

"Yes, I do, most definitely. And if he orders you to stop, for the good of the company, what will you do then?"

There was a long pause. He rolled over and looked up at her; her brow was drawn into a concerned frown, and her dark eyes were serious.

"I think Jeremy is a good man, and he also very much loves classical music. He has a conscience. I think he will understand when I tell him some of the incredible story they told to me. That violin is Daniel's heritage. You know, there is much more—how can I say it?—at risk than just getting something back. I think Daniel will play it, learn how to play it well, and want to play it for the world. There are other wealthy sponsors, but a talent like Daniel's, a *virtuoso* talent, that's generational, it comes along maybe once in a lifetime!"

She stroked his hair and smiled down at him.

"And I think you're a romantic and a very good man. A much better man than Jeremy Browne, who will see his sponsorship disappearing out the door to another opera company. Sergei supports them because of you, he doesn't live here, he believes in *you*. If you destroy that, he'll walk away and Jeremy won't care a jot for some kid and his talent."

Chapter 41

Mayfair, London
October 2008

Sleep was an elusive luxury for Sergei Valentino and he didn't always take chemicals. Sometimes he used the long night hours to work or think or listen to music. On this night he wandered around the underground vault in his palatial Mayfair mansion. Soon after his grandpapa's death, he'd returned to the dacha and found the hidden treasures where he'd been told they would be, in a hole under the floor of the summerhouse. He knew it was all war loot, things his grandpapa had brought back from Berlin and not handed over to the Motherland. Sergei's father would've been furious at the deception against the Party, and his aunt would've demanded their return, but to whom? The owners were long since dead, and who knows how many German hands they'd been through before they reached his? There were two beautiful paintings—one he knew was extremely valuable— some silverware and jewelry and three illuminated manuscripts. He'd added to the collection over the years and divided it between his homes, but the original treasures remained in London. In a moment of generosity, he'd given the wonderful string of natural pearls to Tatiana and they looked magnificent against her skin. But, as always, his favorite was the Guarneri. It had the strongest power to draw him, and he spent countless hours sitting beside the case, holding it in his arms.

"I think he's going to play it," he said, looking at the photo of his aunt. "You would like that. An American playing your violin, probably the first American to ever play it! Maybe the first child to play it, who knows. If it could talk, it could tell us so much." He sighed. "It could tell us so much."

Roberto di Longi vividly remembered the first time he held a violin. His mother had taken him to Harrods to look at instruments while his father, a tailor, was working at the shop on New Bond Street. He was nearly five, and the piano dwarfed him. Then the helpful shop assistant had shown him a cello, but that was cumbersome and uncomfortable. The flute felt cold and strange against his tiny face, and his mother said no to the drums before he even sat down. Then she put a small violin into his hands, and he fell in love.

Every week he had a lesson from Mrs. Moretti, who spoke Italian with his father and instructed him in broken English, using a large ruler to point to the notes on the page. He knew he'd never be a virtuoso, and playing in the school orchestra convinced him he didn't want to be a jobbing musician. But a world without his beloved instrument was impossible to contemplate.

Music was his favorite subject at school. In his university thesis, he described the violin as a three-dimensional combination of architecture and mathematical precision, unique in the extent of its ability to influence emotion through sound. What fascinated him most was the fact that in half a millennium, since the founding of Andrea Amati's workshop in 1560, the basic design of the violin had changed little, and many of his friends would argue it'd been improved upon nearly as much. It was timeless, a classic concept born of the maker's passion and artistry.

After graduation he moved to Italy and immersed himself in the culture and history of Cremona, marrying a local girl, the daughter of a well-known luthier. As the years passed his knowledge grew, and the more people who needed his expertise, the more he learned. In 1990, he opened a small shop in West Hampstead, selling and repairing violins in conjunction with a well-known luthier. He attended auctions and bid on behalf of buyers wishing to remain anonymous, and his reputation for gaining a bargain grew in tandem with his knowledge base. His life was enjoyable, he was passionate about his business, his marriage was strong, he had three talented children, and he could give them all they'd ever want. He was a contented man.

And then one day he heard Tatiana play what was called the "Valentino Guarneri." When he consulted the program notes, something in his built-in radar, his professional compass that processed the stack of accumulated knowledge and memory, told him the notes were wrong. It began as a casual curiosity and grew into a matter of principle, a question of his honor as an expert. He told himself that the fact he didn't like Valentino was irrelevant. What mattered was the opportunity to solve a musical mystery and to be seen to be right.

On a late October day he sat at his desk, pieces of a violin lying on a green cloth in front of him. Slowly and gently he picked up each piece and examined it, an eyeglass in his left eye and white gloves on his hands. The pieces were battered and scratched, the varnish dull and worn into patches. He put them together like a jigsaw puzzle. A middle-aged woman appeared in the open doorway.

"I know you said not to disturb you, sir, but there's a phone call."

He looked up.

"Ask them to call back."

"Normally I would, sir, but it's Maestro Gomez and he asked me to tell you it's about a small needle in a continent of hay. He said you'd understand."

Roberto put down the piece in his hand and smiled.

"Thank you, Dorothy, put him through."

Across the Atlantic Ocean, Daniel was in the living room of his grandparents' house. He looked at the photos from the shoe box and listened solemnly to his poppa and his *feter* Levi as they explained the full story of their violins, what their papa had done to the Guarneri and why, and then what had happened to it. It was like a puzzle; all the snatches he'd heard over the years fell into place beside all this new information and formed a picture.

Maestro Gomez had told them that he believed the violin Tatiana played was their violin. Now he understood about the man who was so sure the label was wrong, because it was. He wasn't a bad man, just intense, and right. Daniel nodded slowly as he remembered his own reaction to hearing the violin at the symposium. He'd felt compelled to tell the maestro about the instrument and the special sound it made. Now he wanted to tell them.

"It's the best violin in the whole world," he said, "better than any Strad I've heard. It made the hair stand up on the back of my neck."

He looked over at the table where his parents sat. His mother was obviously dying to join in the conversation, and he felt guilty because he couldn't help hoping she wouldn't. His father's hand was very firmly on her knee. When Daniel turned back to his poppa, he could see that there was something more, something he was hesitating to say.

"What is it, Poppa?"

"We have a special favor to ask of you, Daniel, something we need you to do for us."

"I'd do anything for you, Poppa," he said simply, "and you, Feter."

"We need you to play again. Maestro is going to ask the Russian to let you play our violin, but you need to play well to convince him. Maestro has a plan to get our violin back, but it won't work unless you play for him."

Daniel's violin case lay on the table. He hadn't asked why they were bringing it. He'd assumed it was another attempt to get him to play, and he was too sick of the fighting to say anything until he had to. Now he got up, walked to the table, opened the case, and picked up the violin and bow. It felt right. His mother started to say something, but his father touched her arm firmly and shook his head.

"It doesn't mean I've given in," Daniel said, looking at them. "I'm just doing it for Poppa and Feter."

His father nodded. Daniel could see the gleam in his mother's eyes, and he knew that no matter what he said she'd see this as a victory. It annoyed him but there was nothing to be done; he couldn't refuse. His family needed him. He was the only one who could do this, and it felt good to be important to them. He went to his poppa and held out the instrument.

"Will you practice with me, Poppa?"

The old man didn't take the violin.

"Play me something, Dan."

Daniel played a note and fiddled with the pegs. Levi rose and went to the piano.

"Come, tune with me."

When he was satisfied, Daniel started to play Debussy's "The Girl with the Flaxen Hair." The notes flooded back and he had to hold himself in check as his desire to play made him race ahead. When he finished, his poppa nodded.

"Very good and you haven't played for some time. This piece is a prelude, from a series, but they were written to be played as individual pieces. It's harmonically complex and very lush. What you need to think about is what Debussy was thinking about. He wanted you to find the essence of beauty in this piece. It's about love, intense and passionate love and yet very tranquil at the same time. So you have to be thinking about smoothness and control, long flowing bow, and gentle transitions."

Daniel put the violin to his chin again.

"Did you play this piece, Poppa?"

The old man smiled at him fondly.

"I played this piece the very first time I played my Guarneri, for many of my papa and mama's friends in our wonderful music room. It feels like last night!"

"How old were you?"

"I was fourteen, same age as you, but not as good as you. Now, play it for me again and remember, watch the timing."

Chapter 42

Washington, D.C.
October 2008

It was performance day, and Rafael was having a catnap on the sofa in his dressing room at the Kennedy Center. His tails hung next to the crisp white shirt, white waistcoat, and red cummerbund. His white bow tie lay on the coffee table with the gold cuff links and his score for *La Traviata*. The thoughts juggling for supremacy in his brain banished any hope of sleep so he stared at the painting on the wall. There was a soft double knock on the door.

"Rafael? It's Jeremy, may I come in?"

He swung his feet onto the floor and sat up.

"Certainly," he called out.

Jeremy wore a gray suit with a saffron-colored lining, a charcoal shirt, and a yellow tie. He looked as immaculate as ever, apart from his trademark wild hair.

"I heard you were looking for me," he said as he crossed the room and sat down in an easy chair. "Is there a problem?"

"No, no, not at all . . . well, not with the production."

"Anything I can help with?"

Rafael hesitated.

"How vital is Sergei, really, his money and so on, to our financial position?"

Browne gave a slight frown and cocked his head to one side.

"Why? Have you done something to upset him?"

Rafael could hear the barely hidden concern in the man's tone and felt a sinking sensation in his stomach. Perhaps Mags was right.

"Not yet. But I might, perhaps, be about to."

"Do tell. Is this about *Parsifal*?"

"No. It's a long story, and I won't have enough time right now for all of it. It's about the Guarneri. I know from whereabouts it . . . er, came. Who it belongs to. Before Sergei's grandpapa. And perhaps he doesn't have as much right to it as he thinks."

Jeremy chewed on his bottom lip. "War loot," he said suddenly.

Rafael nodded.

"Absolutely. Berlin 1939. It could be, I think, a watertight claim and with a survivor alive to identify it. But I know that nothing will happen unless I make it happen."

"Have you met the survivor?"

"Yes, he is very credible, knowledgeable . . . musical even. No question he'll recognize it. And those great instruments are so individual."

"You'll upset Sergei." Browne's voice was full of caution.

"I think that is putting it mildly. He will never forgive me—"

"Don't do it. Everyone here has too much to lose, Rafael, including you, especially you."

His expression was set; Rafael could see he'd made up his mind.

"I know that. But what does the Horowitz family lose if I don't? I mean, haven't they suffered enough? Lost enough?" Rafael asked, more to himself than to Jeremy.

"And what about the people you work with, the orchestra, the singers, the backstage crew, the symposium—don't you owe something to them, too?"

It was an argument he'd expected, but somehow when he had it with himself it was easier to refute.

"Leaving the opera company aside, you conduct concerts for him and, presumably, he pays you very well. Can you afford to lose that?"

He ignored the question and the irritation he felt at the intrusion.

"There's another side to it, Jeremy, an important side. The survivor has a grandson and he could be virtuoso, a talent beloved by a generation. He won the Samuel Hillier when I was chief judge, back in February. But now he refuses to play, because his future frightens him. You know, if we can get that violin back, it may just inspire him to play again."

"Does he matter more than the violinists in your own orchestra?"

Rafael got up and began to pace the room.

"That's unfair and you know it. Sergei is not the only donor we have—"

"But he's by far the largest, by millions. We're the envy of every company, and it's because of you, his friendship with *you*. We depend on that; surely that matters most."

Rafael could hear the anger in Browne's voice and the deter-
mination to prevail over a higher argument. Somehow it seemed
to represent the prejudice that had cost the Horowitz family so
much, and it crystallized his thoughts. He stopped and faced the
Englishman.

"I'm sorry, but I can't give it up. It's wrong, Jeremy. What
happened to them is so, so wrong and this opportunity . . . a
chance to . . . to put something right. I just can't ignore it. That's
not me. Who I am. I could not look at myself again."

Jeremy got to his feet and walked to the door.

"Put it out of your mind for now; you need to concentrate.
I believe Sergei isn't here tonight, but he is in the house for the
final two performances. Think long and hard about it after this
run is over, Rafael. If you were after my blessing, you don't have
it. I think you need to reconsider your priorities."

Daniel sat on his bed listening to music on his iPod. The sounds
of Beethoven's Fifth Symphony rolled around his head and he
imagined Rafael on the podium in the recording studio, encouraging and demanding the melodic majesty from the orchestra.
It helped him to keep his mind off the other emotions that he
found hard to control. He hadn't hesitated for a second when
his poppa asked for his help, and the more he thought about
it, the more he felt important. He was the only one who could
do this. It was hard to imagine what his poppa's life had been
like; he had no frame of reference in his own world. Except for
the music, his passion for the violin—*that* Daniel understood
only too well. The rest was like something from another planet,
some remote history lesson he'd heard in school, and yet, they
were his relations in those old photographs. He fingered the
dimple in his chin; Poppa had it, Great-Grandmama had had
it. Great-Grandpapa had also been passionate about this par-

ticular violin. They were real flesh-and-blood people and they'd died terrible deaths, and now, maybe, he could make something right for them. And because of his decision his parents were very happy and his mother kept hugging him. He wished she wouldn't, but it was far better than yelling and crying and arguing all the time.

But what about the baseball? Was he kidding himself? Had he actually lost a battle or the war? Was he back playing for good now or was he just helping out and when the violins were safe, where they belonged, could he reestablish his position? Was it, as Aaron had said, a tactical retreat to consolidate his front line?

Maestro would know. Tomorrow Daniel was off to England to start the big adventure, with his father and Maestro Gomez, the people who seemed to understand him and fight in his corner better than anyone else. Yep, Maestro would know. When the time was right, he'd ask his hero about the baseball, about whether he'd surrendered or just made a tactical maneuver.

Chapter 43

Sochi Hall, Sussex
October 2008

"Ladies and gentlemen."

From his position in the doorway Rafael could see Sergei in front of three hundred seated guests. He was waiting patiently until the buzz of conversation died away and they all turned their attention in his direction. It was an early fall afternoon and the Russian stood in the ballroom of his Sussex home, a microphone in his hand. Behind him sat an orchestra of young musicians, all award winners or graduates from past Washington symposia, and Rafael knew they would acquit themselves well.

"Thank you so much for being able to come to my little concert. To start proceedings, this wonderful orchestra will play the beautiful intermezzo, from *Cavalleria Rusticana* by Pietro Mascagni."

Polite applause followed as Rafael strode into the room. He shook hands with Sergei and mounted a podium placed in front of the orchestra. Sergei took his seat in the front row. Rafael made eye contact with the musicians and tapped his baton on the stand, drawing their mental focus to him. He gave them an encouraging wink and raised his baton. On the downward stroke, the gentle melody filled the room and began to swell, carried by the strings, until the piece came to an end with one long sustained note. The audience clapped loudly and Rafael raised his hands, palms upward, telling the orchestra to stand, and then he turned to receive the applause. He could see Daniel sitting beside his father, his eyes glowing with excitement, clapping enthusiastically, and he gave him a wink.

"Thank you very much, ladies and gentlemen. Now we have a special treat. Tatiana is going to play for us. She plays the Guarneri del Gesú violin, and she's going to play a composition by Pablo de Sarasate. He was a virtuoso violinist and a composer also. He was born in my country, Spain, in the middle of the nineteenth century. He played in public for the first time when he was just eight, and when he was twelve, he was sent to study at the Paris Conservatoire. He won their highest honor when he was just seventeen. His work influenced many composers, and he had amazing technique. If we could only hear him at his peak, but alas, there were no recordings. In 1883, he wrote this piece called the 'Carmen Fantasy,' on themes from Georges Bizet's famous opera, *Carmen*."

While he was speaking Tatiana had walked through the door and into the room. She wore a shimmering silver dress that flowed over her curves like mercury, and her hair was pulled back into a ponytail. She held the violin by the scroll and the bow, both in her right hand. She gave a shy smile in the direction of the conductor, tuned the violin briefly, tightened the screw on the bow, and took her stance. The orchestra came in first, but she was only seconds later. The melody was a mix of heavy drama, designed to show off the technical skill of the violinist, and a soft, delicate gypsy sound. At one stage Rafael put his finger to his lips to bring the orchestra down to an aching pianissimo. He and Tatiana made regular eye contact and exchanged smiles; when she was playing alone, she had his full focus. The first half finished with the familiar tune of the sexy "Habanera" and the audience burst into wild applause.

Rafael turned to face them, a wide grin on his face, and he took Tatiana's hand and kissed it. *She was good,* he admitted to himself, *and oh, she knew how to make that violin sing!* He thought that one of the most exciting things about a violin like the Guarneri was that you never knew for sure how it would sound on any given day and today it was making music fit for the angels.

They waited for the clapping to subside, and then she took her stance again, violin under her chin, for the second half. The songs of *Carmen* echoed seductively around the room, both the erotically inviting "Seguidilla" and the frenetic gypsy dance. The music became more and more complex and demanding, the accelerating pace reflected in her body movements. Horsehair came loose on the bow and flew about her as she built to a spectacular finish.

Daniel sat spellbound all the way through, afraid to move or breathe in case he woke and it was just a dream. The sound was so superior to anything he'd ever heard before and so versatile; it commanded and pleaded and rejoiced and flirted with him and flooded his senses. Then it was over and he felt completely drained. All around him people were on their feet, clapping and shouting, "Brava!" He sat very still and stared at the woman who was holding the violin and bow in one hand and acknowledging the crowd with a nod of her head. Rafael took her hand again, held it aloft triumphantly, and then kissed it.

"Ladies and gentlemen, Tatiana."

Still Daniel didn't move. She was playing *his poppa's* violin, the violin that belonged to— He felt a sharp nudge in his side and the moment was gone. His father was looking down at him, frowning. He stood up and clapped.

The next morning Rafael collected Daniel and David in Sergei's Rolls-Royce and they went back to the mansion. The car swept up the long graveled drive and stopped at the bottom of the broad steps. The driver got out and opened the rear doors for the two men and one teenaged boy, who carried a violin case. They were shown into the library. The center of the large room was dominated by a long and intricately carved Elizabethan table, but the rest was comfortably decorated with a piano, four leather armchairs, a Persian rug on the polished wooden floor, and a magnificent fireplace and was lined floor to ceiling with bookcases full of books. Sergei flung open the double doors at the far end of the room.

"Good morning, Raffy. Nice to meet you, David, and especially good morning to you, young Daniel."

He shook hands with each of them and gestured to the service laid out on the table.

"Tea or coffee or some Coca-Cola?"

Rafael observed Sergei as he put the child at ease, talking to Daniel about music, composers, his school, the symposium, mathematics, and even baseball. For a man who'd never had children, he was remarkably skilled at connecting with, and listening to, the boy's opinions. David was cautious and protective. Rafael could see that he was watchful for any comment on the family violin, but Daniel knew he wasn't to mention it and he stuck to the script beautifully.

"So," Sergei said finally, beaming at Daniel, "you're going to play for me, no?"

"Yes, sir."

"And what are you going to play?"

"Some Debussy and some Paganini, sir."

Sergei laughed delightedly.

"Wonderful choices, some of my very favorites."

Daniel prepared the violin and tuned at the piano with Rafael, then when they were both satisfied, he turned toward Sergei.

"This is Debussy's 'The Girl with the Flaxen Hair.' It's a prelude from a series, but they were written to be played as individual pieces."

"Quite right. When you're ready, my boy."

Rafael knew Sergei's routine and watched him settle into the chair and focus his attention on the child, blocking out everything else. Daniel began to play the lilting melody, slowly and expressively, and when he finished, all three men clapped.

"And now which Paganini?" Sergei asked.

"Caprice number twenty-four and then some of the first movement of Violin Concerto number one in D Minor."

"Goodness me, Caprice twenty-four? One of the most difficult pieces ever written for solo violin. Even after many years of study, most players lack the technique needed for this piece."

Rafael smiled and gave the Daniel the note to tune again.

"Listen and be astonished, my friend," he said.

This time Daniel seemed to play as if his soul were on fire, his fingers flying over the fingerboard at dizzying speed and his bowing strong and confident. Seated at the piano, Rafael could see Sergei but not Daniel, and halfway through, the Russian leaned forward and stared intently at the performance. With the concluding note, Daniel's head went back and his arms dropped to his sides. Sergei was on his feet instantly, clapping.

"Bravo! You are a truly exceptional talent."

He walked to the boy and put his huge hand on Daniel's shoulder, took the violin from him, and examined it. Then he looked over at Rafael and smiled.

"You're right, as I knew you would be. This child is a genius. And now I have something to show you all."

He led them down a series of corridors at the back of the house to a solid metal door with a keypad instead of a handle and lock. He punched in a number sequence, and the door slid back into the wall. They followed him in, and he swept his arm expansively around the room; it held three glass cases and nothing else.

"This is the prize trio of my whole collection. Meet Amaretto," he said as he walked to the nearest case. "She is a 1715 Stradivari violin, and this is Lucetta," he continued, moving on to the next case. "She is a 1611 Maggini viola, and of course, the one I call"—he was at the third case and he gazed lovingly into it—"Yulena. My 1729 Guarneri. Come meet her, Daniel."

They watched as he punched another sequence into a keypad on the case and the lid sprang up slightly. Then he carefully lifted the violin from the satin and handed it to Daniel. It felt heavier than the boy had expected and very smooth, almost silky under his fingers, and surprisingly cold. He ran his hand over the back and stared at the perfect grain in the maple as it shimmered with the intense color of the red/yellow varnish. His forefinger traced the scroll and the long *f* holes, and he felt the fingerboard under the strings. Very gently he plucked one. Sergei held out the bow.

"Play a scale."

He put the violin to his chin, looked at Rafael, and played a simple G major scale. He hadn't expected to be allowed to hold it, let alone play it. The sudden sound bounced off the walls, loud in the enclosed space, and David turned away for a moment. Daniel wanted to go to his father and hug him, but he knew he couldn't. Neither he, nor his father, had ever seen his poppa play a violin and here he was, holding the very one the old man had played when he was a young boy. When David composed himself, he pulled a small digital camera from his pocket and stepped forward.

"May I take a picture of him, sir? For his mother?"

Sergei beamed with obvious pride. "Absolutely, you may."

"Thank you."

Rafael smiled at Daniel.

"Try a two octave, the B major," he said gently.

Daniel played the more complicated scale, hesitated and fiddled with the pegs, then closed his eyes and started to play some of the Paganini. It sounded harsh, and he stopped abruptly and handed it back to Sergei.

"Don't worry, son, she is very hard to play and you have to be fearless, like Tatiana. But you will learn. I will get Maestro Montenagro to help prepare a piece or two and when you're ready, we will have a little concert!"

Daniel retreated to stand beside Rafael; he knew that he was trembling, and that made him feel ashamed. His head pounded with complicated emotions, and he wanted to run out of the room. What surprised him most of all was that he wished his mom was there. Then he felt Rafael's hand touch his head for a brief reaffirming pat and all was well.

Chapter 44

Vermont
October 2008

Rafael left Daniel and David in a London hotel, flew to New York, hired a car, and drove straight to Simon and Levi's home in Woodsville. He felt humbled by their delight in seeing him.

"Could I have another look at your shoe box?" he asked as they sat at the table and drank coffee.

"Certainly."

As Simon fetched the box, Rafael drew an envelope out of his jacket pocket.

"But first, I have something to show you."

He handed two five-by-seven-inch photos to Simon.

"Oh, my!"

The old man almost dropped them, then grasped them tight and brought them closer to his eyes.

"Daniel."

"Yes, Daniel, and the Guarneri; he did very well."

Simon caressed the picture with his finger, then handed the bottom one to Levi.

"Look at it, Levi," he said without taking his eyes from the image.

"It is yours, yes? Do you think?" asked Rafael anxiously.

Simon didn't answer immediately, and when he looked up, his eyes glistened with unshed tears.

"Yes, Maestro, it's her. I haven't seen her for sixty-nine years and she hasn't changed at all."

Levi opened the shoe box, picked up the photo of the two boys, and passed it to Rafael.

"Nearly eighty years separate these two photographs," he said softly, "and it is the same instrument."

Simon spread the contents on the table.

"Most of this came in the pouch with Levi to London, so he should explain it."

Levi shifted, and Rafael was reminded of the discomfort he'd seen when the old man spoke about himself on their previous meeting.

"This is a letter of introduction my papa wrote to a man who ran a bank in London, but when I visited, he refused to see me. These two sheets are a list of our possessions, written in my papa's handwriting; the ink is faded, but you can still read them. These are two portraits, of Mama and Papa. This drawing was done for me by my sister, Rachel. It's me playing the piano, and there's a poem she wrote about me on the back. These were my identity cards when I first came to England. And this little pouch contained some precious family jewelry. Most of it was used to buy my freedom, and what was left has been given to Simon's wife, Ruth, or his daughter-in-law, Cindy. I never married."

Rafael picked up the list.

"Thank you. Are the violins on this list?"

"Yes, halfway down page one, under musical instruments."

Rafael read the list silently, shaking his head in amazement as he came to the end.

"A Flemish double virginal. An Italian lute, an ivory serpent; you know, I've heard about the serpent but never seen one. Good Lord, what a room that must have been!"

Simon touched his arm. "Oh, it was, Maestro. The walls had music notes in gold leaf all over the wallpaper, I used to try and make them into a tune. There was a huge Steinway grand and such a chandelier. It was Austrian, of the finest crystal, and my, how it sparkled. The instruments were in gold-bound glass cases—"

"He doesn't want to hear all that!"

Levi's voice was a harsh mix of impatience, guilt, and the pain of loss. Simon removed his hand, and his shoulders slumped, his eyes downcast. It was a reflex reaction to disapproval, and the poignancy of it pulled hard at Rafael's heart.

"These are beautiful," he said as he picked up the miniatures. "You know, I can see why Daniel is such a good-looking boy."

Elizabeth Horowitz's proud beauty was perfectly captured in the small likeness. She was turned slightly sideways and her smile was enigmatic, her skin translucent. Benjamin had sparkling eyes, a round face, and an enormous mustache.

"That is how I remember them," Levi said.

"That is how I like to remember them," Simon added softly.

"And this is all you have left?"

"Not quite, Maestro."

Simon retrieved a bundle of faded yellow envelopes tied together with blue ribbon from the sideboard.

"After you left last time, Ruth reminded me that my aunt had given me these. They're letters written by my mother to her sister-in-law in New York before the war. My aunt had kept them all. Avrum left Berlin in 1925 and settled in New York. He married a wonderful American woman, Esther, and my parents never met her. But my mother loved to tell her about life in Germany, what we did and where she shopped and the parties she had. I think she was showing off a bit, but the letters mention the violins a lot, especially the Guarneri. When Levi and I settled in New York, Avrum and Esther were very good to us both; we were family. When Avrum died, Esther gave me the letters; they are written in German and without her husband to translate, she couldn't read them."

Rafael turned the bundle over in his hands.

"That's wonderful. What a thing to have. Simon, can you have translations made for me? Of the list and the parts of the letters that mention the violin, and a copy of that photograph?"

"Of course, Maestro."

"Good. I want you to come to London. There are some people I want you to meet. Will you come?"

"We'd be only too happy to."

He smiled at the two men. "You know there will be many people looking over your grandson's shoulder when he plays these pieces. Important people from years ago. And he will feel their presence. You will need to help him with that."

Thousands of miles away Daniel was in the music room of Sergei's London home, holding the Guarneri in his playing stance. Two feet away a small, middle-aged man sat on a high bar stool and examined him from head to toe. Daniel tried not to look as if he was scrutinizing back. The man was Italian, bald, with a small gray goatee beard and round steel-rimmed glasses. His movements were quick and precise as he darted forward and made a minute change to the angle of the violin relative to Daniel's body and then moved his fingers on the bow slightly. Then he sat back down on the stool.

"You begin now," he said solemnly.

Daniel started to play a scale. Halfway through, the man held his hand up, palm facing Daniel.

"*Va bene,* now we address the technique."

As he drove back to New York, Rafael played a game of moral Ping-Pong with himself. At one end of the table was an angry-looking Jeremy, and behind him all the employees of the opera company and the soloists on contract and the audiences who attended performances. At the other end were Simon, Levi, Daniel, Cindy, David, and Roberto. Rafael was the ball, and he flung himself from one end to the other listening to all the arguments.

The most important thing to remember, Maestro, is that surviving the camp doesn't make you better than all those who died. On one level it was about a strange kind of fate, an arbitrary and completely unpredictable sort of . . . karma.

And what about the people you work with, the orchestra, the singers, the backstage crew, the symposium—don't you owe something to them, too?

Sergei supports them because of you, he doesn't live here, he believes in you! If you destroy that, he'll walk away and Jeremy won't care a jot for some kid and his talent.

If I can help, I'd be only too glad. I might narrow down the haystacks a little, but it's still a bloody small needle in a continent of hay, and while you're thinking about it, consider this. If Valentino's little masterpiece isn't a 1729, what is it? When was it made? Is it the priceless missing 1742?

What was he doing? What had he started? There was no doubt in his mind that Sergei's instrument had belonged to the

Horowitz family prior to the war. His conscience told him that
it'd been stolen, twice, and they'd never willingly relinquished
ownership of it. But Sergei was his friend and they'd shared
some long late-night sessions over a vodka bottle. He knew that
Sergei's beloved aunt had been given the violin by her father and
she'd played first violin in the Moscow Philharmonic, been a
favorite of Shostakovich, and a decorated war heroine, a pilot,
but most important the closest thing he'd known to a mother.
For all his bravado and bluster, Sergei was a human being and
he'd had people ripped away from him, too.

Rafael knew what that was like, how the grief slowly sank
into your bones and seemed to settle there; just because you got
used to it didn't mean you ever got over it. Speaking of grief,
how much of this dedication to Daniel seeped from behind
the door permanently shut in his heart? Miguel, his son, could
have been a concert pianist—his future had been tantalizingly
close—but Rafael grieved for the child, not the musician. He
sighed deeply and frowned. However unpalatable it was, the
decision was made and the ball had decided on which side of the
table it wanted to be; there was no going back.

Chapter 45

Covent Garden, London
October 2008

Five men sat in comfortable armchairs drawn up to the table in a meeting room at the Covent Garden Hotel. Above them hung three red light shades; between them sat water glasses and bowls of sweets. Rafael was at the head of the table, Simon on his left, and Levi on his right. Beside Simon was an excited Roberto di Longi, and beside Levi was a cautious Maestro Carlo Montenagro, the violin tutor. An enlargement of the image of Daniel playing the Guarneri lay in the center of the table. They were all listening to Maestro Montenagro, who spoke slowly and precisely, giving his words due consideration and translating his thoughts from Italian in his head as he went.

"Several years ago I was invited to play, by the mayor of Genoa, both Il Cannone and the Vuillaume replica of it. I have also played once the Lord Wilton, a 1742 Guarneri. They share some, how do you say it? . . . common manners. And this one, she is same. The sound box is short, and the box and belly are thick, remarkably thick—that is because he put so much wood in the resonator. She has the 1742 flame grain in the maple and that very deep orange-red on old-gold ground luster, in the varnish. The 1729 was more a honey color."

Roberto was nodding, and Rafael could see the joy on his face. It was the first expert confirmation of his theory he'd ever had.

"Most important, she has temper," Montenagro continued. "Did you know Paganini called the Cannon 'terribly angry'? He named her for sound she sometimes made, the explosive power, like cannon shot. The boy, he had terrible time with her at the beginning, she not like him at all. He was very nervous of course and so she had a wolf note on the top C on the fourth stri—"

"For me as well!" Simon cried excitedly and then raised his hand to his mouth. "Oh my, I'm sorry, gentlemen; you must forgive me. I battled that wolf note so many times."

Rafael touched his arm. "Don't apologize, Simon. You know that note; that's a good thing."

Montenagro waited a moment and then resumed.

"But when he relax, she tunes herself. Such a thing is what a 1742 Guarneri does. So I agree with you, Roberto. I did not look at her label, but she sounds and looks like a 1742. I have thought this for some time."

Roberto cleared his throat. "Thank you, Maestro. I can't tell you what it means to hear you say that. I would like to add a couple of other points, if I may. The *f* holes are longer, so obviously a Guarneri trait, but these are so much more elegant than his usual ones. He took such care. And look at the scroll; it's rugged and it has his tool marks, but it was clearly made after Giuseppe Giovanni Battista Guarneri, his father and mentor, died and we know that was either 1739 or 1740. His scrolls changed dramatically after his father died, and this is obviously a later one."

Montenagro took a photograph from his pocket and laid it on the table next to the other one. The two violins looked identical.

"This also is most interesting. This violin, it also has one-piece maple back and an orange varnish on old-gold ground. It's a famous 1742, known as the Wieniawski, after Henryk Wieniawski, one of the greatest virtuosos of the nineteenth century, and owned by Mary Galvin since 1998. There are two things about it you should know."

Everyone was staring at the picture of the second violin.

"Guarneri del Gesú, he used to make his violins in pairs, sometimes, not always. There are violins that look almost identical, but this one, it has no pair. I believe very much that this, the Wieniawski, is companion violin to the Guarneri that Sergei Valentino owns."

"Have you told him this?" Rafael asked sharply.

Montenagro hesitated.

"No. And second, it has interesting history. Richard Talbot bought it in 1932, at Anderson galleries in New York for the princely sum of sixteen thousand dollars. Some French and American soldiers stay at his mansion in Aachen in 1944 and they say a French solider, he finds violin in a hidden vault. He begins to play. An American hears him and offers to buy the violin. So the French solider, he sells it for some packets of cigarettes. Then in 1948, the American GI, he takes it to Rembert Wurtlitzer at the Wurtlitzer office in New York to see if it is worth anything. Rembert recognizes it, of course, and wires London, to Hills, and asks if they know what happened to the Wieniawski Guarneri. They wire back and say it has been stolen from the Talbot house in 1944 and is still missing."

"What happened next?" It was Simon, and his voice was raw with suppressed hope.

"Many negotiations, but eventually it was returned to Richard Talbot in Aachen, the rightful owner."

Rafael saw Simon's fist clench and then relax.

"That's promising, I think," he said firmly. "In law, they call it precedent. Roberto, tell us about the label."

Roberto nodded enthusiastically.

"I believe the label has been altered to read 1729, to obscure the true value. Like the Sloan that was repaired by Bein and Fushi in the 1990s, it read 1734, but they believed it was a 1742 so they changed it back and repaired it. We would need another expert to authenticate that. Comparative acoustic tests and dendrochronology tests to establish the exact age of the wood; those sorts of procedures are easy and reliable."

Rafael turned to Simon.

"Simon?"

The old man looked across the table at his brother, who gave him a little nod, then sighed deeply.

"If it is our violin—and it is—then the label will read 1729. But the true age is 1742. My papa had it changed by an expert luthier in Berlin in 1935. To make it seem an inferior instrument. He was going to hide it, but I couldn't bear to stop playing it . . ."

His voice trailed off. Roberto thumped the table with his fist.

"I knew it!"

Rafael smiled at him.

"I know you did. Now, if we all agree that it is a 1742 and that it belongs to Simon and Levi, yes? The question next is, what are we going to do to get it back?"

"Rafael's right," Roberto said. "There are two separate issues, proving that it is a 1742 and therefore it is the instrument that these gentlemen lost, and then persuading Sergei to give it back. I have to say, and I know that this is not what you'll want to hear, I'm certain that there's nothing any of us could say to him, to persuade him—"

"But it's ours," Simon interrupted him, and Rafael could see the intensity in his eyes.

"I know, but he has a family provenance as well, from his grandfather."

Rafael moved uncomfortably and picked up the photo of Daniel playing. Roberto continued on, seemingly unaware of the emotional hornet's nest he was entering.

"I suspect the best way will be an official claim. My research has taken me in several directions. The Holocaust Claims Processing Office in New York is one. Also the American Association of Museums has been very active in this area; they have guideline—"

"May I ask something?" Levi spoke for the first time.

"Of course." Rafael nodded. "You don't need our permission."

"How would a claim prove to anyone that the violin is ours? Surely it will come down to our word against his? And we are old men; time is not our most abundant resource, gentlemen."

He spoke with a quiet dignity and frankness. Simon watched him and nodded sadly.

"To know for sure that it still exists and not to have it, play it, own it, is harder than when we thought it had gone forever," Simon said suddenly. "It's more than just an instrument, it's a symbol . . . a symbol of what we had, what we lost, the people we lost. Nothing reminds me more of my papa than his pride and joy, that violin. It was not just our physical possessions they took; it was the whole fabric of our lives. They robbed us of our family."

He paused and Rafael could see he was collecting his thoughts, finding the words to make them understand. "Many years ago I watched a German, like me—a music lover, like me—lift it out of its case and play it. Then he told me that I shouldn't own such a thing and my papa was probably dead. Do you know what I did? I punched him, broke his nose! The wonder is he didn't shoot me, but it was only 1939. Instead he called me a dirty Jew bastard and hit me with his truncheon, broke my left hand. For five and a half years I survived the worst hell humankind has ever known and I did it by keeping alive my memories, by willpower and by my ability to play the violin. I swore to myself I *would* find my violin, and you think I'm going to give up now, just because I'm an old man?"

Chapter 46

Mayfair, London
Late October 2008

The nights had begun to close in more quickly, and a chill wind swirled around the buildings and shook the leaves from the trees. Indoors the heating was going on, fires were lit, and people were starting to think about the long winter ahead. Upstairs, in her bedroom at the Mayfair mansion, Tatiana was brushing her hair and complaining.

"But if he plays well, people will want to hear him. He's five years younger—"

Sergei smiled at her indulgently. "Not nearly as pretty!"

"No one cares about that. There are so many wonderful violins. Why does he have to play the Guarneri?"

"Because it's the best, and he deserves to learn how to make beautiful music on her."

"Why does he 'deserve'?"

"Because he's put years of work into building his skill and he's very good."

"Is he better than me?"

"Is it a competition?"

"Of course. You might want him to play instead of me."

He was standing behind her now and stroking her hair. She didn't want him to but didn't feel secure enough to ask him to stop. No matter how many talented musicians Rafael had brought to Sergei, he'd never let anyone else play the Guarneri, so what had changed?

"Don't worry about him, princess. He's a talented boy and he'll play her just once in public. To convince him to keep playing, and I think it's working, from what Raffy says. If he graduates, well, I may lend him one of the others to play and record, but *you* will play her for me forever!"

Tatiana put the hairbrush onto the dressing table and gave a small smile into the mirror, saying nothing and showing nothing in her leonine eyes.

Downstairs and toward the front of the house, in the music room, Daniel was having a lesson with Maestro Montenagro. He was playing the allegro from Vivaldi's Concerto in B Minor and the man paced around him constantly, judging his technique from all sides. Over in one corner David sat on a stool watching. He could see sweat beads gathering on his son's forehead, and he could imagine how much Daniel's fingers and arms must be aching with the effort.

David remembered how his father used to sit, silently, and watch his lessons. Had Simon longed to join in, to correct and encourage, all those years ago? Had he, in turn, remembered his own lessons in the glorious music room and the pride of his papa? This simple act of watching a violin lesson connected them back through the generations. David missed playing, and he'd often thought about taking it up again, but Daniel's talent was so beyond anything he'd ever achieved, he felt intimidated. Over the past few weeks his loyalties had torn him in two; he understood his wife's motivation, and he felt for Daniel. He knew the toll not playing and constant arguing was taking on the child. And he'd learned more about his father's war experiences in the past month than during the rest of their relationship. How could his father and uncle tell so much to Rafael—

Suddenly the door swung open, and Tatiana walked in. Without making eye contact, she stalked over to Daniel and pulled the violin and bow out of his hands.

"Attenzione!" Montenagro leaped forward but not fast enough to stop her. The Russian put the violin to her chin and started to play the same piece. She played with a deft touch— *making a point,* David thought. When she finished, she handed the violin to Montenagro.

"That is how she wishes to be played," she said, turned on her heel, and walked out, slamming the door behind her.

"Excuse me, Maestro Gomez, I was wondering, could I have your autograph?"

Rafael and Magdalena were sitting at a table in the hotel bar, sipping wine and watching the world coming and going. Groups of people observed him and gossiped among themselves; every so often someone smiled shyly at him, and he returned the smile. Finally a middle-aged blonde got off her bar stool and walked timidly toward them.

She held a paper napkin and a pen in her hand. He reached out for them.

"Certainly."

"Are you here for a concert?"

"Yes, but it is, unfortunately, a private one. What's your name?"

"Katherine. I love opera and symphony music. I've seen you conduct many times; you're just amazing to watch."

He signed the paper with a flourish and handed it back with a smile. His eyes flashed at her and she flushed.

"Thank you very much, and there you are, Katherine."

"Oh, thank you, sir."

Reluctantly she moved back to the bar, still watching them. Mags gave a sigh, and he could see the humor, patience, and indulgence in her expression.

"So what is your plan for Saturday night, Maestro Manipulator?"

"Daniel will play and then Simon and Levi will know for sure what it is, that it is theirs. We find them a very good lawyer and, I think, lodge a claim. They have a very strong case. Then the public reaction will help."

"Won't that take ages? You're not going to try and persuade Sergei first?"

"At the moment he has no reason to hide it, but if he thinks that people want to take it away, it'll go into a vault somewhere and never see the light of day again."

"Maybe his conscience would prevail . . ." Her voice trailed off thoughtfully. Rafael took a sip of wine.

"Fond as I am of him, I think Sergei has no conscience."

"Raffy, aren't you concerned for Daniel? It's a lot of pressure on a young kid, and he's had quite a break from performing."

He nodded.

"I know. Carlo says he's doing very well, though, and he loves to play it. The hard part for him is when he has to give it back. He's a performer, it's in his blood. You know, the only thing I worry about is that it means *so* much to him now. He knows his poppa will have a very hard time not reacting when he sees it and I think that possibility, it is frightening for Daniel."

Roberto di Longi loved a captive audience. He sat across his display table from two elderly gentlemen who were as crazy about musical instruments as he was. The thought of sharing all the precious masterpieces in his vault gave him an itch of anticipation and vanity. Between them lay a long strip of green baize, and on it sat three violins. He picked one up and handed it gently to Simon.

"This is a Nicolas Lupot, made in Paris in 1798, nice red varnish on a golden-brown ground. Lupot was a very talented maker, and his instruments command a good price on the market today."

Simon turned the instrument over in his hands and then passed it to Levi without comment. Roberto picked up a second one.

"This is a Giovanni Battista Guadagnini, made in Parma in 1767. Two-piece back and look at the narrow curl of the scroll. I'm going through the authentication process with this little beauty, and it could well be worth at least a hundred thousand pounds. Lovely golden brown tint. He made cellos and double basses as well. Rich sound."

Simon took it from him. "It's a beautiful instrument," he said simply.

"Yes, it is. I often wonder at the artistry of these men. Given when they lived and the limited resources and technology they had, and yet, think of the masterpieces they created. All by trial and error and instinct. If you did it now, with computers and precision cutters and so on, the sound would be no *better* than the sound they created."

Simon handed the violin to Levi, who'd put the Lupot down on the table.

"And this," said Roberto proudly as he picked up the third, "is true genius. This is a 1730 Strad."

He handed it over reverentially. It was a deep red color and had flames in the grain running vertically down the back.

"Antonio Stradivari," Simon whispered as he took it. "I've never seen one, in the flesh."

Roberto watched him as he did the standard examination, ran his finger over the back, traced the scroll, checked the bridge, and plucked the A string.

"Hello, my beauty," Simon murmured.

Roberto picked up a bow and handed it over.

"Play something."

Simon's eyes opened wide in what looked like astonishment. Roberto couldn't help the feeling of power his position sometimes gave him; he knew only too well what a thrill this was for the old man. Such experiences built trust, and that would be vital if he ever got to handle a sale for the family.

"Really?"

"Why not? They were made to be played, and you won't do it any damage; you know what you're doing."

Simon hesitated and Roberto wondered what his reluctance was.

"It doesn't matter how you play; they're a lot more forgiving than the Guarneri."

"I know. It's just I haven't played since . . . for many years. Since 1945."

"Then it's time you did, and a Strad is a very fitting way to warm up for a Guarneri."

The two men exchanged knowing smiles, and Roberto walked over to the piano to play A above middle C. With his help Simon tuned the four pegs, then tightened the screw on the bow, and played a simple scale. The sound was crisp and clear.

He hesitated again, and Roberto and Levi waited patiently. Then suddenly he launched into Vivaldi's "Winter," followed by snatches of Mendelssohn, Massenet, Mozart, and Bach. The violin responded to each minute change of tempo and technique as the luscious tone rose and fell away to pianissimo, only to build again. Finally he stopped and handed the violin back to Roberto with a shy smile.

"Thank you, sir."

There were tears in the Englishman's eyes.

"I don't think you have any idea how good you are," he said gently.

Simon smiled again, and Roberto could see what looked like a flush of embarrassment.

"I was expecting you to say that I should practice hard and then I might become very good, and give me a lump of rosin."

Roberto couldn't keep the surprise from his voice.

"Really?"

"Just a wrinkle in time, another life, another world."

Chapter 47

Mayfair, London
Late October 2008

"Mom. Stop fussing."

Daniel put his hands to his throat and pulled Cindy's fingers away as they fiddled with his bow tie. She ruffled his hair instead. He licked his palms and patted it down again.

"I'm very proud of you for doing this, for your poppa; you do know that, don't you?"

He smiled at her.

"And I like it much better when we're not fighting too. I have to warm up now, and Maestro will be here soon. You go find Dad."

"Are you sure you don't want me to stay?"

"Yes, absolutely, certainly, definitely sure."

She reached out and touched the violin case on the table and seemed about to say something more, then changed her mind and kissed him on the cheek. He felt a surge of relief.

"Good luck, precious boy."

*   *   *

Outside people were streaming up the steps and through the open doors to Sergei's London mansion, laughing and chatting happily as they came. His team of uniformed butlers stood in a row in the vast reception hall to receive their coats and gloves. Slowly they moved through the double doorway and into the music room. Five hundred chairs were set out in rows at one end of the long room, facing the platform where the orchestra would sit. At the other end the guests circulated, drank champagne cocktails, and nibbled on miniature hamburgers, hot dogs and bagels, beluga caviar, and Neufchâtel cheese savories. Sergei was in full concert mode, kissing women on each cheek, shaking hands, accepting congratulations, and repeating the story of his amazing "find," who was the youngest competitor ever to win the Samuel J. Hillier.

Simon and Levi, both in brand-new suits, stood with Ruth, David, and Cindy and watched the huge Russian work the crowd. Cindy kept brushing her black taffeta skirt nervously with one hand.

"I should be with him," she repeated, in David's direction. He shook his head firmly.

"He's better off with the maes—"

She started toward the door. "Nonsense, no one knows his routines like I do. I should—"

David grasped her wrist in his hand and looked into her eyes.

"Cindy, listen to me. He doesn't *want* either of us there right now. The maestro will know what to say, and do, and Rafael promised to keep an eye on him. He'll be just fine."

"Sometimes family makes you more nervous." Simon smiled at her. "David's right; he has a performer's temperament, and he will be fine."

*   *   *

Rafael stood outside the closed door and listened to the violin and piano together. It was an amazingly sweet sound, and it filled him with pride in his achievement. He couldn't escape the fact that this boy was here, tonight, doing this huge and emotional thing, in front of all these people, because he, Rafael, had made it happen. For better or for worse, this was all his doing and he'd live with the consequences. The music stopped and he knocked on the door. There was a pause, and then he heard Montenagro's voice.

"Yes?"

He opened the door and went in. Montenagro rose from the piano.

"Nearly finished?" Rafael asked.

"*Sì*. He's yours and he's ready."

Montenagro shook Daniel's hand as he walked past him.

"Enjoy yourself, young man. That is very important. Let her sing to you and she will sing to everyone else, *sì*?"

"Yes. Thank you, sir."

Montenagro looked Rafael in the eye and nodded. They both knew that to say more would only increase Daniel's nerves.

"We will talk later, *sì*?" he said and then he left.

Rafael turned his attention to Daniel.

"Put her down and come sit with me," he said as he concertinaed his long body onto the sofa in the corner. Daniel did as he asked. The boy's face was pallid, and his eyes were full of apprehension.

"How do you feel?" Rafael asked.

"Okay, I guess."

"Remember that conversation we had, back in the hall, at D.C.?"

"About me giving up?"

"And about sports. Baseball and football . . . soccer."

Daniel nodded.

"I want to tell you a trick, Dan. When you're out there to-night, imagine that you're, you know, walking out onto Wrigley Field. And the violin, she is whichever you want, the ball or the bat. You take your stance and the crowd falls silent."

He could see Daniel was fascinated.

"So when you start to play, it is like you wind up, yes? All your energy and concentration, it is focused on what you do, and then you score. It is a home run. Or it is a strike, the perfect pitch. As you play tonight it will be the best game of baseball ever. The crowd will cheer and you'll be the hero."

Daniel laughed. "Do you do that?"

"Oh my God, yes! I start to conduct and I am on the right wing for Real Madrid, Champion's League final. I run and I run and the ball, she is at my feet, and I beat defender after defender until at last I curl her into the back of the net. Over the goal-keeper's desperate leap."

They were both laughing.

"But you don't tell anyone, okay? It is our secret, that we play sport while we make music, okay?"

"Okay, no matter how much they torture me, I'll never tell."

"Good boy."

The laughter subsided.

"Dan, there was something else I wanted to say. You know, you are doing a good thing tonight, for your family. Whatever happens, and I don't think anything will, apart from lots of cheering, don't be frightened. You know the violin, she means a great deal to your poppa and he will have a hard time seeing her again, and seeing you play her, but sometimes emotion like that is a good thing. It can be, for us, a healthy thing. You are not hurting him, you are helping him, yes?"

Daniel nodded.

"I know. Dad talked to me about that. He explained what a really hard time Poppa had in the war."

"Yes, he did, and he is a very brave man. You know, you should be very proud of him. He is extremely proud of you, and so am I." He pulled himself to his feet and held out his large hand. "And now it is time for us to go play some sports."

Chapter 48

Together they walked through the hall, Rafael carrying his baton and Daniel, the violin and bow. Large portraits and paintings stared down from the walls on either side, and the thick carpet beneath their feet muffled their footsteps. In the doorway they stopped, and Rafael surveyed the huge room, the battleground.

The orchestra sat, tuned and ready, full of eager anticipation. The crowd had been directed to their seats. He knew Sergei was very pleased with the mix, potential managers and agents, reviewers for magazines and websites, professional musicians, luthiers and students, friends and fellow businesspeople, a sprinkling of celebrities with a well-known passion for classical music and Daniel's family.

Tatiana was absent, and he was relieved Sergei had taken his advice; her presence would increase Daniel's nerves and it wasn't fair to her. He knew Sergei had been most displeased by her demonstration during the music lesson, and things between them seemed strained. Rafael wondered what she'd thought of her "treat," a ticket to see *Hairspray* at the Shaftesbury Theater, a night at the Hilton, a wad of cash and instructions to go shopping. According to Sergei, she certainly intended to, judging by the size of all the suitcases she'd taken with her.

Roberto di Longi sat in the third row. His last comment to Rafael had been all about hubris and justice and how far people will go to keep what they desire and how satisfying it is to be proven right. It'd occurred to Rafael at the time that just because he admired the man's expertise, that didn't mean he had to actually like him, and if he saw anything close to a gloat, Roberto would feel the lash of a Spanish temper.

Two seats along from Roberto sat Rafael's darling Mags. He knew she had serious doubts about the whole enterprise, but she loved him and understood him, and she admired the fact that doing what was right was fundamental to his personality. He'd come very close to telling her what he actually hoped would happen, and then he decided it was too much of a burden. The fate of the evening was his load alone.

Simon, Levi, Ruth, David, and Cindy sat in the front row. The sight of the two old men, sitting so straight and staring at the orchestra, tugged at his heart. Time must have been moving at a leaden pace for all five of them, ticking by almost in slow motion through a mist of pride, excitement, fear, and anticipation. Suddenly the lights dimmed and a buzz went around the room.

"Kick off!" Rafael whispered to Daniel, and the boy grinned up at him, excitement in his dark eyes.

As applause broke out, the maestro walked quickly across to the podium at the edge of the platform, smiled warmly at the orchestra, and turned to the expectant crowd.

"Good evening, ladies and gentlemen, and a big welcome to this very special performance. To begin, shall we make a little music of the night?"

He turned back, tapped the top of his music stand, waited

for the orchestra to focus on him, and gave them his signature wink. The familiar opening to Mozart's Serenade no. 13, K525, more commonly known as "Eine Kleine Nachtmusik," rang out crisply, and the audience settled comfortably into their seats.

Daniel stood in the doorway from the hall, the violin and bow in his hands, his foot tapping in time to the rhythmic music, the nerves evaporating. What a genius Mozart was! It sounded like a musical game of questions and answers, one phrase responding to another, a piece of frivolous party music, written while the composer was deep in the middle of the opera *Don Giovanni,* and yet it'd become one of the most recognized and loved compositions of all time. That was the amazing thing about music; there was always something more to discover and love.

He watched Maestro Gomez from his side angle and was, as always, mesmerized by the way he made the complex job seem so effortless. He'd taken the maestro's advice and spent some time by himself just sitting with the violin, holding it, talking to it, playing bits and pieces as they came into his head, and now it felt more like a friend, not like some huge task at which he might fail. It was a member of his family, he told himself, just a piece of wood that was at home in the hands of a Horowitz, nothing mystical or symbolic.

The piece came to its conclusion, and the maestro motioned to the orchestra to stand as he turned to take his own bow. Then he stepped off the podium and walked into the space between the orchestra and the audience. Before he spoke, he glanced sideways at Daniel and smiled. Daniel gave him a nod to show he was ready. *As ready as I'll ever be,* he thought.

"My friends, it is a real joy for me to tell you a little about the performer you will hear play now. I first met him about eight months ago, when he made the finals of the Samuel J. Hillier competition. You know he was only just fourteen and the rest, they were much older! I was the conductor that night and chairman of the judging panel and, in the finals, he played the piece he's going to play for you first tonight, Paganini's Allegro maestoso, the first movement of Violin Concerto no. 1 in D Major. He won that competition, and as one of my students is so fond of saying, 'daylight came second.'"

There was a rumble of laughter and appreciation around the room.

"So instead of me *telling* you about his talent, I shall let you hear for yourself. He also plays a very, very special instrument tonight. It has been loaned to him by our wonderful host, Sergei Valentino. Without Sergei's generosity, none of this could happen, no? It is the extraordinary 1729 Giuseppe Guarneri del Gesú violin.

"Ladies and gentlemen, please join me in giving a warm welcome to Daniel Horowitz and the Guarneri!"

Daniel felt a light touch on the small of his back, and he stepped forward and walked toward Rafael, who was extending his arm toward him. The crowd was applauding and he bowed to them. He could see his family smiling and clapping and his mother nodding and tears on her cheeks, and his poppa's gaze locked on the violin in his hands. Rafael shook his hand, then mounted the podium. Daniel took his place, to Rafael's left, in front of the concertmaster. The pianist played an A and he tuned the violin, tightened the bow, and gave Rafael another small nod. The orchestra had quite a long introduction. After a tiny pause, he began to play, sweet, clear, strong notes that gave way to a lilting melody, punctuated by complex runs.

His body moved gently, and at times his eyes closed and at times he glanced at Rafael, who was constantly apace with him, almost breathing for him. Out of the corner of his eye, he saw his poppa start to rise from his seat as, four minutes into the piece, the continuous trills spilled forth and built to breathtaking high notes. His uncle put his hand on his poppa's shoulder and pushed him back down, and his nana grabbed his poppa's hand.

The last two minutes were almost entirely solo, ending with just a few accompanying notes from the orchestra, and the applause started before the piece concluded. Everyone was on their feet, and the noise was deafening. Daniel turned to Rafael, who stepped off the podium, took his hand, and raised the two joined hands in the air.

"Ladies and gentlemen, Daniel Horowitz."

Still the clapping continued and shouts of "Bravo!" Daniel bowed and smiled happily at his family. Cindy was still crying and Daniel knew she hadn't stopped, but it gave him a sudden jolt to realize that his nana, poppa, and *feter* were crying too. He wanted to go to them, hug them, show them the violin, but Maestro Gomez still held his hand tightly. Finally it slowed down, and Rafael let him go and gestured for him to walk off, back to the doorway. He could see a woman waiting there with a bottle of water and a towel to wipe away the sweat.

Rafael turned back to the audience, now seated. He could feel their energy and enthusiasm matching his own racing heart.

"I won't say, 'I told you so,' but it makes you glad, yes? Before he plays for us again, I want to tell you a little story. A few months ago I heard that Daniel wasn't sure if he wanted to keep playing the violin. As I know all of you will appreciate, it takes a special level of dedication to play like that, and it is a hard thing, to be fourteen and have such incredible talent. But he is here tonight for a very special person in his life. Daniel's poppa, Simon Horowitz, is sitting over there."

He gestured toward Simon, who, along with the rest of the family, was staring back at him in a state of shock over this departure from the script. He could also see Sergei, who'd leaned slightly forward, all his attention focused on the speech.

"Simon is a German Jew who grew up in Berlin. In 1939, his father had his bank taken away from him by the Nazis and his house, it was looted"—there was a growing noise as individual audience members reacted to the story—"and all the boys and the men in the family were sent to Dachau. The women were later sent to Auschwitz. Simon survived for five terrible years because he was made to play the violin for the guards. But the most remarkable part of this story is that Simon's father had a genuine Guarneri del Gesú violin, and, you know, the Nazis took it in 1939. Simon hasn't heard one played for nearly seventy years and tonight he is, by his own grandson!"

Spontaneous applause burst forth and people began to stand. Rafael walked across the gap to the front row and embraced Simon in a warm hug. He could feel the frail body quivering.

"Trust me," he whispered softly in Simon's ear. "Go with your instinct."

Then he pulled back and shook the bony hand. Ruth was crying softly, and he kissed her gently on each cheek, then shook Levi's hand. As he turned he saw Sergei. The Russian was standing and clapping. His round face was as white as Rafael had ever seen it, and the pale green eyes glittered at him with what he knew was cold rage . . . and something else. Knowledge and understanding. In that split second, Rafael's instinct hit him squarely in the gut. Sergei knew. He knew where his violin came from; he knew something about the story he'd just heard.

Chapter 49

Rafael mounted the podium and led the orchestra through Rossini's "William Tell Overture," as he had with a hundred orchestras all around the world. That experience and training carried him through as his mind raced ahead. The audience's response was polite, impatient; they wanted to hear from the star attraction again. *So,* the maestro thought, *let the games begin, and whatever happens, happens.*

"Time to hear from our prodigy again. This time he will play for us Debussy's 'The Girl with the Flaxen Hair.'"

Daniel walked back into the room to yet more applause. He tuned the violin briefly, and before he took up his stance, he nodded to Rafael.

"Daniel would like to say something to you all."

The boy was looking over the heads of the crowd, as Rafael had suggested to him; any direct eye contact would've been too difficult.

"I would like to dedicate this piece to my poppa and to all my family I never knew."

It began with an achingly soft melody, haunting and smooth.

About two minutes in, a loud collective gasp cut across Rafael's intense concentration and he swung around, the baton raised. Simon was standing right in front of Daniel but not looking at him; he was looking at the violin, his head slightly cocked to one side. Daniel's eyes were open, and he'd stopped playing, the bow on the string and his fingers in the air. Levi started out of his chair, but David shot to his feet and grabbed Levi's arm to hold him back. Simon raised his arms and took the violin and bow out of Daniel's hands. The boy took two instinctive steps to his left, and Rafael came down off the podium and put his arm around him. The room was completely silent.

Simon caressed the body of the instrument with his finger, tracing the purfling and up the fingerboard to the scroll. Then he laid his cheek against the back and mumbled some words in Hebrew. Finally he put the violin to his chin and started to play the Debussy, slowly and carefully, his stiff fingers searching for the notes and the bow jerking over the strings. He rocked on his feet and moved to steady himself; his eyes closed and he smiled.

Then in one fluid motion he stopped, his arms dropped to his sides, and he sank to his knees. Six decades of rage, grief, humiliation, and frustration burst forth in a howl that sounded more like an animal than a human being. It was a keen, a funeral lament for his father, his mother, his brother, his sister, his uncle, his aunt, and his cousins, for all the lost years, all the shiva he'd been denied, all the agony he'd been forced to hide in order to survive.

It took Sergei almost another full minute to come out of his shock and move swiftly across to the kneeling man, but before he could take the instrument, Rafael intercepted him.

"No," he said firmly, "we need to talk, privately. But for the moment, he holds it."

Sergei recoiled, and Rafael could see the shock and anger.

"Never!"

Rafael spoke into the Russian's face, his voice deep and full of menace.

"Be careful, Sergei, this is very public, and in a battle for hearts *you* will not win. Keep it private. Be sensible and come with me."

He gestured to David to come to him.

"We need all your family and I think Roberto and Carlo. Follow Sergei, now."

As Levi helped Simon to his feet, all hell broke loose in the audience. People were talking loudly and standing up, pointing at Simon and arguing. Rafael climbed the podium and held his hands up.

"Ladies and gentlemen, please. Please. Can I talk to you all, *please?*"

Eventually people started to turn to him and stop talking. Many were still watching the group following Sergei out of the room.

"Thank you, may I apologize for this, please. There is going to be a break, perhaps for a while now. I am hopeful that the concert will continue, but for now there will be more champagne and food for you all."

With that he turned to the orchestra.

"Eat and drink and relax a little; as soon as I can I'll let you know."

Before they could react, he was striding after the last figure disappearing through the door.

Chapter 50

Sergei was pacing the room. As soon as Rafael appeared at the doorway the Russian turned on him.

"You knew this," he snarled.

"Keep calm, Sergei—"

"You set me up! You will *never* work—"

Roberto came between them, his palms raised.

"Now let's just—"

"You!"

The Russian spun around and poked his finger into Roberto's chest. "What part have you played?"

Rafael grabbed his hand by the wrist.

"I know you're angry and you feel betrayed, yes? But we need to talk, all of us, sensibly, calmly."

Sergei wrenched his arm away and focused on Simon sitting in a chair, clutching the violin and bow to his body.

"Why should I want to talk? Give it back to me, now!"

He strode toward the old man, and his intention was obvious. It was Carlo Montenagro who intercepted him and stood in his path.

"Listen to them, just for five minutes; listen to what they have to say."

"Why? They have nothing I want to hear."

"Make sure of that."

Rafael looked around the room. Daniel was standing between his parents, and they each had an arm around him. He looked frightened. Ruth stood beside Simon's chair, and Levi was only a couple of feet away. Carlo Montenagro gestured to the others.

"Please, everyone take seat. Please, *now.*"

They all gave a little start and moved quickly to seats at the table. Sergei's ice-cold eyes swiveled from face to face, and Rafael felt them pierce his veneer of calmness.

"So. Who is going to tell me what this crap is all about?"

No one moved.

"Rafael? My friend?" His voice was heavy with sarcasm.

Slowly Rafael pulled himself to his feet; he needed to be taller than the immense man if he was to have any chance of appearing convincing.

"I'll start, and I think others will add. Sergei, this is Simon and Ruth Horowitz. They're Daniel's grandparents, and this is Simon's elder brother, Levi. Their father was a banker in Berlin before the war and he was also a very good musician. He collected many wonderful instruments and he had, also, an Amati and a Guarneri. But in 1939 the bank was taken, the house was looted, and the family was sent to concentration camps. They believe that this"—he pointed to the violin that Simon still clutched—"is their Guarneri."

Suddenly Simon looked up at him as if snapped awake by what he heard.

"*Believe?* I *know* it is. I would know this instrument anywhere."

"And how on earth are you going to prove this, after all those years?" Sergei asked, glaring at the old man.

Roberto answered for him.

"Actually, it would be remarkably easy to identify their violin. It has a highly unusual, even unique, history. In 1935, Benjamin Horowitz took his Guarneri to a Berlin luthier and had the label changed, so it would read 1729. It was a misguided attempt to conceal the true value of the instrument. In effect, what he created was a violin with its own individual quirk. It looks and sounds like a 1742, the year it was truly made, but the label reads 1729."

Roberto looked smug, and Rafael could see that he was enjoying himself.

"Where did your grandfather get the violin from, Sergei?" he asked suddenly.

Sergei was glowering at the elderly Horowitzes, as if sizing up an enemy, and he ignored the question for several seconds. Rafael wondered how they should position themselves to stop him from getting the violin into his grasp and ordering them out.

"He bought it, in Berlin. From little music shop that had survived the bombing; he drove a very hard bargain. Maybe it was the same luthier that your father took his violin to." He directed the last comment at Simon.

"Impossible. Amos's shop was destroyed. I saw it happen, the night of the Kristallnacht pogrom."

Levi nodded. "I saw the ruins too."

Suddenly Sergei stood up.

"Enough!" he roared. "I have been patient and I have listened to this rubbish. Now I want my violin back, and I want you all to leave. If not, I call the police."

As he spoke he moved with surprising speed around the table and came at Simon from behind, reaching out for the violin.

But the old man was prepared, and his hands were still agile. Almost instinctively, he grabbed the scroll in one hand and with a flick of the wrist threw the instrument to Levi. As soon as it reached his cupped hands Levi passed it on to Rafael, who was already standing. He held it securely in two hands. Sergei stared at him.

"Raffy? Is it really worth your career? Are you prepared to sacrifice everything for these . . ."

Rafael raised an eyebrow. "Jews?"

He saw the shock in the Russian's expression.

"No. I may be many things, but I am not an anti-Semite. I was going to say 'people you don't know.' It belongs to me; I own it, and police will support my rights."

"Before the police are called, perhaps we better show you our evidence," Levi said.

"What evidence?" Sergei's voice was harsh, with a note of desperation that was not lost on Rafael. Levi opened a blue pocket folder and drew out the documents. He described each one as he placed them on the table.

"A photograph of us, Simon and me, with our two violins. A list of our possessions, compiled in 1938; the violins are on page one. And many letters, written by my mother to her sister-in-law in New York before the war, in which she talks about the violin often, describes it."

Rafael watched Sergei as the Russian raised his eyes from the row of papers and returned the old man's steady gaze. He could see the barely contained fury. There was no hint in the expression that the Russian was lying about his grandfather, and yet, somehow, Rafael knew he was.

"Carlo, you're an expert; what year do you think this violin was made?" Roberto asked suddenly.

Sergei turned to look at the maestro.

"Carlo? You know this violin for long time; what do you say about all this?"

"I do, and I would say, in my opinion, although the label, it say 1729, the evidence, it tell me 1742."

Rafael feared that Sergei would lose what little self-control he had left if Roberto pushed this angle too hard. Then security would be called and the opportunity he'd so carefully crafted would be lost. But the Englishman pushed on determinedly.

"The authenticity of the date can be verified by tests. If the label has been altered, that will prove it beyond doubt. If it hasn't, then it can't be the Horowitz violin. If it has, then there is only one conclusion," Roberto added with finality. There was a long pause. Finally Rafael cleared his throat.

"So we have disputed ownership of a violin that is priceless—"

"Hardly that," Sergei sneered. "It's insured for over five million pounds."

There were reactions all around the table. Clearly only di Longi and Rafael had had any idea of its true worth.

"But why insure it for so much if you think it's a 1729?"

Sergei stiffened, but it was too late, they'd all seen his reaction. The realization propelled Roberto to his feet.

"You know. You know it's been altered. You've had it checked."

"I've checked nothing; the label, that is your fantasy. I insure all my instruments for what experts tell me they are worth."

"No credible expert would tell you a 1729 Guarneri is worth five million pounds. That's ludicrous."

Roberto came around the table and eyeballed him, only inches from the Russian's vast bulk, but he was a tall man and adrenaline spurred him on.

"You have no right to this instrument and you know it! I've researched cases like this; some make claims and go to court, some get tried by the media. How many journalists are there in that room, only a few hundred feet away? They know about violins, and they know how to write a story like this. Shall we invite them in, show them the evidence, let them make up their own minds? We could go to the *Chicago Tribune;* they've a history with this subject and they'll crucify you."

Sergei's fists clenched, and Rafael started forward; one good punch and Sergei could kill Roberto.

"My family has owned this violin for over sixty years!"

Roberto pointed to Simon.

"Bad call. His owned it for over a hundred and fifty years before that. Wait until CNN gets the story—"

Rafael stepped between them.

"Enough, gentlemen. Sergei, I have a question for you, and I want an honest answer, yes? If you suspected that the instrument was more valuable than a 1729, that the label, it was wrong; if experts tell you it is worth five million pounds, too much for any violin except a 1742, why didn't you get it investigated? Tested and restored?"

Everyone waited for the answer, seconds passed. Sergei shrugged.

"I thought about it, but I will never sell it, so what was the hurry?"

Rafael shook his head.

"But how could you claim the insurance if anything happened to it? Any company would want to know why the value was so high."

Sergei didn't answer. Rafael could see the emotional tussle, the desperate search for a way out, being played out on the normally impassive face.

"This is bullshit." Roberto spat the word out. "You knew that if it was verified as the last 1742, *everyone* would want to know its history and you couldn't risk that. You *knew* that ridiculous story of your grandfather finding a music shop, in a bombed-out city under gunfire, would be laughed at."

Roberto put his hands on Simon's shoulders.

"Look at him, Valentino. Do you honestly believe the musical elite will side with you? You give so much money to so many arts organizations and at the same time you keep a violin torn from its rightful owners? Before most of them were shipped to death camps? And you think *time* is on your side? For God's sake, man, you think sixty years means more than over a hundred and fifty? Admit it, *you are never going to win this one.* Your reputation will be in the gutter from the moment this man gives his first interview. I've heard him speak and he's very eloquent. That first interview is about half an hour away unless you give him back what belongs to him."

Still Sergei looked at Rafael.

"Why did you not come to me? Talk to me, tell me this? Why did you publicly humiliate me?"

He had a point, and it made Rafael feel uneasy.

"I apologize. I, we, thought that if we tipped our hand, you would hide the violin somewhere and refuse to discuss it."

Sergei sighed heavily. "How could I hide her? Everyone knows I own her."

Again there was silence. The Russian turned his back on them and gazed into the empty fireplace. When Rafael spoke, his voice was gentle.

"I know what she means to you, this instrument. I know who she reminds you of. You must understand, my friend, it is the same for these men, yes? They watched their father play her when they were children. The same father, you know, who Simon saw shot dead in the camp. He also lost his mother, his sister, his brother, all murdered by their own people. Just like Yulena."

At the sound of his aunt's name, he swung around to face Rafael, and there were tears in his eyes.

"This violin, she is all I have left."

"I know, but she is all they have left as well. It's time to do the right thing."

Sergei turned away again, and Rafael knew there was nothing more that could be said—the case was closed. Then all of a sudden Simon stood up and held out his hands toward Rafael. His dark eyes were very calm and he smiled as he took the violin, put it to his chin, and began to play, the allegro from the Concerto in E by Bach. As he listened, it occurred to Rafael that Simon knew what it was like to play a violin for a hostile enemy when everything he held dear was on the line.

"Papa loved that piece," Levi said softly, with immense sadness in his voice.

Sergei made a noise, an almost involuntary gasp of pain.

"The tears of an angel," he said.

Simon stopped playing. "What did you say?"

Something in his voice made Rafael concerned, and he moved closer to the old man. Sergei swung around.

"I just happen to know. Guarneri del Gesú used that phrase to describe the sound his violins made, the tears of an angel."

"How do you know that?"

Sergei frowned. "Doesn't everyone know that?"

"No, they don't. Who told you that?"

"My aunt, when I was young and she played for me. I believe my grandfather told her when first he gave her the violin."

Simon studied the instrument between his hands, smiled, and said nothing more.

"Why do you ask this question, old man?"

There were new notes in Sergei's voice, impatience and confusion. Finally Simon looked up at him and nodded slowly.

"Many years ago my papa took me to see the luthier, Amos, and I played for him. He told me that del Gesú described the sound of his violins as the tears of an angel. I loved that story, I was so proud to know it. Years later a *stabsmusikmeister* asked me what the Guarneri sounded like, before he tore it away. I told him the only thing I could think of in that moment, that it sounded like the tears of an angel and that was a quote from del Gesú. But that's not where the story ends. Amos was also sent to Dachau and he told my papa that he'd invented the quote, all those years before, because it sounded Italian and he knew it would make me happy."

There was a heavy silence.

"So he didn't say it. What is your point?" Sergei was defensive; the balance of power had shifted.

"I was so disappointed that I never told another person. If your grandfather heard it, he must have heard it from the man I told, the *stabsmusikmei*—"

"Not necessarily, he could have told many people," Sergei said angrily.

Roberto was a step ahead. "Not very likely, especially if he was hiding the violin as some sort of postwar insurance."

Again a stifling silence enveloped them, broken by Levi.

"If you think about everything it has seen, the tears of an angel is not so far from the truth."

"You mentioned an Amati, what year?" Sergei asked abruptly.

"1670," Simon said quietly.

Sergei nodded slowly, and Rafael wondered if he could see the beginning of a solution.

"A beautiful instrument. Do you know where it is?"

"In a private collection in Lyon, we think—"

"Lyon? Jean-Pierre Clavelle, I presume? He would own such a thing. We are friends."

"The description of the Clavelle Amati fits our instrument."

Rafael watched Sergei studying Simon. The Russian was a clever man. He would find a compromise if he could, and this was what Rafael had been banking on—back Sergei into a corner and he'll come out with a deal. The faint sensation of optimism was rising in his chest; *come on, Sergei, work this out!*

"What if I bought the Amati and gave it back to you. And I guarantee that Daniel can play the Guarneri whenever he needs to. When he is a concert violinist, he will need an instrument."

Before Simon could respond, Rafael cut in.

"You said you would never sell her. If you keep ownership for your lifetime, then on your death, you must will her to Daniel, yes?"

"I have no children, so I am happy to do that. I would have left her to a museum somewhere anyway. And I ask in return that when he records his first CD, he dedicates it to my aunt, Yulena, and continues to name the violin after her. She would have been a great concert violinist had she lived."

Rafael looked inquiringly at Simon, who exchanged glances with Levi, then nodded with a small movement of his head.

"But what if they want to sell it? You give them no way to get any real financial compensation for their losses!" Roberto blurted out, his anger still evident.

"We would never sell her." It was Simon's turn to sound indignant. "People who own such a thing for generations never consider selling."

"So we are agreed," Rafael said quietly.

"What about Tatiana?" It was David who asked the question, and everyone turned to look at him. Cindy glared and he shrugged.

"She obviously considers the violin to be hers to play by right; should we just ignore her?"

Sergei sighed.

"Like me, she is mistaken. My friend, your son is a more gifted violinist than Tatiana will ever be. I will find her an instrument that will please her. Now, if we are to share her, Mr. Horowitz, I have something to tell you that I think you will want to know."

He sat down opposite Simon and held out his hands. The old man handed the violin to him without hesitation. Sergei turned her over and over, stroking the wood lovingly as he spoke.

"My memories of her go back to when I was small child, also. We lived in Moscow, and my aunt played to me. My mother died when I was born, and she and my grandmama raised me. In 1965, my aunt was murdered by the KGB, here in London. They said she was trying to defect, but I know she would never have done that; she had promised me. Although she wanted to live in the West and learn from great teachers, she would never have left me."

He looked up at Simon. "Were you there, when the Nazis took her?"

"Yes."

"Do you remember? The men?"

"Until my dying breath. There was a *stabsmusikmeister*. He played her, badly. He swore at me and he played her. I hit him, punched him, broke his nose, and he broke my hand with his truncheon."

Sergei smiled with understanding, and Simon smiled back. These men shared more than one connection, Rafael thought to himself as he watched, fascinated.

"Good for you. Before my grandpapa died, about eighteen years ago, he told me a secret that I swore I would never tell. But you will want to know this. As Berlin fell he was there and he interrogated a Nazi spy who was carrying a genuine Guarneri violin. The man admitted to being a music captain in the army. He boasted he had looted it from a wealthy family of Jewish bankers in Berlin at the start of the war. He was running away, deserting his homeland. My grandpapa kept the violin."

"And the man?"

Simon seemed to hold his breath as he waited.

"He was shot, as a deserter."

Simon closed his eyes. "Thank you, sir."

"But not before he showed where he had hidden some other treasure."

His words were ambiguous and didn't become clear to everyone straightaway. It was David who spoke.

"Your grandpapa brought back more than just the violin?"

Sergei turned to look at him.

"Yes, he hid it in the summerhouse at his dacha on the Black Sea. I think he was deciding what to do with it, and then it just became . . . too long, too hard to explain where it came from. He told me about it also on his deathbed, and it was there, as he said."

"If it came from the same German, it could have come from our house?" Simon phrased it as a question.

"It's possible, I suppose," Sergei said. "I'm not a criminal, Mr. Horowitz. I believe my grandpapa would have returned it, had he known there was anyone alive to return it to. I have the original items here, in my vault. Come, I show you."

Chapter 51

As soon as Sergei switched on the lights, it became obvious that it was more than a possibility.

"Levi, look!"

Simon went straight to the portrait on the wall. It was a handsome young man with shoulder-length curly brown hair, wearing the colorful garments of a German nobleman at the turn of the sixteenth century. His eyes were hazel and his bearing proud.

"He was mother's grandfather, but many, many generations before. It hung in our entrance hall."

Levi was studying the painting, and at last he addressed Sergei.

"You own an original Albrecht Dürer and you do not display it publicly?"

Sergei returned the accusing gaze without flinching. "I knew it was stolen."

"So why did you not hand it in, so that the owners could be traced?"

"My understanding was the owner and his family were dead."

"He was a clever man, this German officer, using the chaos to hide valuable things for himself."

Sergei nodded.

"There will always be corruption in war. I believe the Russian and American armies found hundreds of these private treasure stacks."

While they were talking Simon had gone to the other painting.

"This is not ours," he said simply and moved on to the glass case displaying the silver. They saw a silver-and-gold teapot, two silver bowls decorated with inlaid enamel, and one large silver box, with the initials "ERH" on the lid, intertwined and surrounded by delicate engraving.

"Mama's box! It sat on her dresser. She kept her jewelry in it. The other pieces I don't recognize; we had so much silver."

Levi had gone to the case containing the three illuminated manuscripts.

"Papa's books. Simon, come see; remember these books? Papa always wore his white gloves when he read them, and we were never allowed to touch them."

The old men bent over the case together, grasping each other's forearms, joy and sadness on their faces, tears in their eyes.

Rafael had stood to one side watching in wonder. He looked over at Sergei and their eyes met again; the Russian's expression was a mixture of grief and pride.

"Thank you, my friend, you didn't have to do this."

"Why would I not? These things belong to them also. My aunt, she had strong ideas about what happened to the Jews. She had very close friends who were Jews, and they were persecuted under Stalin and forced into exile for their faith. Had she known where her violin really came from, she would have made it her mission to see if the real owners were still alive. Had she known about these things, she would have done the same . . ."

His voice trailed off, as if he'd thought of something.

"Mr. Horowitz."

They both looked up at him.

"Do you remember anything of your mama's jewelry?"

"Her pearls!" they answered in unison.

Sergei smiled and nodded.

"A very long string of the most beautiful pearls; I suspected as much. I have them here; Tatiana has been wearing them, but they will be returned to you. There are some other pieces I think you will—"

"She had a diamond brooch my papa gave her, in the shape of a violin."

"Ahh, yes, I'm sorry. My aunt, Yulena, she was buried with that brooch. My grandpapa had given it to her. It was the only piece of the jewelry he took out of hiding, in spite of the . . . he could not resist the urge to give it to his child. He adored her."

Simon smiled at him. "And I'm so very glad he did, sir. I'm happy that it rests with her."

"And I am glad that you will have some of your possessions returned to you."

He turned to Rafael.

"This deal stays between us, Raffy; the details never leave this room—no press, no interviews, no sale, ever. We will need to sign an agreement; my lawyer will draw one up, but no one else will know. And you will speak to di Longi?"

"Leave Roberto to me," Rafael said quickly. "He knows better than to bite the hand that feeds him customers. Plus, I suspect he will have an Amati to sell. For my part, I'll support your concept for the *Parsifal* in Egypt. Together we will persuade Jeremy of the brilliance of the idea, and they will get their money's worth, yes?"

Sergei grinned delightedly. Rafael held out his hand.

"Still friends?"

Sergei shook it and then embraced him.

"Of course, best of friends. Once Daniel has graduated, the violin will be available whenever he needs it, and for agreed concerts before that. Otherwise, it lives with me until I die."

Suddenly Daniel cleared his throat.

"Excuse me."

For a second it wasn't clear who had spoken, and then everyone swung around to look at him. He walked uncertainly across the room to face Rafael. His face was very pale.

"Excuse me, Maestro, but I have a condition too."

"That's fair. You played magnificently; did I tell you that?"

"No, but I'm sure you would've."

Daniel smiled shyly at him, and Rafael felt a stab of guilt. In all the drama of the confrontation, he'd forgotten about the child. After so much practice, his concert had been interrupted, and the precious violin, the piece of musical history he was responsible for, had been taken from him. He had seen Sergei very angry with his poppa, and no one had stopped to ask him if he was okay, if he understood what was happening. Or that, in Rafael's case, it was exactly what he'd wanted to happen.

"Everyone's talking about my career and after my graduation and my concerts. I agreed to play, to help get the violin back for Poppa. I want to keep playing, especially if we have the violins back, but I *really, really* want to play baseball too. So if there is no baseball"—he paused—"there is no career."

Rafael hid his amusement and addressed David and Cindy over the boy's head.

"I'm afraid a deal is a deal, my friends. He's fourteen and he knows his own mind. I can tell you the risk is really very small."

Sergei nodded.

"Raffy is right. Let him have his passions; he will play better if he loves life. Maybe he and I could buy a baseball team! What do you say, Daniel?"

Daniel grinned up at him.

"Cool! Definitely the Cubs, the Chicago Cubs."

Sergei looked at him thoughtfully.

"These Cubs, are they good investment?"

"They will be, if we own them. We'd need to talk about transfers."

Rafael couldn't help it; the laughter spilled out of him. It was an incongruous idea, but Sergei just might make it happen and it broke the tension. David shifted and looked at Cindy. She took it as a cue and opened her mouth. Her husband laid his hand on her arm.

"No, dear, this one is mine. If we say no, he'll only find another way to play; he's a Horowitz and we're very determined. Of course you can, you've earned it."

Epilogue

Thirty-five years later, much-loved violin virtuoso Daniel Horowitz sat on the terrace of his Italian summer home and turned an open violin case toward the ghostwriter of his autobiography. His famous Guarneri lay inside, the oil varnish still glowing brightly.

"Oh, my lord! When you see it up close, it's truly magnificent."

He gave her a satisfied smile; he never tired of seeing the first reaction to Yulena, nor was he oblivious to the effect he was having on her.

"She is, isn't she? Magnificent and sexy."

As they spoke their words appeared on the screen of her electronic tablet and she pulled her finger across the device to change the font size. She was recovering her composure, and he waited patiently.

"When did you start to play the violin, Maestro?" she asked eventually.

"The day I turned four. The same age as my father, my grandfather, my great-grandfather. A family tradition."

"My goodness! Did you ever want to stop?"

He hesitated and smiled at the memory.

"Yes, and that's why I've always invested in baseball teams."

She frowned, and he could see the association was too obscure and obviously confused her. Daniel picked up the violin and stroked it.

"For a short while my passion for baseball overwhelmed my passion for music, but then this beauty came into my life, and I became content to own a part of a professional baseball team. I was there during the great Valentino years with the Cubs!"

She nodded slowly. He couldn't help but smile again; this was clearly not where she'd expected to start, nor was he the intense musician she'd assumed he would be. Mention of the late Sergei Valentino brought the memories flooding back, and he hid his emotion by carefully laying the violin back in its case. Where on earth did he begin to do justice to the amazing men who had secured his beloved violin, guided his early career, and made it possible for him to balance his passions?

"The opening sentence should be, 'This is not so much *my* story as the story of a German Jew, a Spanish Catholic, a Russian agnostic, and a rather special violin called Yulena.'"

About the author

About the book

Read on

Insights,
Interviews
& More . . .

Meet Julie Thomas

Victoria-p.com

JULIE THOMAS lives in Cambridge, New Zealand. She wrote *The Keeper of Secrets* over a seven-year period while writing and producing television and film full-time. On turning fifty, she sold up, semiretired to the country, and became a full-time writer. She adores music and lives with her highly intelligent and very manipulative cat. ∾

Reading Group Guide

1. Who is *The Keeper of Secrets*?

2. Worried that their son will hurt his hands and, ultimately, his promising career as a violinist, Daniel's parents forbid him to play baseball. Do you think they are being overprotective? What would you do?

3. What draws Daniel to music? What separates his gift from those of other talented musicians? Do you think he understands the gift he has? Why is baseball so important that he would risk his future over it?

4. Describe Maestro Rafael Gomez. What does he see in Daniel and the way he plays? Talk about his relationship with Daniel. What lessons does he impart to his young protégé? He tells Daniel, "We must find that violin and we will find your heritage, Dan. *Then* you'll play for the whole world." Why was he so sure that they could find the missing Guarneri?

5. Why did the Horowitzes believe they would be immune from the ravages of the Nazi regime? Why didn't they leave Germany? When the violin is confiscated, Benjamin tells his son Simon, "One day you will play it again; believe in that, son, because that's faith and it will keep you sane." Was he correct? Does faith have the power to hold back insanity? Where does such faith ▶

originate? Would you say that Simon had faith or did he stop believing?

6. Compare Daniel to his grandfather, Simon. What did music and the violin mean to Simon? Did he do the right thing playing for the German officers in the camp? Were you surprised to learn of the bond between the officer and Simon and his father? Why did Simon give up playing after he was liberated from Dachau? What would finding the Guarneri violin signify for him?

7. Think about Simon's time in the concentration camp and the depravity he witnessed. Do you think you would be strong enough to survive such horrors? Besides playing the violin, what did Simon do to survive? Do you think he suffered survivor's guilt? How does losing everyone you have ever loved affect your beliefs and the person you are? How did his experience change him even as he was in the camp?

8. Can we ever make up for what victims like Simon lost? How much do we owe such victims? Do you think we will ever forget the horrors of the Holocaust? What would it mean for humanity if we did?

9. What is Rafael's relationship with Sergei Valentino? How are the two men alike? What are your impressions of Sergei? Why was

the violin so precious to him? How did the violin come to be in his possession?

10. Talk about the bond Sergei shared with his aunt Yulena. What would his aunt have wanted him to do?

11. How does loss connect the various characters—Simon, Rafael, Valentino? Talk about the hardships they faced in their lives.

12. Who is Roberto di Longi and what role does he play in the story?

13. If you could hear "the tears of an angel," what would they sound like to you? Do you enjoy classical music? If so, do you have a favorite composer or piece? Share it with your reading group.

14. If you knew little about music, what did you learn from reading *The Keeper of Secrets*? ⤳

The Lost Violins

THE VIOLINISTS in the Horowitz family—Benjamin, Simon, and Daniel—may have sprung from my imagination, but their experiences are all too real. They are representative of hundreds of thousands of Jewish families who suffered the unimaginable cruelty of the Holocaust and have lived with the injustices ever since.

The 1742 del Gesú violin may sing only on the pages of my book, but it is an example of the thousands of rare musical instruments ripped from their rightful owners by marauding Nazi music specialists. Beethoven's piano, Stradivari, Amati, Gagliano, and Guarneri del Gesú violins and cellos were shipped back from the occupied countries to Berlin. When the Third Reich fell, these precious examples of creativity were looted a second time, by the conquering armies.

I stumbled upon this fascinating story when researching looted art, a more well-known Nazi war crime. I happened upon a magazine article about a missing 1742 Guarneri del Gesú. Further research explained the reasons why such violins can be almost impossible to trace; in one instance the date had been changed on the maker's label to hide the true value, in another the modern day owner refused to confirm he owned the instrument.

The more I read, the more enthralled I became. My late sister-in-law's mother was born Jewish and her family fled to

Palestine from Lithuania before the war. She married a New Zealand soldier, became a war bride, and converted to Christianity. This novel is dedicated to my late sister-in-law: she was a music teacher and her five children are very musical. My niece has just finished her Masters of Music in Amsterdam on the harpsichord. My nephew is a talented violinist and also plays piano, guitar, and electric violin. When he was eleven he wanted to play cricket, and his mother said it would damage his fingers, so they compromised and he played soccer instead!

My mother and her identical twin sister sang on the stage throughout their early life in the 1920s and 1930s. I grew up around music and fell in love with opera when I twelve. All these things combined to feed my fascination for this subject. I began to wonder what it would've been like to own such a magnificent thing as a Guarneri del Gesú violin and to be able to play it . . . and to have it forcibly removed by people who had no right to it and then, by a miracle of coincidence, to hold it again.

So the story and the characters began to take shape. Rafael Gomez is the game changer—the man of principle and Daniel's guide—and I based him on the opera singer/conductor I admire the most, Plácido Domingo. Sergei Valentino was based on Robbie Coltrane's portrayal of Valentin Zukovsky in the James Bond film *GoldenEye*. I needed a Russian who was the antithesis of his upbringing, someone who'd emerged from the gray morass of Soviet Russia to become a ▶

The Lost Violins *(continued)*

shining example of the appetites of the Western world, a man capable of great cruelty and yet with a heart.

As I started to research the Holocaust in detail, the entire Horowitz family began to emerge. I read accounts from survivors who said that their parents were blind to the growing risk and didn't escape when they had the chance. I read accounts of prewar escapes from Germany and found Levi. The heartbreaking story of the resistance in Berlin, such as it was, gave me Rachel and Elizabeth's story. The couple Rachel worked for were real and so was their fate when the spy ring was broken. Maria Weiss was a combination of several real, incredibly brave Gentiles. Simon took years and he often made me cry. He is, perhaps, the character of which I am most proud. I really didn't want to kill off Benjamin and yet the story didn't work so well if he survived—I cried for a day. The Dachau section is the result of hundreds of heartbreaking stories and I hope I do them justice. Chapter twenty-seven, the liberation chapter, is based on a letter written home by a real first lieutenant in the 45th Infantry Division and archival footage that was almost too hard to watch.

The Valentino family also took shape as I researched Soviet Russia. General Valentino was a fictional sidekick to the very real Marshal Zhukov. The character of Koyla solidified when I read an astonishing letter written by a *zampolit*, a political officer, to

Comrade Stalin in which he bitterly condemned his own family as traitors. Yulena was Koyla's foil and vital in Sergei's story because he must have his own valid reason for his actions.

They all became very real to me and I will love them forever. ∾

From Julie Thomas's Bookshelf

BECAUSE I WAS BORN with a serious congenital heart defect, I spent the first four years of my life in bed and my mother read to me for several hours a day. I was a precocious reader from an early age—the Paddington Bear books, the Biggles series, *Swallows and Amazons*. By the time I was seven I was reading newspapers, magazines, and books. When I was ten my dad gave me a leather-bound set of Jane Austen books and I fell in love with *Pride and Prejudice*. There is no greater gift you can give a child than a love of reading; they will never be trapped in their physical surroundings and will face the world with an educated, open mind and a compassionate heart.

(1) *The Pillars of the Earth* by Ken Follett
(2) *Pride and Prejudice* by Jane Austen
(3) *Schindler's Ark* by Thomas Keneally
(4) *Perfume: The Story of a Murderer* by Patrick Süskind
(5) *The Professor and the Madman: A Tale of Murder, Insanity, and the Making of the Oxford English Dictionary* by Simon Winchester
(6) The Cazalet Chronicle: *The Light Years, Marking Time, Confusion, Casting Off* by Elizabeth Jane Howard ∾

Don't miss the next book by your favorite author. Sign up now for AuthorTracker by visiting www.AuthorTracker.com.